MOON BEAM

Travis S. Taylor
Jody Lynn Nye

Peachtree

BAEN

MOON BEAM

A Baen Books Original

Baen Publishing Enterprises
P.O. Box 1403
Riverdale, NY 10471
www.baen.com

ISBN: 978-1-4814-8252-3

Cover and interior art by Dominic Harman

First Baen trade paperback printing, July 2017

Distributed by Simon & Schuster
1230 Avenue of the Americas
New York, NY 10020

Printed in the United States of America

10 9 8 7 6 5 4 3 2 1

Prologue

"The Bright Sparks just aren't the same without Pam," one of the bloggers' floating holographic heads said, her round-cheeked face contorted with intensity.

"No! They'll be better! You'll see!" insisted a young man with long eyes and a waterfall of shining black hair. The others burst out in protest. Their voices echoed over the silent, twilit Iowa farm fields surrounding Barbara Winton.

The tall, brown-haired girl put the online chatter mostly out of her mind and focused intently on the problem at hand. With silent finger commands, Barbara motioned her personal data engine, PDE, to adjust its position and to alter the lighting a bit. The hand-sized supercomputer tilted and hovered closer under the hood of the harvester, casting the white cone of light across the grease-covered, grimy circuit box. Barbara removed the last screw in the faded, zinc-plated sheet-metal cover. She could feel the rush of air from the four silent fan jets on the ultralight PDE as it moved about.

"I don't agree," another one of the other bloggers, an adolescent male with short, knotted, crimson-dyed dreadlocks, insisted. The holograms from the Web site cast dancing hues of colored light that mixed with the flashlight function of the hovering PDE. "I don't think Pam ever fit in anyway, and besides, Dr. Bright will be putting Dion in charge, just wait. You'll see."

Barbara frowned, squinting down into the mass of electronic components. The smell of burned capacitor made her eyes water. The teenager dashed away the tears with the back of her hand and wiped them on the front of her denim coverall.

"Fido, I can't see the alternator diode bridge. Project that schematic for me again. And do a cross-correlation between the image and the schematic pictures and see if you can pinpoint it." Barbara was perplexed. She wasn't sure if it was the lighting, the grime, or if she was just lost in the circuit, but for whatever reason she wasn't finding the components she was looking for.

"Yes, Barbara," the PDE replied. "Please give me a moment to cross-reference images and to extrapolate position angles." On the air above the miniature spotlight, diagrams of circuits flashed one after another, rotating and spinning in search of the correct orientation.

"Right." Sweat trickled into her eyes. Barbara rose and wiped it off her forehead with the back of her hand, and, she guessed, smeared grime on her forehead. The late afternoon Iowa sun had heated the trademarked tractor-green painted metal on the enormous satellite-guided harvester like a cake pan in an oven and, at the moment, she was the cake. Even though the Sun had set an hour earlier, the heat continued to radiate from the vehicle. Barbara suspected it was over forty degrees Celsius under the hood of the beast, but was afraid to ask Fido to find out for sure. She really didn't want to know.

"Here it is, Barbara," the hovering supercomputer said, shining a laser-pointer beam into the depths of the tractor's circuitry. A tiny red dot danced on the component she was looking for.

"So, the diode bridge is here in this corner of the box on

this board, and the high-current lead goes this way. . . ." She traced the cable with the tip of the screwdriver in her right hand while her two-generation-old PDE did its best to track the motion and keep it lit. She really was asking a lot of poor old ancient Fido. "Right about here is where the voltage regulator should be. Yeah, gotcha." She tapped the cover of the regulator with the metal end of the screwdriver, making a hollow *tapping* sound as she did.

"I don't think Dion is the man for the job. I think the job needs a woman," a tattooed female blogger put in. "I like Jan. She's the one who can do it. The way she rewired that computer-controlled electromagnet was nothing short of genius."

"How about two leaders?" asked another woman, dark-skinned in a high-necked white cotton blouse. "Jan and Gary are the Nerd-Twins. They work together so well. I admire their teamwork."

"You think two heads are better than one? I think that'll be a disaster! Gary can't make decisions."

"Fido, I need you to go ahead and handshake with the diagnostic computer on this combine and start up the engine," Barbara said, pointing. "Monitor the phase interval. If this regulator is out we should get a lot of ripple on top of, oh, thirteen point seven volts right here at the input to the drive motor."

"Starting the engine, Barbara. Please be mindful of moving parts and sparks."

"Safety first," she said. She pulled her hands free of the engine and rested them on her hips to make certain they were out of the way. Her knack for understanding power systems included a healthy respect for what high amperage could do to human flesh.

Barbara waited until she heard the whir of the electric drive kick in and watched the graphs of voltage and current from systems throughout the tractor engine on yet another holoprojection from Fido. Just as she had expected, a curve suddenly went sporadic and oscillated randomly about a dotted line, marking the optimum level at thirteen point seven volts. She nodded. That regulator was shot. That was really bad luck.

"Barbara," Fido said, in his conversational tone, "there is a temperature sensor warning on the high voltage tripler rectifier for the right front drive motor."

"*What?*" Barbara swiped at the projection in front of her to access the menu. She frantically pulled up the diagnostics for the gears and drives. On the third screen, she spotted a vibrational mode that shouldn't have been there. That could fry the whole system! "Shut it down, Fido! Shut it down!"

"I'm attempting to override the power system, but there seems to be a malfunction in the interface," Fido replied, still maddeningly casual. "The oscillating current is causing the motor to vibrate due to the back electromotive force being induced."

"I get that. We have to shut it off! Dad will have a cow if we blow this motor!" Barbara pawed through the canvas tool bag next to her with one hand, searching for anything that would do the trick. She needed to cut the power to the drive before it could go out of control and burn out the windings, but she didn't have any insulated wire cutters that could cut through the centimeter-thick cable. Besides, fifty amps running through the wire would likely weld whatever tool she attempted to cut the wire with right to the tractor, just adding to the problem. An axe would work, but she would have to run back to the barn to get one.

The engine began whining, rising to a frequency that hurt her ears. She cast around, looking for any shutoff or switch she could close.

"Fido, this thing is about to burn out if we don't stop it. Shut it down!"

The PDE sounded infuriatingly calm. "I'm sorry,

Barbara, but something is wrong and I cannot. You will have to do it manually."

"I know! I know!" Barbara thought quickly. She should call Dad for help. No. It was nearly dinnertime, so he was back at the house already. He couldn't make it out to her in time. What would Dad do in this situation? The bright spark of an idea flashed into the edges of her mind. The idea was risky, but it could work. I got this, she thought. "Fido, do you still have throttle controls?"

"Yes, I do."

She waved her arm. "Kick it in! Full throttle on the front right side, now!"

"Barbara, that will cause an overload on the power circuit."

"Do it! That's what I'm hoping for."

"Very well. Activating full throttle."

Barbara swiped up the voltage and amperage graph in an adjacent window and crossed her fingers. She watched the thermal data with all her nerves tuned to high. The voltage continued to swing wildly, and the current rose like a rocket ascending to the Moon. The vibrational modes in the motor continued to worsen and the horrendous noise could have shattered glass.

"The motor will burn out before much longer, Barbara," Fido warned. "Should I begin deceleration?"

"Full throttle! Don't stop!" Barbara stared at the readings, hoping she knew what she was doing.

". . . Jan *knows* what she's doing and is a good engineer. But I think the Sparks are in a rut. That particle accelerator experiment they did was a disaster," a deep, thickly accented voice said. Barbara twitched at the word "disaster."

"That's not true! Neil posted some data on the membership boards this morning that was amazing!"

"I can't afford the membership area," someone replied, sourly.

"Me, either," Barbara muttered to herself, staring at the rising graph. "Me, either."

"Well, there was apparently some feedback in one of the superconductor magnets that caused the aim of the proton beam to be off. Wasn't their fault."

"They should have planned for that kind of contingency!" the deep voice insisted. The debate raged on. Barbara did her best to ignore the background chatter, but it was difficult. Dr. Bright's Bright Sparks had it great, and they were doing great things, and on the Moon, of all places! Barb had been one of their biggest fans all her life.

She had watched Dr. Keegan Bright's show ever since it began, when she was a little girl. The Bright Sparks, young people ranging in age from fourteen to twenty-two, had lived and worked with him for years. She knew all of their names, when they joined the program, when they left it, and where many of them had gone since. They were brilliant and had all kinds of fun scientific and engineering resources at their fingertips.

The most exciting moment had come a handful of years before, when Dr. Bright had left Earth for the new international moon base named Armstrong City, and taken the most current crop of Bright Sparks with him. There had been a couple of new additions and subtractions from the team since then, like Pam. Along with all their other Earth-bound fans, Barbara had followed all of the Sparks' exploits on social media, as they settled in on a literally strange new world, adapting to their environment and adapting the environment to suit themselves, all with the latest scientific technology, their wit and ingenuity. The first videos of them bouncing around in lunar gravity as they put together their first project had nearly made her explode out of envy. How she wished she could be one of them! She could work on particle accelerators, or anything else for that matter, rather than broken down, decades-old tractors that were about to blow drive motors at every turn.

But, she thought with a sigh, *somebody has to take care of old tractors*. Farming wasn't just pushing dirt around. It was one of the most important jobs there was, and over the decades had fallen into fewer and fewer hands as farm sizes increased and people dropped out of the backbreaking work it took to keep an agribusiness going. She always reminded herself that every job was important. People had to eat. That was what her dad and her grandpa had taught her and her brothers since they were old enough to listen. One day she'd get to the Moon and visit the Sparks' laboratory classroom. One day.

The screeching sound in the motor rose to a point that was so unbearable that Barbara clapped her hands over her ears. It drowned out the bloggers' heated debate in the background. Just as she covered her ears, something mechanical let out a loud *click*. Barbara jumped back in case something was about to blow. Instead, the electric current graph dropped instantly to zero. The shrill scream spun down to a whining moan. As Barbara held her breath, it dropped to a low hum. Suddenly, the system stopped altogether. She closed her eyes and sent up a silent plea.

Please be all right, please be all right, please be all right!

Barbara took in a deep breath and opened her eyes, hoping that she hadn't just destroyed a seventeen-thousand-dollar tractor drive motor that her family most certainly couldn't afford to replace. They couldn't afford the thirty-nine dollars a month for the private membership area on the Bright Sparks website, and they most certainly couldn't afford to lose a harvester right at the end of growing season.

"How bad is it, Fido?" she asked the floating rectangle.

Fido displayed a circuit diagram with all the gates in the positions they were supposed to be.

"The diagnostic system says that there was a power overload on the right front drive motor and the safety circuit breakers have been tripped."

"Yes!" Barbara cheered, waving her arms in the air. She wished her PDE could high-five her. Her idea had worked! By driving the failing regulator at full power, she had shorted through the diodes that had been causing too much current flow until the safety circuit breakers triggered, cutting off the power before the engine could burn out.

She traced the diagram on Fido's projection until she found a mechanical breaker that looked as though it had burned out. That was no big deal. The breaker and diodes only cost about fifty bucks. Barbara smiled. "Okay, Fido, data-dump all this to the mainframe in the house so I can show Dad."

"Yes, Barbara," Fido said. The PDE paused for a moment. "Your dad is calling."

"Really?" Barbara asked, with wide eyes. "Amazing timing. Put him through."

Her father's image appeared over Fido's screen. Like her, he was tall and rangy, but his light brown hair was going a bit thin on top. His eyes crinkled as he smiled at her.

"Hey, big girl. What's going on with Harvester Seven?"

"Were you spying on me or have you developed psychic abilities you haven't told Mom and me about?" Barbara said with a laugh. Lange Winton's eyebrows went up.

"Uh, no. Just curious about our predicament. Why?"

"I just finished with Seven. Fido just dumped the data to the house. It's going to need some parts ordered before we can fix it, unless we can scavenge them from something we're not using right now. I also think it needs a firmware update because Fido couldn't shut it down remotely when we needed to. That's some kind of fault."

"Hmm," Dad said, with a shrug. "That's timing for you. Harvester goes out just before the harvest. The repair money will have to come from somewhere. Oh, well, we'll figure it out. Good job, sweetheart."

Barbara smiled. "Is that all you needed?"

"As a matter of fact, no. We just got a delivery for you at the house. It needs a thumbprint and signature before the man will leave it."

"What is it? I haven't ordered anything."

Dad beckoned to her with a grin. "Well, you won't know until you open it. Get up here so this young man can go on his way. Besides, between school work and that tractor, you've put in over a ten-hour day already. Mom says to call it a night."

Barbara blew a wisp of hair out of her eyes.

"On my way."

Barbara reached up, grabbed Fido out of the air, and slid him onto the magnetic band on the left shoulder of her coveralls. She hoisted her tool bag onto the other shoulder and swung it into the bed of the beat-up old pickup truck, then closed the tailgate. The old green and white truck with patches of primer on the hood and various other places didn't look like much, but it was hers. It gave her the freedom to drive anywhere on the farm she wanted, and even into town every now and then. Even though she'd gotten her license two months before, she had been driving that truck around the farm since she was fourteen. The truck, once an abandoned wreck stashed behind the barn, had been her first big fix-it project, probably inspired, she realized with a smile, by the Bright Sparks making their first Moon buggy. It had taken her years of work and buying or cobbling together spare parts to get it running. One day she might even consider painting it, but she kind of liked the patched quilt look.

The truck's batteries showed full once she started it up, and the drive kicked in silently. The old farm vehicle had been out in the sun all day while she worked on the harvester, so it was fully charged. Pleased, she calculated that the diesel engine backup probably wouldn't have to kick in until the middle of the week unless she had to haul some big loads or pull something out of a rut.

Harvester Seven had been on the front side field about three kilometers from the house. The drive home took just a couple minutes up the baked dry dirt road, past the transmitter repeaters on stalks that talked to the field equipment from the central mainframe. Barbara lowered all the windows and let her hair blow in the wind as she listened to the bloggers continue their argument about the Bright Sparks and Dr. Bright. She thought of a comment or so, but didn't bother to ask Fido to post it for her this time. The passion the bloggers put into their posts made them feel as though they were involved. Most of them also participated in the science and engineering competitions that Dr. Bright posted every week, accumulating points on the Sparks Meter. Barbara answered every quiz and entered her ideas for new projects that the Moon-based students could undertake. She thought she'd posted some really good ideas, and gotten praise for them from her fellow bloggers. It was the closest she was ever going to come to being part of the program. In a year, when she applied for college, her high rating on the Sparks Meter should add to her appeal as a potential student in the STEM Fields, maybe even get her a scholarship.

When she rolled into the long drive, her headlights lit up the rear of the delivery truck that was in her parking place. She parked in the knotted grass close to the ancient tire swing instead. Her father came out on the porch and waved her up.

"Barb, you look like you've been wrestling a greased pig," Dad said with a laugh. He hugged her and handed her a yellow shop cloth from his back pocket as she walked up the porch steps into the light. He didn't look much better, with his thinning hair slicked down with sweat, his coveralls daubed with rust and dirt, and a black smear on the side of his face where he must have dabbed it absentmindedly with axle grease. Barbara guessed he'd been working in the shop behind the house on one of the million other broken-down pieces of equipment. She felt a rush of cool air hit her in the face as she opened the door. The familiar squeak as the damper pulled it closed behind her and the orange-and-white cat zooming in and nuzzling up to her leg reassured her that she was home.

"That's my good kitty, Tabitha." Barbara scratched the cat behind the ear and rubbed under its chin. The cat purred her satisfaction.

Her mother, still in the tailored suit she wore that day to her law office, came up to give her a peck on the cheek. Anji Winton was small and curvaceous, with long dark hair and eyes she inherited from her Ojibwa mother. Barbara had inherited her looks from her father, but her determined streak and her brains, or so her father insisted, from her mother.

"Sweetheart, there's a plate for you on the table once you've signed for your package," Mom said. She clicked her tongue in disapproval at Barbara's appearance. "Oh, what a mess you are! You've got grease all over your face and hands. You better wash up. And don't sit on my good couch with those grungy coveralls on. Your brothers won't be home until after practice. But for pity's sake, sign for this package so this nice man can get on his way! It must be important if they didn't send it by drone." She gestured to the delivery man in brown shorts and button-down shirt who hovered nervously by her elbow.

"Yes, Mom," Barbara said, turning to him. "Hi."

"Can I get your thumbprint here, ma'am?" He held out a flat touchpad and a stylus.

"Sure," Barbara replied. He looked anxious and ready to get on his way. She touched the plate's surface in the little square he indicated. Her fingerprint appeared in black, and a green checkmark etched itself over it. "Like this?"

"Right. And sign here and initial here please." He handed her the stylus. She scrawled her name in the box, and the screen changed to a colorful graphic with the delivery company's logo. "Thank you. Here you go." The delivery man handed her a container the size of a cereal box. "You have a nice evening."

He rushed out the door and ran down the front steps to his vehicle. Barbara watched him go, feeling bad that she had held him up.

"What is it?" asked her mother, tapping the box.

"Let her open it," Dad said, but he came to stand at her elbow.

Barbara glanced down at the carton, puzzled. Her name and address were on the front, but no return code was printed in the upper left corner. She tore through the packing tape and turned the box on its edge. A small silver plaque slid out into her hand. It was the same size but half the thickness of Fido. A message tablet!

"What in the world?" she whispered.

"Well, are you gonna play the thing or stare at it?" her father asked.

"Uh, right." Barbara depressed the ON button and the screen cover removed itself as the small device took to the air. Projector lasers at the corners of the device cycled through several colors, then the three-dimensional image of a very familiar smiling man's face appeared before her, a man with thick blond hair, blue eyes and an infectious grin. Barbara's heart nearly stopped beating as she recognized him.

"Hello, Barbara Winton. I'm Dr. Keegan Bright. I'd like to congratulate you on being such a well accomplished young lady. Your academic records, standardized test scores, and your performance on the online science and engineering challenges have placed you at the top of a very exciting list."

"What list?" her father said as he looked at her with raised eyebrows.

"No idea!" Barbara shook her head, baffled. But, no idea or not, Dr. Keegan Bright had sent her, *her*, a message, and she wanted to hear every word of it.

"Shhh!" Barbara's mother said.

"What list, you might ask?" Dr. Bright raised an eyebrow and paused, for dramatic effect.

"Well, I'll tell you," Dr. Bright continued, with a smile. "What was *not* released as public knowledge is that the online science and engineering challenge that you joined in was actually a worldwide competition. It was intended to find just the right person that I've been looking for. And Ms. Winton, you've won that competition hands down. There's only one thing left to do before we can be certain. If you're willing and able, and your parents are okay with it, I would be very excited if one week from now you could report to the astronaut training facility and Bright Sparks Central Earth in Houston, Texas. There, you'll spend the next three months training as an astronaut and learning how things work in space. As soon as your training is complete and you've met all the requirements, I'd like to offer you a job. I would like for you to join us here at Bright Ideas Laboratory and become the newest member of the Bright Sparks." He cocked his head playfully to one side. "So, what do you say, Miss Winton, do you want to go to the Moon?"

Barbara gawked at the hologram. All of her hopes and dreams fulfilled with one single question? What did she say? What else could she say?

"Weeeeehdrooooooh!"

Chapter 1

"... And if you look out the window on the starboard side, you will see your first close-up view of the far side of the Moon," shuttle captain Morris Joon announced over the loudspeaker. "In about four and one half minutes, we'll be turning the port side toward the Moon, then doing our orbital insertion thrust maneuvers. So, buckle up, sit back, and relax. We will be in lunar orbit for about another thirty minutes or so. Once we get clearance we will start our final approach into Armstrong City Spaceport. Captain out."

Reluctantly abandoning the oblong porthole, Barbara swam-floated into her seat as the seat belt sign turned on. She managed to pull herself into place partway above her chair, then the magnetic harness points on her white EVA suit aligned it with the harness on the chair and pulled her the rest of the way down. The south pole magnetic surfaces on the straps locked in place against the north poles of the seat with rapid clicks. She made sure her helmet was in easy reach in case of emergency.

Barbara's stomach quivered. It felt as if she had a million butterflies flying around inside, though not because of the microgravity. After months of training and instruction at

Houston, too busy even to stop and think, she was hours away from joining the Bright Sparks.

She felt nervous about actually meeting Dr. Keegan Bright. She was just as nervous about actually meeting the other Sparks. Dr. Bright's show and his company were known worldwide, with millions of views and likes every day. They were all honest-to-goodness celebrity superstars. And now, Barbara was expected to just swoop in and be one of them. She had no clue how that was going to happen.

"Don't stress over it, big girl," her father had advised her. "Approach the job like a broken tractor that needs fixing, or any other problem you face in everyday life: check things out, make an assessment of the situation, then get to work."

Her dad had made it sound so easy. If she was honest with herself, she was scared out of her wits, but hoped it wouldn't show.

When she had left Earth a couple of days before, the near side of the Moon had shown a crescent of sunlight, but that had receded into a sliver. She could see the Moon's outline, a gray shadow against the starlit sky. As they neared it, more details began to spring into view.

She managed to settle down and tried to relax for just a moment. She tapped Fido in his pouch on the shoulder of her spacesuit. The PDE sprang to life and projected her desktop of choice in front of her: walnut-sized icons floating in easy reach depending on how often she accessed them, with a holo of her family and Tabitha-cat in the background.

"Fido, go polarized for privacy," she whispered softly. She reached in her other sleeve pocket, pulled out her polarized lenses and placed them on the bridge of her nose. "Data entry pad mode."

The device projected a hand- and finger-driven menu before her. The QWERTY keypad hologram displayed on the seatback fold down table as she dropped it in place. She tapped at the virtual keyboard for a bit and waved through the menus until she connected to the shuttle's wireless router. With a glance to one side at her sole seatmate, Nelson, an ebullient, dark-skinned man from Cote d'Ivoire on his way to the Moon to negotiate for mineral shipments who was intent on the latest news in the *Financial Times*, she opened the Bright Sparks Web site and turned on the talking blog posts.

For weeks while she was in training, Dr. Bright had teased the big announcement he was going to make with a thirty-second video explaining that a new Bright Spark was about to report for duty. The bloggers had been in an uproar of speculation, trying to guess who that would be or where s/he would come from. About six hours before Barbara was due to land in Armstrong City, Dr. Bright had revealed her name in a worldwide live post that went out over the Internet, terrestrial television, and over the Bright Sparks app.

The net had exploded immediately with speculations and comments even before he had finished talking about her, and filled her new Sparks inbox with questions, congratulations, complaints, images, and memes. Barbara ignored all the negative comments. The most famous scientist on the Moon was welcoming *her* to his hand-picked group of young scientists and engineers. Dr. Bright went on to sing Barbara's praises and his hopes for her future. She played the recording over and over again.

The crew of the shuttle had floated back one at a time to congratulate her. Barbara couldn't help but beam with pride; yet, at the same time, she hoped she could live up to expectations.

Captain Joon's voice interrupted the headphone audio.

"Ladies and gentlemen, we're about to begin orbital insertion thrust. Please be prepared for a bit of a jerk and then continuous acceleration for a couple of moments."

Barbara waited for several seconds with her hands gripping the arms of the seat until she felt the slight kick of the electromagnetic engines. The EMdrive thrust peaked at close to one gravity and pushed her down into her seat. For the first time in days, she finally felt her normal weight—her Earth weight. Almost as soon at the thrust started, it was over. Within a couple minutes, the shuttle was slowed down and locked into lunar orbit, resuming microgravity once again. The butterflies in her stomach fluttered back to life.

The training period had been intense but awesome. Barbara assembled every day with a group of adult scientists, technicians and specialists, all preparing to go to the Moon for their various projects who needed to learn the ins and outs of living there. Though she was by several years the youngest person in the group, they all treated her with the same respect they showed one another. At Dr. Bright's request, she had kept the secret of why she was going, but it helped buoy her through the hard work. When the group 'graduated,' the center held a small party. Barbara desperately wanted to blog about it, but knew she couldn't. Not yet. Now, she could tell the world—in fact, the whole solar system.

In her luggage in the hold of the shuttle, Barbara had packed her best party clothes and best sandals and some cosmetics, but she had never been much of a fashionista. It wasn't just that she couldn't afford fancy clothing, but she really wasn't that interested in it. She found it perfectly natural and comfortable to spend all day in coveralls, much as she would have done on the family farm. What was going on around her was far more interesting.

". . . On final approach to Armstrong City Spaceport," Captain Joon said pleasantly. "To port, we're now passing by the Apollo 12 and the Apollo 14 landing sites. If you look closely, you can see crews working on the museums going up there in the future sites for Conrad and Shepard Cities.

Please remain seated and we'll have you on the ground momentarily. Thank you."

Barbara stared out the window, afraid to blink because she might miss something. The shuttle was slowly decelerating toward the bright lights ahead. The first thing she could see over the rim of one of the larger peaks was the edge of the city. The Armstrong Hotel and Casino triple towers stood as twenty-two-story mirror-image buildings that were lit up like holograms Barbara had seen of Las Vegas on Earth, another one of the million places she had never yet gone. That thought made her a bit giddy. She had lived only a four-hour maglev trip from Las Vegas, but she managed to visit a place four hundred thousand kilometers away from home first.

Armstrong City lay mostly underground, so from above it looked like an arrangement of crop tunnels covered in pale gray lunar regolith. The multicolored lighting seemed to have no particular plan or scheme to its design. Running through the city from top to bottom (north to south) and side to side (east to west) was the "cross of corridors." Like the center of a complex spider web, smaller "strands" spread out in all directions seemingly at random. Barbara knew from studying the map of the city that the two main travel tubes were big enough to drive a flatbed cargo truck through. The tubes were the main highways of the city. Though she couldn't see it yet, at the middle where they met was a ring of tunnels surrounding Tranquility Base Park and Museum where the Apollo 11 landing had taken place so many decades ago. The flag and statues of Neil Armstrong and Buzz Aldrin in spacesuits stood there, marking the first Moon landing. The hotel brochure pages claimed you could see the park from every room on that side. A replica of the Lunar Excursion Module had been rebuilt there, too. Barbara craned her head, trying to spot it out of the porthole.

The shuttle looped around the city in a holding pattern as it continued to slow its descent, and made a slight dogleg maneuver, clearing the hotel and the habitat center. Barbara gazed at the city, trying to pick out other landmarks. Farther south and east, the three large satellite communications dishes were surrounded by larger buildings. On one of them, the largest, she spotted the blue and red logo identifying it as the NASA Lunar Headquarters. Barbara could see what appeared to be gravel roads spreading out from the buildings and heading out from the edge of the city every which way, skirting craters and mountains as they snaked off to remote and as yet unpopulated regions of the Moon.

As the city grew closer, she thought she could make out the Bright Sparks Central habitat area just south and west of the hotel towers. It was the last thing she was sure of identifying before bright blue lights came on around a large concrete square, the spaceport's landing apron. The shuttle's engines vibrated under them. Barbara clutched her armrests.

At the apron's edge were a set of three concentric circles of blue lights with a big green lighted X in the center. Just as the shuttle crossed into the landing zone to the north of the apron, Barbara could make out the domed center point which was the Apollo 11 Museum. The actual historical landing site was just below her. She let out a crow of excitement when she glimpsed it.

"Fido, zoom in on the statues, please?"

"Of course, Barbara."

Her glasses focused instantly, pinpointing the two spotlit figures in the round park underneath the dome. There they were: Neil Armstrong and Buzz Aldrin, standing beside the American flag that they had planted there in lunar soil more than a century before. And now, here she was, Barbara Winton from Iowa, flying over the very spot where humankind first set foot on another world, about to follow in their footsteps. She hoped they weren't too big for her.

Comments from Bright Sparks Weblog:

Choco327—They should have just brought back Pam. She was awesome.

GaMeRgirl873—Dr. Bright thinks she's up for it. That's enough for me!

SwitchViewDan—Why her? Why not me? I'm jellous.

ZetaMoto—A farm girl. From Iowa! Go Hawkeyes!

BeamGrill—Hope she doesn't mess everything up.

Jan—Looks like I'm getting a new roommate today. Can't wait to meet her!

Keegan#1fan—Dr. Bright rules!

Chapter 2

Barbara concentrated on running as fast as she could, staring at the blank beige-enameled wall in front of her. The clear plastic mask on her face made every breath louder than normal, but she felt exhilarated. With every step, she bounded high above the track of the treadmill. She could almost fly! The Moon's gravity, only one-sixth of Earth's, seemed barely enough to hold her down. In a way, that felt more alien than zero-gee aboard the shuttle.

"All right! You may stop." Dr. Devi Singh came around to the front of the treadmill and reached up to put the disk of her stethoscope on Barbara's chest above the edge of her blue cotton examination gown. Barbara straightened up involuntarily at the touch of the cold metal and bounced a little off the table. Goosebumps rose along her arms, and she couldn't help but shiver slightly. If the doctor found something wrong now, she might send Barbara right back to Earth on her very first day. "Breathe in again . . . and now, out."

Barbara pulled off the mask and let her head drop back. She inhaled a lungful of the air scented with rubbing alcohol, cleaning fluids and an unfamiliar sweetness like the smell of synthetic fabrics. For a medical exam room on the Moon, it looked amazingly ordinary, with its plain blond-wood counter, its metal sink, the sphygmomanometer attached to a frame in the wall, and the poster showing the muscles and blood vessels of the body taped to the back of the door. Somehow that seemed weirder to her than having it full of bubbling retorts and futuristic life-restoration cabinets. Even the jar full of cotton balls next to the tongue depressors and latex gloves seemed too Earthlike to Barbara, almost taking away the wonderful alien feeling of being on the Moon.

"Very good, young lady." Dr. Singh let the end of the scope drop to her ample chest. Her dark eyes crinkled as she smiled up at Barbara. "Your heart and lungs sound good. All your scans and your records from Earth agree. You're in good health. You may go now. If you have any concerns, always come back to me or call. Be *very* careful of your oxygen levels, and don't be too brave to ask for help."

"Okay." Barbara picked off the wired electrodes, then hopped off the treadmill to stretch. At almost 173 centimeters, she was a good 15 centimeters taller than the colony physician, and taller still than the slender girl at the doctor's side, her daughter and one of the younger Bright Sparks.

"Come with me," said Daya Singh, holding out a tiny hand. She was a smaller, slighter version of her mother, with plump lips and large, long-lashed eyes. Her black hair was braided into a long plait that fell down her back, but escaped wisps floated around her heart-shaped face. "The others can't wait to meet you!"

"I can't wait to meet them."

"Let her get dressed first!" Dr. Singh laughed, and plumped lightly onto her rolling stool to enter information onto the tablet propped on the steel table attached to the wall. "I would bet that after days on the shuttle she would like a real shower."

"I really would," Barbara agreed.

Daya led Barbara out into the changing room and turned her back to give the tall girl privacy. Barbara carefully stepped into the glass walled booth and let the water wash away all the accumulated sweat and dead skin cells. She squirted lightly scented moisturizing cleanser from the dispenser bolted to the wall above the controls into her palm and rubbed it all over her skin and hair. It felt so good to be clean again.

The shower was a closed cube, three meters tall by a meter square, with a floor that rose a few centimeters in the center. The condensation and droplets that touched the ceiling drained slowly down the walls in the one-sixth gravity and dripped into slots along the edge of the floor, to be collected in a graywater system for reuse and recycling, or so the information about the colony had said.

She toweled her short brown hair until it was just damp. It would dry quickly; the humidity of Armstrong City's atmosphere was far lower than Earth normal, particularly the Florida coast where she had spent her last few weeks. In fact, part of her training and briefings before her flight there had warned her to drink fluids, moisturize all exposed skin often, and to use lip balm regularly to avoid a dry skin injury. There was so much to learn about living in space. She had only just begun to take it all in.

"Did you like your trip from Earth?" Daya asked, eagerly, still talking to the wall. Barbara, wrapped in a towel, retrieved her new clothes and fresh underwear from the third of the row of metal lockers. "Did you get sick? Everyone gets sick on the second day in space."

"I did," Barbara admitted with a grin, pulling on underwear and a purple coverall with her name embroidered in black over the left breast pocket and on the upper right sleeve. She stuffed her dirty clothing into one end of her duffle bag behind her toiletry kit. Daya was just as nice as she had seemed in the weblogs. Barbara had liked her on sight. "It wouldn't have been so bad if it hadn't been so cramped in the compartment. I was embarrassed by being sick right in front of other people like that. There were four of us coming up with a ton of cargo. And our luggage. I was surprised how much of my own stuff they let me bring."

"There's lots of room for things that aren't temperature or pressure sensitive," Daya said, her head nodding as she spoke. "We leave things outside in the vacuum under tarps all the time. The only equations that matter are how much room there is in the shuttle, and how much extra thrust it needs to lift the ship from Earth. But there's usually plenty of both."

"Are you studying engineering, too?" Barbara asked. She reached for the heavy-soled boots and pulled the tapes to secure them. The crisp sound of the fasteners told Daya it was all right to turn around. She smiled up at Barbara.

"No, medicine. My mother was a medical school professor at Johns Hopkins before she took the assignment here in Armstrong City. But I'm in Dr. Bright's program, and I pick up plenty of science along the way." She pointed to the wristwatch-like gauge that Barbara had yet to fasten on. "Keep that on at all times. It shows your oxygen and CO_2 levels. You must be religious about it, not just for your safety, but for those around you. You might be the first to notice when something is wrong."

Barbara pulled the band snug. She had a lot to get used to. All her training had told her what it was going to be like to live on the lunar surface, but not what it *really* felt like.

"I have to keep reminding myself I'm really here," she said, shouldering her duffle bag. "After so long, I almost can't believe it."

"Come on!" Daya said, reaching for her hand again. "The others must be bouncing off the walls to meet you!"

She pulled Barbara along behind her, covering the length of the room in four long bounds. As part of her preparation,

Barbara had spent two weeks in NASA's undersea training facility, so the buoyancy wasn't as disorienting as it might have been. Even though the floor was solid, she felt as though she was walking on a trampoline, bobbing partway to the curved ceiling with every step.

Daya grabbed hold of a U-shaped handle near the door to steady herself and slapped the panel. The door slid aside, and four bodies tumbled toward them, knocking one another over in a cheerful jumble.

"You took long enough!" exclaimed a thin teenage boy with longish brown hair and freckles across his nose as he pulled himself to his feet. Behind him were a young woman with sharp cheekbones and almond-shaped eyes, a tall, dark-skinned man with the bulk of a football player, and a slim, broad-shouldered young man with flared nostrils, dark blue eyes and a strong jaw. She knew them all!

"Hi, there," she said, her heart pounding in excitement.

The boy steadied himself on another wall cleat and stuck out his free hand.

"Hi! I'm Neil Zimmerman. This is Jan Nguyen and Dion Purchase and Gary Camden. You're Barbara Winton." He said it almost like an accusation.

"Call me Barb," Barbara said, shaking Neil's hand and the others that were suddenly proffered. The Bright Sparks! All of them wore jumpsuits like hers, but in different colors and conditions of wear. Neil was the shortest of the four. Jan and Gary, the self-styled Nerd Twins, were almost exactly the same height, about 170 centimeters, both with shining dark hair cut short and whip-thin bodies. Dion stood at least thirteen centimeters taller. He had beautiful, dark brown eyes with long, curling lashes. Barbara found herself staring into them until Dion grinned self-consciously. She broke off her gaze and glanced at the others. "I know all of you from the weblog and Dr. Bright's show! It's amazing to meet you at last!"

"Welcome to the Bright Sparks," Jan said. She had a low,

musical voice like the song of a wooden flute. Barbara had heard it a million times on the vlog, but it sounded different—prettier—in person. Her jumpsuit had been fuchsia once, but it had faded to rose pink, especially around the knees and elbows. "Come on! We'll show you to your quarters. You're rooming with me. Not that we're going to get to spend a ton of time there."

"I won't want to," Barbara said, spinning in a circle with her arms out. "I'm on the Moon!"

"That's the right attitude," Neil said, pleased. He pulled a thin gold-cased PDE out of the pocket of his jumpsuit. "Hold it! Great! I'm uploading the picture to the page now. 'Barbara's here!'"

Barbara stopped spinning.

"Can I see it before you post it?" she asked, in alarm.

"Sorry!" Neil looked sheepish. "Too late! I'll let you see the next one, okay?" He turned the screen toward her. Barbara peered at the image. He had caught her in mid-spin, with her brown hair flying outward from centrifugal force. She wrinkled her nose at the uninhibited expression on her face.

"It's all right," she said. "I look geeky, but I'm embracing my inner geek."

"Sorry. Sometimes I just move too fast. Come on. I think I saw the loader carrying your luggage toward the dorm."

He bounced off down the domed corridor. Jan laughed at him. The others set out more slowly in his wake.

"Don't mind Neil. He's always in a hurry to get to the next thing. We'd say he was ADHD if we didn't know better. What do you think of Armstrong so far?"

"I haven't had a chance to see much of it," Barbara admitted. She had kept her eyes glued to the viewport on the side of the shuttle as long as she could once it made orbit. "I only landed about forty minutes ago. They ran the four of us into the infirmary in a cart for our checkups. The light on the spaceport was so bright I couldn't see much beyond the plain. There were other craft out there. Six, I think?"

"Yes," Dion said. "They belong to NASA, ESA and the colony administrator, Ms. Reynolds-Ward, plus the hotel shuttle. Tourism's getting to be a big deal up here. I help with vehicle maintenance, even though my specialty is biology. That's how I got my scholarship from Dr. Bright. What was your project?"

"Smart meters," Barbara said. "My program helps make power sources more efficient, especially renewables. I've been incorporating organics into the matrix. I used them to make our satellite guided tractors use less power back on the farm at home."

"That's bright!" Dion said. It was one of the group's catchphrases along with "we got this." Barbara grinned.

"That sounds good," Gary said. "I thought of going into electrical engineering, too, and I read your bio. Do you want to work on a project with me? I've got some ideas for expanding the colony grid."

"I . . ." Barbara hesitated for a moment, then realized this was *exactly* the kind of opportunity she had been looking forward to. "Yes, sure! But, do we have to talk to Dr. Bright about it first?"

"Nah. He'll check in on us now and again when he needs to," Gary said.

"Come on!" Neil called, beckoning with his whole arm from ahead in the corridor.

"He's just hyper," Jan said, but Barbara could see it was with exasperated affection. They followed.

"We'll throw ideas around later," Gary promised.

The corridors had high arched ceilings and a flat, level floor. Barbara knew from the settlement handbook that all the passageways were round tunnels that had panels fitted in to walk on. Below them ran conduits, pipes and heating elements in a thick cradle of insulation.

"You can't see much of the colony buildings from the shuttle portholes because of the sunlight," Barbara said. It looked like a big spiderweb with occasional buildings that rose above the rest. "It's like being out in the desert."

"You mean Earthlight," Jan said, with a grin. "We're moving into nightside here."

"How big is this place?" Barbara asked, glancing around. "I mean, the city."

"One might could say it's as big as the Moon!" Jan laughed. "Or maybe it will be someday."

"Getting bigger all the time," Dion said. "I can send you the most current map, if you want." He held up a wafer-thin, silver PDE, the same shape as Neil's. Barbara noticed with a touch of envy that theirs were of a much fancier model than hers, sleek and trim, with an optical sensor as well as the usual buttons. She was almost ashamed to take her smaller and less complicated device out of her pocket, but he waited until she did. Her screen lit up with a notification of a file. She touched it and let go. Fido hovered in the air before her. A chart with a key in the corner unfolded into a three-dimensional moving image. The colony had a lot more buildings and structures than showed on the surface. It looked as if the servers had even picked up her shuttle landing on the strip. Following Dion's gestures, she could use both hands to pull the image apart to examine it layer by layer as they walked.

"Thanks!"

"There are about three thousand people here right now," Dion said, as she scanned the diagrams floating above her screen. He pointed to a circle that seemed to stand out above the mottled gray landscape. "That's counting the hotel right next to the spaceport. We get a lot of scholars up here for study programs, engineers, scientists, people looking to create industry up here, documentary producers, and tourists." He screwed up his face as if he didn't approve.

"There's even talk of them making a big movie up here soon."

"What's wrong with all that?" Barbara asked, puzzled. "I'd have come up before if I could have afforded it."

"It's not that . . ." Dion seemed reluctant to say more.

"Are the tourists the problem?" Barbara guessed.

Dion's round cheeks relaxed from their scowl.

"Yeah. They come four hundred thousand kilometers and think it ought to be just like it is at home. But it's so far from *being* like on Earth, you'd think they'd be completely into it!"

The gray corridor abutted a red-walled corridor, this one with thick plexiglass windows set into the sides. All the doors and hatches had silver metal clasp locks and wide latex gaskets. Barbara glanced out of one of the windows, but could see nothing but gray lumps through it. The section seemed so primitive. None of the entries on the Armstrong City website or Facebook page showed this much detail.

"Why is this part different than the part near the spaceport?"

"It's older," Dion said. He plucked her PDE out of the air and touched it, then touched his own device. Both screens lit up, and he let hers go. The hovering chart became more detailed, color coded by zone. "The original landing zone for the colony was adjacent to this part, in gray. Armstrong looks like one big unit when you see it from the sky, but it's been put together out of a bunch of old project huts and things, and joined by the tunnels. There's new construction going on all the time. That's yellow. The Bright Sparks dorm used to be in this section after they moved ground control to the new tower, in blue." He waved at a line of doors on the left. "Now we have a pod with rooms connecting around a lounge where we can hang out and talk. And our own kitchen."

"You like to cook?" Barbara asked.

"I do."

"Ha, ha." Gary laughed, his voice echoing off the plastic walls. "We like to eat!"

"You'll find you need to eat more than you do at home, too," Jan said. "Just staying alive takes more calories. And both of us work out with Dr. Bright. Have you met him yet?"

"Not yet," Barbara said, excitement and nervousness making a cold tangle in her belly. "He sent a video recording to me at home to tell me I'd won a contest I didn't even know I'd entered, and told me about the program. I couldn't believe I was actually hearing him leave a message for me. I've spoken with him a few times since on video calls. I couldn't believe I was actually speaking with him! I've watched his show for years!"

"We all have," Neil said. He had gotten tired of waiting at the far end of the hallway for them to catch up, and bounced back to rejoin the group. "He's cryo."

"He's what?" Barbara asked.

"Cryogenic," Neil said with a cheeky grin. "Cooler than cool. It's our word. We don't even put it on the vlogs. You can use it now, too, Barb. You can talk to Dr. Bright. You'll see. Come on, let's show you your room. Then you can see the rest!"

The walls changed color frequently as they passed through the well-lit tunnels and into various habitats of distinctly different sizes and shapes. A glass door to the right obviously led into a clean-room complex that occupied its own pod. Through the panel, Barbara could see figures in hazmat suits moving between scientific equipment and glass-fronted refrigerators. Screens on the wall displayed images from the electron microscopes as well as images from Earthbound television stations. She knew that there was a broadcast station somewhere in the complex. Dr. Bright's show had been produced from there for the last few years. She had recorded every episode and watched them over and over, feeling that she was part of the group that embraced science with burning curiosity. To think she would actually be working with him seemed beyond possibility. *OMG, it had come true!*

I'm here! The thought added extra bounce to her step as she crowded along with the others. Even petite Daya kept up, bounding along beside her.

Barbara's ears had begun to recover from the roar of the shuttle trip. She became aware of an ongoing hum. When her feet touched the ground, she sensed vibration coming through the floor.

"What's that noise?" she asked.

"What noise?" Gary asked.

"The hum?" Daya asked, with a laugh. "It's the ventilation pumps. The air is constantly recirculated through CO_2 scrubbers to keep it breathable."

"I guess I knew that," Barbara said. "I just never thought about the sound."

"We never really notice it anymore, I guess." Daya shook her head. "It's never completely quiet here. You'll get used to it. You can even use a white noise app. It may help you to sleep through it at first."

Barbara suddenly felt a moment of panic. During her training in the undersea environment back on Earth, if something went wrong with the environmental controls, she could go out through an escape hatch and surface. Here, there was nowhere to go if there was no air.

"Do they ever . . . stop?" she asked. She'd known that, but now she *felt* it.

"No," Dion said, firmly, putting his arm around her shoulders. His grip was firm and comforting. "There are backups on backups. Life support has, like, sextuple redundancy."

"We'll show you the best place to go," Neil assured her, his hazel eyes serious for once. He pointed down. "There on the floor, you see the orange line?" Barbara nodded. "Well, those always lead to a safe air supply. You can follow that and there will be either an emergency air lock or a suit locker. Also, in a pinch, you can pull any of those red levers under glass on the wall and they'll lock down the corridor around you and sound an alarm. Personally, my PDE has an algorithm based on air flow and the Navier-Stokes equations that can guide me to pockets any time I need them to. But then, you have to worry about the carbon dioxide, which I also have an app to override the sensors built in to the PDEs here that tell me the real safety margins . . ."

"Neil," Gary slugged him on the shoulder. "We have things to do."

"Uh, right," the boy replied sheepishly. "I'll show you later. After you check in. Come on!"

Barbara drank in all her surroundings. The air in the tunnels felt warmer than she expected. It smelled of chemicals, cooking aromas, stone dust, human sweat, cleaning fluids, and the sharp odor she associated with electrical circuitry. There was also a faint hint of machine oil or some other lubricant in the background of all of it. The floors and walls were not perfectly smooth, which would have made them easier to clean. She recognized that the texture was intended to help generate and retain heat, a vital trait on the cold lunar landscape.

"Even the smell isn't what I imagined." She shrugged. "Stranger than I expected."

"Like what?" Dion asked.

"I bet it's the ozone from all the printers and electrical components," Neil added. Barbara shook her head.

"No. Not ozone. It's something else. Something more, well, dirty or earthy. It reminds me of the machine shop I go some times to have parts made on the CNC or the metal sintering devices," Barbara explained.

"Eureka!" Neil shouted. "Lubricants! They're on everything up here."

"Really?"

"Yeah," Jan added. "You see, moving parts tend to collect lunar dust because of static electricity and all. They get into the parts and clog stuff up. So everything is constantly being lubricated and relubricated. You'll get used to that. You'll learn quickly that any of your projects with mechanical parts better be checked often for wear or they'll seize right up."

"Or they'll get sanded down to nothing." Gary said. "That happens a lot."

"Machine oil mixed with pine-scented cleaners? It's everywhere?" Barbara asked. "That sounds kind of awful."

"You'll get used to it," Jan told her.

The tunnels sloped downhill from the old section. Soon, there were no windows on the sides, but light came from daylight-equivalent LED fixtures in the ceiling alternating with faceted crystals as thick as her thigh, that she realized were catching the brilliant light reflected from Earth.

Each section had a set of large massive metal hinged doors with environment sealing gasketlike fixtures about the door jamb that either stood open or had to be cycled like an automatic airlock door. There were some thin, clear, not airtight polycarbonate doors, that slide aside as the youths approached. Barbara recalled from her reading and training that if there were an air leak or an over or under pressure situation that sliding doors would be stuck and couldn't be opened. Hinged airlock doors, in contrast, had mechanical jacks that would force a crack in the seal and could then be swung free. She often wondered why the city designers just didn't put bleed-off valves on the sliding doors, but had never known who to ask. *Maybe Dr. Bright would know,* she thought.

Alongside all the doors were enameled, permanent posters containing detailed emergency instructions and mounted cases containing oxygen masks attached to small tanks. Barbara glanced at them with a feeling of alarm. She hoped she'd never need to use any of those things.

The next section, painted dark green, was filled with private apartments. Some of the inhabitants had dressed up the otherwise utilitarian plastic-coated entryways with decorations. A number of doorways had a pair of large green potted plants on either side. One modest door had a bronze ornament high up on the frame that Neil identified as a mezuzah. Kids' toys lay against the wall in front of several. Everywhere, there was a light film of gray dust. It was the lunar regolith, Barbara realized. Moon dust. On Earth, Moon rocks were precious relics. Up here, the lunar soil was everywhere—absolutely everywhere—and it had to be dealt with.

Small, white, disk-shaped robotic cleaners scuttled along the corridor on the floor or clinging to walls, brushing it into themselves. That would account for the stone smell. She thought about that for a moment and recalled that there was a lot of titanium oxide in the lunar dust and wondered if it had a smell. She'd seen titanium oxide paint and sunscreen before but it either smelled like paint or coconut oil. Moon dust didn't smell like either.

The next room was a high-domed chamber full of tables where people sat over trays talking with one another or immersed in books or tablets. The long wall to Barbara's right was a cafeteria line from which savory aromas rose. A couple dozen other people were collecting items for their breakfast, dishing eggs out of a covered, rectangular steel pan or pouring coffee from a cylindrical samovar. Her last meal on the shuttle suddenly felt as if it had been days ago, but she ignored the pangs. She had to keep up. Neil took a hard left and headed toward the farthest right of three widely spaced blue doorways. It slid aside at his approach.

"We have proximity sensors for this hallway," Jan said. "It helps if you have your arms full. We have to give a palm print ID or an iris scan for the others."

"Cryogenic," Barbara said, trying out the word. Jan gave her a grin of approval.

Alternating to the left and right were narrow hallways, each ending in a brightly lit room. According to the map shimmering above her PDE screen, each indicated a round pod divided into segments around a central chamber. At the fourth archway, Neil turned right. Barbara opened her stride to keep up with him, and bounced into an oval chamber. Its ceiling was lower than the cafeteria's, but well illuminated by an array of prisms and LED fixtures. The dark brown stone floor had twenty-centimeter rectangular niches cut into it. Barbara realized they were there to anchor the furniture in place. Two big couches and a handful of padded chairs stood around a low, round table that doubled as a bookshelf. Tattered paperbacks leaned against big hardcover books, some with dust jackets. She was surprised that people still read paper books. She was even more surprised that somebody wasted their launch mass allotment on them when they could simply download all the books in the world onto a small solid state drive ten times smaller than one book. Her family had thousands of books on the family mainframe that she could download into Fido for reading or listening. This was the most high-tech place human beings lived, but they still kept books.

Four doors were set into the walls. As Gary had mentioned, there was an open kitchenette with all the familiar appliances. The wall opposite the kitchen had smooth plastic-coated shelves set into it. More plants, many of them trailing vines, shared space with oddments and a mechanical clock that ticked audibly over the rushing sound of the ventilators. A wide porthole was set into the far bulkhead. It all looked smooth and seamless, so it seemed pretty clear to Barbara that it had been printed rather than built or machined.

Lights from the exterior flickered through the porthole and Barbara hurried to look out. It gave her a view of the next round dormitory pod and a winding walkway half covered by drifts of gray dust. She jumped in surprise to see a solemn, bronze face looking back at her. She realized that it was a statue, a replica of Savannah's Bird Girl, with small bowls in her outstretched hands.

"Word to the wise," Gary said over her shoulder. "Don't open the window."

Barbara spun around to retort that she wouldn't be that stupid, and saw that they were all grinning at her.

Dion flopped down on one of the big sofas in the center of the room and crossed his long legs on the arm.

"Don't worry. They did that to me, too, when I got here."

"Why is the statue there?" she asked.

"Just to give us something to look at," Gary said. "And a reminder. When her bowls fill up with regolith, it's time to sweep the paths. Of course, there's no wind. But the force from ships taking off and landing stirs up the local dust."

"And every time the day-night line passes over us every twenty eight days or so a wave of dust follows it." Jan said.

"Really? Why?"

"Well, it's thermal physics," Neil started explaining. "You've got searing heat from the Sun inches away from freezing cold in the shadow, so a horizontal whirling cloud of dust forms. It's kind of like a dust storm but only a meter or so high. You'll see. It's neat."

Jan put her palm on the plate of the door to the right of the kitchenette, and beckoned Barbara over.

"This one's ours. Check in so it'll recognize you."

Barbara approached the door with confidence that she didn't really feel, but she planted her hand on the big rectangular plate. It beeped and turned red. A bar behind the glass rose up, then down. A slot to the right of the plate lit up.

"Identity card, please?" a polite female voice asked.

Barbara fumbled in the pocket of her jumpsuit and came up with the card she had been issued during orientation. She ran it through the slot as though it was a credit card. The plate turned green.

"Welcome, Barbara," the female voice said. The door slid open.

"Thank you," she said reflexively.

"You're in," Jan said. Barbara followed her inside.

Her bags had beaten her there. Apart from the sealed window in the curved wall, the chamber wasn't that different than the dorm she had shared in Houston. Two beds lay on opposite sides of the room. A low, black-topped table with padded edges stood between them. A couple of plain desks with adjustable LED lamps were tucked in beside built-in closets. All horizontal surfaces were filled with personal items: plants, coffee cups, tools, and small pieces of electronic equipment, some of it disassembled. Barbara looked around with dismay. Jan began to gather up the piles of books and clothes that lay all over the plastic 3D printed bed on the left.

"Sorry," Jan said. "I got used to having the place to myself. I'm like a slime mold. I tend to spread out and take up all available space."

"Aren't there empty rooms?" Barbara asked, stepping in to help her collect it all. "You could keep this one, and I could stay somewhere else."

"I guess there are." Jan grinned. "Dr. Bright prefers us to have roommates. It helps to keep you out of your own head as well as fostering a sense of community. Besides, maybe it'll help me to break some bad habits. You're not a neat-freak or something?"

"Uh," Barbara hesitated. "Maybe a little," she admitted, hoping it wouldn't put Jan off.

"Do you want me to help you unpack?" Jan asked. "I managed to keep from filling up your closet or the bureau."

"Sure." Barbara smiled. "Thanks." She undid the combination locks on her cases and pushed one toward the other girl. "Wasn't there someone else in here before? Pam?"

Jan tossed her long black braids back over her shoulder and dug an armful of T-shirts out of the suitcase. She kept her back to Barbara as she pushed at one of the bureau drawers to unlatch it.

"Yeah. Pam lived with me."

Following the blog, Barbara had seen entries from Pam, but they had gotten fewer and more terse over the course of some weeks, then stopped completely. She couldn't help but voice her curiosity. The group seemed so friendly, and Barbara admired Pam's brains.

"Where is she now? Did she graduate? Transfer to another program?"

"I don't know," Jan said, flatly. "She . . . didn't fit in."

Barbara stood quietly for a moment, stacking clothes in a drawer. Part her of really wanted to ask what Pam had done. It had to be something pretty bad for it not to have been mentioned on the Bright Sparks vlog when Pam left. Whatever it had been, it had clearly rubbed Jan the wrong way.

Worry added to the tangle of emotions in Barbara's belly. She wanted desperately to fit in with the group. To be accepted into the Bright Sparks seemed like the apex of everything she had ever worked for, then she was starting to figure out achieving her place was only the beginning. She had the opportunity to work in an environment open to so few that it was on a par with winning the lottery. Who wouldn't do everything they could for the chance to do science on the Moon?

"Well, I'll fit in, don't worry," she said, shutting the drawer with a firm hand. She smiled at Jan. "What do you want to do now?"

"Let's ask the others," her roommate said.

"We can take you on a tour of the whole settlement, if you want," Dion offered, when they emerged into the common room. "There are plenty of amazing things to see. What do you want to see first?"

The others chimed in, all shouting suggestions. Barbara looked from one to another, unable to make up her mind. Neil held up his hands.

"Hey, quiet!" he yelled, his voice echoing off the top of the dome. "I know where to take her. The lake."

The others nodded eagerly.

"Oh, yeah," Jan said. "Let's get our suits."

✧ ✧ ✧

TomCat76—Hah! Neil got her! Him and that camera.

StrTrk4FR—She looks happy. *I'd* be happy.

CombatBallerina—Look at her credentials. She's good.

OSay5477—I still miss Pam!

ButchFel9—I think she's hawt. I can do her.

Ninochka—You think they're all hawt.

Chapter 3

"I've seen the lake in the vlog and on the Moon website," Barbara said, as they trooped out of the dorm pod in bathing suits, sandals and robes, with towels over their arms. "I know it's possible, but it still *feels* unbelievable to have a lake of liquid water on a planetoid with no atmosphere."

"It's because it's far enough underground to be insulated," Gary explained. "You're warm enough walking around without a protective suit in the tunnels, aren't you?"

"Uh-huh."

"Well, thank the lake for that."

Barbara tilted her head. "How do you mean?"

"The Moon isn't volcanically active with a molten core like the Earth, or at least we don't think it is, so we can't get heat from underground. . . ."

Neil raised his voice to interrupt Gary.

"Where do you think all the heat from people, machines, doorways, generators, electrical systems, HVACs, power plants, and everything goes?" Neil asked, giving her a look of wide-eyed disbelief. "It would be a waste to let all that waste heat just radiate out into space. It'd be hard to do, too. So it's all stored in the lake. Everything at Armstrong City that has to be cooled is cooled with water, and that water is pumped into filtration systems around the bottom of the lake, then into the lake itself."

"I see," Barbara said and then shook her head. "Well, not exactly. Not yet, anyhow. Is there so much waste heat that it keeps the lake at swimming temperatures?"

"Oh, yes!" Jan smiled. She dodged around a gigantic cart full of merchandise being pushed toward one of the stores in the arcade. Thanks to the light gravity, the woman driving it seemed to be able to move it all with one hand. "In daytime it's absolutely balmy—almost thirty degrees Celsius. At night, it drops down to about twenty-three. It's a little cool for me then so I wear a wetsuit or don't swim. But the boys don't seem to care. The Sun set two days ago and it's just now starting to cool off a little, but it isn't cold enough for a wetsuit yet."

"So does the lake just cool off because it isn't used as much at night?" Barbara asked. "I mean, it's dark for almost twenty-eight days, so why doesn't it get a lot cooler?"

"You need to read Dr. Bright's analysis of the system. It works just like it was designed to," Neil said proudly. "At night, the heat in the lake is pumped through exchangers and used to keep the facility air temperature at a stable twenty two and a half degrees Celsius. In daytime, the water takes heat out of the HVAC system to keep it cool."

"Ever any chance of not generating enough heat?" Barbara asked. She was beginning to get how it worked, but she was realizing that she had a lot more to learn about living on the Moon, things that the Sparks seemed to take for granted as everyday life. It was all so strange to her. She knew they'd probably be impatient with her, but Barbara didn't like feeling like the kid holding the class back. She thought she'd known everything about the Moon and the Bright Spots. She was finding out that *being* there was a lot different from reading about it.

"Nah," Jan elbowed her playfully. "Quit worrying about

it. The nuclear fission reactor system that powers the city needs a whole bunch of cooling, and that thing will run for another hundred and fifty-seven years without need of replacement rods. We're good."

"Oh, okay. So how deep is it?"

"Pretty deep in spots," Gary said. "And it's warmest at the bottom where the heat exchangers are buried."

Barbara started to do the calculations in her head, and was overwhelmed by awe.

"That's amazing. I'd love to check that out."

"Everything here is amazing when you first see it or hear about or experience it. But you'll get used to it pretty soon," Dion said, with a kindly grin.

"Maybe, I don't know. I mean, my forebrain gets it, but the limbic system's still panicking," Barbara admitted.

The main corridor to the lake was wide enough to drive a flatbed through and ran from one end of Armstrong City to the other with the larger buildings attached to it on either side. The hotel lobby double doors were on the north side and were always open. As the Sparks walked by, Barbara got her first view of the plushest area on the Moon. She glanced curiously into the lobby of the hotel. Overstuffed chairs covered in damask brocade and tables that were the cutting edge in sleek modern design, down to the complex electronics, were arranged in conversation groups in front of the registration desk, a floating, jet black tabletop.

So far, the hotel was the only place that had elegant furnishings in it that she had seen. Everything else was pretty basic, but considering what it cost to get things up there, she wasn't surprised.

"Hey, before we get there, you can swim, right?" Neil asked, stopping and pointing an accusatory finger at her.

"I'm a good swimmer," Barbara assured him. "But, I like to know I can surface into the air or check the level on my tanks."

"You a scuba diver?" Dion asked, looking pleased.

"Ever since I was a kid," Barbara said. She had noticed the red and white PADI flag patch on his dark blue and white swim shorts, but she already knew he was a diver, too, from the vlogs. "I qualified for cave diving so I could go to the NASA training facility off the Florida coast."

"That's cryo," Neil said, tapping away with both thumbs on his PDE. He hit SEND. "Our readers will find that interesting."

"We can all swim," Gary said, "but Dion's the real merman. Water's his element."

"I got my master and teacher certifications," Dion said, a little embarrassed at the compliment. "Learning to breathe with a respirator and a CO_2 converter meant it was a piece of cake to adjust to spacesuits. I'm hoping to get a permanent job up here when I have my bachelor's degree. There's a bunch of colleges that will let me work for my master's and doctorate with remote learning."

"You're a biologist, isn't that right?" Of course, Barbara knew them like she had known them all of their lives. Only a few months prior she had never really expected to even meet them. Not only the light gravity made her feel as if she was walking on air. "You've been helping out with plant hybridization?"

"You been reading up on us." Dion grinned, to show he didn't mind. "Yes. It's been a privilege to be able to study the effects of lunar gravity and radiation on Earth fruit-bearing trees and edible vegetation. Dr. Bright attracts some pretty prestigious colleagues to come up here. I've had a cryoblast working with them."

"And I have been able to sit in on experiments performed by noted medical researchers," Daya said. "It's a small community, but a diverse and fascinating one."

"Wow." Barbara felt her heart swell with happiness. "I can't wait to start."

Jan shook her head, as if pitying her. "You'll be sorry you said that. We work pretty hard. We had the morning off to greet you. I was kind of surprised Dr. Bright wasn't waiting in the module for us."

The route to the lake went past a darkened room with a bar behind a number of small tables and a wall of blinking video games. Loud music poured out of the door. Except for a couple of people bent over the glowing screens of portable computers, the room was empty.

"Why isn't anyone in there?" Barbara asked.

"Too early," Gary said. "It's just after nine a.m. local time."

"Nine? I feel like I've been awake for hours!"

"Shuttle time's something all its own," Jan said. She captured her floating PDE and put it in her robe pocket. "We're synched with ground control in Houston, Texas and payload operations in Huntsville, Alabama. They're both on Central Time, minus-six hours GMT. It just makes it easier to have one time zone."

The corridor next to the bar had only one name on the direction plate: Selene Lake. The passage was wider and sloped down even more markedly than other tunnels in Armstrong City. Barbara was having a bit of difficulty adjusting her gait to account for the lower gravity and the downslope of the corridor.

"Why are we going so far down?" Barbara bounced clumsily a time or two to keep up, worried her sandaled feet might go out from under her. "Don't the tourists complain?"

"Sure, but you'll get used to it. The lake is where you go if there's a problem big enough to affect the entire colony," Neil said, his mobile face serious for once. "It's deep underground, to protect against solar radiation and almost any surface strike except maybe a big asteroid. The temperature is regular, there's water and oxygen-giving plants. But otherwise," his expression brightened, "it's just the place most people like to go and hang around."

His voice sounded more and more hollow the farther down the corridor they walked. The floor wasn't carpeted, adding to the echo. Instead, the stone had been cut into a cross-hatched pattern and sprayed with an anti-skid long-chain polymer coating. Barbara started to smell water, and the air began to feel pleasantly humid. According to the colony map, which she kept running on Fido, the rumbling in the wall to her right came from a huge water-purification plant. The corridor widened still further until they walked through a set of open doors four panels wide.

Inside, the expanse of dark, shimmering water stretched across more than half of the cavern's floor. It was difficult to grasp the scale of the lake, but small jetties and piers jutted out into it along its rim. The expanse of water had to be a full kilometer across at the least. Barbara breathed out in awe.

A couple of men in T-shirts and board shorts sat on the nearest pier with fishing poles in their hands. Colorful canoes and kayaks were stacked against the near wall beside a rack of oars and life vests. Three red kayaks plied their way along the water near the far wall, their female operators wearing lycra body suits and bright yellow life vests.

In her imagination, Barbara had pictured a body of water like a massive swimming pool, but the cavern, well lit by daylight-equivalent fixtures, looked more like a woodland glade. Young trees rimmed the left edge of the pool, giving way to reeds and other water plants. A clutch of water lilies spread white blossoms across their broad green leaves. She could just smell their sweet scent among the odors of moss, algae, and the water itself. The tiling ended in a small lawn of tangled grass mixed with knots of weeds, purple deer clover, and wild flowers growing up through gray sand.

Barbara's eyes were wide as she scanned the room, taking in every detail. This lake had never been aired on the Bright Sparks website, though one short, tantalizing video of it was on the Armstrong City feed. Neil turned, the ever-ready camera PDE in his hand. Barbara caught him just in time.

"Don't you dare take a picture of me in my suit!" she warned him. Neil lowered the PDE, looking chastened.

"You have a really expressive face," he said. "We like to show everyone how people react to life up here."

"Well, photograph my face," she said. "Leave my body out of it, okay?"

"You have a nice body," Neil said, with a cheeky grin. "But it's up to you." He stuffed the PDE into his robe pocket and tossed the robe onto one of the chaises laid out in long rows on the side of the lake. "Last one in is a tricephalopedalus!"

He ran in big low gravity bounds and jumped in a long slow arc into the water and plunged face first into the deeps, his arms flailing wildly. As the water splashed up and about it caught Barbara off guard. The water appeared to fall in slow motion. Dion and Gary followed more slowly, but still made huge slowly falling splashes that looked more like an explosion than a splash. Barbara shook herself. The lower gravity affected *everything*.

"The water's colder the farther down you dive and then it turns over at about twelve meters as you start to near the heat exchangers on the bottom over there," Jan warned her, pointing to the left side of the lake. Barbara automatically thought of it as the west side, then checked her PDE to see which way north was. She realized she was completely turned around. The heat exchangers were on the east side. Now she had a bearing to go with a landmark.

"No way you could make it to the thermocline without gear, though," Jan continued, as she and Barbara put their PDEs away and shed their robes. The grass underfoot tickled Barbara's feet. Jan pointed to a visible current in the water near the edge closest to the wall. Numerous life-rings were attached to posts driven into the stone. "Stay away from the colony intakes on the north side. See the rock wall jutting out of the water in a circle there?"

"Yeah."

"That's to keep you out of the intake area. The suction's fierce there. You won't get sucked into a pipe or something because of the grate covering it, but you could get caught in the vortex and drown even with a lifejacket."

"Thanks for the warning," Barbara said. She waded into the water up to her knees. The shallows were warmer than the air. The Sparks were right. It felt wonderful. She squeezed the soft bottom sand with her feet. Small ripples moving on the surface caught her eye. "What's that?"

"Fish," Jan said, with a laugh. "The lake has been seeded with a lot of oxygen-producing plants, including reeds, lakeweed, even freshwater kelp. Moss grows on the rocks all along the bottom of the lake. It sucks up the CO_2, but it tends to get out of hand. The fish eat it. The fish also nibble at the rocks, so the lake gets a fraction deeper all the time. There are snails, too. Don't get grossed out."

"I won't," Barbara promised. The lake was definitely not like a big pool as she had expected. It was more like the pond on the south field back home. She wondered if there were snakes in it as well, but she didn't want to ask yet another question.

She followed her roommate into the depths. The water was at least ten degrees cooler than the air, making her shiver slightly as her body adapted. But she would have braved it if ice was actually floating on the surface. *I'm swimming on the Moon!*

Her wonder must have shown on her face. She caught the expressions of two guys fishing on the pier. They grinned and nodded indulgently at her. Barbara laughed. They knew what she was feeling.

A shout came just before water hit her from one side,

drenching her hair for the second time that morning. She paddled in a half-circle to glare indignantly in the direction from which it had come.

"Gotcha!" Neil crowed, leaping up out of the water like a dolphin.

He and Gary started splashing her furiously. Barbara had no choice but to retaliate, sweeping waves of water at them.

"Watch out!" Daya shouted, standing on the lake's edge in her bright pink suit. Too late, Barbara felt her feet being yanked down into the depths. She sucked in a big breath before she was dragged under the water.

Oh, my God, I'm going to drown in outer space! she thought, fighting hard to kick free of the bond around her legs.

Under the water, which was clearer than any lake she had ever swum in, the band around her legs let go. She blinked hard to clear her eyes. It was Dion who had pulled her under. She swam at the big youth, who kept easily out of her reach. Having seen the width of his shoulders, Barbara didn't expect such slim hips and rippled abdomen. He had a natural swimmer's physique. Dion stopped, swishing his arms from side to side to stay in place, then used hand signals that she recognized from dive training, and touched his forefinger to his lips. She stopped. He gestured toward the other two boys' legs, which she could see about six meters from her. She nodded, making her hair swirl in the water. Together, she and Dion swam toward them, arms out. She grabbed Neil around the knees as Dion tackled Gary. Barbara couldn't help laughing at the astonishment on their faces when they pulled them down under the surface. Her breath exploded out of her in a gout of bubbles. She surfaced, breathing in lungfuls of the sweet, moist air, laughing. Neil came up almost under her chin.

"No fair!" he sputtered.

"What's not fair?" Jan asked, flutter-kicking her way over and thrusting armfuls of water all over the smaller boy. "You splashed her. She got you back. Hurray for you, girlfriend."

Neil shielded himself, but it was useless. He shoved waves back at Jan. The two girls buried him in a tsunami of water.

"Okay, you win!" he yelled. He gave Barbara a mischievous look. "Welcome to the group."

"Thanks," Barbara said, lying back on the surface of the water with a sense of satisfaction. She felt more buoyant than she did in Earth waters, and it was wonderful. "I think I'm going to love it."

"And this is *my* favorite place in the whole colony," Jan said, at last. Once they had dried off and cleaned up, the Sparks took her on through the main hydroponics garden, into the grand hotel lobby and the entertainment center again, then cruised by one side of the small but chic shopping mall. Just past the last of the administrative offices under the big dome, the others stepped aside at a set of double doors to let their new member pass inside. Barbara stepped in and looked around at the big chamber, almost holding her breath as the strange sense of familiarity overwhelmed her. "This is our lab and workshop and classroom, all in one."

"I know," Barbara said, her eyes wide. "I've seen it on the web series. It's . . . it's . . ."

"Cryogenic," Gary said with a laugh. "Yeah, it is."

Neil took pictures of her incessantly as Barbara walked around. She paid no attention to him. The room was so familiar, but at the same time unreal, like the set from a television series. She kept expecting to look behind a piece of equipment and see stagehands holding it up.

The huge chamber was well-lit, with plenty of work lights

and table lamps to supplement the overhead lights and deck prisms that would have admitted and spread sunlight if they were on the Sun side. A couple of electron microscopes sat on a battered basalt-topped table near the wall. Beside them was a closed glass cabinet with lights shining inside. Refrigeration units, glass-fronted or stainless steel: hummed at the rear of the chamber, alongside massive shelves on which lay, in no particular order, lengths of conduit, coils of cable and wire in innumerable gauges, boxes of connectors, soldering irons and flux, circuit boards, laboratory equipment she didn't recognize and infrared laser heaters. She ran her hand through a bin of loose LEDs and capacitors. Heavy shop equipment with plastic shields pulled down over blades and drill bits was attached to the floor. Hand tools and dozens of pairs of safety goggles and ear protectors were hooked on a plastic wire grid on the wall. According to Gary, the lockers and boxes marked with masking tape held works in progress or finished projects that had been put to one side for the time being. A Tesla coil two meters high, like a gigantic steampunk mushroom, stood idle in a corner next to a similarly scaled shiny metal ball atop a plastic tube.

"We're not allowed to run the Tesla coil anymore," Neil said, with evident disappointment. "It kept blowing out the rest of the colony's lights because the electric field kept inducing too much charge onto the room's power conduits. Apparently, they need to be grounded or shielded or both a little better. Maybe someday." He eyed her. "Maybe *you* could make it work."

Maybe I could, Barbara thought wonderingly.

Across the room, computer desks with multiple flat projector screens and touchpads faced one another in a circle. Barbara noticed there were half a dozen individual stations. Nearby, a trio of enormous screens was attached to the wall over a line of numerous smaller ones. One of the big screens had a world map showing the Moon's position and the day-night meridian. Hundreds of small points on the map were illuminated.

"You can have this desk," Neil suggested, pointing to the chair that had its back to the big screens. He flopped into the seat facing the map. "This one's mine. I keep the group blog. And the vlog. Daya helps out with that."

"I know," Barbara grinned. "I subscribe to the free channels. This is awesome."

"Sit down," Jan suggested, slipping into the chair next to the empty station. "Let's log you into the system. You'll have full access from now on."

"To the subscriber area?" Barbara asked, hopefully.

"Yeah, of course," Jan said. "You'll be contributing to it. You have to have access."

Barbara smiled.

The projector screen lit up at her touch, crisp and bright. The colorful logo in the middle, a yellow-white nuclear starburst with multiple faces in each of the rays over a field of electric blue, filled the screen.

"Do you see?" Daya asked, pointing to an image in the ray that stuck out at 2:00. "We have already added you." Barbara peered at the cartoon drawing. It wasn't a bad likeness, although she always hated pictures of herself. She managed to spot three of the other Sparks: Gary, Daya and Jan.

"Who are all the others?" she asked.

"Sparks from past years," Gary said, sliding into the station on her other side. He logged into that computer, and a photo album appeared in the lower corner of Barbara's computer screen. The "cover" opened itself and flicked through page after page of faces. She knew some of the faces from the web series and the blog. "Some of them are scientists now, working all over the world. Once in while they come back to visit. Dr. Bright started the program back on Earth a long time ago and we've only been up here a few years, you know. Dion's been in it the longest."

"I'm hanging in until they throw me out," Dion said. "I started when I was fourteen, like Daya."

"I've been taking the tests since I was ten," Barbara admitted.

"I was lucky," Gary said. "My folks work for Armstrong City, so I was already up here when my application was approved." He nudged Jan. "We started on the same day."

"Twins," she agreed, and fist-bumped him.

"Open that folder," Neil said, as a yellow arrow-shaped cursor moved into Barbara's field of view. It pointed urgently at an icon on the left margin. "That'll show you what we've been doing this year."

"I've been following the show and your blogs," Barbara protested.

"This is some of the cryogenic stuff that we couldn't post yet," Jan explained. "But since you're part of the program now, you can see all of it."

When she clicked on the icon, it exploded into running images. "Ore sampling in craters," one was labeled. "Effects of radiation on shielded microcircuitry," read another. "Effects of low gravity on neurological development." "Deep-space imaging." Her mind whirled too much to concentrate on one of these fascinating projects. She looked up at the others, her eyes shining. Her new colleagues looked pleased at her evident excitement.

"So what will we be working on now?" she asked. "What can I do?"

"I'm glad you asked that," said a new voice.

Barbara glanced up, and her heart almost stopped in her chest. She would have known the voice if she had been on the surface of Pluto. Dr. Keegan Bright stood there, not on television or on the other side of a computer screen, but in person, right in front of her.

She was struck hard by how good-looking he was, with a square jaw, wavy blond hair and blue eyes that squinted humorously at her. She had had a serious crush on him since she was a little girl. To her surprise, she discovered that he was only a few centimeters taller than she was, but broad-shouldered for his height. His biceps strained at the material of his jumpsuit sleeves. Barbara felt flustered.

"I, uh, I'm . . ."

Dr. Bright came toward her with his hand outstretched and grasped hers firmly.

"You're Barbara. I'm glad that you're here at last! We're going to get a lot of work out of you, young lady. But you'll be helping out in the name of scientific exploration and astrophysics. I hope you're ready for it."

"Yes! I mean . . ." Barbara stopped, as the words tangled in her brain. "I, um . . ."

"She was talking normally just a minute ago," Gary said, with mischief on his long face.

"Are you sure?" Dr. Bright asked, bending down to peer at her mouth. He had a warm tenor voice softened by a Southern accent. "All I hear is squeak, squeak, squeak. Maybe we should send her back to medical and have them take a look at her?"

The teasing made Barbara indignant for a moment, then she relaxed.

"It's the way we talk on Earth now," she said, offhandedly. "English is so last decade."

"Well played." Dr. Bright laughed. "Things change pretty quickly when you're out of touch. I'd better run to keep up with you!" He gestured to the others to sit down, and hitched a hip onto the edge of a steel table. "Have a seat. Most of you have heard some of this briefing, but I'm going to give you the full rundown. We're ready to start Project Moon Beam."

The Sparks cheered. Barbara looked at them with curiosity brimming inside her.

"What's that?"

"So glad you asked," Dr. Bright said.

✧ ✧ ✧

TeamSparks090—Give me a break!
Y no pix of swimming?

HeloFanAx—She must have come out of the
stone age. That PDE is ancient. Sad.

RutaAust—Is that a new bank of machines in
the arcade? Awesome!

KeeganMarryMe—Welcome, Barb! #Handsoffmyman

Chapter 4

Keegan took his state-of-the-art PDE out of the cargo flap on the side of his jumpsuit trousers and aimed it at the main screen. The file he had selected transferred to the classroom server and loaded. The new girl, Barbara, stared at the spinning Bright Sparks logo with shining eyes. The others pulled up their notes from previous discussions, but they all looked eager to start. He was fond of the kids. Jan and Gary, his Munjojerry and Rumpleteazer, like twins from two different moms, nudged each other with their elbows. Dion, the big mother hen, glanced at all the others before turning his attention to the front of the room. Daya had the self-possession of a woman four times her age. She was a born doctor, just like her mother, and a good listener. Neil had to calm down a little, but he was going to be a great force for good in the science world one day. The teen knew how to get people's attention, and he was passionate about the program.

This is why I love my job, Keegan thought. *Everyone gets so excited about solving the hard problems. They'll work themselves to death for the sake of it. And to top it off, we're on the Moon! It's their dream come true, but it's mine, too.*

"Okay, now," he said aloud, tapping the PDE screen to open the file. "You can all read up on the background later, while you're traveling. You're going to have a lot of time for that, so don't worry about it.

"Humanity has launched a number of telescopes into orbit over the years: Hubble, Chandra, Kepler, Webb, Darwin, Agile, INTEGRAL, Iris, Swift, Gaia, Aldebaran, Sagan, and so on; but all of them are around Earth. Two major problems with them: one, orbiters are vulnerable to damage from space debris, and two, they're so close to Earth that the planetary atmosphere, radio waves and albedo interfere with their effectiveness. But all a telescope really needs is a dish, a power supply and a feedhorn. We have a grant to construct one right here on the Moon."

"We're going to launch a telescope into lunar orbit?" Barbara asked, eagerly.

"No," Keegan said, watching her with anticipation. He'd had the fun of springing the surprise on the other five when the grant came through. Now he had a new audience, and the others were waiting to see how she reacted to the news. "No, we're going to build one right here on the surface."

"Build one?" Barbara echoed. Her expression of flat-out astonishment was everything that he would have hoped for. "How? Where?"

He pointed at the big monitor, where the architectural rendering of a lunar cityscape filled itself in. "On the far side of the Moon. We're establishing a second research center there that we're calling Aldrinville.

"We have all these readymade craters and we have identified one on the far side that's the perfect size and almost the ideal shape to build a combination radar/radio telescope."

He flicked the small device again, and the computer mockup of Project Moon Beam spread out across all three

screens. The left screen showed a topographical map of that area of the Moon, rotating in three dimensions. With thumb and forefinger, he enlarged the center portion to fill the screen.

"Bright Ideas, my company, has obtained the grant from the National Science Foundation and some private investors to finish the excavation on this crater here in the Compton-Belkovich region of the far side of the Moon. All the way back in 1998—ancient history right?—NASA's Lunar Prospector probe orbited the Moon and took detailed pictures of the area. The really cryo part is that the probe revealed a highly reflective plain lying between two ancient impact craters. This Compton-Belkovich region of the Moon contains thorium and other silicate rocks, and is actually much more reflective than the normal lunar regolith. If you look at this small unnamed crater here it's a perfect candidate for a radio telescope dish. Our small imaging satellites orbiting the Moon have mapped it in fairly good detail and it's already almost a perfect parabolic shape. It shouldn't be hard to turn it into an ideally shaped spherical reflector dish using just small excavation equipment." He paused for a breath and looked at the Sparks to make sure he wasn't losing them. He wasn't. They were all glued to every single word, even the ones who had heard it several times already.

"Hey, what's that big dome-shaped thing not too far from the crater?" Barbara asked sheepishly, not sure if it was okay to interrupt.

"Aha, good eye." Keegan smiled at her and was glad to see her relax a bit. "None of them caught that until I pointed it out. Would you be surprised if I told you it was an ancient alien moonbase?"

"What?" Barbara asked in shocked disbelief. "No, it isn't."

"Okay, okay, you're right." Keegan laughed. "It isn't. It

turns out that this region of the Moon was once very volcanic with special types of volcanos called silicic volcanoes. And that dome is what happened when they almost erupted but didn't quite make it. The large dome formed from the pressure and then solidified as it cooled, but the fun part is that the silicic lava then receded back underground or to the basin. Voila! The Moon made us a dome habitat for free. That, my dear, is the future location of the main body of Aldrinville. It's only about two hundred kilometers from the excavation site."

"That's so cryogenic!" Barbara almost cheered. Keegan could see thousand-watt light bulbs going off behind her eyes with all sorts of ideas. He was beginning to think he'd made the right choice in her. There had been so many to choose from.

"Very cryogenic. I agree. So, back to our project at hand, as we survey and excavate the one-hundred-thirty-meter diameter crater we'll create very high resolution surface maps to overlay with the satellite maps. We'll measure its reflectivity across a large portion of the radio spectrum, set up some infrastructure, and install this mechanism, a mobile feedhorn with state-of-the-art low-noise blockdown amplifiers and filters." He tapped again, and the center screen showed the telescope completed and operating. A framework like a three-legged, albeit very bowlegged, spider arched over a perfectly smooth spherical dish. The feedhorn, a radio waveguide antenna sealed into a protective radome, traveled along one of the uprights. Simulated beams coming from or going to the feedhorn ricocheted off the spherical dish and bounced off into space.

"It looks kind of like a hula hoop, doesn't it? But based upon the size of the crater, the transmitter/receiver has to be mounted high, at a proportion of the radius divided by two. Because the Moon revolves, the mechanism needs to be able to move freely, so we can keep it directed at its target. It will not only listen to the stars, but it will be able to beam data into deep space, as well as radar beams to map nearby space and the planets. And we're on the far side of the Moon away from all the radio noise of Earth, thus making it a more versatile device than other Earth-based or orbiting telescopes. Not to mention the biggest in space!"

"Bigger is better when it comes to radio telescopes," Neil grinned.

"Absolutely right, my good man." Dr. Bright smiled at the young Spark.

The framework image enlarged, and the elements exploded outward to rotate individually. Keegan enjoyed the new animation program that kept everything in proportion and with metadata scrolling up alongside each piece. "We'll mount the arches on spherical bases, kind of like beachballs. They're inflatable, to keep them as lightweight as possible. They'll move smoothly along the surface of the crater's rim, powered by electric servo motors. The power will be supplied by solar power and, when it's not on the dayside, stored battery power. The output will have feeds by lunar satellite and landline to both Aldrinville and Armstrong City as well as Earth. And you'll be interested to know that I didn't design this program, Barbara." He pointed at the other Sparks. "They did."

"Really?" Barbara asked, looking at her new colleagues with delight and surprise. The Sparks' expressions varied between modesty and open pride.

"It was Gary's idea," Neil said, "but we've all been working on refining it."

Barbara turned an admiring glance his way. Gary tried to look modest, and failed. He grinned instead.

"I suggested the inflatable spheres," Jan said, pointing at the diagram. "We work with those a lot. It seemed like the obvious solution instead of installing heavy rollers. You can push the frame with one hand. That keeps the power requirements down. We've been researching every aspect for efficiency. That's one of the reasons we were glad you were coming."

"I thought you were directing us," Barbara asked Keegan. "Aren't you overseeing our education on this program?"

"I wouldn't put it that way, no." Keegan shook his head. "That's a common misperception. I steer you, but you tell me what you want to study next. I'll teach you and find you resources, but *you* direct *me*. This isn't so much a classroom as it's an incubator. I'm guiding you so you won't fall off the edges, but you're going to take the chances and reach out on your own. Maybe next time we'll be working on one of *your* designs. I'm looking forward to that." He raised his voice to include the others.

"Meanwhile, you'll all be happy to know that the rest of the equipment we need to get started arrived on the shuttle with Barbara. The sections of the arches, plus the Lunar Bobcat for excavating are all waiting inside the loading dock for you. The Bobcat's been adapted to run off battery and solar power instead of internal combustion, but it sucks a lot of electricity. You'll be moving into the Sun side of the Moon as the Armstrong side begins to face away, so you'll have to depend a bunch on your solar array."

"Is the array already assembled?" Barbara asked.

"Not yet," Gary said. He tapped at his computer keyboard, and the view on the big screen changed. "Here's what's on site at the moment. Not much."

Not much was an understatement. Barbara saw a ridged crater, an irregular black blotch on the lunar landscape. She understood why it had been chosen. It was almost perfectly round. The perimeter had already been roughly smoothed down, but she couldn't see anything else manmade.

"Wait a minute," Barbara looked concerned. Keegan watched but kept silent. "That crater is a hundred thirty meters in diameter, right?"

"Yes." Neil said triumphantly. Barbara frowned. Her gaze fixed on a point above the screen.

"So, doing all the excavation with a Bobcat will take forever. The surface area of the crater is, let me see pi times sixty five squared is . . ." She pulled out her PDE and opened a plotting calculator app. "That's like thirteen thousand square meters. And if we assume we're going on average ten centimeters deep in the crater," the figures rose into the air in a column around a graph of an inverted empty hemisphere, "then we have to move one thousand three hundred twenty seven cubic meters of lunar regolith around."

"So what?" Jan asked. Barbara held out the small device to her.

"Well, I watched my uncle dig a swimming pool with a small dozer like that and it took him all of a four-day weekend to do it. I'm guessing the swimming pool was only about two hundred cubic meters of dirt. So that's two hundred cubic meters divided by four days which means you could move about fifty cubic meters of dirt per day. So, one thousand three hundred twenty seven cubic meters divided by fifty cubic meters per hour is, uh, twenty six and a half days. Are we going to be driving that thing around for three weeks?"

"That's a very good seat-of-the-pants analysis, Barbara." Keegan nodded. He was impressed by how fast she could calculate in her head. "But our initial analysis of the crater from our satellite imagery suggests that the crater shape is very close to what we need, so we will just be knocking down humps and filling in low spots. The team has simulated it and believes the crater can be smoothed out in ten days. Besides, they've all been practicing on the Bobcat simulator, and hopefully they'll be more proficient than your uncle at driving the thing. No offense to your uncle."

"Okay, I see. And no offense taken," she said, with a

sheepish grin. "He'd never driven one before he rented it. But what about recharging the Cat? How long will that take?"

"We can charge it overnight. Our plan is to use a power car," Dion said. "It's got stacked arrays of batteries underneath a series of expandable solar panels that fold up for transport, and we'll be on the Sun side almost the whole time." He brought up a list of equipment and showed it to Barbara. He pushed the holo for each device to one side as it popped up on his PDE until he was surrounded by hovering images. Barbara studied them all with curious eyes.

Keegan stood back with his arms folded, watching the others bring the newcomer up to date on the project. The more independent they were, the sooner they would be able to go out into the world and run their own experiments, gather their own groups of peers. It was becoming more important every year to expand the scientific reach of young minds. The motivated ones like the Sparks inspired the ones back home who never thought of themselves as leaders or innovators in the field. But, now, they were going off on a dozen tangents. He had to pull them back.

"So, here's the list of tasks you'll need to complete before you leave tomorrow morning. Hey!" Keegan said, shouting to be heard over the eager chatter. "Here's your task list."

The young people subsided and turned their attention back to him. He double-clicked on his PDE's home button. The file went out to five of the Sparks, who began scrolling down their screens. Barbara looked at the others in bemusement, then at her old PDE in her hand, then up at him.

"Oh, yeah, I forgot," Keegan said, with a smile. He reached into one of his many cargo pockets and came out with a new special-issue PDE, still in the box. He handed it to her. "This one's yours. Maybe it has a little more versatility than the one you have now. Jan can show you how to beam your Per Dee's persona, contacts, and files from the old one to this one. It's actually not that difficult. Give it a password, something that's hard for anyone else to guess, and change it often." He aimed a thumb at the console. "Same goes for your desktop unit. I don't want to see any stick-it notes on the side of the case, you hear me? We have too much classified material going around, most of it protected by nondisclosure agreements and government regulations."

The tall girl opened her mouth to protest, then shut it again. Keegan was glad to see she wasn't the kind who would lie to herself. Leaving your password around was the most common mistake in the book. He had already lost some valuable data in past years that cost him and the Sparks not only a contract, but a marvelous opportunity. That wasn't going to happen again on his watch.

Barbara took the slim, blue-silver device out of the box and handled it with an air of reverence. At her touch, the screen lit up, and four emitters at each corner of the flat device created the hologram of a spinning nebula. Keegan watched closely as she followed its prompts for getting started, generating a tall white page of text. After sign-in, the little computer would automatically take her on a tour of its capabilities. Its simple appearance was deceptive. The power and capacity of the device was far beyond any other PDE made to date. The custom PDEs he and the Sparks used pushed Moore's Law to its outermost edges. Less motivated youngsters would probably reduce them to overpowered gaming machines and selfie-generators, but these kids made use of their tools. They wouldn't be in the program, otherwise.

Barbara made an involuntary intake of breath, telling him she had reached the page with the PDE's stats. She tapped the two discreet buttons on the right edge, and became engrossed in what she saw on the screen. A grin spread across her face. She ran a finger up the resulting hologram to scroll it, her eyes moving rapidly over the text.

"You can play with it later," Keegan said. His voice yanked

her out of her reverie. "Let's get to the tasks at hand. You have a lot to do before tomorrow morning. We're kicking you in at the deep end, but I understand you're a pretty good swimmer anyway. I believe that you can handle it. Take a look at the list."

"Yes, sir," she said, looking a little embarrassed, and pulled the correct file open. The roster popped off the screen and hovered in the air.

"We've gone over the schedule a bunch of times," Keegan said, moving into the center of the circle of PDE access servers and beckoning the kids to turn and face him. "This should take you about two weeks. The site is two thousand four hundred nineteen kilometers from here along a continuously improving packed regolith road. At an average speed of ninety kilometers per hour it will take about twenty-seven hours of drive time to get there. You'll stop halfway for a sleep cycle and take breaks as needed. That means two days out and two days back of hard driving. The team has estimated ten days for excavating the crater and setting up the equipment. That means surveying, roughing in the spherical shape, surveying some more, smoothing it, final survey, assembling the mechanism, testing and checking in with us back here in Armstrong City. Total of fourteen days. Still good with that?"

"I think so," Gary said, concentrating on the file. Jan nodded, too. "If we have any schedule slip or unforeseen disruptions, it shouldn't add more than a day or two. We'll have enough supplies for even longer, if we need them."

"We have redundancy on top of our redundancy," Dion said.

Keegan clapped his hands together.

"So, who's doing what?"

Neil, as usual, blustered his way through the organizational list. He gestured casually at the list hovering in midair.

"Daya and I have got this under control," Neil said, dragging the smaller girl into the discussion even though she hadn't said anything yet. He poked a finger toward the slim young man. "Gary, since it's your project, you can run operations here and monitor our progress while we go out to the site."

Dion waved a disapproving hand.

"Not you, little bro. You're not allowed to go on construction missions yet," he said, with an admonitory head shake at the younger boy. "You two get to stay here where it's safe. You're running Mission Control for us."

"That's not as important as helping with the construction!" Neil sputtered.

"You'll be helping," Dion said, his deep voice soothing. He leaned toward Neil and tapped the younger boy on the arm. "You're overseeing construction via the comsats and imaging satellites to make sure *we're* getting it right. And who else is going to disseminate the information to scientists on Earth? That's you. The blog has your name all over it. Settle for it, little brother."

Neil looked disappointed. Keegan would have been surprised if Neil hadn't tried to get himself on the away team, but he didn't qualify yet. Children under sixteen weren't allowed in danger zones. The lower limit had originally been eighteen, but Keegan had argued with NASA and other bodies to allow well-trained, sensible sixteen- and seventeen-year-olds like Jan and Gary on operations as long as they were under his nominal supervision. In countries outside the U.S., the age of maturity was lower, and this was the Moon. Neil had a year to go yet; maybe longer if you counted emotional maturity.

That was the problem with this group. It was tough for them to get it together efficiently. He had had a lot of faith in his last candidate to help organize the Sparks, but Pam had been abrasive and dismissive. She hadn't lasted three months. No one had been sorry to see her go. Keegan had been sorry for the wasted potential, but the Sparks needed to function as a unit. That wasn't so easy with so many strong personalities. He sat on the edge of a desk and listened, and hoped.

"Oh, so *you* want to lead this operation?" Neil countered, his hands on his hips, looking like a flea challenging a big dog.

"I didn't say that," Dion said, raising his brows. "It's Gary's design. How about you, Gary? Do you want to be in charge of the project?"

"Me?" Gary looked flustered. "Uh, sure," he said. He glanced at the list. "We'll pack everything this afternoon, then we can check and see if we're missing anything. I'll, uh, I'll drive the wide hauler with the framework. Dion can drive the cargo car. Jan, you want to take the power truck?"

"No way," Jan said, tossing her braids. "The power truck fishtails all over the place! That regolith is like slush."

"I ought to take the wide hauler," Dion said. "One of the senior technicians told me that it tends to lose power when you drive it uphill. I'm strong enough to hold the wheel if it starts to slip. Jan should come with me. She and I can fix it if it breaks down."

"That's possible," Daya said. "But what about the inflatable habitat and the water tanks? Four vehicles. You'll need a fourth driver."

Keegan watched the interplay between the Sparks, with an eye on Barbara. She had been reading through the list of things to do and items to go. He waited and watched the wheels turn in her head. She looked up from her PDE, her brow furrowed.

"I can drive the power truck, if someone will give me a quick lesson on the controls," she said. "I learned to drive a car in Iowa in the winter, so I've been in slush plenty of times. Is all this stuff in the cargo bay with the new equipment?" She gestured at the list.

"I'm not sure," Gary said, glancing at the others. Dion shrugged his huge shoulders.

Barbara glanced at Keegan. She looked tentative. He gave her an encouraging nod, waiting to see if she knew how to follow through.

"Why don't we go and run down the inventory now?" she said. "It doesn't make sense to load it until it's all there in one place."

"Right," Jan said. By the smug look on her face, her newfound friend was living up to her expectations, too. "Then, we'll have to pack our personal items."

"I'm the newbie. I'm kind of at a loss." Barbara's eyes widened. "What am I going to need on a mission like this?"

"Stick with me, and don't worry about it. It's all figured out already." Jan pulled Barbara's arm toward her and scrolled down the project manifest with one thumb. "Take a look. There's a checklist for personal items, too. You probably brought most of it with you. We'll take what you don't have out of general storage. And we'll need to test your environment suit to make sure it's spaceworthy."

"It's fine. I just got off the shuttle!"

"That's a must." Jan shook her head. "We always test every suit before every EVA. It can mean life or death. Better safe than frozen."

"Or asphyxiated," Neil said, darkly.

Barbara shivered.

"Right," she said. "Will you help me put together my kit?"

"Of course, I will." Jan grinned, her dark eyes full of humor. "Happy to help, roomie."

"Thanks," Barbara said, warmly.

Not a whit of jealousy or competitiveness there. Keegan cheered to himself. *Looking promising*, he thought.

Barbara looked down at the file again. The others

gathered around her. "Okay, we got this. It makes more sense to get our own luggage together first, bring it down to the cargo bay, and start going down the checklist of everything else we need to assemble. You can show me how to test my suit in there. Neil and Daya, will you do a comm check to make sure that the satellite links are clear between here and Aldrinville? I'll need to see how to get in touch with you to give you updates. How does that sound?"

Keegan's smile broadened. His hunch about Barbara was dead on. Looked like the Sparks had a leader.

They had pretty much forgotten his presence. On his PDE screen, he switched on the audio pickup so he could keep on monitoring their conversation in the lab and on the hidden app on their handhelds, then slipped out of the room.

The project was in good hands.

✢ ✢ ✢

> Captain86—Project Moon Beam sounz awsum!

> NeroliFox—Why is she leading? She just got there!

> GaryFan—A crater telescope theyl find aliens

> M0on1969—They're all gon die. Don't go!

> TeamSparks090—"We got this?"
> Grammar much, Barbara?

Chapter 5

Barbara clutched the padded wheel with her white-gauntleted hands and peered out of the windshield of the power truck. The music she'd downloaded onto her PDE blasted in the sealed cab of the truck, and she sang along. She preferred the classic pop music that her parents listened to even though it was over sixty years old. The lyrics were so silly. How could a song know what you did in the dark? She had no idea what that meant but the song had a cryogenic beat, and if she ever danced she figured it'd be a good one to dance to.

The seats in the power truck's dove gray-walled cabin were high-backed, padded benches made wide enough for three people in full EVA suits to sit abreast, like a semi-trailer's cab on Earth, but the big, square, double-paned windows and the oversized doors were gas-sealed to protect the inhabitant from the frigid vacuum outside. At the beginning, Barbara felt nervous that the seals would give way, leaving her to suffocate in the scanty lunar atmosphere. After a few hours, she had gained faith in the integrity of the big vehicle. It even handled with relative ease, far smoother than her family's farm vehicles or her old truck. If she didn't know she was hauling tons of batteries and solar panels in a truck the size of an eighteen-wheeler, she would have thought she was in an upscale family van. The sound system was awesome. If she cranked the bass, every bone in her body vibrated with the rhythm.

The road that had been cleared between Armstrong City and the Aldrinville site had looked clean, but within a mile or so, the gray regolith dust kicked up by Gary in the wide cargo hauler at the lead going at ninety kilometers per hour had started to settle on all the vehicles following. The legs of the feedhorn segments sticking out from under the tie-down tarpaulin stirred up a cloud that made it difficult to see. Jan and the broad, upright cylindrical tank truck hit that and tossed more to the rear past its rounded sides. To top it off, Dion was just in front of Barbara in the heavy cargo car, stirring up his own cloud of regolith. Barbara drove in a virtual dust storm. If it wasn't for GPS, she would probably have run off the road by then. Of course, there was no wind. The regolith outside the reach of the convoy's oversized wheels lay undisturbed in its eternal heaps and dunes only meters from the roadway.

"Fido, kill the music and update me on route status," she said out loud. The screen the new PDE in its clamp mounting on the dashboard of the vehicle lit up, and a wavy line traversed across the face of it in multiple colors.

"You have completed two hundred seventy kilometers, Barbara," the PDE explained in a friendly female voice, only a little mechanical-sounding. Dr. Bright had assured her the voice would smooth out in a short time. "You have a scheduled fifteen-minute rest stop in fourteen minutes nine seconds."

"Okay. Time to check in on the others. Call Jan."

"Okay. Calling Jan Nguyen. Is that what you want?"

"Yes."

Instead of a burr for the ringtone, Barbara had programmed a high-pitched jingle sound that could be heard over the hum of machinery. Naturally, there was no click when Jan answered, but the other young woman's face appeared superimposed on the windshield. Jan's heads-up display activated at the same time. When she saw Barbara, she grinned.

"Hey, girlfriend!" Jan's voice boomed out of the speaker system of the truck. Barbara hastily adjusted the volume. "You doing okay back there?"

"Yeah. We're coming up on our scheduled fifteen-minute break in about thirteen minutes. You and Gary doing all right up front?"

"We're both fine. Just talked to Dion and he says he's got to go to the bathroom."

Barbara chuckled. "Me, too, actually. I'd rather not do it in the suit unless I have to."

"*That's* what Dion said." Jan twisted her lips in a smug smile.

"Well, I can hold it until the break, if he can. I'd hate to get off schedule." Barbara wanted to stick to the timeline for driving she'd mapped out. She'd driven across North America once with her parents to go to Walt Disney World in Orlando, Florida, to see Dr. Bright's exhibit at Epcot Center. She understood her limits driving. She could do almost ten hours on her own, with breaks for lunch, walking around, and snacks. But that was on Earth, without major dust storms, and where if she broke down there would be recharging stations, convenience stores, and anything else she might need. Here on the Moon, there was nothing but dirt and stone as far as one could see—when she could see. In between checking her route, she had been reading manuals on how to fix axles or oxygen leaks in her vehicle. "I'll call him next."

"Okay, then. I'll pass the word to Gary. Coffee in thirteen. Talk to you then, Barb."

"Roger that," Barbara said, as she had heard the others

say. She decided that she liked Jan so far. She hoped that they might be friends for a long time. Instead of using voice command, she reached over to the PDE stuck to the dashboard and hung up by touching the screen with the conductive material in the tip of her glove. She closed one connection and opened the next.

"Dion, it's Barbara."

"Hey, lady," his warm voice boomed out. "We stopping soon?"

Barbara glanced at the corner of the display.

"Twelve and a half minutes. Can you hold it until then?"

"If you can, I can," he said, with a wink. "You run a tight ship! Not that that's a complaint," he added, as he saw her concerned expression. Barbara worried again that she had overstepped the bounds. She felt keenly aware of her situation as the newest Spark. Dion seemed to understand that, and was giving her every benefit of the doubt. "Dion out."

"Barbara out," she said.

The connection closed. The warmth of reassurance that the others accepted her gave her more energy. She bounced a little in the pliable shock padding of the seat.

"Resume music?" Fido inquired.

"Yes!" Barbara said. "Rock on, Fido." The music swelled, washing her in sound.

As she continued to drive, she noted how the brilliant sunlight overhead cut sharp, black shadows alongside each of the cars and the crater edges to either side of the road, but they were quickly becoming obscured by the dust accumulating on the windshield. The sunlight made everything look much crisper with sharper contrast and detail than the earthlight did. They had passed the day-night line over two hours prior. She was glad of that because any EVAs would be less taxing on the suit's batteries in daylight—no need of lights and heaters.

"The stupid Moon dirt sticks to everything," she mumbled to herself as she cycled the windshield wipers again. She fully suspected that once she stopped and stepped outside the truck that she would track the dust back in. Barbara prepared herself mentally for the pristine truck's interior and the crisp whiteness of her suit to become coated with the claggy gray dust. That would be soon, because on her break she intended to put her helmet on and walk around all the vehicles for a visual inspection and to just stretch her legs a bit. But, before that she had to go. Pretty badly.

After over three hours of driving across the lunar surface she knew that the predominant colors on the Moon were the gray of regolith, the white of anorthosite, and the black of the ancient lava that had hardened into basalt, but occasionally, other colors, like bright orange, winked out at her from boulders. When she'd asked her PDE about it, Fido had told her that early settlers on the Moon—that was to say, within the last thirty years—had found a wealth of rare earths and radioactive minerals in greater concentrations than on Earth. Unfortunately, the most common substance anywhere on the surface was the dust. She had been told by the techs that had been out to the site many times that the dust changed colors as they approached the ancient silicic volcano regions, but so far all she saw was just gray lunar regolith. Every time she thought about it, she got excited, knowing that only a few people had ever seen these sights with their own eyes, but the reality of a long, bumpy drive in a vehicle on which she had had only a brief lesson in driving weighed more on her mind than the novelty. On top of all that was the, well, internal pressure. But relief was coming soon.

"Turn it up, Fido," she said. "We've only got a short way to go."

The music rose around her, and she leaned over her controls.

✧   ✧   ✧

"Just like in the training," Barbara laughed to herself as she unzipped the bottom panel of her suit around her backside and up between her legs in the cramped cubicle. The thick compression material *schlurped* as she pulled it away from her skin. The cold air of the power truck's cabin rushed in and gave her a sudden chill. She winced as she barked her elbow on the metal wall. "Ow! This was easier at home, rather than in this shoebox-sized travel toilet."

"I'm sorry, but the travel toilet is as big as it needs to be," her PDE chimed in, almost scaring the pee out of her prematurely. She'd forgotten she had left it on conversation mode.

"Forget it, Fido." She laughed at how silly she was, complaining about the built-in potty on an oversized lunar rover. There were nearly eight billion people on Earth. Fewer than ten thousand of them had been to the Moon, and she was one of them. After all, that put her in the top ten thousandth of a percent of humanity. Everything she did there was a new experience, even this, although it would be a lot less embarrassing to mark other occasions. She was also grateful that Neil and his ever-present camera weren't in the cab. Nobody needed to see an image of her struggling with outer space plumbing.

"That's that," she said as she finished up. She placed her elbows against the closely spaced walls and managed to push herself up from the narrow seat. With the back of her wrist, she tapped the recycle button, and the toilet made a very slow whirling and swishing sound beneath her. The instructor had cautioned all of the trainees *not* to be sitting when the vacuum system engaged. She rubbed her hands with cleaning gel from a wall-mounted squeeze bottle and shook them until they dried.

Barbara untucked her suit from the hook and ladder hasp at her belt, clasped a zipper pull with each hand, and slid them down between her legs before she let go. Then she grabbed the pulls from behind her legs and pulled them up to her waist. Barbara tapped the compression control on her wrist and the suit tightened back against her body. She could feel a faint rush of air forced up around her neck and in front of her face. She opened the toilet door and eased her way out. Whew! Even going to the bathroom required almost as many steps as putting together a truck engine.

She unhinged her helmet from the hook and then placed it over her head, slapping the faceplate down. It sealed with another *schlurping* sound as the neck garment tightened and compressed against her skin. She could feel the helmet suck tight to the back of her head and ears. The semi-malleable compression helmet formed to fit her perfectly and felt like a second skin or a well-fitted but heavier swimmer's cap. She had shed the gloves on a small shelf under the helmet hook. They sealed so tightly to her fingers that they felt like a second skin.

"Fido, prepare the cabin of the main door for egress." The PDE was connected wirelessly to all the truck's controls. Immediately, pumps started pulling the air back into storage bottles for later use.

"The cabin air pressure is dropping. Please seal your faceshield and gloves," her PDE said.

"Roger that." She ran a gloved fingertip around the softseals just to make sure. All were properly engaged. The heads-up display readouts kicked on so she could see the suit's status projected in front of her eyes in translucent blue and red letters. A bar graph showed her power storage, oxygen recycling, and a host of other stats. "Suit seal is good. Pressure stable. Open the door."

"Cabin door is cycling now." The hatch slid aside with a rumble of servomotors.

Barbara leaned forward and looked out the door at the lunarscape around her. She had to pause for a moment just to take it in.

For the first time, she didn't have a windshield, a window, or a shuttle porthole between her and the view, only her faceplate. The clouds of dust hung in the air at about waist-level, settling slowly down around the four trucks in the low gravity. Now that they were past the day-night line, the undulating fields of regolith glowed bright silver-gray in the increased sunlight. She glanced to the sky toward Earth, beginning to disappear below the horizon the farther she and the others drove toward the far side of the lunar orb. While she knew Earth would be much larger than the Moon was at the same distance, it still gave her a jolt to see the huge blue-white sphere surrounded by its white halo in the blackness of space. It seemed at once near and very far away. Her breathing, contained by the protective helmet, sounded loud in her ears. A faint circle of condensation appeared and disappeared over and over again on the translucent shield before her mouth. She swallowed, feeling her neck muscles constrict.

Unbelievable, she thought. *I'm making history.*

The top step to the truck was about a meter above the ground. In lunar gravity, that was a simple jump for her, but the moment was one she wanted to remember for all time.

She stepped off the truck and dropped gently to the surface. She was surprised at how little Moon dust she kicked up.

"That's . . . one small step for a girl, and one giant leap for mankind," she murmured to herself. Like Neil Armstrong so long ago, she was leaving her footsteps on the Moon—a long way from Iowa. She stared at her booted feet, wondering if her prints would look like Armstrong's.

"Hey, girl," Jan said, almost scaring her out of her suit. Barbara's heart pounded like a triphammer. She hadn't noticed Jan in her suit and helmet at the front of the truck before she had jumped out.

"You startled me!"

"Sorry." Jan glanced down at her boots, then smiled up at her. "Your first time to walk on the Moon's surface, right?"

"Yeah," Barbara said, trying to find the words to express how it felt, but couldn't summon the words from the depths of her soul. "It's . . . its cryogenic."

Jan's dark eyes filled with humor.

"You said it, didn't you?"

"Said what?"

"You know, the whole 'small step for man' thing."

Barbara felt her cheeks burn.

"Uh, maaaybe." she said sheepishly. Jan laughed.

"Ha-ha! Don't worry. *Everybody* does it. I'm sure if we took a survey, more than half the people say it. Maybe more than half."

Barbara's heart slowed to a normal pace.

"Well, I guess I at least fit in with half of the people. Did *you* say it?"

"As far as I know, we all said it." Jan turned as Dion, massive in his white suit and helmet, leaped from the cargo car and bounced toward them. Gary followed, loping along behind, his long legs covering the distance like a gazelle's. "Even Dr. Bright."

"Really?" Barbara felt even better.

"What're you two jabbering about?" Gary asked, coming to a halt. A cloud of regolith rose around his feet and settled very slowly.

"Just stretching our legs," Jan replied. She aimed a conspiratorial grin at Barbara. "How are you doing?"

"A little stiff, and thirsty," Gary admitted. He looked from one girl to the other. "Well?"

"Well, what?" Jan asked, putting one hand on her hip.

"Did she say it?" Dion asked, a mischievous smile lighting his face in the clear-fronted helmet. He held up his PDE in his gloved hand. "I just got a text from Dr. Bright. He wants to know."

Barbara opened her mouth, but she couldn't bring herself to say anything. Jan came to her rescue.

"Of course she said it," Jan replied. "Barb's one of us."

"How's it going up there?" Daya asked. About two hours past their second break, the younger Sparks checked in on them for the tenth or twelfth time. Barbara could see the smaller girl's face and Neil's projected on the windshield of the power truck alongside the images of the rest of the crew. They were back on the road again. Barbara felt fortified from both the camaraderie of her new colleagues and plenty of good, hot coffee. They hadn't teased her about her declaration—much.

"It's kind of boring," Gary replied, making a long face. His dark hair had been pulled back so it wouldn't catch in any of the EVA helmet's seals. "Not much scenery, as you can tell." His image was replaced briefly by the picture of the side of a crater they were passing.

Barbara laughed.

"At least *you* get some scenery," she said, looking past the images to the front window of the cab. In spite of the steadily brightening sun, her view was becoming more obscured by the kilometer. "All we've been getting is your dust."

"Well, if you led the way, you wouldn't see a lot more," Gary said, with an offhanded wave of his glove. "You think this is bad? You should have seen it when we did our initial survey of the site a couple of months ago. The graders have been out grinding down the anorthosite ever since. The road's a lot better than it was."

"This is better?" Jan asked, wide-eyed. "My tailbone can tell you there's not a lot of difference between this and an avalanche. My rear's getting hammered flat."

"At least you get to *be* out there," Neil complained. "We're stuck back in Armstrong City!"

"You want to come out here and wrestle these trucks for hours on end?" Jan asked, with a lift of her eyebrow.

"I could do it," Neil said, but he looked uncertain. Barbara felt sorry for him.

"The wide hauler's not fishtailing too much," Dion said, flipping a palm upward into the view of his video pickup. "I was afraid it would be worse."

"But you're strong enough to drive with one hand," Barbara said. "I'm impressed. I'm having to put a lot of muscle into my turns. I don't understand why these trucks can't be driven by wire instead of mechanical feedback."

"Well, I dunno either." He looked a little embarrassed by her praise. "The challenge is keeping me going."

"Don't let him snow you," Gary said. "He could carry one of these vehicles on his back."

"I kind of feel like I am," Dion retorted.

Nine hours had sounded like a reasonable length for the first day's travel, but Barbara had to agree that it was extremely tedious. The drive had been uneventful so far. In spite of the others' complaints about the condition of the road, or possibly because of it, she was being lulled into a trance.

"How do you stay awake?" Barbara asked, blinking hard to drive away the drowsiness. "Between the windscreen wipers and the white noise from the ventilation system, the sound's almost hypnotic. Even my music can't keep me alert."

"You need more coffee," Jan said, laughing.

"I've had too much coffee," she said. "I don't want to stop again too soon. We're almost to the halfway point."

Gary tossed his head back in a cavernous yawn. Barbara yawned in sympathy.

"An hour and a half for lunch and two fifteen-minute breaks aren't enough," he said, blinking. "If I couldn't see all of you on vid, I'm pretty sure I would have fallen asleep at the wheel."

Barbara eyed his image with concern.

"Will you make it the rest of the way?" she asked.

"I guess," he said. His gaze went unfocused for a moment, probably as he corrected the angle of his vehicle. "I feel sluggish. If it had just been me, I think I would have stopped sooner."

"Am I pushing everyone too hard?" Barbara asked, concerned.

He yawned again, but swallowed it, and met her eyes directly.

"No. I'll make it. We've got only about half an hour left before dinner and sack time, right?"

Barbara glanced down and to the left at her chronometer. "Twenty-seven minutes. Are you hungry?"

"Ha ha," Jan giggled. "He's always hungry."

"No!" Gary protested. He held up a handful of plastic wrappers. "I've been snacking all the way."

"Well, that's why you're sluggish," Daya said. Her lips pursed primly. "You're flooding your brain with too many carbs."

"Hey, I'm fine! I've got protein snacks, too." Gary produced a couple of red-and-yellow-wrapped meat sticks. "I'm staying on the road. That's all I need to do for another half hour."

"Twenty-five minutes," Barbara added, then blushed as all of them stared at her. "Sorry. I do numbers. My mouth goes on autopilot sometimes."

"I can confirm you're on track," Neil added. "The imaging nanosats have snapped a picture of you at least every ten minutes or so. If Dr. Bright would hurry up and approve my EMdrive Drone project we could have followed you and had real-time video the whole way."

"EMdrive Drone?" Barbara asked, raising her eyebrows. That was a project she hadn't heard of. "What's that?"

"You know, E, M, drive as in electromagnetic cavity propulsion, like what powers the shuttles?" Neil said.

"We've gone over this fifty times, Neil," Dion said, in a very patient tone. "It takes too much power to fit it on a drone."

"Not true. I've done the calculations," Neil retorted, frowning. "We just have to make the drone very lightweight! Since we're on the Moon with lower gravity, it could be done."

"Power is a problem?" Barbara asked.

"No," Neil immediately responded.

"Yeah, it is," Jan said at the same time. "EM drives on the small end don't produce much thrust, something like a couple of newtons per kilowatt. So, if it's solar powered you'd need a one meter by one meter solar panel just to give you a couple of newtons of thrust. In other words, the solar panel would be required to power the drive to make enough thrust to fly the engine, the solar panel, and the vehicle. All of that would have to weigh less than, uh, I don't know, like, a liter of water in order to fly."

"We could do it," Neil insisted. "I have the solid model of the prototype already finished. We just need to print it out and test it."

"Maybe we will someday soon, Neil," Barbara told him, trying not to laugh at his dismay. "Sounds fun."

Gary yawned again, almost showing his tonsils.

"Guys, I hate to interrupt such stimulating conversation but we're here," he said. "I'm ready for a nap."

"Me too," Dion agreed. "We stopping?"

Barbara checked the latest nanosat image that Neil and Daya had beamed to them. They were a few minutes short of her schedule, but she knew she had to learn to be a little more flexible.

"Sure," she said. "We're halfway there. We can make camp for the night. I say we get stopped, take time for restroom breaks, and then get the tents inflated."

"Sounds good to me, Barb," Gary said. His shoulders

worked as he pulled the hauler to a stop at the side of the road. "Nice to have someone being definite for a change other than Neil."

"Hey!" Neil protested.

Gary grinned at him. "Let's get over to the side. While I don't expect any traffic on the future mega-highway between Armstrong City and Aldrinville, leaving a vehicle parked in the middle of the road just doesn't feel right even if this road's on the Moon a thousand kilometers from anybody. Here goes." He pressed his lips together and stared hard into the middle distance. Barbara heard the servos of his control system die down. He looked up at something she couldn't see. "Okay, team, I'm at full stop. Dion? Jan? Barb?"

"Pulling in," Jan said. "Dion?"

"Stopping now," Dion replied. The sound from his engines dropped from a whine to a grumble. Barbara checked his location on the moving map application. A blue dot for Jan halted only a few meters from Gary's dot and then Dion's pulled in just behind them. She steered carefully, feeling the heavy vehicle start to drag as the acceleration tapered off. The last of the dust cloud settled onto her windshield. She ran the wipers just once more to clear it. "Barb?"

"I'm here. Engine off." Barbara told him. "Power supply at eighty-six percent."

"Nice going," Dion said. "I'm about the same. You did pretty good for the first time driving that kind of rig."

"Thanks!" Barbara felt a glow of pride.

"We can charge to full overnight if you run the leads out to the rest of us."

"Will do," Barbara said, already planning the best way to hook the other trucks up to hers. The heavy coiled cables were on massive spools in the side of her trailer.

"I'm reading all your vitals," Daya spoke up for the first time in a while. "You're all in great shape; just tired, it would appear."

"Thanks, Daya," Barbara said. Then a thought struck her. "Are you going to watch us sleep, too?"

"Well, I was going to," the girl said. "Why?"

"Uh, well, to be honest," Barbara squirmed a little, "it sort of creeps me out."

"Don't worry, she only sees charts and graphs, Barb." Gary laughed. "Besides, it's a required safety protocol. Don't forget you're a Bright Spark now. Everybody's watching."

✧ ✧ ✧

HeloFanAx—Why do they have to stop?
They only have to go another thousand klix?

Jurgen0925—Boring pix, Neil! It's all grey!

M4r1a—I'd be scared.

YuBaitu—History is made one journey at a time.

Chapter 6

"Don't forget the fact that I'm a Bright Spark, he says!" Barbara slid her pajamas over her bare feet and pulled them up. The light blue pants with pink kittens scattered randomly about the flannel material gave her a much younger look than her actual age. She straightened the long blue-and-pink sleep shirt over them, and pulled thick sleep socks onto her feet. "And the fact that we're in an inflatable tent in the middle of nowhere on the Moon—well, that just won't stop rolling around in my head."

"You'd think you'd get used to it, but I never have. Nice PJ's, by the way." Jan pulled the hair band from her long black hair and untied the braids. Barbara watched her as she started to drag a brush through her hair. Jan wore dark blue pajamas with a colorful picture of Saturn on the top.

"Thanks," Barbara said as she looked out the transparent window section of the tent once more before she brought down the curtain to block out the brilliant sunlight. There was nothing on her side but Moon as far as she could see. Gray lunascape with jagged hills and crater rims in the distance looked cold and exciting at the same time. Then it hit her how far away from everything she was. They were twelve hundred and eight kilometers from any other humans and about four hundred thousand kilometers from the rest of humankind.

"Oh, you're welcome. I like kitties. Wish we could bring one up here," Jan said. "I miss mine. Ms. Scruffles."

"How can I help you, Jan?" her PDE replied in an alto voice.

"Sorry, Ms. Scruffles. Cancel." Jan laughed.

"I miss my cat, too. Tabitha's almost as old as I am, though," Barbara said. She sat down on her sleeping bag spread out on the inflatable bunk and pulled her knees up to her chin. "You seem very calm about everything here."

"How do you mean?"

"I mean, this is kind of scary to me." Barbara ran through all the things that could go wrong in her mind. "The tent could spring a leak or there could be a solar flare or we could have a power failure or . . . I don't know. Probably a million other things could happen that could kill us. Oh, my god!" Her throat tightened. She stared up at the other girl. "I never realized how dangerous this is. My parents would be freaking out if they knew all the details of the things that I do. I'm not so sure we should be out here like this all by ourselves."

In her mind's eye, she saw the bulging, rounded wall of the tent split and the moist air escape in a gust of ice particles. The cold rushed in like an Arctic gust, surrounding the two girls before they could even move, freezing them into blue-skinned statues with glassy, sightless eyes. Barbara clenched her hands and sucked in a deep breath. Why hadn't she taken more precautions? She couldn't surface into atmosphere; there *was* no atmosphere. Her breath began to come in short gasps. She tried to stop, but she couldn't. They were all going to suffocate!

Jan threw herself onto the bunk next to her and grabbed her by the shoulder.

"Barb. Barb! Snap out of it!" Jan shouted, her nose almost touching Barbara's. Barbara flailed at her with both hands. With a flick to the chest, she knocked Jan back a meter or so, and immediately felt ashamed of herself.

"Oh my god! I'm so sorry!"

"It's okay." Patiently, Jan bounded back and sat down again. "Calm down! You're not in serious danger. In fact, you're not in any danger as long as you stick to your training and what you *know*. While the Moon is a harsh environment, we understand it and are prepared and well trained. *You* are well trained. There are no monsters here that are going to get us. If a micrometeor hits the tent, we'll fix it. If there's a power failure, we'll fix it. Whatever goes wrong—and it will; it always does—don't panic. We'll fix it. You'll help. We Got this."

"I, uh, I . . ." Barbara tried to pull herself together. She was breathing so hard it felt like her chest was going to explode. Jan put a sympathetic hand on hers.

"Listen, we all go loony our first time. God knows I did. It took me a couple hours to get past my first trip out here without Dr. Bright chaperoning us. It's sort of a panic attack, agoraphobia, and isolation all wrapped up in one big smack in the face. This is the ultimate test of your confidence in your own ability to function without someone else telling you how to." Jan squeezed her hands, giving her a necessary connection to hang onto.

Barb clutched her friend's fingers. What she was saying was almost word for word from the panic training they had received on Earth. She nodded. Jan smiled. "Take a deep breath before you hyperventilate. The tent can't explosively decompress. Physics just won't allow it. Look at it. Look!" Jan pointed at the wall.

Reluctantly, Barbara turned to see. It looked like plain cloth.

"It's a densely woven canvas of mixed fibers, treated with

sealant made to be flexible at sub-zero temperatures," Jan continued. "The pressure is only at two-thirds of an Earth atmosphere and the material is too thick and rugged for it to split. Plus, the inflation system would just compensate for a leak with overpressure. Also, you've learned, and I saw you do it this morning, to put on your compression suit in thirty seconds or less. These new suits are so easy to get in and out of. Strip down, slip it on, zip it, then slide the helmet on, then the gloves and boots. Easy. The hardest part was getting over stripping almost naked to put it on." She grinned. Barbara smiled weakly at her.

Jan held up her wrist. Little lights twinkled from the band. "Look at your bracelet. All green. That means we have plenty of oxygen."

Her calm recounting of the steps to put on their survival suit soothed the rising terror in Barbara's belly. Eventually, the panic subsided and Barbara relaxed.

"Okay, okay, I'm sorry." Barbara let out a sigh and plopped onto the air bed, feeling as though the air had been let out of *her*. But when her bottom hit the mattress, she bounced back up almost twenty centimeters then, and slowly came to a rest on it. Gravity. It made her chuckle ruefully. She met Jan's concerned gaze. "I've got it under control. I do. Just . . . the training, even the emergency exercises, can't prepare you for this. The truck seemed more, well, solid. And doing EVAs in the suits is temporary, like scuba-diving. But the tents, well, they don't seem solid or temporary. I just need to get used to them being all that is between us and space."

"Think of it as camping out." Jan smiled, her dark almond eyes lighting up. "Minus the mosquitoes and the scary outhouses."

Barbara felt ashamed of herself. She glanced up at Jan. "I really freaked out, didn't I?"

"Yes," Jan said, brimming with satisfaction. "Right about

on schedule. We all did it. You recovered pretty well. It won't be the only time, but don't worry. We're all here to help you and each other. We're self-rescuing princesses around here."

At that, Barbara had to giggle. "How do Gary and Dion feel about being called that?"

Jan made a wry mouth.

"Do you think I give them a choice? I think it's a fair exchange for all the times I've been called 'you guys.' But, really, I don't think they mind. Gary especially. It's the hair."

Barbara let herself laugh heartily, partly because it was funny, and partly because she could relax again. She had known she might have a panic attack. Some of the screening she had gone through was to ensure that she knew what to do, and not to let it freeze her into being nonfunctional. This was one of the big reasons why no one was allowed to go out into the lunar landscape alone. Jan wrinkled her nose humorously.

A hollow-sounding voice interrupted them.

"Barb, this is Daya. Please respond?"

Barbara looked around for its source, then realized her PDE was still attached to her compression suit. She bounced once, flinging herself up and almost hitting her head on the top of the tent, and windmilled to a stop near the zipped door where her suit was hanging. She pulled the PDE from the sleeve pocket and returned to the air mattress with a dive onto her sleeping bag. Jan bounced high, but held on as the inflatable bed settled down. Barbara looked into the screen at the smaller girl.

"Barbara here, Daya. What's up?"

"Um, I'm seeing elevated levels in your vitals. Are you feeling okay?" Daya asked, her huge dark eyes full of worry.

Barbara frowned. She was out of her suit with all of its monitors. How could the younger girl know she was agitated? Then she looked at the instrumentation bracelet on her left wrist.

Darn it, I forgot about that thing. Little sister Daya is always watching us.

"Oh, I'm okay," she said, feeling her cheeks warm with embarrassment. "I was just, uh, uh . . ."

"Daya, this is Jan," the dark-haired girl said, leaning over Barbara's shoulder so Daya could see her. "She's fine. We were just, um, talking about cats." She giggled and winked at Barbara.

"Are you sure?" Daya replied, her eyebrows lowered in concern. "Because the readings here would suggest the onset of a panic attack!"

"Oh, no. Nothing like that." Jan screwed up her face. "It was cats."

"Any cats in particular?" Daya asked. From the tone in her voice, Barbara wasn't sure Daya was buying it.

"Uh, no. Just cats in general." Barbara added. "My cat Tabitha. And Ms. Scruffles."

"I got some new pictures from my mom at home, Daya," Jan said, with a wicked glint in her eyes. "Want to see them?"

From the panicked look on Daya's face, Barbara guessed that she had had to endure holoslide shows of Jan's cat pictures more than once.

"Not now."

"I'm okay, Daya," Barbara assured her. "Really, I am."

"Uh huh." Daya said. They could tell she wasn't convinced. "Just take it easy and get some rest. And, I guess, quit talking about cats, then."

"Right, will do, in about never." Jan laughed. The younger girl made a little face at them.

"Good night, Daya," Barbara told her and shut off her PDE. She slid it into the jacket pocket of her pajama top. "Thanks for covering for me, Jan. I, uh, just couldn't handle it if they thought I was washing out of the program or something like that."

"Washing out? You are so far from it." Jan waved a

dismissive hand. "Hey, besides, what're bunkmates for? Just think of it like, even the NASA astronauts get motion-sick on their first microgravity experience. I mean, I know I did."

"Yeah, I did a little."

"See," Jan said, with a friendly grin. "No big deal. Now, let's get some sleep, okay?"

"They don't actually call me 'rookie,' Dad, but I'm sure they're thinking it," Barbara told her father. Their images hovered above New Fido's screen. Jan was wearing earphones and listening to music to give her some privacy, something that was proving to be in short supply on the Moon. It was good to see her parents' faces in this remote place.

Lange Winton smiled. "I'm sure they think you're just great, big girl. Otherwise, Dr. Bright wouldn't have chosen you to do the job."

Barbara relaxed. Her dad always seemed to know the right thing to say to make her feel better.

"That's right, Barb honey," her mother added. "You're the smartest young lady I've ever met and all you have to do is show them that. They'll accept you. It sounds like they already have."

"I know, I know, but I'm still the new kid. And, it's, well, very isolated up here." Barbara forced a smile to her lips even though she could feel them quivering. "It's kinda like camping out on the western fields at the edge of the property, you know what I mean?"

"Yeah, we understand that. You're more than just kilometers away from anywhere," her father replied. He gave her a rueful smile. "Speaking of the western fields, Harvester Seven died out there again. It drove up to the edge of the field and then lost its mind and turned into the swamp and kept going 'til it got stuck all the way up to the top of the axles. It think it misses you."

"Probably the GPS board went on the fritz again,"

Barbara guessed. "You'll have to get someone to pull the main access router from the computer box under the rear access panel. It won't be cheap, Dad."

Her father waved a hand.

"Don't you worry about that, big girl! We'll get it figured out. You need to stay focused on what you have going on out there."

Her mother interrupted them. "Are you having fun, sweetheart? I bet it's the time of your life. You made it to the Moon!"

"Yes, Mom," she said. She glanced at Jan, grateful for her roommate's tact, but realizing she had to show similar consideration. "We need to get to sleep. I love you both. Can I see Tabitha?"

"Uh, hold on." Her father slipped away from view for a second, then returned with the orange and white cat that had lived on the farm about as long as Barbara had. The cat seemed annoyed at having been picked up from whatever it had been doing.

"Hey, Tabby." Barbara smiled. "That's my kitty. I miss you, old girl. You miss me?"

The cat gave her a long-suffering look and kicked out of her father's arms. He looked embarrassed.

"She was purring, I swear," Lange Winton said.

"It's okay, Dad. Love you and Mom." Barbara chuckled and settled down in her bunk to go to sleep.

Barbara found herself looking up at the tent ceiling more than once throughout the night. The inflatable bunk wasn't as comfortable as a real mattress. She found herself holding her neck rigid to compensate for the pillow sliding around under her head. There had to be some way of coping with it. Part of her sleeplessness was due to the lower gravity and thinner air, the same as she had experienced sleeping in the mountains. The air was also far drier than she was accustomed to breathing, in spite of the humidifier built into the ventilation system. She hoped she'd get over it soon. Beside her, Jan slept like a log.

Barbara put her arms behind her head. She wished she could relax. While she had been exhausted from driving all day, she still couldn't shake that alone-in-the-wilderness feeling. The monsters that Jan assured her were not out there were the demons in her own mind. As the hours passed, Barbara got impatient with herself. She had achieved her heart's desire. She was on the Moon, on a mission with Dr. Bright's Bright Sparks. All possible precautions had been taken. The physics were under control. She had *peeps*. They would all take care of each other, and they would get the project done. Dr. Bright would be proud. All she had to do was deal with the psychology's soft science.

After her meltdown earlier in the night, Barbara promised herself there would be no more incidents like that. She had a job to do and she was going to do it better than anyone else. She didn't want to end up like that Pam girl. She certainly wasn't going to screw up an opportunity working for Dr. Bright!

That led her to mull over the details of the excavation and construction that they had scheduled to begin early the day after tomorrow. Dr. Bright had said that the crater was almost perfect for their purposes. Barbara began to do calculations in her mind to make certain they excavated it into the ideal parabola for the radio-radar telescope. The formulae filled her mind until sleep finally came.

"Yip! Yip! Yip! Wake up, Barb! Yip! Yip! Yip! Wake up, Barb!"

Barbara's eyes flew open. The dream in which she was at the bottom of a crater with a shovel vanished.

"That's your alarm clock," Jan mumbled into her pillow. "Ms. Scruffles, cancel wakeup call."

"Yes, Jan," the PDE said.

"Yip! Yip! Yip!"

"Quiet, Fido," Barbara said.

"Yes, Barbara!"

"Hey, you guys up yet?" Neil's voice came from both Fido and Ms. Scruffles at once. Barbara fumbled for the PDE. She dragged it up to eye level and squinted at the screen. The two younger Sparks sat side by side at their computer desks in the lab. On the wall behind them was a satellite view of a gray landscape with four long dashes and two round dots thrown into relief by the angle of the sun. Peering at it bleary-eyed, Barbara realized it was a snap of the trucks and their tents as seen from a long way up.

"Are you two all right this morning?" Daya asked. She wore a bright orange jumpsuit. The color was almost painful on Barbara's sleepy eyes.

"Yes," she said.

"You don't look like you're up," Neil said, peering at her skeptically. He had on a bright blue jumpsuit that was almost as hard on the retinas as Daya's. "I could play you the Marine Corps reveille." He started to reach for a button.

"No way!" Jan said, swinging her legs over the side of the bunk. "I'm up! I'm up!"

Feeling the strain of the day before in her arms and shoulders, Barbara sat up and worked her neck back and forth. Her back ached a little.

"Me, too," she said, letting out a gush of breath. "We're fine. We'll be on the road on schedule. You can tell Dr. Bright."

"Great!" Neil said. "We'll get the guys going now. Have a great day!" The PDE's screen went blank.

Barbara shot an exasperated look toward Jan.

"When we get back, couldn't you just strangle him?" Jan asked, shaking her head. "Nobody should be that cheerful at this hour."

"Yes!" Barbara said.

Jan rose and stretched, then undid one of the gear packs they had brought into the tent with them.

"Hey, roomie," Jan said as she tossed Barbara a folded white packet about the size of a sheet of copy paper. Barbara caught it in mid-air. "Dry shower? You can clean up while I hit the head." She nodded toward a portable potty unit that sat in the corner.

"Thanks," Barbara said. No way to hit the snooze button and go back to sleep now. She got up to use the cleansing packet, and turned her back to give Jan privacy. She could hear Jan zipping the curtain around the toilet but there was no escape from sound in such close quarters.

"Fido, some soothing morning music please."

"Yes, Barbara." A soft piano sound filtered into the tent that was soon accompanied by a guitar and a woman's voice. Barbara loved that song. It was one of her mother's favorites. The plaintive music made her a little homesick.

Barbara turned her attention back to the task at hand: cleaning away the dust. One side of the cleansing packet contained a flat tube of "shower in a box" cleanser that was a strong enough surfactant that the small tube could clean an entire human body. On the upside the cleanser was strong but not too harsh on the skin, and the other side of the packet contained a large drying cloth. She used both, then finished up with her own toiletries and skin cream. Anything resembling a real shower would have to wait until they set up the habitat near the construction site and piped in the water tank. She had been warned when packing for the Moon to steer clear of anything that contained perfume. In small quarters where the air was constantly recycled, you could get tired of your own smell very quickly, but it was rude to inflict strong perfume on everyone else. It felt good to be clean. She pulled on her suit and fastened the seals.

When Jan was finished with her own dry shower, she

rolled up the envelopes and cloth and stuffed them into the portable toilet.

"They break down when they hit the septic solution," Jan explained. "Everything we use is biodegradable, reusable or recyclable." Barbara followed her example.

She saw what Jan meant when they opened up the breakfast rations. The clear screwtop containers for milk and juice were so sturdy they could be sanitized and refilled an infinite number of times back at the settlement. The empties and lids went back into the box. The clear vacuum-pack wrappers holding pastries and breakfast sandwiches were bioplastics that were treated the same way as the shower cloths.

"The Moon is never going to end up with the trash problem Earth has," Jan said. "Not if we have anything to do with it."

Together, the girls emerged from their tent in blazing sunlight to do walkaround inspections of the vehicles and cargo. As they trudged through the deep regolith dust, Gary waved to them from the top of the wide hauler. He swiped a hand to clear the dust off his faceplate. That stuff just got everywhere! He was ready to roll, but Barbara still had her checklist to go through.

"Inflation on tires, good," Fido acknowledged, as Barbara narrated the answers to her checklist. Following her list, she did a visual examination of each of the seals, then climbed the inset U-shaped rungs to the top of the trailer to have a look. "Pinhole leaks in cabin, negative."

In all, everything looked fine. Her inspection revealed no undue movement or wear and tear. The only task Barbara had to undertake was to sweep the Moon dust off the exposed solar panels and roll up the cables that had recharged everyone's batteries. Her power storage read one hundred percent. She snapped the big reel back into place with a feeling of satisfaction, and closed the safety bar.

Once everyone had cleared their personal goods, Dion took charge of deflating and repacking the tents. Barbara was impressed by how quickly he got the collapsed bags rolled up and stowed.

"We're good to go," he said, via the PDE intercom function. Barbara glanced toward his truck as he gave her a thumbs up and swung into the cab, surprised that he sounded as if he was standing next to her. "Load up!"

"Roger," Barbara said. She brushed as much regolith off her suit and boots as she could before she climbed inside her own vehicle. They'd never be free of all the dust. She simply had to cope with it.

For the first part of the drive, Barbara didn't activate her playlist today. Instead, she stared out at the lunar landscape, just getting back into the pace of driving. Everyone over the group circuit was oddly quiet, only speaking to give orders to their PDEs to control one system or another. Barbara suspected the others were as tired as she was. She concentrated on following the satellite map and what little she could see of the anorthosite trail through the others' dust. Now and again, she still glanced at the jagged craters on her left and right with a sensation of delight.

"The road's a little squishy ahead," Gary warned them an hour into the drive. "We've got a kind of tight right turn coming at the base of that crater five kilometers up, so take it slow."

"Acknowledged," Barbara said. The others chimed in as well, then fell silent. They were all too intent on getting to their destination. She was still taking in the landscape out of the side windows and enjoying the journey.

The screen filled with an overhead image from the nanosats from time to time, a contribution from Neil back in Mission Control. The fourth dust cloud in line was the power truck she was driving. The crater Gary mentioned loomed enormous quite a distance to their left. They had to divert around that and a cluster of three smaller, overlapping ones beyond it to reach their goal.

"You're on target for on-time arrival at the site," Neil said, his face appearing on an inset on the image forty-seven minutes before they were due to stop for lunch. "I posted the series of images on the blog. The number of hits is blowing my mind! The number's almost half again as large as our last big project got."

"Will you be willing to answer questions from some of the comments we're getting, Barbara?" Daya asked, her own picture appearing in the other corner.

"Me?" Barbara asked.

"Sure!" Neil said. "You're the newest Spark. Lots of people want to get to know you, hear what you think."

Barbara drew in a sharp breath. After being one of those people who wrote in to Dr. Bright's show or asked questions on line, she hadn't anticipated being one of the ones who *answered* those questions. But she was having experiences that would be the envy of fellow science nerds back on Earth. It was a humbling thought.

"Yes . . . I guess so."

"Good," Daya said. "I will accumulate the more interesting ones and beam them to you in a file. Take your time. You can dictate them to your PDE if you like."

"Uh, thanks," Barbara said.

"It's all right to record them over and over until you get the entries the way you want them. I often send out sixth or seventh drafts."

"You can also listen to your email," Neil added. "Just tell your PDE to read it to you. Or you can tap into the movies and TV show archives we have."

"Um, maybe later," Barbara said, still absorbing Daya's request. "Out."

For about half a minute, she thought about catching up on superhero movies, then decided against it. Driving a power truck almost the size of an eighteen-wheeler across an unimproved road on the Moon took all of her concentration. Every now and then she had to hit the wipers, as the dust would make the windshield too opaque to see through. A little music wouldn't hurt, though. She usually studied with the walls of her dorm room vibrating.

"Fido, playlist number five, I think."

"Yes, Barbara."

The music rose around her, and she started an oldies headbanging song her grandparents liked that had a good driving beat. The bleak landscape looked better with a good bass and shredding guitars. Maybe she could post the songs she played in a downloadable file. *Lunar roadtrip playlist,* she thought with a giggle.

But the PDE hadn't played more than half a song before Fido's voice interrupted it.

"Barbara, you have an incoming call from Dr. Bright."

"Oh, wow. Okay," she said. She sat up straighter and gripped the wheel in both hands. "Answer it in projector mode."

The scientist's face was projected onto the windshield head's up display. Barbara felt her heart flutter.

"Ms. Winton, how are you doing this morning? I hope all is going well?"

Barbara smiled shyly at the HUD image.

"I'm doing fine thanks, sir. How are you? We're . . . we're moving along pretty well so far. No problems with the trucks or the tech." Her words piled out on top of one another like a basket of puppies as she described the trip. Part of her said he had been following their travel on satellite, and he already knew everything, but she just couldn't stop talking.

"Great!" He gave her a toothy television smile as if he was going to laugh. He was so full of energy that Barbara found it infectious. She smiled nervously back at him. "Good report, Barb. Sounds like you're managing the group like a trouper."

"We're on schedule and will arrive at the crater site around six p.m.," she responded cheerfully.

His blue eyes studied her thoughtfully.

"That's good to know. So, what do you think about those tents, huh? I got to tell you, they weird me out sometimes. I mean just looking out the window at the emptiness of the Moon all around you and nobody around for hundreds and maybe thousands of kilometers and you start to thinking that there's nothing but a flimsy bit of fabric between you and cold dead space." He raised his shoulders and shivered. "Brr! Gives me chills thinking about it now. You just have to not think about it and focus on the task at hand."

Barbara had never talked that long with him before. She had never really thought about him having human emotions like a normal person. After all, he was *Dr. Bright*. He was larger than life, a super genius, astronaut, pilot, and celebrity scientist. Barbara was surprised that the tents might creep him out too.

"Yeah, I did sort of have a hint of that at first, but I got over it." She wasn't sure she should have told him that, but he waved away the notion.

"Hey, wait 'till you are out there and you look up and see the Earth for the first time rising over the limb of the Moon and shining full in the sky. Then you'll forget about everything else and just realize how beautiful it all is," he said. She could tell by the look on his face and the sincerity in his voice that he was speaking from experience.

"I can't wait," she replied, and she meant every word.

"Great!" He smiled his exuberant smile again, then leaned in a little closer to the video pickup. "Now listen, I want you to keep an eye on everyone for me, okay? I mean, this is a long drive, and if you feel like you should take more breaks or rest longer, don't feel like you have to follow the scheduled timeline exactly. Sometimes these things look better in a presentation or on a schedule than they do in real life. You've got to see what people need, and respond to it."

"Yes, sir." Barbara licked her lips nervously. It was like the bloggers were saying, that she was considered in charge of this project. That couldn't be right. She was the newest member of the group! But she wasn't going to let him down. "Right now, we're doing fine."

"I knew you would be," he said, sitting back with that companionable chuckle. "Listen, I've got to go right now, but I'll check in later. And Barbara, don't you hesitate to call me if you need anything, any time."

"Yes, sir! Have a great day."

"You, too. Barb." He nodded and the feed shut off, leaving the screen clear of anything but the dust cloud and the road ahead. Barbara shook herself in disbelief.

"That was an interesting conversation, huh, Fido?" she asked.

"I'm sorry, Barb. I was not listening. Do you want to tell me about it?" Fido replied.

She laughed. The new PDE was not only efficient, but discreet. "No, thanks. Never mind. How about some music? Fast-paced and loud."

"Okay, I will play some music."

Triumphant chords rose around her. Barbara felt as happy as she had ever been in her life, but humble and nervous at the same time. Dr. Bright trusted her.

Keegan shut off the video call and leaned back in his desk chair. He exhaled through pursed lips, making a motorboat sound. The four vital-statistics feeds for the previous evening displayed on one of the screens of his private office were those belonging to the Sparks traveling toward the crater, and the one on the far left was Barbara's. He looked at the brief spikes and smiled as he overlaid his own first open-Moon EVA data over it. Barbara had handled her first space-panic attack in a fraction of the time he had, and with much less intensity. He bet she didn't even break out in cold sweats. Keegan recalled getting so freaked out on his first EVA that he thought he was going to have to change his shorts. Compared to the other kids, only Pam had fared better.

But that girl had been an emotionless robot. He'd gone too far in that direction choosing her. Barbara was different. She was more emotional, but logical at the same time. It was a quality about her that he didn't quite know how to describe but he knew he liked.

"Kids these days!" He laughed. "Well, Leona, looks like we've got ourselves a keeper."

"Yes, it would appear so, sir," his PDE responded.

"But, keep an eye on her. And make sure she calls her parents again sometime today. I think that'll help her morale. The last call seems to have done her some good."

"Yes, sir. I have sent a reminder to Fido to suggest it."

"That's the way to do it," Keegan said. "I don't want to steer her too much, but it's too easy to forget about the little things that help keep a mental balance."

"Dr. Bright?" A knock at the door broke his train of thought.

"Yes?" He closed out the biodata files with a wave of his hand. The assistant producer leaned in the open door.

"We're ready for you on the set, if you are."

Keegan kicked his chair back from the desk and gave the young man a grin.

"Be right there." He picked up his PDE and put it on silent. "Time to pay the bills."

"How did you not see that hole?" Gary was shouting at Dion as Barbara bounced to them over the dusty road. Jan stood a few meters away from the boys, examining the heavy cargo car's passenger side rear dual wheels. Both huge tires were completely off the ground, and the axle was resting on a larger, glassy, smooth-looking boulder. Two massive, wide ruts had been plowed through the regolith thirty meters off the main road. The car vibrated in place as if frustrated. Heaps of Moon dust were scattered outward as if a bomb had gone off, leaving bare, dark rock underfoot.

"Is everybody all right?" Barbara asked, looking at each of the others in turn for signs of suit damage or injury. Through the PDE circuit, she had heard the whole argument from the moment Gary had climbed out of his vehicle. She took a long running leap and bounded to land right between them in a low cloud of dust. "Nobody's hurt, right?"

Gary took a step back as she approached, then turned and stomped away a few paces, although stomping was a relative term when each forceful pace made him rise a few centimeters above the surface. Barbara, too, got caught by the light gravity and found herself bouncing uncontrollably back and forth. She steadied herself by putting her hand on Dion's shoulder. Gary loped back and caught her around the waist. Together, the two young men helped her settle to the surface.

"Thanks," she said. They both looked angry, but not at her. "What happened?"

Dion threw up his hands in annoyance.

"It was so quick," he burst out. "I didn't intend for it to happen."

"And he ran off the road! I warned you!" Gary said, leaning toward the taller youth. "I missed it. Jan missed it. Why didn't you?"

"Okay, back up a little." Barbara forced them each to take a step slightly apart from the other. She looked back along the road to where her own vehicle was parked. She could hardly have missed the swerving tracks the heavy car had left behind it on its way to its current resting place. "Was anyone hurt?"

"We're okay, Barb." Dion nodded. "I, uh, I don't know, maybe I nodded off or something."

"Highway hypnosis probably," she said. "I should have stopped us earlier for a break. I'm really sorry."

"This isn't your fault, Barb," Gary almost shouted. He gestured towards Dion. "It's his."

Barbara stayed between them.

"Hey, it could happen to anyone, Gary. It could have happened to me in the next hundred meters. So let's quit thinking about what happened and start thinking about what we need to do next."

"This thing is stuck pretty good." Jan bounced from around behind the cargo car. "Both wheels on the back driver side are buried in about a meter of regolith. I hope the rock banging against the axle didn't warp it."

"Bah, warp it?" Gary gave a sarcastic laugh and shook his head. "That frame was cold rolled and heat treated. I bet that rock would break before that axle would."

"Well, how much you think it weighs with all the cargo on it?" Barbara asked, trying to get him to think instead of react. "I mean, can we push it off that rock? I've still got my Earth muscles, at least for now."

"I doubt by hand. We might be able to winch it off, if we had a winch," Dion said.

"Well, I don't remember seeing that on the manifest," Barbara said. "Fido, do we have one on any of these vehicles?"

"Nope," Jan replied, before Barbara's PDE could answer. "I'm not even sure we have a tow rope or a chain. Boy, that's shortsighted, isn't it?"

"No kidding," Gary said. His burst of temper had dissipated. Like Barbara, he had gone into problem-solving mode. "I didn't think of including a winch. Maybe we could use a jack somehow. We've got those."

"Not to get a meter of play we couldn't." Dion turned to

Barbara. "I'm sorry, you guys. I just don't know how it happened. It was all so fast. Gary said 'watch out for the hole on the side of the road,' and the next thing I knew, I was here. My tire hit it, and knocked me off the graded surface."

"It's all right." Barbara chewed at her bottom lip, trying to think. She looked up and down the road. It was empty apart from their four vehicles. "What would Dr. Bright do?" She wondered if she ought to call him. She opened her mouth to tell Fido to make the connection, then stopped. She didn't want to disappoint him by calling for help without trying to solve the puzzle first. More to the point, she would disappoint herself. Barbara tried to clear her mind and examine the situation without emotion.

"Who knows what Doc would do?" Jan shrugged. "Improvise, I guess."

"Yeah, he'd probably take a paperclip and some bubblegum, and build some sort of device that the ancient Egyptians used to build the pyramids or something." Gary laughed and held his palms up. Barbara gawked at him.

"That's it!," she said. She turned and bounced toward the rear of the wide hauler.

"Huh?" Jan asked. They all followed Barbara. "He'd use an ancient Egyptian pyramid building thingy?"

"What're you talking about?" Gary asked. Barbara could tell they thought she was losing her mind. "I was joking. Dr. Bright couldn't use a papercl—"

"No, he wouldn't, or maybe he *would* use a paperclip. I don't know exactly." Barbara interrupted, the idea forming in her mind. "But he'd use what he had at hand. I've seen him do it on the show where he had a problem and used stuff around him to fix it."

"Yeah, so what?" Gary asked. "We've seen *him* do it on lots of episodes. How does that help *us*?"

"We'll use what we have." She leaped up onto the rearmost uncovered part of the wide hauler and patted the bright yellow fender of the small vehicle there. "*We* have a Bobcat with a front end bucket on it." She glanced at the forward edge of the digger. Too sharp, but it might work.

"We can't dig the car out," Dion said. "It's hung up on that boulder, not mired in the regolith. Maybe we ought to turn back and get help. They've got mobile cranes for building construction in the settlement. If we could borrow one, we could get the car off the rock."

Barbara turned and looked down at their puzzled faces. They were all inventors. She was surprised she had to spell out her idea for them so specifically. Maybe none of them had grown up on a farm and had to do stuff like this as she had.

Well, no, they hadn't. They were all city kids. They were smart and creative, but hadn't had to deal with a situation like this before. She had.

"We don't have to go back. We're not going to dig the car out or even build up under the wheels," she said, looking for the controls to lower the rear gate. "And we don't need a crane. We have all the lifting power we need right here. We don't need to move the rock, we just need to lift the truck. We'll simply hoist it off with the Bobcat's bucket. Dion, would you download the manual on that car and figure out where the hardpoints for the frame are? If we lift it in the wrong place it'll tear it up."

He grinned widely, understanding immediately where she was going.

"Sure, just like changing a tire," he said. "I didn't even think of that."

"I've never changed a tire," Gary said. "I never even had a car. You don't need one living in Brooklyn."

"I have," Jan said, eyeing him. "Where do we have to lift from, Dion?"

"I'll sic Candy on that." He tapped the PDE on his sleeve. "Candy, give me full schematics and crane lifting points for this vehicle."

"Roger that, Dion," his PDE replied in a sultry female voice. "Whatever you need."

Barbara stared at him and rolled her eyes. She hadn't heard his PDE's voice before. He gave her a sheepish grin.

"Gary, Jan, we need to get this dozer unloaded," she said, beckoning them over.

"Don't worry about the dozer. I've got it." Dion said, flipping open a control box at the car's bed level. "Can you and Jan clear the ramp and lower it?"

"No problem." Barbara nodded to him.

Gary jumped from more than three meters away and landed on the edge of the hauler beside her. A rooster tail of shiny Moon dust trailed and glistened in the sunlight behind him. Barbara noted how much shinier the dust had gotten. She figured they were approaching the silicic region of the Moon. They had passed the limb of the Moon more than an hour earlier. Officially, they were now on the far side. Barbara scanned the sky and saw only stars and the Sun. She was out of sight of the Earth for the first time in her life. She felt a frisson of fear mixed with excitement, but she would have to wait for a while to commemorate that milestone. They had a problem to solve first.

"Hold it right there!" Barbara shouted while holding up a closed fist motioning Gary to stop the dozer in between the two tails of dust a couple of meters past the base of the ramp. "That's good."

"Hey, Barb?" Jan said, calmly, in a low voice.

"Yeah?" Barbara asked.

"I was just going to remind you, very gently, that we're all connected through the comm link and you don't really have to shout."

Barbara turned to her roommate, who stood ten meters away from her, to the side of the truck gate. She was right. Barbara felt abashed.

"Oh, sorry, guess I got carried away. I'm just used to doing things as I did back on Earth. Dozers should be loud!"

"Well up here sound doesn't carry," Gary continued, grinning at her over the controls of the Bobcat. "And nobody working around them is wearing helmets that are connected by wifi to everybody else."

Barbara laughed at herself.

"You're right," she said. "I won't shout any more. Fido, remind me to start thinking like I'm on the Moon."

"Roger, Barbara," Fido said. "Reminders set."

Dion came over to show the three of them a diagram on Candy's screen. Without the particulate matter in atmosphere to give them body, the holograms were far more limited than they were back in Armstrong City, or even in the cabs of their trucks.

"The hard points are here, here, here, and here." Dion pointed at the image, then at four struts on the bottom of the vehicle, which lit up in blue. Round-headed rivets were visible on the truck frame. "You see them?"

"Yeah, good." Barbara thought for a moment. They couldn't just raise the bucket up into the struts. That might tear the metal and compromise it. They needed a buffer between them. Had she been back at home, her dad would probably have used a fence post or a four-by-four chunk of tree stump as a pad. "Hold on. We need to put a board or something softer than steel across there to protect the bottom of the frame from the bucket, like a piece of wood."

"Trees don't grow out here," Gary stated flatly. She wasn't sure if he was trying to be funny or not.

"Well, we need something." She thought hard, visualizing the pieces of equipment moving around in her mind. *What would Dr. Bright do?*

"Let's go take a look at the gear we brought," Jan suggested, when Barbara hesitated. "Maybe there's something that will jump out at us."

The four of them rummaged through the gear on the wide hauler, the stuck cargo car, and the power truck. One after another, Barbara rejected their suggestions as unworkable. Some were too easily dented or damaged, some were too narrow, and others would cause more damage if they burst on the sharp teeth of the Cat. The four of them gathered at the wide hauler one last time, hoping to brainstorm some sort of idea.

"I give up," Dion said. "Sorry, guys, I've let you down and now we're stuck. We'll get the car down, but we might damage it enough to leave it inoperable." He sat down on the spare tire for the hauler and propped his chin on his elbow in the "Thinker" position.

"You've got to quit being so negative, Dion." Jan slugged him on the shoulder, making him lose his balance on his prop. He windmilled his arms and seemed to swim in the air until he was upright again. Barbara was fascinated. The effects of low gravity were fun to watch. Jan plopped down on the tire next to him and bounced lightly. "We'll figure it out."

"I say we take the chance metal to metal," Gary said. "How much damage could it cause, anyway?"

"Well, I saw our neighbor lift an old tractor once like this. He didn't use anything as a bumper pad, and when he sat it back down it was lopsided," Barbara told them. "That tractor never drove right after that."

"Well, in that case, I give up too." Gary put his foot on the far side of the tire, looking like George Washington in the famous picture of him in the boat crossing the Delaware River.

Barbara looked at him, thinking how funny that would look on that painting if Washington had been in a space suit. For that matter it would be a great picture of Gary just standing in that heroic pose in his space suit with his foot propped up on a spare tire for one of the construction vehicles. It was so perfect, she had to preserve the image for posterity. She took her PDE out of her sleeve and pointed at the three of them.

"Say cheese!" She snapped the picture. "I'm sending it to Neil. This is perfect for the blog."

"What? The Bright Sparks defeated?" Dion shook his head in disgust.

"Nope." Barbara smiled and nudged Jan over with a flick of her hip. She sat down beside them. "The Bright Sparks so close to an answer they wouldn't know if they were sitting on it!" She patted the tire under them.

Jan looked down, startled, then laughed. "Just proves what parts we're thinking with, sometimes."

"That's it! Perfect," Barbara said, as the spongy spare tire slowly made contact with the hard struts on the underside of the stranded cargo car. She signed to Gary in the driver's seat of the Bobcat, who raised the bucket still further. The soft material in the bucket of the dozer met the framework and indented, but did not crush. So far, it was working! "Good. Keep it coming."

The cab started to rise. The electric winch motors driving the bucket started to strain slightly, but the weight of the car was nothing for the little dozer. It lifted over the rock. When it was almost clear, the wheels dropped to the bottom of the suspension. It was strange not being able to hear any of the vibration unless she rested her gloved hand on it. All the cues she was following were visual.

"Okay, Dion, put it in neutral," she said. Almost instantly, the cargo hauler started rolling forward. "Hold the brakes!"

"I've got it," Dion replied from the cab.

The car stopped rolling forward. Barbara could see the front wheels turning to the left.

"No, wrong way!"

"You are shouting, Barbara," Fido said, in a gentle voice.

"Right, sorry," she said, dropping her voice at once. "Dion, you have to drive *with* the pushing bulldozer as opposed to away from it. Like driving in snow."

"How? There's no snow in Georgia where I grew up."

"Cut the wheels the other way," Jan beat her to the instruction. The wheels almost instantly turned to the right. "Yeah, like that." She shared a look of triumph with Barbara.

"Okay," Barbara said, backing up out of accident range. "Now, when I count to three, ease off the brakes, Dion. Gary, you push forward a little." With her eyes on the double tires, she held up a hand so Dion could see her in his mirror and Gary could see from the Bobcat. "One, two, three!" She dropped her hand.

The car started to slide forward, then the wheels started to roll. In no time, they had pushed the rear bumper plate of the cargo car past the boulder. The little dozer couldn't go much farther because it was now bumping against the enormous buried rock. Gary had to work the controls several times back and forth, pushing the tail end of the cab sideways so he could get the bucket clear enough from the boulder to lower it.

"How's that?" he asked.

"I think you can get it down now, Gary," Barbara told him. "Let's see."

"Okay, keep a watch and don't let me get the car door hung on that rock again."

"You got it." She smiled. "Bring it down slowly." The car eased down, to Barbara's admiration. "Gary, that's perfect!" He must have spent hours in the simulator practicing.

The bucket got the car just low enough that the back wheels started to touch the ground on the passenger side before the bottom of the scoop hit the side of the rock again.

"That's as low as you can go, Gary," Jan said.

"Okay, let's see if we can get that tire out from under the car now," Barbara told them.

She and Jan threw their arms around the body of the tire. They worked and worked trying to pull it out, but the weight of the car was still on it. Barbara thought they needed another six centimeters of play at least. She backed off, panting. They had wiggled the dozer about as much as they could, but the bucket was jammed against the side of the rock. It could go no further until the car was off of it. Somehow or other that car had to get six centimeters lower to have its weight on the wheels and not on the strut resting on the spare tire that was lying on its side in the dozer bucket.

"Darn it. We're so close!" Jan said as Barbara turned and walked around to the other side of the car. She studied the way the two vehicles were jammed together. It looked like the result of a terrible collision involving the boulder, although nothing irreparable had happened to any of them yet. She started to do calculations in her mind to get the two of them apart.

"Maybe I could just drive it off," Dion suggested.

"Not a good idea," Gary said. "It might tear up the spare and could possibly even rip the back end of the car off on the edge of the bucket. May have to raise it back up and try to wiggle it some more."

"We'll do no such thing." Barbara jumped up into the cargo area of the hauler and hopped down again with the electric scissor jack cradled in one arm. Her impact on the Moon's surface kicked up more dust, but it had scarcely any impact on her lower legs or knees. She knew she was going to enjoy the lower gravity. "We've already used the spare. Might as well use the jack, too."

She plopped the squat metal frame on the bucket beside the tire and depressed the red UP button. Once it extended to almost the right height, she worked it into the hardpoint closest to the tire, then pressed the UP button again. The hardworking little device's electric motor vibrated under her hands.

The edge of the car rose. As it did, the tire bounced back to its normal shape. Gary and Jan bounded forward to slide it out from between the car's strut and the dozer's bucket. As soon as it was free, Barbara hit the down button on the jack. The electric motor vibrated in her hand as it brought the weight of the car downward. When the wheels touched the Moon, the weight of the vehicle sank onto the suspension. Once the jack was completely collapsed, Barbara slid it out from between the bucket and the car. Gary leaped back into the dozer's seat and rolled it out of the way. The heavy hauler was free and clear.

"Tranquility Base here. The Eagle has landed," Barbara said triumphantly. The others cheered. "Pull it forward now, Dion. Slowly."

"Roger!"

The car eased forward. Once he was certain that it was free of the rock and the bucket, Dion pulled it back in place behind Jan's water hauler. Barbara couldn't help but grin and feel proud of herself. Here she was on the Moon using a spare tire and a scissor jack and a bulldozer to get a lunar rover unstuck from a boulder. That was just something you couldn't do back in Iowa. Jan blindsided her with a big hug. The two of them bounced around on the roadside like a couple of soap bubbles.

"Great work, roomie! You were brilliant."

"Nah, I wouldn't go that far," Gary said as he got down from the Bobcat and patted her on the shoulder. "But it'll do."

"Thanks." Barbara looked at her PDE in her sleeve and blanched at the time. The accident had put them way behind schedule, and they still had several hours of driving left to do. "I think we should go ahead and make camp here tonight instead of pushing on. We don't want this to happen again."

"I'll be fine," Dion insisted. He jumped down from the cab and walked back in their direction. "I can make it."

Barbara turned to look him straight in the eye.

"Maybe, but *I'm* tired. And we've already killed two hours here." Barbara looked around them at the empty Moonscape then at Fido's map. "We can be at the crater by lunchtime tomorrow and be well rested to unpack. We're not scheduled to do anything but set up camp tomorrow anyway. We'll be safer doing it this way."

"Maybe we should call Dr. Bright and ask him," Gary said. He sounded unsure at a change in plans.

"No." Barbara shook her head. Their dithering only made her more certain that what she was doing was right. "I don't need Dr. Bright to tell me if I'm too tired to drive or not. Only I know that, and only you, Dion, and Jan, know that. We're stopping here for the night."

"Uh, well, okay. I guess you're right. I'm pretty tired of driving," Dion admitted. "I did go off the road. That has to mean I'm not making all the right connections."

"I could eat," Gary added, in a hopeful voice.

"You can always eat." Jan punched him on the shoulder.

He planted gloved hands on his chest and affected an innocent expression.

"Hey, I'm a growing boy."

"Good. It's settled then." Barbara turned toward the vehicles. "Why don't we divide and conquer? Gary and I will put the gear up. Jan and Dion, get the tents out and set them up."

"Roger that," Dion said. He gestured to the others. "You heard the boss lady."

"I'm not the boss," Barbara said.

"Yeah, I kind of think you are," Gary said, with a grin. "That's okay. In fact, it's cryogenic."

✧   ✧   ✧

ChooChoo54—Dion caused the first car accident on the Moon!

SalchichaPequena—Espero que los Sparks no tomen dañados.

5X5Power—The tire was hilarious!

ButchFel9—She's even more hawt.

Chapter 7

Neil leaned over the console, putting his face closer to the embedded console camera and fixing it with a cheerful gaze.

"So, that's the latest from Bright Sparks," he concluded. "This lunar excavation is one of the greatest projects ever undertaken on the Moon, and we're all proud to be a part of it. Daya and I will keep you up to date on progress on the radar-radio satellite dish. Sparks out!" Neil leaned back in his springback chair, satisfied. "That podcast will get over a million hits in the next few days. What do you think?"

"'Daya and I'?" the girl beside him said, crossing her arms on her thin chest. Her dark eyes were full of reproach. "It would have been nice if I had appeared any time in the podcast. It's supposed to be a group effort!"

Neil felt a surge of guilt. "I'm sorry. I just got so excited that I just kept going."

Daya's expression softened from irony to sisterly exasperation. "I know. You are impulsive. I should be used to it by now."

"I really am sorry," Neil said. He hated it when she made him feel guilty, but this time he deserved it. "I'll tell you what: you can present the next podcast the day after tomorrow. You'll be the leader then. I promise."

Daya shook her head. "You won't remember. You'll just grab the mic and begin, without thinking about it."

"I will!" Neil protested. "Hey, Einstein!"

"Yes, Neil?" his PDE responded from its place flat on the desk beside the computer keyboard. It had an old man's voice with a slight European accent.

"I want you to remind me that Daya gets to be the lead in the next update on the weblog, okay?"

"Yes, Neil," Einstein responded. "Should I stop you if you attempt to open a post?"

He grinned. The AI really learned from experience. The PDE program, which had been written by Pradesh, a Spark who had left the month Neil had joined the group, adapted itself as it went. "Yes. That's a great idea. If Daya's voice isn't the first on the pod, delete it. Even I ought to figure it out after one or two files disappear on me. Is that all right, Daya?"

Daya let out a musical trill of laughter. "Very well, I accept your apology. I don't want to argue with you." She fixed her huge, dark brown eyes on him. Neil squirmed a little. She could be pretty intense. He always felt as if she wanted more from him than just being colleagues, but he felt she was still a little immature for him.

"So, you two, how's it all going?" Dr. Bright swung into the room and slid into the chair opposite the two of them. The pockets of his beige jumpsuit bulged with gadgets and various electronic components. His PDE, Leona, peeked out from the top of his left breast pocket. "Making progress?"

Neil turned to him, enthusiasm brimming again. He wanted to impress Dr. Bright with the way he—he meant, *they* were doing. Maybe Doc would try to ease off the age limit restriction preventing Neil from going on EVA missions, if Doc was pleased with the way that he and Daya handled Mission Control on this project.

"Very well, sir," Daya said, regarding their mentor with shining eyes. "The podcast has just gone out." She shot a disappointed look at Neil, which Dr. Bright could not have failed to notice. "And we have heard from the EVA team. They had a minor problem with the vehicles."

"What kind of problem?" Dr. Bright asked. He sounded calmer than Neil would have been.

"A small road accident, or so Barbara tells us," Daya said.

"Dion ran his car off the track," Neil said. "Einstein, show Doc the overhead images."

Daya tapped on her mousepad. Dr. Bright studied the sequence of satellite pictures that appeared on the screen, and nodded.

"Yeah, the engineers told me there were some holes in the roadbed. They'll fill them in over time. Anyone hurt?"

"No, sir," Daya said. "The wide hauler hit a rock, but the team pulled it off again."

Dr. Bright grinned. "That'll make some good telling later on," he said. "I can't wait to hear it."

"It took them hours," Neil said, disapprovingly.

"Did they ask for help? From any of us?"

"Well, no . . ."

"Was it bad enough to report to me or the colony administrator?"

". . . No. . . ."

Dr. Bright waved a hand.

"Then, they got it solved. I don't need details now. We get an ETA for them to reach the construction site?"

Daya ran the simulation program that served as a trip planner for the convoy. Neil kept an eye on her, but she did it right. The four miniature rectangles wriggled along the snaking line of the road in the direction of Aldrinville, halting at the designated crater which was marked as a brilliant blue circle.

"It will take them another four hours of time on the

road," she said. "But they have stopped for the night. By their vital signs, it was the right choice to make. All of them showed increased respiratory and cardiac activity. It would be a good idea for them to eat more carbohydrates tonight and a high-protein breakfast before they set out. They should arrive at noon."

Neil opened his mouth to chime in, but Daya had already covered everything.

He found it hard to get past the envy of the older Sparks. Sometimes he felt as though he could explode with envy. This wasn't Earth. He shouldn't have been held back by something as arbitrary as birth dates. The rules ought to have been different here. He had been on the Moon for more than a year, and had never been to the Aldrinville site or many of the other places that the older Sparks had visited. Only when his parents, Dr. Bright, or another adult accompanied him had he had a chance to see anything but the Armstrong City complex. He was starting to have claustrophobia, and there was a whole planetoid out there to explore! It wasn't what he had envisioned when he had signed up for the program. He wasn't being *used* the way he had hoped. He wanted more action.

He glanced up, and caught Dr. Bright's eye on him.

"Uh, would you like to review the podcast, sir?" Neil asked.

"I would really like that," Dr. Bright said, kicking back and putting his feet up on the nearest computer table. "Put it on the main screen, all right?"

"Welcome to the Bright Sparks podcast!" Neil's own face, blown up to over a meter square, looked out at them. Neil watched with a critical eye. "We've got a lot to tell you about today. Our team is halfway through its trip to Aldrinville. . . ."

Neil let out a breath as the image faded and the outro music played over the credits and web contact information.

He hadn't mispronounced anything, or said "um" once. The automatic filter wiped out any glint of red-eye and concealed most of his ubiquitous and myriad freckles. On the other hand, he was all too aware of Daya sitting just inside the edge of the frame behind him with her PDE in her hand, ready to add her news, and he hadn't given her a chance. He felt his face flush with embarrassment. He turned to Dr. Bright, fully expecting the older man to take him to task.

"Well, you're doing just great," the scientist said. "Good stuff! That's informative, succinct and friendly. I can tell people are going to enjoy it. One day, you're going to have a science show of your own, and I hope you'll let me be a guest once in a while."

"We would be honored," Daya said, beaming, her resentment clearly forgotten.

"Do you want to add anything to today's entry?" Neil asked, eagerly. "We could add an appendix to the podcast."

"Nope," Dr. Bright said, giving him a slap on the back. "I don't want to interfere. I'm glad to see that you're taking turns on hosting. That's good practice, too."

"Um, yes, sir," Neil said, and dropped his gaze. Daya let out a crow of laughter.

"One thing you can include for tomorrow is a schematic of the mobile framework," Bright went on, seemingly unaware of Neil's humiliation and Daya's triumph. "That part of the project's already protected by our patent. I'm even fielding queries from some corporations about adapting it for other extraterrestrial applications, which could bring in some funding for our future operations. It's the electronics for the dish and the feedhorn that are still pending. Just keep that part among ourselves for now."

"Yes, sir," Neil said. "I'll put it in the next blog." Then, as Daya stared at him pointedly, "I mean, Daya will. She's presenting the next entry."

"That's right," Daya said, with satisfaction. "I hope to get entries from Gary and the others about the trip. Do you want us to mention the accident?"

"Don't make a big thing out of it," Keegan said, flashing her his famous smile. He had already known about it. Leona had been monitoring the well-being of the team without invading their privacy. There had been a few tense moments, but they'd gotten through it all right. "But it's part of the adventure. As long as everyone's all right, no harm in describing what they did to problem-solve on the far side of the Moon. It'll give the viewers a true picture of how dangerous it is out there. We may sound like it's all in a day's work to set out to create a scientific facility out there, but it's a hundred eighty degrees around from normal. I'm proud of them for rising to the occasion. Meantime, how's your project doing?"

Neil was happy to leave the podcast behind.

"Hey, Einstein?"

"How can I help you, Neil?" the PDE asked.

"Put up the database so far, okay?"

"Of course, Neil."

The Bright Sparks logo blinked off the main screen. It was replaced by a grid full of hyperlinks superimposed over a photographic map of the Moon. Armstrong City was in the center of the orb. Its own logo, a golden A cradled in a big white new-moon crescent, glowed from the heart of the blobby gray sprawl. A compass rose lay in the upper right-hand corner of the grid. North and south corresponded with those of Earth. A snaky blue line angled out about west-northwest from the settlement. Two blue dots, just wider than the body of the line, appeared at two-thirds and the end of the line. Bright lights of jewel colors passed within twenty degrees north or south of Armstrong City around an artificial equator.

"Those are the satellites beaming us images," Daya said. "The dashed lines indicate their transits if they're orbital.

The stationary satellites at L2 are ringed with red. If you run a cursor along those lines, you can see the stored images from their cameras." She demonstrated. Computer-generated images overlapped one another along the dashed lines, then vanished. "We're receiving pictures of the convoy from Lunasat 5 and MoonCom Prime." She pointed to a violet pinpoint and a yellow pinpoint. "Lunasat is in position to give us the most current image. Would you like to see?"

"Sure would," Keegan said.

"Achi, please show us the last position of our convoy?" Daya said.

"Of course, Daya," the soothing voice of an older woman replied. Keegan wondered again if Daya had used her own grandmother's voice as the model. He'd just never thought to ask.

At the second blue circle on the map, a single frame appeared and widened out until it filled the screen. Keegan could easily pick out each of the four vehicles, now in a line at the edge of the graded roadway. He clicked his tongue again at the sight of the mess in the regolith at the side of the road. The two round tents had already gone up as of this image capture. Looked like it was a good idea to stop. He couldn't spot the long shadows of any of the EVA party. Just as well. That brilliant, endless sunlight made it hot in those suits.

"We haven't got anything yet, but we'll be monitoring the construction from tomorrow on," Daya said. She ran her slim hand down the trackpad, and the image changed to show the round crater chosen for the telescope. Keegan was struck all over again by how perfect it was, like the Moon intended it for such a purpose. All it needed was a little cleanup, and it would be ready to go. "We will be packaging the data for dissemination for NASA, ESA, JSA, CNSA and other scientific concerns to download. The comsats and imaging satellites will give us fresh pictures every time they pass over."

"The best part," Neil said, almost climbing over his desk in his eagerness to contribute, "is that TravelSat will send us updated LIDAR data every hour. We've constructed a 3D model of the crater itself. From that information, we'll be able to have a top-down view to tell Gary and the others where to dig next. That way, the dish and the rim road for the feedhorn will be perfect."

"Perfect?" Keegan smiled. "Perfect is the enemy of the good enough. Nothing works out perfect, Neil, but we'll get as close to it as we can. Don't beat yourself up if there's a flaw or two. We're working with natural materials and human error, after all."

"Right," Neil said, though his face clearly said he didn't believe it. "Well, once the dish is operational, we'll have the control infrastructure here. The portal to connect Armstrong City to Aldrinville was put in place on the last survey trip. It took almost two hundred site-to-site repeater stations with Yagi antennas mounted on ten meter poles."

"Yes, I recall, Neil." Keegan smiled at the boy. "I seem to remember us doing an episode where I installed one of them. The battery packs and solar panels were a bit cumbersome to carry up the pole."

"Uh, yes, sir." Neil felt sheepish. "I mean, I was just repeating for thoroughness. Anyway, we can send and receive TCP/IP information packets all the way to Aldrinville as soon as there's something there to send and receive it."

Daya brought up a three-dimensional model of the crater that tilted from side to side to show the rough basin and the jagged rim thrown up thousands or millions of years ago by the unknown rock that had formed it. "This is the computer-assisted design rendering."

"Your calculations look good," Keegan said, with an approving nod. It looked stunningly accurate, almost photographic. "I'll want to see the printout when it's ready."

Daya's eyes danced. She and Neil exchanged a conspiratorial glance.

"We have a surprise for you, Dr. Bright!"

Neil dashed to a table in the middle of the lab facility covered with a green dropcloth, and pushed it to Keegan's side.

"Ta-daaa!" he announced, whipping the cloth away. "The shared solid printer in the main Armstrong lab rendered a 3D image of the dish for us."

Keegan stood up and surveyed the model on the rolling cart. Around 60 centimeters wide, the dove-gray plastic dish looked almost exactly like the geologic feature that he had surveyed and hiked through with Gary. He crouched down at eye level to admire it.

"Almost like being there," he said.

"It took four days to print," Neil said. "But it was worth it. You can see every subcrater and boulder."

"We will laser out the irregularities as the construction progresses," Daya said, "as we update the CAD rendering."

"Well, that's excellent work," Keegan said, standing up. "I'm proud of you. I want to put you two on next week's show with this. We'll do a short feature close to the end of the episode, so everyone can see it." The young ones swelled with pride. "In the meantime, how's the weather looking?"

Neil grinned and plopped back into his chair. "Well, for Armstrong City, the forecast is steadily increasing Earthlight, with sunlight returning in about a week. For Aldrinville and the satellite dish, brightly sunny, with no rain in the forecast."

Keegan laughed.

"Are you watching those sunspots?" he asked.

Daya turned the screen over to an image with an NOAA image in the far corner. The wall filled with the near-perfect yellow-gold sphere of the sun, its corona whipping and heaving across the blackness of space like trees in a high wind. A sprinkle of black masses across the center and lower hemisphere became visible, each with a numeric designation and metadata. She ran the cursor to the largest, near the solar equator.

"Of the four we can see, only one is particularly active. So far, no coronal mass ejections have been observed, or any other noteworthy events. We have alerts on all feeds from the major space centers and solar observatories to let us know in case anything changes."

"Good," Keegan said. "Keep the EVA team informed."

"We will," Daya promised.

✦   ✦   ✦

NeroliFox—Good report, Neil. Now shut up.

TeamSparks090—Barb didn't answer my question!

HeloFanAx—Look at those legs! I mean, the telescope. Awwwwwsummmmm

HCMDevil—These kids are supposed to be smart but can't even drive a space-car. Smh.

KadtheKonqueror—Where do they find these losers haha.

MouseCat—Ugh, I could have had them half-way to NEPTUNE by now and I would have let the girl actually talk.

Chapter 8

Barbara stood on the lip of the crater and surveyed it as though she was prepared to dive into it. Instead of looking like a defect, the depression appeared to have been excavated by a cosmic ice-cream scoop. On the one hand, it was a small crater compared with others they had passed on the way from Armstrong. On the other, it was a full geological feature, bigger than her uncle's largest soybean field. She started doing some calculations in her head. The volume of the crater was four thirds pi times the radius cubed divided by two. Luckily, they didn't have to dig out the whole thing.

"Will ten days be enough?" Jan asked, bobbing up to join Barbara on the rim. She kicked a small stone. It bounded down the softly rounded slope to knock into a cluster of rocks at the bottom. A plume of regolith dust rose and settled delicately over them.

"More than enough, I think," Barbara said. "We're only doing some finishing work in the bowl. Most of our efforts will be to make the road and set up the habitats."

"Ten days will be plenty," Gary protested. Barbara looked around. She was still getting used to hearing someone's voice as though he or she was next to her, when the person could be kilometers away. In this case, Gary was a third of the way around the rim. He and Dion were working on unloading the heavy equipment. He lifted his head and aimed his faceplate toward them. "It'll go faster if the two of you help."

The girls laughed, and bounced their way back to the vehicles.

A device like a skid loader on oversized wheels was in the rear of Dion's car. On the narrow flat bed, Jan and Barbara worked together to pile soft, flat packages each the size of a king mattress. On Barbara's checklist, the five packages were the habitats that would form the control center and living quarters for the dish. Once it was up and running, the telescope would be made to be monitored remotely, but in the meantime, astronomers and astrophysicists could operate it on site.

"Take them to that spot over there," Gary said, pointing to a higher ridge along the south edge of the rim. "We can get the first habitat module set up today. Do I need to send you the schematics?"

"No, I've got them in Fido," Barbara said, tapping her left shoulder. "I've looked them over. We inflate them one at a time with gas canisters, the way we do with our tents?"

"They're a lot like the tents," Jan said, with a mulish expression. "It shouldn't be that hard."

"There's a lot more to them than that!" Gary said, defensively. He and Jan went faceplate to faceplate. Barbara was struck again by how similar they looked. "These are part of a permanent installation. Don't be careless."

"I'm not careless!" Jan exclaimed.

"Hey, hey," Dion said, abandoning the wheeled grinder he was unloading to step between them. They both bounced backward. "This is Gary's baby. You know that. He's been planning this while the rest of us were working on other projects."

"You mean *he's* acting like a baby," Jan said. "We're not stupid or inexperienced."

"Well, I am." Barbara called up the schematics on Fido in her heads-up display. The domiciles did look like the tents, but they were far more complex. She had run over the plans during a couple of the breaks, and had looked over how to assemble them, but a few leading questions might help defuse the tension. "Do we have to roll one of the water tanks down that slope today?" she asked, holding her screen out so the others could see. "I can see how the power truck can run everything on a trickle charge for the time being, but what about physical connections?"

Gary produced his own PDE and started marking the diagram. The information spread out to the others' devices.

"We don't need water until we start to occupy them. Until the first one is ready, we'll live in the tents the way we have been. All of the modules are going to radiate out from the central control room around the water storage," he said. The lines he drew appeared on Barbara's image, too. "The first one is the biggest of the habitats. Central control will be in there."

"Why over there?" she asked, glancing to the rim on her left. "It looks like more rock we're going to have to bulldoze."

"No, that's the beauty of it," Gary said, eagerly. "Back there is a minor crater that was made before this one. It's a natural dished arc that faces the telescope—the perfect place for the control room. That ridge will act as a backstop to the cluster before we dig them in and bury them."

"Won't people need access to the rear wall at some point in the future?"

"No," Jan said, crowding around to her other side. The Nerd-Twins' spat was forgotten in a matter of minutes. It always was. "That's a dead zone. All the technology will be accessed from one side or the other. No vital boxes or plumbing access will be against the rock. Gary's plans call for

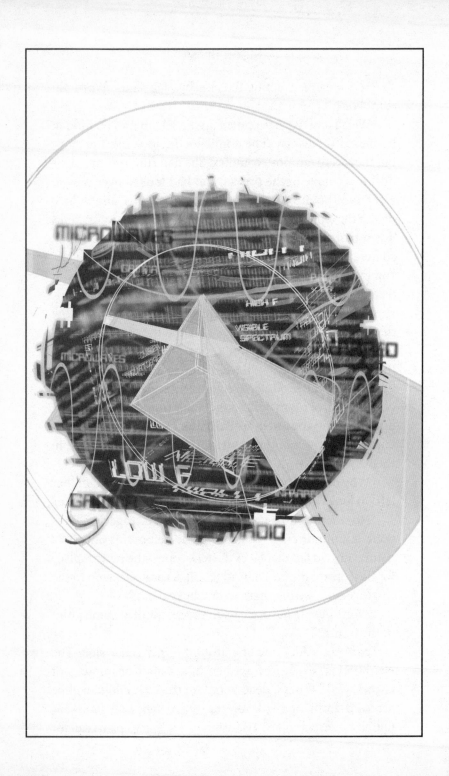

insulated conduit for the two chambers that will be completely contained. The rock will help protect the habitat from radiation and micrometeors. It's a natural protective barrier."

Barbara scanned the instructions for the modules. The power requirements for each section allowed for redundancy on redundancy. That meant the site could expand in time. The team had chosen well. She could feel her excitement growing.

"Why can't we bury the modules the first day?" she asked. "The stats show they have enough internal pressure."

"Not at first. They'll collapse under the weight of the regolith unless we constantly keep them under pressure," Gary said. "Partly, if not completely. Once you inflate them, the polymer in the walls begins to harden, like glue. It takes a minimum of twenty-four hours until they're rugged enough to support the weight of dirt and rock without inflation pressure, but after that, they're solid. In fact, they ought to last centuries. This way we don't have to keep pumping air in them if nobody is there. And if they spring a leak they won't collapse. But they need the sunlight to cure. That's part of the reason for doing this mission in the daytime. Turing, send them the stats, will you?"

"Right away, Gary," his PDE replied in a light tenor with a cultured English accent.

"That's fantastic!" Barbara said, beaming at the others. "Let's get started. I bet we can get the first shelter up before bedtime."

Dion's massive shoulders held onto the air gun as it shot an anchor peg into the cleared floor of the rock. With every round, he and the nailer were catapulted backward, like a movie cowboy in a barroom brawl. Barbara and Gary, sweeping eons of accumulated regolith and small stones into tall heaps with the Cat and a metal rake, laughed so hard they almost fell over.

"Ha ha," Dion said, picking himself up. His face ran with sweat. The back of his white suit was gray from the Moon dust. He raised a hand to wipe his face, and knocked his gauntlet into his faceplate. That made Barbara laugh again. Dion gave her a disappointed look. "This is hard!"

"I'm sorry!" she gasped. She blinked to clear her own sweat out of her eyes. "How many more do you have left to do?"

"Two," the big youth said. Resolutely, he set the gun against the ground and pulled the trigger. He tumbled backward, the tool in his hand. Jan, attaching tie-downs to the eyes of the shining anchor pegs that would connect to loops all around the base of the module, gave him a hand up. "One. Done."

When he completed the final anchor, the others cheered.

"Now, we'll pad the site with a level bed of regolith, isn't that right?" Barbara asked, pointing her rake at the space between the pegs. "To give it an even base?"

"Right," Gary said, rolling the small dozer forward. He dumped bucketsful of gravel and dust into place, and Barbara raked them level. When the mass reached the level of the peg eyes, Dion and Gary spread the first habitat shell over it. They arranged it so it was facing the correct direction and attached it to the tie-downs. "I'm getting hungry."

"We can stop for dinner as soon as we inflate the module," Barbara said, straightening up. Hours of fetching, carrying and shoveling had left her arms feeling as limp as noodles. She was going to hurt that night.

"No problem," Jan said. She bounded down the slope with a long green gas cylinder wrapped in her arms. On Earth the metal tube would have been too heavy for one person to carry, but on the Moon, it was no problem. "Let's pump it up!"

The wheat-colored material was a good deal crisper than the fabric from which the tents were made. It had door panels and knock-outs for technical access formed into the sides, each of which would be replaced with permanent portals once it had stiffened into shape. Jan clipped the gas canister to a waiting connector. At Gary's nod, she unscrewed the valve.

Barbara couldn't help but expect to hear the hiss of gas, but the silence of space kept the sound confined to the module. The only sound in her ears was her own breathing and that of her companions, plus the occasional burr or chatter from their PDEs.

It hadn't looked that large when they unfolded the envelope, but as the habitat rose against the lunascape, it seemed to grow into the size of a circus tent. In fact, it was fifteen meters in diameter. According to the manifest, it had been made with internal walls, starting with an airlock-mudroom leading into a main chamber with smaller rooms for storage and sleeping, an insulated engine room that would house the technical and environmental equipment, and included its own toilet and shower facility. To make those work, all they had to do was install the plumbing and run the water to it from the tank. Waste would run into a septic storage that would be emptied periodically and brought to Aldrinville or Armstrong City for recycling. Eventually, once all the modules were in place and buried, nothing would be seen above the ground except the solar panel array and the airlock entrance. Inside the airlock was an airshower to blow the dust from their suits. The air was sucked through vents in the floor where the dust was captured by filters that required cleaning about every other day. The air pressure light turned green and the oxygen level was in the green when it was working properly. And eventually, Aldrinville would have its own sewage recycling system. As Jan had said, the Moon would never have the waste problems of Earth, if they could possibly help it.

"Take a good look," Barbara said in satisfaction, as the bubble stopped swelling. It seemed to crackle in the brilliant sunshine as the polymer began to stiffen. "You're seeing something that no one else will ever see again. Once this thing is ready it will be covered with lunar regolith forever."

M4r1a—Kewl! That makes my camping tent look sick!

KeeganMarryMe—I want to go there! What about tours?

GaMeRgirl873—Sparks rule! Look how fast that went up. The dish will be a piece of cake!

Chapter 9

". . . And today's episode is 'The Moon is a Harsh Mirror, part one.' Here he is! *Live from the Moon* with Dr. Keegan Bright!" Leona's warm, matter-of-fact female voice poured over the soundstage speakers as the show's heavy rock-based computer-simulated orchestra and band played the theme song.

"That's my cue," Keegan said softly to the production assistant checking his lapel microPDE. He waved the young man aside. The assistant retreated. Keegan put on his television smile and cleared his throat. At just the right beat of the music, he burst onto the live set, waving his left hand at the imaginary audience just as he had done five days a week, about thirty weeks a year, for the past seven years. He still felt the rush of excitement, as if this was the first time he had done the show.

"Hello, hello! And to all you folks back home: greetings, Earthlings!" He laughed his trademark infectious chortle. "We've got a really exciting show for you today. In a bit, we'll check in on a shuttle that's inbound from Earth with our very special guest today, and then we'll talk to our newest Spark, who is at this very moment leading some of the other

Sparks on an expedition to the far side of the Moon! How about that?"

"That does sound exciting, Dr. Bright!" Leona's computer persona image appeared on a large screen to Keegan's right. The lifelike facial expressions the artificial intelligence's attractive female avatar made always amused Keegan. Today, she was pictured as an alien with bright blue-green skin and antennae sticking up from her forehead. Keegan's audience loved to speculate among themselves in the website comments section what Leona would look like from day to day. Maybe tomorrow, he'd make her an elephant.

Although her looks were ever changing, Leona was one constant that had been with the show from its inception back on Earth. In those days, the show was prerecorded. But for the past few years the main part of the show was beamed out live, with prerecorded segments when there were experiments that took more time to set up.

"Yes, it is, Leona," Keegan said, with a grin for the camera. "And the fun part is, our newest Spark, Barbara Winton, has absolutely no idea we'll be talking to her. Shh. Our little secret."

"TRIVIA!!! TRIVIA!!! TRIVIA!!!" a chorus of children's voices from middle school through teen chanted in unison. Keegan made a gesture to empty space where he could see on the monitors was a graphic of the word dancing about. He clapped his hands together.

"Aha! It's trivia time, Leona. What have you got for us today?" Keegan asked.

"Dr. Bright . . ." the AI began in a dramatic tone, as the computerized band began playing gameshow-style music in the background.

"Yes?"

"What was . . . the first satellite to orbit the Earth?" Leona's expression was devious. Keegan put his chin in his hand and tapped his cheek with his forefinger.

"Hmmm? Not sure. Let me think on that. . . .I'd guess it was Sputnik. Yes. It would have to be Sputnik because that was the first spacecraft ever to orbit the Earth." Keegan raised a triumphant eyebrow at the image on the screen. "That was in 1957. It was only 58 centimeters across, and broadcast radio signals in low Earth orbit. . . ."

A blare of sound interrupted him.

"I'm sorry, Dr. Bright. That is incorrect," Leona replied.

"What?" Keegan asked, outraged. "No, I'm certain Sputnik was the first satellite put in orbit."

Leona sounded smug. "While it is true that Sputnik was the first manmade satellite put into orbit, the Moon had already been orbiting the Earth for billions of years. Therefore, the correct answer is 'the Moon.'"

"Leo, you are such a Lunartic. That was not a trick question at all, was it?"

"I do not understand what you mean."

The invisible studio audience laughed uproariously.

"You never do!"

"I'm sorry, Dr. Bright. There was no trick implied. The question was quite straightforward."

"If you say so." Keegan turned and gave the camera an outrageous wink. He knew the answer, naturally, but a large percentage of his young audience did not. And letting the ones who did know feel a little superior to the grown-up scientist wasn't all bad, either. "You heard it here first, folks. The Moon was indeed orbiting the Earth before Sputnik."

Leona touched the elaborate silver device sticking out of her left ear as if she was a spaceship communications officer.

"Dr. Bright. Our connection to the incoming shuttle is ready. Your special guest can speak to you now."

"Great! Patch her through." Keegan waited as the image of a middle-aged woman, with curly black hair and a dimple in her chin, wearing a blue NASA astronaut flight suit appeared on the screen to his left. She beamed at the video pickup.

"Shuttle Commander January Harbor here. Dr. Bright, do you copy?"

Keegan smiled back.

"Commander Harbor, we copy and have your image perfectly displaying at ten megapixels per frame at seventy five Hertz. Do you have me? Over."

"Affirmative."

Keegan turned to the camera and made an elaborate gesture toward the screen.

"Ladies and gentlemen, meet the first person to step on Mars, and the person who set up the first real-time video feed that always streams live from the Mars Communications outpost Ares One, Dr. January Harbor. Commander Harbor, meet everybody else."

"Hello. It's very nice to meet all of you!" January waved and smiled. The invisible audience cheered her. Keegan knew she was a pro. She had been on air so many times before that speaking on camera was second nature to her. He found something magnetic about the way she carried herself, even if she was floating about the cabin of the shuttlecraft and her hair was bouncing to and fro. "It's my absolute pleasure, Dr. Bright."

"So, Commander," he said, "tell us why you're on your way here to the Moon."

January leaned in with the air of a friendly conspirator.

"Well, that's a very exciting topic, Dr. Bright. I'm coming to the Moon to lead a project where we plan to build the largest optical telescope ever made and test it. This new telescope will have a primary mirror an amazing thirty meters across. A mirror this size would sag far too much under the Earth's gravity and would be very difficult to manufacture in a high Earth orbit. So, we plan to build it right here on the Moon just outside of Armstrong City. If it works well, we'll build a second one near Aldrinville to supplement the project I hear *you're* working on."

"That's awesome. Leona, bring up a graphic of the Large Lunar Telescope, or LLT, for the people at home to see."

"Right away, Dr. Bright."

"Commander Harbor, just building the telescope on the Moon isn't the only interesting part about this project, is it?"

January smiled.

"No, you're right, Dr. Bright. We will be using a brand-new technique that will use the titanium oxide dust found all over the Moon as material to feed a special three-dimensional sintering printer. The laser head of the printer will turn the titanium oxide into a molten titanium material and then it will lay it up into the parts needed to build the giant mirror for the LLT." As Dr. Harbor described it, Leona displayed animated schematics that solidified into full-color graphics on the second screen.

"Do we expect the mirror to be perfect once the printer is finished?" Keegan asked. It was a loaded question that the two of them had discussed prior to the show.

She shook her head, looking resigned. "No. I wish it were, but although the mirror surface will be very harsh for optical standards it would work fine for radio waves, but that's not our intended purpose. Once the rough surface is printed, we will then have to excavate the mirror from the lunar soil and very carefully place a special polishing machine on it that will smooth the surface of the mirror to within a few billionths of a meter!"

"I can't wait to see that." Keegan said. "That must be some special polisher."

"Yes, in fact, it will consist of wirelessly guided robots and laser photogrammetry imagers," Commander Harbor said. The image of a boxy device appeared in the midst of the dull dish. A brilliant red net of laser beams spread out before it

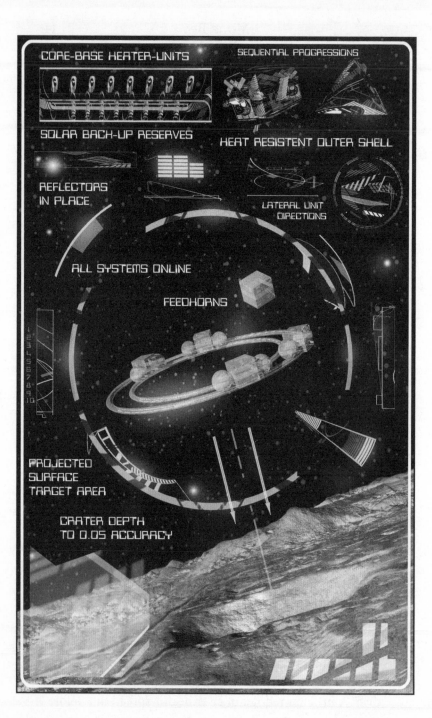

as it moved, polishing and grinding with myriad small tools. For the young audience, the animation had sound effects, which would be absent during the real project in the lunar vacuum. "We're pioneering some new wrinkles in older technology to create this dish. We'll be able to control the finishing process with a degree of precision that has never been seen before."

"I can't wait to see that, either!" Keegan raised his eyebrows. Commander Harbor laughed at his eagerness.

"And the images we will get from this telescope will be unprecedented in all of astronomy," she said. "We believe we'll be able to image planets around other stars. Imagine that!"

"Wow. That's great. Again, I can't wait."

January shook her head.

"Well, I'm sorry, but you'll have to, Dr. Bright. It will take us almost a year to complete the telescope's construction."

"Oh, no!" Keegan said, in mock horror. "You must let us visit the site along the way! I'm sure our viewers want to keep up with the project." He paused and tapped at a control panel, bringing up a graphic of the shuttle's approach vector to the Moon on Leona's screen. "So when do you arrive?"

"We're currently about twenty-three hours out."

Keegan grinned.

"That'll be just in time for tomorrow's show. Hope to see you land."

"Until then." Commander Harbor nodded. "Harbor out."

Keegan turned back to the camera.

"Wow, can you imagine a telescope made from lunar regolith and thirty meters in diameter?" He paused for effect as Leona zoomed out, showing the LLT image to scale on the map of the Moon. It covered a large section of the surface. Armstrong City, beside it, helped give the viewers the scale. "That's one Large Lunar Telescope. But, that's a telescope that uses visible light that we can see with our eyes. We scan the universe with more than one kind of telescope: infrared, ultraviolet, x-ray and radio telescopes among them. The Sparks and I have come up with a way to use the Moon itself as a telescope to pick up radio waves. Everything in space emits energy somewhere on the electromagnetic spectrum."

A graphic appeared on the monitor as if the spectrum was floating in front of him. He pointed at different regions on the imaginary graphic as he spoke. Sections of the graph illuminated where he gestured.

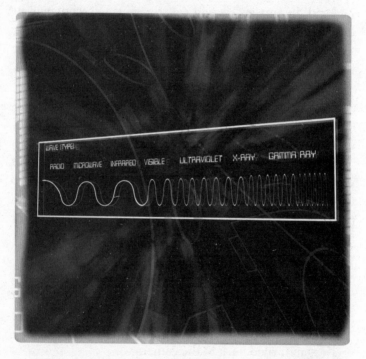

"This part here is the visible light part of the spectrum," he pointed to the center, "where all the colors of the rainbow exist and what the LLT will be looking for is light from stars and planets from deep space. If we were to think of light as a wave then the distance between the peaks of the waves of light would be between about four hundred to seven hundred billionths of a meter, four hundred to seven hundred nanometers. Now, light isn't really a wave, but that's a much more detailed discussion for us to revisit another time.

"For radio waves," he continued, as the illumination moved to the left, "we can see that they're much farther down on the spectrum and their wave's lengths, or wavelengths, would range between many tens of meters down to centimeters. This is the part of the spectrum where *our* telescope will function. This type of telescope is called a radio telescope. Our fun trick is that we will be using an already existing meteor crater for our receiver dish. Just like your small satellite receiver dish back home but much, much larger. Like Commander Harbor's, this one is groundbreaking, in more ways than one. My buddies Neil Zimmerman and Daya Singh can explain it with a very interesting model they've created. Maybe they can 'spark' our imagination." On the second screen, the image of the Bright Sparks' laboratory shimmered into view, with Daya and Neil eager and bolt upright behind their desks. "Sparks? Over to you."

"Do you ever feel you're out of touch, living on another planet?" Barbara asked, trudging across the landscape ahead of Jan. Trudging through the regolith was like walking through knee-deep snow. The guys were having to dig out plenty of drifts of it in the corners of the craters.

She took the theodolite off her shoulder, balanced it on its pointed legs, and set it toward a point on the cleared roadway around the large crater. The tall, brass-cased optical device had a multiplicity of uses, such as in rocket launch technology, meteorology and complex construction. She used it to measure vertical and horizontal angles of the section of the crater in order to show Jan where to place reflective cubes at precise locations along the lip. Measurements using readings from the cubes would be read by LIDAR satellite telemetry by TravelSat and beamed back in the Sparks' mission control center to keep the away team from excavating too much and spoiling the near-perfection of the natural depression.

"Not really," Dion said, sounding as though he was next to her, despite being hundreds of meters away, digging out huge rocks with the Cat. "We're close enough that there's only a few seconds' lag in between conversation on a digital link. I hear from my family all the time."

"You've got a big family, too, right?" Barbara asked. It seemed kind of weird to be talking about normal stuff while they were building a space telescope, but she really couldn't think of any momentous topics to bring up. Besides, she had to concentrate on getting her task finished. Small talk didn't distract her from siting the cubes where they needed to go.

"Six brothers and sisters," Dion replied, cheerfully. "Y'all think this peace and quiet is spooky. I think it's refreshing. It was never quiet at home. Always someone hollering for Mommy or Daddy or me to come fix something."

"You're the oldest?" Barbara asked. "That's right. I read it on your profile. So am I. I've got two younger brothers."

"Me, too," Jan said. "Well, the older of two. I have a younger sister."

"Me, four," Gary added.

"I've got an older half-brother and half-sister," Neil put in. "Twelve years older than me."

"Which half is the brother and which half the sister?" Jan asked. The others laughed.

"I *mean* they're twins," Neil said, with a groan that said the four older Sparks were all sadly obtuse. "But they're so much older that I kind of grew up by myself. Daya's an only."

"I could have said that for myself," Daya said. She sounded hurt.

"So, we're all eldests, in a way," Barbara said. "What made you apply for this program?"

"Are you kidding?" Jan asked. "A chance to work on the Moon? I've been a fan of Dr. Bright since I was little."

"I always felt like no one in my school got me," Gary said. "They weren't interested in science, or anything else that meant something to me. There weren't any magnet schools close enough. Dr. Bright's program sounded like heaven. Then I met my twin here."

"Yeah!" Jan agreed. "Even if our specialties aren't the same, we're still fellow nerds."

"Identi-nerds," Gary said.

"Nerd twins," Jan said.

"This is my second family," Dion added. "One's blood. This one's brains."

"But we're kind of isolated, even back in Armstrong City," Barbara said.

"From what?" Neil asked, scornfully. "We're connected to *everybody*. We get all the latest entertainment. All that's been transmitted by microwave to cities for years. We can get bounce from satellites when we're facing them. And petabytes worth of data comes up on solid-state drives from Earth with every shuttle, every visitor, every supply ship. It's a pain if you're in a hurry, but we're never really out of touch. By the way, you have e-mail, a whole bunch. I just sent it to your PDE. Do you want Fido to read it to you?"

"Later," Barbara said, feeling comforted by the thought of mail from home. She stooped to sight through the theodolite. Jan moved into her field of view. At exactly the right moment, she gave Jan the thumbs up, and her roommate set another of the shining crystals in place.

"You're so slow!" Gary teased them, as they moved toward the next designated site. "We'd have finished planting those crystals in half the time it's taking you!" Barbara turned to stare at the white-suited figure in the middle of the wide crater, raking regolith to fill in one of the shallow depressions. Every one of them was working as hard as any farmhand. She opened her mouth to protest, but Jan jumped in first.

"Oh, yeah, like speed is the only thing that matters," Jan

taunted Gary back. "Remember when you wound the mechanical dynamo too tightly in that experiment, saying that it would spin faster, and the cable snapped, taking out the inside housing?"

Barbara listened avidly, glancing from one Spark to another.

"I think I remember that experiment," Barbara said. "I didn't see any problems on the show. Do you have to hide the mistakes you make? I mean we make?"

"Hide it?" Jan asked, sounding hurt. "No, we don't really hide things. There are a lot of misfires and drudge work in any scientific project. You ought to know that."

"I do," Barbara said. "But wouldn't it be educational to make that info public?"

"It's public," Neil put in. "All the logs of our activities are available. Anything that's not protected by a patent or sealed by a lawsuit is open to read. It's just that most people don't want to read the day-to-day boring stuff."

"I would have read it," Barbara said. "How did I miss those logs?"

"It's easy to miss," Daya said, her gentle voice breaking in over Neil's explosive protests. "There's a link on the website."

"Yeah," said Neil. "It's not fancy. All those tiles on the home page? The purple one in the lower left corner contains the archives."

"Sometimes I read 'em late at night," Dion said, steering the Cat in a wide arc with a scoopful of rocks and sand. "They help me get to sleep."

The Sparks laughed.

Conversation ground to a halt as afternoon wore on and everyone's energy began to flag a little. Neil and Daya stopped communicating after lunch. When Doc Bright's show was live, Neil had bragged that the two of them were going to give a live report, and they needed to write up the script and run it past the production crew. Barbara wondered when she'd get a chance to watch the show being videoed live. She had been watching it for years. Her cheeks burned a little at the memory of meeting Doc in person for the first time. A good thing she hadn't gone into full fangirl mode. He might have sent her right back to Earth.

Barbara stopped halfway along the broad pathway and leaned against the theodolite she had been carrying over her shoulder and drew a few deep breaths. Hauling equipment all over the landscape, even at lower gravity, was exhausting, but as Fido's screen showed her, she had managed to keep the work done right and on schedule.

She checked the chronometer. Twenty-four minutes to their next break time, and she could hardly wait. Sweat ran down her forehead. She couldn't wipe it, but she blinked and shook her head to get the droplets out of her eyes. With one arm, she hoisted the device again, ready to help Jan place the next cube. Only a few more to go.

Dion rode the Cat inside the smaller crater, clearing the debris to build a pad for the second inflatable habitat. He had spent the last couple of days leveling the road around the edge of the crater, clearing and smoothing the path on which the feedhorn assembly would ride. Now it was level enough to place the reflective cubes while he and Gary did one of the other jobs on the list.

The agenda didn't require the team to work straight through on one task, or be on top of each other the whole time. It was proving better for morale to break the jobs up into sections. As she came around the lip, she watched Gary raking stones and rubble out of the way after Dion did the earth-moving, or rather, moon-moving. The next day, Barbara had them scheduled to raise the second inflatable. The first inflated habitat was curing nicely. Its shell only needed a few more hours to cure before it was safe to bury. With the interhelmet system, they could all talk whenever they wanted to, regardless of whether they could see one another. Every so often, Fido had to remind her not to shout, but less than it had the first day.

The big dish was looking good. They had spent the morning together excavating a massive boulder at the heart of the crater that Gary speculated was all that remained of whatever had caused the impact billions of years ago. Now while he and Dion worked on smaller obstructions and imperfections, she and Jan placed devices to help measure the dish remotely. Neil had showed them the 3D model he and Daya had made of the crater. Every scoop of rock would change the parabolic pattern of the natural crater. She didn't want to make any mistakes.

"How's it going, Gary?" she asked, careful not to raise her voice.

For answer, he turned and gave her a thumbs up. She was pleased.

They all took turns doing the grunt work as well as overseeing their individual specialties. For her own part, she'd inspected the power truck first thing that morning, to make sure its solar collectors were aimed directly toward the Sun and clear of regolith. That pesty gray dust invaded every nook and cranny of the vehicles, the tents, and the ports on the equipment. The regolith had been pulverized by micrometeorites for billions of years so it was finer than talcum powder and even somewhat conductive. That meant it could knock out circuits or clog up moving parts, and it mixed with almost every lubricant to create a perfectly hardened mess. With long-handled brushes that they carried in the cabs of the trucks, she had cleared them all.

The gauges on the power truck showed all the batteries at full. The rest of her list was almost all checked off, too.

She tried at first to organize who handled what task, but they traded off assignments all the time without telling her. It irked her, but as long as everything was done on time she figured she had to let them do it their way. She didn't want them to think she was a slavedriver. She just wanted to run a tight enough ship that Dr. Bright would be impressed once the project was finished. It wasn't easy to bite her tongue when someone else reported a job done she had assigned to someone else, but she did it.

Day five of a two-week expedition, and she was already sore and physically tired, but she was still very much mentally fired up and gung ho for the effort. What the Sparks were doing here was the first of its kind. As young as they were, they had been entrusted by Dr. Bright and the Lunar Administration with a major scientific mission. Her fellows were great people: smart, funny, considerate and as driven as she was. She didn't want to let any of them down. She could do it. She could put one foot in front of the other until they were done.

It's simply a situation of mind over matter, she thought.

As soon as the phrase crossed her mind, an alarm bell went off in her head, reminding her of her astronaut training. If she started feeling too physically tired, whether she thought she could handle it or not, that was usually when accidents happened. They'd already had one on the drive out because she was pushing too hard and focusing on meeting a schedule. Safety absolutely had to come first. Barb stopped in her tracks and set down the theodolite on the rim of the crater. She took a deep breath and closed her eyes. She opened them as she exhaled slowly.

"Everything all right, roomie?" Jan asked from behind her, down the rim a bit. Barb scanned about and smiled down at her roommate, thinking how much she liked the Sparks and being one of them herself.

"I'm good. Just taking a short breather. It's almost break time."

"Yay!" Dion cheered, from the cab of the Cat. Barbara glanced toward him with dismay.

"You don't think we're pushing too hard, do you?" Barbara asked. "I mean, I don't want anybody getting too tired and causing an accident."

"Oh, you are such a good mother hen, you are." Jan smiled up at her. "That's usually Dion's job. I'm fine, but if you'd like we could call for a break and have the guys check in."

"Uh, no, that's okay. We'll be okay to stick to the schedule. The LIDAR satellite will be flying over in an hour and we need to have all corner cube reflectors placed in the exact right spots before that. I think once the flyover is done we will be done excavating and surveying for the day. Then we can focus on setting up the feedhorn booms and rollers until we get the 3D analysis back from TravelSat."

"Makes sense to me." Jan agreed. The guys chimed in their agreement. "So, we keep moving?"

"Yep," Barbara said. She extended the legs on the theodolite and bent to arrange its lenses. "I'll have the location for the next cube in a—"

"Barbara, you have an incoming call from Dr. Bright." Fido interrupted her. "He's requesting an immediate video chat."

"Uh, okay, put him through and turn on the camera." Barbara held the PDE so she could see herself in the viewer. Then an image of Dr. Bright appeared on the screen. He was dressed the way he always did for his show, in a white lab coat. Barbara glanced at the digital clock in the corner of the screen, and suddenly realized what the reading meant. It was actually time for the live show to air. Her mouth dropped open in shock.

"There she is!" Dr. Bright boomed through her PDE, not really talking to her. "Ladies and gentlemen, meet Ms. Barbara Winton. Say hello, Barbara."

"Uh, hello, Barbara?" she stammered. Her throat tightened. She was live on television for millions to see! She wondered if any of her friends or her parents back home were watching. For a moment, she hoped they weren't. Her hair was in her face, and she was sweating. She swallowed hard.

"Ha ha. Clever." Dr. Bright laughed. "We just had Neil and Daya explain the Moon Beam project with a three-dimensional model, but nothing is better than seeing the real thing to gather the magnitude of the project. So, if you would, I'd like for you to pan your camera about the Aldrinville Crater and tell us a little about what's going on out there on the far side of the Moon."

"Uh, yes, sir." Barbara wrung her brain out trying to think of what to say. That wasn't fair! Dr. Bright had really put her on the spot. Her legs started shaking as her stomach knotted up. She took in another deep breath. *Focus*, Barbara thought. She had done many science fairs and competitions when judges had pressed her with hard questions. She had gotten through *those* without making a fool of herself. She could do it now. She moved Fido in a smooth arc to show the crater.

"As you can see in the distance, the boys, uh, Gary and Dion that is, are using an electric mini bulldozer to move boulders and lunar regolith about. We surveyed that spot this morning and there are a few low spots. We're using the spoils piles from the high spots to fill those in. Once you step into this place you realize just how big this crater is. And it's a relatively small one as lunar craters go."

"How big is it, Barb?" Dr. Bright asked, encouraging her. Statistics and numbers were her strong suit. Her confidence resurged.

"The crater is almost exactly hemispherical already, with a diameter of one hundred and thirty one point four seven meters at its largest part. That means it's a little bit elliptical because its smallest diameter that we have measured thus far is one hundred twenty seven point two three meters. Not perfect, but almost. And, we're smoothing it out to within a half meter or so of flatness all the way about it." She showed the camera a view of the roadway.

"How in the world do you know if the surface of the crater is within a half meter one way or the other the same shape as a spherical satellite receiver dish?" Dr. Bright asked. Barbara assured herself that he must most certainly know that answer and that he was feeding her things to talk about.

"Well, that's what Jan over here and I are working on right now." Barbara panned to the theodolite she had been carrying. "We're using surveying equipment to map the floor of the crater. That equipment then wirelessly feeds the information through my PDE back to Neil and Daya where they update their data as we change the crater through our excavation. Jan is placing small reflector cubes. Show them one, Jan." She panned the camera to Jan who was holding the suitcase full of reflector cubes. Jan waved. Barbara paused the camera until her roommate dug one from the case.

"Here you go. One highly reflective laser corner cube." Jan said as she held one of the shiny glass cubes near the PDE camera.

"So, she's placing the corner cubes at precise locations about the crater. A laser ranging and imaging satellite will fly over us in about an hour and will accurately map this place to within a few centimeters of accuracy. The cubes will allow Neil and Daya to precisely map the satellite imagery data to the surveyor data we send them. Once the two sets of data are tied together the computer can generate an exact replica of this crater to within a centimeter or two of accuracy. We will use that to analyze and determine if we need to do some more digging." Barbara realized she was repeating herself a little, and stopped talking.

"Excellent!" Dr. Bright applauded her. "We can't wait to get more updates from you. Be safe! I know with that satellite coming you've got work to do, so I won't keep you any longer. Thanks, Barbara."

"You're very welcome, Dr. Bright!" Barbara beamed from ear to ear.

"Bright out." Her PDE closed the connection.

"Whew!" She would have rubbed her forehead if she hadn't been in a spacesuit. "I hope I didn't mess that up! A little warning next time would be great."

"You did awesome, girlfriend!" Jan slapped her on her back. Barbara flew a couple of meters, then picked herself up again, dusting regolith off her knees. "But get used to it. He never lets us know ahead of time unless it's something that takes setting up and rehearsing."

Barbara gawked.

"Wow, I had no idea. You and the others always seem so natural on the shows."

"Nah. We're as nervous as you were. But you get used to it." Jan looked at the PDE on her wrist. "The younger Sparks will be going on pretty soon, too. Clock's ticking, Barb. LIDAR on the way. Let's drop the rest of these and take a break."

"Right." Barbara grinned, her composure returning. "Everything's under control again."

✧　✧　✧

Choco327—Wow, she's rough.

HalifaxNox—Give her a break, why don't you?

CombatBallerina—I'm getting tired watching them work! How long til they finish?

MOon1969—I totally love those habitats! And the little road around the crater is cool.

Jurgen0925—Space revolution. Two new telescopes soon. Marvelous.

Chapter 10

"And here he is, Dr. Bright! Dr. Bright? Dr. Bright?" Leona asked, again and again.

Keegan looked out at the brilliantly lit studio and shifted impatiently from one foot to the other. The anxiety of doing a good show made him antsy. The shining lenses of the two cameras glinted at him.

"Hurry up with the mic," he said, without looking down at the sound tech who was wiring him. The spotlights were whirling around, looking for him. He had to hit his mark before the music stopped. "I've got to get out there. I'm going to miss my cue!"

"Uh, Dr. Bright, there's no place to put it," the tech said.

"What's wrong with you today?" Keegan asked, glancing down at him. "Just put it in my pants pocket, like always."

"Uh, well, you're not wearing any pants!"

"*What?*" Keegan looked down and realized from the waist down, his jumpsuit was missing. He was wearing nothing but a pair of undershorts. He looked up in horror to find all of a sudden he was standing in front of the cameras before millions of people. Wild laughter filled the studio. He froze in horror. How could he recover from a gaffe like that?

"Dr. Bright!"

Leona's voice broke through his dream state. Keegan's eyes flew open. To his infinite relief, he wasn't in the studio. Millions of people weren't laughing and pointing at their screens. He *was* wearing nothing but underwear, but safely under covers in his own bedroom away from the cameras and the millions of viewers. He groaned and rolled over to look at the digital clock. 4:17 A.M. Armstrong time. Outside his window, it was lunar night, with a steadily broadening slice of bright blue Earth in the far distance.

He'd had that dream, or something like it, over and over again since his school days.

Had some modern psycho-babble-ist analyzed it, there was no telling what complexes and parent issues they might suggest he had. But, as everyone since time began or at least since clothes had been invented had had the "nude-in-public" dream, Keegan always dismissed it as common anxiety that had to be overcome before public speaking, or something else of which he was uncertain. He wondered if cavemen and cavewomen had dreams of going out scavenging without wrapping up in their animal fur loincloths.

He guessed what his anxiety was all about. Almost certainly, he was suppressing worry about sending the four older Sparks out to the far side of the Moon. In his heart, he knew they could handle it. They were bright, motivated and, above all, sensible kids. The project was going along well. He was proud of them.

"Dr. Bright? Are you awake? You have an urgent incoming call," Leona's voice announced over his bedroom's intercom speakers.

Oh, that's right. Leona's voice had awakened him from the anxiety dream. Keegan blinked his eyes several times and exhaled, making the motorboat noise. The exhalation released the tension from the nightmare.

"What, uh, who is it?"

"It's Neil."

Keegan peered at the clock again.

"What's Neil doing up at this hour? Is he sick?"

"I am not certain, Dr. Bright. But his hail is encoded as extremely urgent."

"Okay, hold on for a second," he cleared his throat and threw the covers back. "Lights at thirty percent." His feet hitting the cold, smooth floor jolted him fully awake. He slipped on a pair of sweatpants and slid into the rolling chair in front of the screen over his desk. Just as he sat down, an automated voice blared over every intercom speaker in Armstrong City.

"WARNING! WARNING! WARNING!" Three deafening buzzes came from the emergency response computer. Keegan smacked his keyboard. The screen came to life, displaying a bright red graphic with the same word repeated in huge black letters, and text in huge, readable letters scrolled up the screen. "This is not a drill. Repeat. This is not a drill. The Solar Activity Warning System has detected a large disruption in the coronasphere of the Sun that is generating extremely harsh x-rays. There is a very high probability of expanding ionic blasts. All inhabitants are advised to tune to the Lunar Emergency Information Network for further safety instructions." The message repeated over and over again, scrolling upward.

"Neil was ahead of the emergency system, wasn't he?" Keegan murmured to himself.

"I cannot say, sir," Leona responded, "but we did receive the notification of his call before the alarm."

"Oh, sorry, Leona, I wasn't really asking that. Patch him through."

The boy's face appeared on his wall screen. Neil looked like he'd been up all night. His wavy, dark hair was mussed up, his eyes were bloodshot, and his face looked pale. A dark stain like dried chocolate decorated one corner of his mouth. Keegan could see a scatter of refillable soda bottles with the dregs of cola on the computer table behind him. He'd been on the youth about his diet and knew he would have to address it again. It was important to him that the kids took the best care of themselves that they could. Not having a wife and kids of his own, the Sparks had become his *de facto* family, and he watched over them like any father might. But hey, he had pulled the all-nighter with coffee and chocolate himself. He pushed the impulse to mention it aside. During an emergency was not the time to scold him.

"Neil! Are you all right?"

"Yes, sir. I guess you heard the alert?"

"Yes, I did, but your call came just before the siren went off. What do you have on it?"

"You know that sunspot activity we've been monitoring? Just a little while ago, there was a huge flare from sunspot 2513. We have a coronal mass ejection coming this way. I think this is just the start of it, but we'll need some more data from the weather satellites." Neil said. He glanced down, and the screen split to add an image from one of the solar tracking websites. Keegan peered at the graphic and the text scrolling up alongside it. All the signs were there of a severe solar storm. "This is going to be a hot one. I'm sending you images now. I'm worried that the magnetic field lines pinched but haven't reconnected yet. I don't think this is going to be just a one-time thing."

Automatically, Keegan shook his head.

"We can't be sure of statements like that, Neil. The universe always does something more or different than we expect unless our models are exact. And what do we say about that?"

"Our models are never exact?" Neil offered, sounding uncertain. Keegan urged him to think.

"Right. So now, which direction is it going? Is it going to

hit us? And how strong is it going to be? And, when? We need specific details. Send me all the data you've got." Keegan started running his own calculations on Leona's small screen, using the links that popped up one at a time from Neil's feed.

"That's just it," Neil said, his eyes wide with alarm. "*Look* at the data. The flare is pointed right at us. We're going to get the full force of it! What're we going to do?"

"All right, calm down. I'm looking at it now, Neil. Good work." Keegan flipped through the slides that Neil had put together. It was solid work. If the boy wanted to be an astrophysicist or an astronomer someday, he certainly had the knack for it.

Keegan followed the video from the early warning satellites that stood at a modified Lagrange point in a straight line between the Earth and the Sun. The satellites used solar powered EMdrive propulsion so that they could sit much closer to the Sun than at a standard Lagrange point. Keegan sped up the video, playing it at a half hour per second. At about 0200 hours, the sunspots appeared to wink, then the large plasma loop shot from the coronasphere, making a giant warped horseshoe shape that continued to expand and then burst.

Purely as stellar videography, the solar flare was amazingly beautiful. The bright white and orange loop danced about, then shot bursts of plasma away from the sun at speeds just over a hundred times slower than the speed of light. Keegan understood the moment he saw it that once those charged particles of plasma hit any object, a decay stream of hard x-rays and other ionizing radiation would follow.

"Leona, overlay the x-ray and particle data on the video. Adjust the density of the cloud for spherical expansion and give me an incident irradiance of the x-rays and a particle count per square meter at the Lunar surface distance."

"Right away, Dr. Bright."

Keegan ran the video again. A CME could be bad news. If it was going to hit the Moon, Armstrong City would be safe because they were on the dark side at the moment, but Aldrinville was facing the Sun. A chill formed in his belly. This CME was strong and moving fast. That meant that x-rays, extremely hard and very dangerous to unprotected humans, were on their way, and lots of them. The electromagnetic field lines expanded. Electrons and ions from the blast spiraled out about the field lines following the Lorentz forces the CME generated. In just twelve hours the far side of the Moon would be washed with them. The model showed the cloud lasting for about eighteen hours, but only time would tell how accurate the model actually was. Keegan's stomach knotted. The Sparks were in the blast's direct path.

"Start a countdown clock, Leona, with optimization algorithms running to constantly update it based on any new data."

"Clock is ticking, Dr. Bright. Current estimate of CME impact is eleven hours and fifty-seven minutes and counting." The female avatar on the wall screen nodded and made an expression that would suggest concern if she'd been real. "What about the away team?"

"They've got to hear this right now! Get them up and ready for a conference call." He turned to the split side of the monitor where Neil's face was frowning. "Neil? Is there something else?"

"No, sir, not really." The boy looked hopeful but resigned. "I've . . . cancelled the EVA you had planned for Daya and me today. For the show. Tentatively. Because of the CME."

"Ah, I see." Keegan had to smile. That was unexpectedly self-sacrificing of Neil. The kids had been looking forward to the chaperoned and live EVA for so long he hated to have to postpone it. But for the moment, Keegan wasn't certain of anything. He needed to absorb and think on the data for a few moments and he needed some coffee. *Lots* of coffee. "Let's wait to make that determination, Neil. We ought to be okay on this side, barring power fluctuations or communication glitches. We've got to make sure the rest of our team is safe first. And, I want you in bed now. You can't go on an EVA if you're falling asleep on me."

"Uh, okay, sir. I'll be fine, but are the others going to be all right?"

"We're going to do our best to make sure of that, Neil. Thanks for sending me the alert. You beat the colony alarms to the punch. We got this! Great work!"

"Let me know if I can help any way," Neil added, his natural exuberance rebounding in spite of his exhaustion. The hope of going outside the Armstrong City shell was better than no hope.

"You already have! Now get to bed." Keegan shut off the call with Neil and turned to Leona's avatar on the small screen. "You got the kids up yet?"

"Yes, Dr. Bright. They are all on standby."

"Good. Start the coffee maker and go ahead and open the call."

The four elder Sparks stared anxiously at the screen. Dr. Bright's blond hair was all over the place, as if he'd been hauled out of bed at a moment's notice, and he hadn't shaved. At his elbow was a huge thermal cup filled with black coffee with steam rising from its surface. Barbara's mouth watered for some coffee. The bad news that they had awakened to needed a solid hit of caffeine to moderate it.

"No, you can't leave the electronics outside at all," Dr. Bright said. "Anything hit by the highly-charged solar wind is going to get fried or charged up. You have to make sure everything is grounded as well. But, mainly, you have less than eleven hours to build a shelter to ride out that storm.

Get air, water, food, and power into the shelter in enough quantity to last for at least seventy-two hours." Dr. Bright sounded nervous to Barbara. That was something she wasn't prepared for. Seeing him so worried left her feeling helpless. She clutched Fido between both her hands as if the PDE was a lifeline. "The model suggests that the CME will last only about eighteen hours, but it's foolish to count that as an absolute. Better to be prepared for the long haul."

"It's too early to bury the shelters," Dion pointed out. "We've got two of them up, but they still need at least another day to cure. They might collapse."

"Well, that isn't exactly true, Dion," Dr. Bright said. Formulae trickled across the bottom of the PDEs' small screens, showing tensile strength versus load-bearing. "Yes, they'll collapse at low pressure, but if you have them inflated to one atmosphere it'll take tens of meters of dirt on top of them to collapse it. There should be enough ultraviolet from the interior lighting to complete the curing process. It will just take several days longer. I'd rather take a chance on damaging the habitats than risk you all being exposed to massive x-rays."

"We'll bury them deep," Gary promised. "I've got the calculations on how much pressure they can take from when I designed the site."

"Good man," Dr. Bright said. "I'm counting on all of you."

"Can anyone come out to get us?" Jan asked.

"Not in time," Dr. Bright said. He took a swig of coffee from the mug in his hand as if it was giving him energy. "We have no shuttles to spare, and believe me, I've been burning the communications circuits to Colony Administration trying to get one assigned to you. Nothing's available in time. It'd take two days to get to you by road, and that's too late. Same if you got into the trucks and started back this way. I'm here for anything you need, but you're going to have to stay put and handle this one right there. I know you can do it."

Barbara sat back with Fido in her hands, numbly staring at the screen. The four older Sparks had gathered in the girls' tent when the alarm came in. Dion and Gary had only taken off their helmets and gauntlets before sitting down on the air mattresses. She and Jan were still in their pajamas. The lunar chill that had come in with the boys permeated to Barbara's very bones.

Over the last week, she had become comfortable with the precautions they had had to take to stay alive and healthy on the remote site during the construction. Every process and piece of equipment they had brought along had been tested for that project. All of Gary's calculations to prepare for this project were sound. They had been checked and rechecked by the entire team and Dr. Bright. She had even begun to like being way out in the lunar back country without anyone else around but the four of them.

This was different. Now her life and the rest of her team's lives were in danger. She had taken for granted the protection that the Earth's atmosphere had given her almost all of her life from the dangers of the system's lifegiving Sun. Now, at a stroke, the pitiless star could send a bolt of radiation and wipe her out because she was exposed on the face of an airless planetoid.

For a moment, she felt as if despair was strangling her, cutting off her air. Then her native stubbornness welled up and chased it away.

No.

She, Jan, Dion and Gary were *Bright Sparks*. They were already doing something that most people considered impossible, living on another planet. They could handle this. They would survive this new challenge. It was time to take action.

"That settles it then," Barbara exclaimed, sitting bolt upright.

". . . I'll keep feeding you data from the . . . what?" Dr.

Bright began, then stopped at her interruption. He gave her a curious look.

Barbara felt abashed.

"Uh, I'm sorry, Dr. Bright, but it's our necks out here. It's time for us to stop discussing and . . . and start *doing*."

"I agree, Barbara." Dr. Bright said calmly, with his left eyebrow raised. She wasn't sure if he was annoyed, pleased, or indifferent to her interruption. "What do you suggest?"

The ideas came to her so fast, she had to spit them out one after another.

"From what you just said, we have no choice. We have to bury the shelters as fast as possible. The two we've set up are at a half atmosphere now. That was enough to cure, but not enough to bury."

She started running calculations in her head, checking them on Fido. "It'll take another, oh, two hours to pump them up to a full atmosphere. Once we've got that done, it'll take several more hours to get the water from the truck piped inside and to pull all the power from the power truck and move the vehicle inside so it won't short out in the CME. Can we make an inflatable garage instead to shield the vehicles?"

"We could," Gary said, "but the fabric's not enough protection against radiation. By the figures that Neil pulled up, we're going to be hit with a ton of solar energy."

"Do you have a better idea?" Jan asked him.

"I'm thinking!" Gary started scrolling through the database on his PDE. "No, not even if we pile the remaining shelters on top of them. The covering won't be thick enough."

"We can bury them, too," Dion said. "They don't have to be in a habitat. If we tarp over the mechanisms to protect them against regolith dust, we can plow them under. If they're up against the side of the shelters, that's one side I don't have to worry about."

Barbara brightened. The calculations she was making in her mind added the bulk of the trucks to the area of the nearly-cured first habitat.

"I think that will work," she said, encouraged by the others' hopeful faces. "It'll take at least three hours at full speed to cover the shelter. Including the vehicles won't add that much extra time to the process. Let's see . . . We can run the hose from the water truck to the shelter and connect it to shelter number one. If we move it as far uphill as possible along the outer slope of the bigger crater, it ought to give us enough pressure to move it from the tanks and through the plumbing system in the shelter even if the pumps go down. Then we can attach the power truck to the shelter and bury it right against the wall."

"Are we, uh, sure the trucks still work again if we bury them?" Gary asked, glancing up from his screen.

"They won't work if we don't," Jan said, with a wry look at her fellow Nerd-Twin.

"They're all electric, Gary," Dion said. "Sure they will."

"They ought to, Gary," Dr. Bright confirmed. "Look at the heaps of dirt they already collected on the way to Aldrinville. Barely a scratch."

"True," Gary said, nodding. "We'll cover them with the tarps to minimize the regolith we'll have to clean off of them."

"We have to keep one of the plumbing lines above ground," Jan said, displaying the schematic of the water system. "The carbon scrubbers need sunlight to function. X-rays won't hurt them."

"Right," Barbara said, making a note on the list. "But the rest need to be under two meters of regolith at least."

"We can get away with one meter if we have to," Gary said. "Two's better. Good numbers, Barbara."

"Keep going, roomie." Jan said, encouragingly. "Sounds like we can handle this."

"Actually, we do have a dilemma," Barbara said, lifting her eyes to her companions. "The power storage is recharged with solar energy, so, once we bury it there will be no recharging until we *un*bury it," she explained. "But if we don't, the charged particles from the CME will destroy it when it hits. What a mess."

"We bury it," Jan said. Dion nodded. After a moment, Gary nodded, too. "We'll keep from piling dirt on the truck until the last minute to charge it as far as we can, and use as little power as possible while we're waiting out the storm. If we have to dig the panels out by hand when it's over, we will."

"I won't even play computer games," Gary vowed. From the expressions on the others' faces, Barbara realized that was a real sacrifice on Gary's part. He held top worldwide rankings in a couple of online games.

"We should have enough power," Barbara said, still not quite grateful to have companions who could grasp complex problems immediately and offer practical solutions. "I think we have enough tarps for the solar panels. I'll make sure there are no power leaks anywhere in the system. The habitat's our primary concern. Without that, none of the rest matters. We'll get on that right away."

"Yes and no," Dion, the biology major, said. "We've got shelter, enough food and water, no problem, and enough power, but if the carbon dioxide scrubbers fail, that's the one thing that would kill us the fastest."

"I see." Barbara understood. Air. She was so new to the Moon that she still took for granted the atmosphere she had left behind on Earth. The nervous part of her was screaming that all was lost, but she pushed it to the back of her mind. She made a few notes on the schematic she was working up, and nodded at the results. "All right, the ventilation system gets priority from the batteries. We should have plenty of power." She looked up at the screen, resolute. "We'll make it, Dr. Bright."

"I think that's a solid plan, Barbara," Dr. Bright said. He still looked worried to death, but not as haggard as he had when he started the call. "The battery arrays are designed to hold a charge through a complete lunar night. So, you have fourteen-ish days in that regard. That's assuming it remains protected from the charged solar wind." he took a deep breath.

"As soon as the CME is done," Dr. Bright continued, "there should be enough power left in the truck to just drive it out from under the regolith once you disconnect the cables from the shelter, or you can dig it out with the dozer. Perhaps you can find a way to mark where the cables and connections are buried so you can undo them first."

"Or push it out." Gary added. "Not sure about the cables."

"Right, or push it out. We'll figure out the cable thing." Barbara smiled. "Now we need to get to work." She stood up, keenly aware that she was wearing yellow pajamas printed with dancing elephants. Not much of a uniform for interplanetary heroics.

"Wait, I want all of you to listen to me now." Dr. Bright said, fixing his eyes on them. At his stern tone, Barbara sat down again. "Pay close attention to me here. We're not worrying about following the details of building Aldrinville. Forget the telescope. I mean it. What we're doing from this moment on is surviving. If you are caught outside during this storm the x-rays could, no, *will* kill you. I wish there was time for you just to drive back, but there isn't. And I can't get a shuttle to get to you in time. You have to stay insulated from the storm. Focus on getting a shelter completed that you can hole up in. I'm sending you calculations now that express how deep it must be buried. You need at least one meter of dirt on all walls, top and sides. That's the absolute minimum. You can't cut corners on that number. Like you and Gary calculated, I'd prefer you double that if you have time. But one meter is the absolute minimum! If you have questions or just need to talk to me, do not hesitate to open a channel."

"Yes, sir," the Sparks chorused. Barbara felt that knot of panic twisting in her belly again, and forced herself to ignore it.

"Dr. Bright, that brings up another issue." Jan said. "Will comms stay up?"

The scientist blew through his lips, creating a buzzing noise.

"I'm going to say I doubt it. Right now, the internet connectivity is from those Yagi pole-mounted router to pole-mounted router via wireless TCP/IP transceivers along the road. You probably saw them up on the lips of craters. The gaps in coverage are filled with satellites, like Lunasat 5. There's no way of knowing if the communications will survive the CME or not. But we will have to shut the satellites down as a precautionary measure to keep their circuits from frying. So, for sure the sats will be off-line for the duration of the CME. The wireless routers were hardened for radiation but not for levels this high. They might survive; they might not. Assume they won't. I'm presently working on a communications contingency just in case. But realize this: you might be on your own out there once the CME hits. Right now, like I said, it looks like it will last eighteen hours or so. Place the radiation sensors outside and drag a wire back in the shelter before you bury it. Do not come out if the sensor has high readings or if it quits functioning. I will find a way to get the message to you."

"Right." Barbara clapped her hands together and pulled her EVA suit off the peg on the tent wall. The others looked at her once Dr. Bright had logged off. "Let's get to work, team. We haven't got much time and we have a lot to get done!"

YuBaitu—What is a CME? Is it bad?

KeeganMarryMe—OMG, is everyone on the Moon going to die?

KadtheKonqueror—LOL why are they worried? Earth gets hit with flares all the time.

HCMDevil—@KadtheKonqueror The Moon doesn't have a magnetic field like Earth's you absolute moron.

Chapter 11

"As we can see here," Daya explained to Dr. Bright, pointing at the three-dimensional virtual image of the side crater and the shelter on the main screen in Sparks Central. "The satellite image and video from site cams shows their progress. Their vital signs are still good, but their heart rates are elevated. They're working hard, but I'm very worried that they aren't progressing fast enough. You can see what they have accomplished so far."

The habitat was still a long way from being buried. Keegan looked at the screen with concern. He wiped one hand down the front of his jumpsuit and took another swig of coffee from his oversized cup. It had gone cold. Small wonder. It had been over two hours since he had heard the news.

The Sparks Central High Performance Computer Cluster ran multiple algorithms at once to create a real-time virtual image of Aldrinville from all the data available. The inflatable shelter was slowly being covered from the back side. Every successive image showed more scoops of pale regolith piled on or against the wheat-colored cylinder.

"Well, they're getting there," Keegan said. The water truck

and the power truck had been moved to opposite sides of the rectangular base of the inflatable structure. It looked like they had built a ramp for the water truck so it would be elevated above the shelter's water intake. That was good thinking, probably on Dion's part, but just as likely on Barbara's. Time lapses of the video imagery showed spoils piles from the larger crater excavation being reduced and the albedo of the shelter changing to that of the lunar regolith. Keegan played the time lapse several times before he leaned back in his desk chair with a sigh. He looked over at the youngest Spark. Daya's long braid was more tightly bound than usual, and her neat peach-colored jumpsuit was buttoned to the neck. Everyone was battening down the hatches to see out this storm.

"Where's Neil, Daya?"

She pursed her generous mouth with amusement. "He should be in bed. I hope he is. He needed to rest after being up all night monitoring the sunspot. I promised I would wake him when we need him."

Keegan looked at the countdown clock. The CME blast wave was only four hours out and he'd have liked to have a projected completion plan. Time-lining was Neil's other expertise. Someday, NASA could use the boy on long space mission planning. For now, Dr. Bright needed him to work out the next two hours of the EVA team.

"Okay, go get him now. You two get on live with Aldrinville and optimize their schedule. They have to beat this CME. I'm counting on you two to make certain they don't forget anything."

Daya's eyes shone with pride.

"Yes, sir!" She was out the door before he had time to add any afterthoughts.

"Good kids," Keegan said, smiling after her. "Leona, keep eyes and ears on all of the Sparks and give me text updates every fifteen minutes. If any of their vital signs show unusual changes I want to know about it. I need to know that they can get the job done under stress. Fear is even more of a killer than radiation."

The AI sounded almost sympathetic.

"I will implement the appropriate algorithm, Dr. Bright."

"Great. Thank you."

"You are welcome, Dr. Bright."

Keegan tapped a few keys on his console and had a multi-split screen showing the suit data for each of the four older Sparks. Daya was right. The data from each of them looked normal so far, even Barbara's. For now, they were managing their situation like professional astronauts. Keegan told himself that he'd just have to trust that he had picked the right people for the job and to move forward with other matters that had to be taken care of. He had no choice. If the rest of the technicians and scientists in the colony weren't busy making sure Armstrong City would be safe, the responsibility wouldn't have to fall on such young shoulders.

"Next time, I don't let them go it alone," he muttered to himself. "My own fault."

"I'm sorry, sir. I didn't catch that," Leona replied.

"Huh? Oh, ignore that. You know the old saying? 'If you want to make God laugh, tell him your plans.' But, uh, what do you think, Leona? We've still got a show scheduled. Do we air a rerun today? A best of?"

"I will help with whichever you prefer, sir." Leona replied.

Keegan gave a rueful chuckle. It wasn't really up to him anyway. He was contracted for a certain number of live shows, and he had a production staff working full time to be prepared each day. For that day he had intended to go outside on an EVA with Neil and Daya and use a small man-made crater to set up for broadcasting a live feed back to Earth. But he wasn't at all certain going outside with the youths during a CME impacting the other side of the Moon and his Aldrinville team was a good idea.

"What do I do?" he asked aloud.

"With what, Dr. Bright?" Leona asked.

"Rhetorical question, Leona," Keegan replied. He shook his head to clear it.

Keegan ran the CME model again on the mainframe. He watched as the blastwave of charged particles and harsh radiation expanded with a spherical wavefront and impacted the far side of the lunar surface. The simulation showed that several satellites in the lunar communications network would be passing through the blastwave just as it hit, but all of them would pass through it many times a day simply due to orbital mechanics. Armstrong had no choice but to turn them all off until the CME was finished and hope that precaution protected their circuitry. Each of them had cost millions of dollars to build and launch. That meant no communications from satellites for anywhere from twelve hours to three days, depending on how long the solar event continued. That worried him. He hated leaving the Sparks out there by themselves with no way to talk with them.

There *had* to be a secondary plan. Keegan didn't have very high hopes that the wifi routers on the poles along the road would survive for very long. There and then, he decided that after all this was over, before any other EVA teams were sent out to Aldrinville, a hardline had to be laid in. They'd need a means to dig a trench and lay cable for thousands of kilometers, but it could be done. It had to be done. He'd get with NASA, the Lunar Administration Council, and Mrs. Reynolds-Ward, the colony's founder, about planning.

All that was still in the future. Keegan needed a plan *now*. He didn't like the idea of his Sparks, his family, being stranded on the far side of the Moon, buried inside an inflated tent, and cut off from any help or being able to call home. If something went wrong, he'd only hear about it when it was too late. Or not hear. He didn't like either possibility at all.

"But how to talk to them?" he asked aloud. "And what do we need?"

His brain refused to sprout any solutions. Keegan felt like slamming his head on the desk. For the first time in a long time, Dr. Bright was out of bright ideas. But Keegan had never let that stop him before, and he wasn't about to let it stop him now.

Somehow, some way, he would figure out something to get through to them. He had to. His family was depending on him whether they realized it or not. An idea would just have to come.

"There's no doubt in my mind, Barb." Jan talked constantly as they dragged immense coils of black insulated cables to connect the power systems to the shelter from the battery stack on the truck. Barbara started a response as she unspooled the lead out carefully from the rear of the power truck so as not to tear the connector loose at the near end. They had replacement parts, but she couldn't take the time to do a repair, not now. Every minute that ticked away was a minute they couldn't get back. She was so concerned she didn't even want to listen to music while they worked.

Behind them, Dion scooped up regolith in the bucket of the Cat, and Gary raked it down in a growing slope in the small crater around the domed habitat. The first loads had already been deposited on the roof of shelter number one.

". . . Dr. Bright is right," Jan said, more nervous than Barbara had ever heard her. "We *are* going to lose all communications with Armstrong City. There's just no way in the universe that the routers along the road will function properly during the CME. They're going to blow. The only question is how many of them will function again after the storm passes. I hate being cut off!"

The team had built a high platform beside the shelter for the water truck, which was already buried in meters of gray dust and rubble. The lines into the first shelter were connected. The second, which they were leaving unplumbed and unelectrified, would act as a storeroom for the rest of the equipment they wouldn't need until after the CME had passed. They would load crates and boxes in, and seal it against the coming storm.

Barbara checked the time. The team still had hours of work ahead of them. None of them were sure they would finish on time. She struggled as best she could with everything that had to get done. But for the moment her hands were full. The five-centimeter diameter power cables were stiff in the cold vacuum of space and were heavy even in the lower gravity of the Moon. The sweat continued to pour profusely from her forehead.

"I think you're right, Jan," Barbara agreed. She blinked her left eye several times reflexively as a drop of sweat rolled into her eye, stinging it. In fact, her helmet visor was fogging up from the inside. "Fido, lower the humidity in my suit!" she snapped. "I can't see what I'm doing."

"Right away, Barbara," Fido replied. Suddenly, the air around her face seemed a little drier. A gentle breeze blew toward her eyes. A light film that had condensed on the inside of her faceplate shimmered and vanished. The coolness made her feel a little better.

"So what do we do about it?" she asked Jan. "You're right. It's dangerous to lose touch with the base. What if we have an emergency? What if . . . one of us gets hurt?"

Jan shook her head. "I have no idea. I've been racking my brain for something, but I just have a big nothing going on there. It's too bad the dish isn't operational yet." Jan sighed.

"Barb, I'm getting brain fog. I'm so tired I can't think straight."

Barbara could tell her friend was frustrated and tired. They were all wearing out from the endless work. They were all scared. None of them liked the thought of being cut off from the rest of humanity during such a crisis. And if they were all that tired, they were going to have to take a break before they made a mistake that could be fatal. She knew they needed to lighten the burden any way they could.

"Okay, then," she said firmly. "Stop concentrating on it. Let's try to think about something else, and maybe our unconscious minds will work it out." Barbara had to force herself to take her own advice, but she came up with a new subject. "Neil sounded heartbroken that he and Daya aren't getting to do the EVA with Dr. Bright today."

"I know," Jan said, with a little smile. She unlimbered a hula-hoop-sized loop of cable to Barbara, who flattened it out in the knee-deep layer of dust that the boys had laid down between the truck and the habitat. Many more loads would bury it deep when they had finished. The cable's stiff casing didn't want to stay down. Barbara laid small rocks on the parts that stuck up to keep them in place until it relaxed. "He's so anxious to be grown up. Sometimes I feel so sorry for him, but then I recall what a pain in the backside he is sometimes." She tossed her head playfully. "Maybe you've noticed that he has a crush on me."

"Oh, yes," Barbara said. As she pulled the cable toward the rectangular panel at knee height on the wall of the shelter, she turned to grin at her roommate. "I hope you don't take it seriously."

"No. He's a serial romantic. Pretty soon, his fascination with my marvelous self will wear off, and he'll imprint on *you.*"

"I hope not!" Barbara laughed. "But I do feel bad about the EVA. He was almost bouncing off the walls of

Armstrong City because we were going out on this mission and he wasn't."

"There will be plenty of other times for him," Jan said, as they arrived at the side of the habitat. She reeled out the last of the cable into Barbara's hands. "Daya, on the other hand, I'm not so sure she could care less. She seems perfectly happy no matter what her situation is. She'll make a good doctor someday. It's too bad she isn't interested in engineering. I don't think she likes to get outside the box that often. And she's a lot more subtle about it, but she's suffering from her own crush. On Neil. Not that he notices."

Barbara grinned. "I've seen the way she looks at him. Of course, he's blind as a bat about it. Kids. So, what exactly were they going to do on their EVA? Dr. Bright was keeping it a surprise from the Earth audience until they actually went out with the television crew. Neil was obviously dying to tell me, but Daya refused to let him reveal the secret."

Barbara put one hand on the big multi-pin connector in the bottom of the panel, and tugged the heavy cable in her right hand up to it. To her dismay, it fell about three centimeters short. She pulled again. It wouldn't move.

She looked back toward the truck. No excess length stood up from the dust, and she knew there had been plenty of extra cable to cover the distance. Gary's measurements had allowed for plenty of slack. She tugged again. No luck. She and Jan hauled on the cable with both hands. It didn't move.

"Oh, that stinks! We're hung on something somewhere down the line. Stay here and keep it out of the regolith, and I'll walk back down the line and see if I can get us some more slack."

"Okay." Jan said, taking the plug out of Barbara's grip. "The cable's probably stuck against the wheels on the other side."

Barbara grimaced at her own carelessness. "Probably. I

thought I'd pulled it free with enough of a service loop. Guess not." She trudged back toward the truck, slowly plowing aside the wall of dust to trace the cable's path with one booted foot.

Sure enough, when she got close to the truck, she saw that the thick black line was wedged between the lunar regolith and the large back wheel. How could she have let it get trapped like that? She blamed the stiff casing, which probably popped up again once they had turned their backs on it. It was something to address with Dr. Bright for future projects. "Found it! So, do you know what they were planning to do outside?"

"Oh, it's really no secret," Jan said, as Barbara reached down and hooked her glove under the trapped portion of the cable. "It's a story about lunar telescopes. Since we're on the light side right now, Armstrong City is dark, which means they'll get awesome views of Earth . . ."

Barbara pulled at the loop. During the brief hour since they had unreeled it, the growing bed of regolith had cascaded down from beside the truck. One big, heavy stone had settled against the free coil, shortening the slack. She wrapped both hands around the cable, braced her foot against the rock, and leaned backward. It wouldn't come. She yanked at it again and again to get it free.

"Come on! Unh!" she grunted. On the fifth tug, it broke loose, sending Barbara tumbling backwards. She bounced a few times on her bottom and came to a stop with gray dust rising all around her. She gasped and clapped her mouth shut. All her instincts told her that she would inhale the dust, but her brain reminded her she was wearing a spacesuit. Still, her heart pounded in her chest. "Aaagh!"

"Are you all right?" Jan asked, alarmed.

"I'm . . . I don't know," Barbara said, feeling anxiously around her body with her gloved hands. Falling down on the far side of the Moon in a spacesuit could be dangerous for all sorts of reasons! She could puncture her suit. Was there any cold coming in? Would she hear a hiss if air started escaping? She could break a limb or sprain something. *Settle down, Barb!* she told herself. She checked the suit health monitor on the screen of her PDE attached at her left wrist. All systems were green. She wasn't injured, just a little winded.

"Hey, roomie, answer me! Over!"

"I'm fine. Really. No panic. Honest. Sorry to scare you. I scared myself!"

Barbara pulled herself to her feet and brushed herself off, scattering a dusting of regolith in all directions. Her heart rate slowed, and the pulsing on the PDE settled to a normal pace.

"Good," Jan said, with a sigh of relief. "Anyhow, they were planning on setting up a mini version of the Aldrinville radio telescope, then broadcast our show live back to Earth through that system instead of microwave link. We dug the crater about two kilometers out from the edge of Armstrong City as practice for this project. It's only about five meters in diameter. Neil printed out an inflatable feedhorn boom to go over it. Not huge, but it's a full working model."

"That's so cryo!" Barbara said. A fizz of excitement and envy filled her chest. "This is why I love Dr. Bright's show. We get to do real science. I mean, this is, too. But most science programs for young people demonstrate simple principles, but nothing practical for the real world. I mean, how many times do you need to create a vacuum that forces an egg into a bottle?"

"Not that too many kids are going to build themselves radio telescopes, though," Jan said, wryly. "Then I think they were going to interview Commander Harbor. She's due to land any time."

Barbara made her way back toward the power panel at the rear of the shelter, moving the extra cable along with her as she went, careful to make sure the length stayed under the soil.

"That's fantastic! I kind of wish we could be back there to meet Commander Harbor. Who wouldn't want to meet the leader of the first manned Mars mission?" Barbara said.

"No kidding," Jan said, just as enthusiastically. "I want to get out there myself one day. But where I really want to go is Saturn."

"Hey, you two!" Gary's voice interrupted them. They looked up toward the roof, where he was raking piles of lunar soil out to the edges. "If you could hurry up with that power box, Dion and I would like to start burying this section. It's bad enough Dion and I can hear your chatter."

"You're free to join in the conversation," Jan said.

"No, thanks," Gary said, shaking his shovel at them. "*We're* working."

"So are we!" Barbara glanced at Jan. "How's it look?"

"Done here," Jan replied as she twisted the locking mechanism on the cable connector once more with her gauntleted hand just to make certain. "Let's get inside and start powering up everything."

"Okay, good." Barbara looked at the panel one last time. Little green LEDs blazed to life on the recessed board. She closed the panel over it. "We're done out here, guys."

"Good," Dion said. The dozer scooted into view, carrying a full bucket of soil. "Come on, Gary. Let's get the truck buried."

"Roger that," Gary said. He bounded off the roof of the habitat with the shovel in his hand and loped toward the Cat.

"C'mon, Barb," Jan said, beckoning her toward the airlock. The door of the habitat had stiffened in the last several hours to the consistency of lucite, although it was far stronger than any plastic.

Barbara shook her head. Even with a CME bearing down on them, part of her thoughts were still back in Armstrong City. Commander January Harbor! Barbara was on the Moon, but Harbor had walked on *Mars*. The astronaut had led the team that built the first high bandwidth relay ground station that would host future missions and an eventual outpost there someday. It was exciting how much progress humankind had made in the last few decades!

An idea began to percolate in her mind. Something from her conversation with Jan had sparked her unconscious, activated the problem-solving neurons, and started the gears turning. Something clicked, and sparked. The calculations began to fall into place. Barbara held her breath. Maybe. Maybe it would work. If there was time. She glanced up toward the sky, but her visor immediately darkened to blot out the brilliance of the sun.

"Fido."

"Yes, Barbara?"

"Where is Mars right now?"

"Keegan, we're on in an hour. What're we going to do?" Jacqueline Feeney, the show's executive producer and director, pulled him into a quiet huddle beside one of the camera tripods at the edge of the greenscreen on the main soundstage set. Jackie was an attractive woman of his own age, only about ten centimeters shorter than he, with golden skin, cascades of wavy dark hair that she kept pulled up in a knot on top of her head, caramel-brown eyes and a pointed, determined chin. She showed him her tablet, on which half a dozen miniature videos were rolling in individual windows. "I have several prerecorded segments lined up and ready to fill. But we still need twenty-two and a half minutes of live segments to stay on contract."

Keegan ran his hands through his hair. Ann Limubwe, a round-faced African-American woman with her thick russet hair in a cascade of twists, was their lighting technician, who also doubled in makeup and hair. Clicking her tongue, she came over with a comb to drag his tousled locks back into place. Keegan waved her away impatiently.

"Come on, Ann! I haven't even had a chance to shower or shave today!"

Ann smiled in a motherly fashion and continued straightening him up. He addressed Jackie over Ann's shoulder.

"I can't believe I let them talk me into signing a clause that demanded a live feed even during emergency situations. What was I thinking?" He shook his head. "I need to be focused on keeping the kids safe."

"Then, do that," Jackie said, firmly. "Go about your business. Find a way to make sure the EVA team is safe. Just do that! We'll roll the cameras unless you tell us not to. It will be real whether it's exciting or not. And since we'll be covering you live, it will satisfy our contract. The network executives will see that it's ratings gold. A crisis on the Moon? If it wasn't so serious, I'd be thrilled. I know the big shots will be. It'll be on every news service across Earth before it even finishes airing. They'll love the publicity. Think of the hits on social media!"

"We could. I guess." Keegan rubbed his chin and felt stubble scratch against his hand. He hated having to consider ratings at a time like this. "Just have the cameras follow me around in the control room, and I'll do my best to talk through what I'm doing as I can. Maybe we could have you and the camera crew helping explain things to fill holes if I get busy. I hope the execs won't make a fuss. But even if they do, it won't matter. This has to take priority."

Jackie smiled, although the expression didn't erase the worried lines in her forehead. "They won't make a fuss. This is an emergency, a *real* emergency. We'll run a statement at the beginning of the show saying just that. We'll back you up. We'll fill in if you get busy, and run video footage and web captures if it gets too hairy. Are you certain the CME will hit before we air?"

Keegan checked on Leona's screen to make certain.

"Yes. It will hit about thirty minutes before. We'll start seeing damage to the communications and power infrastructure on Earth about then, but it looks like it will impact the far northern part of the planet the most. Here at Armstrong City we should be fine. Probably won't even notice any difference at all."

"What about in Aldrinville?"

"It's going to be bad there, Jackie. Bad." Keegan thumbed toward his screen, running formulae over a topographical map of the Moon's far side. "The models are continuously updating from the solar observatory data. This is the biggest event like this to hit us since 1859. And I think it's going to dwarf that event by a long shot."

Jackie's hazel eyes widened in horror as the image of the expanding radiation bubble on the screen impacted the Moon's surface again and again.

"That's terrifying! Those poor kids!"

Keegan felt the guilty knot in his belly twist a little more.

"You're telling me? But, the show must go on. We'll make this work. I'll assign Neil and Daya to capture some live images of the northern lights and any other spectacular footage from Earth as it happens. We ought to get significant veiling. It'll be downright pretty." Three-quarters of his mind was on the away team, but a quarter of it was still focused on making the show work. "Hey, you might put some producers on that, too. Earth could see some blackouts if the CME makes a hit on any of the northern power grids." Keegan did his patented exhale and motorboat sound to clear his mind and give himself a microsecond of meditation and tension relief. He glanced in the direction of Sparks Central, even though he couldn't see it from the studio floor. "At least those two kids will be here by me, not out there."

Jackie pursed her lips.

"Okay. We have a plan, Keegan, so relax. The kids out there will be safe. They're, well, they're the brightest, most self-sufficient youngsters I've ever seen in my life. That's why we chose them. That's why *you* chose them." Jackie placed a hand on his shoulder. Keegan covered her fingers with his own hand and squeezed them, finding a lifeline in her grasp. Her eyes crinkled warmly.

Keegan's breath caught in his chest. They'd felt some strong mutual attraction to one another since they'd started working together at the beginning of the show's run, but they'd channeled it into professional behavior and close friendship. *Maybe we've suppressed it too much*, Keegan thought ruefully. This time, he felt, the pat was a sisterly gesture to show him her support and comfort. They trusted each other, and at that moment, that meant the world.

"Keegan, just do what has to be done." Jackie looked at her watch and whistled a sense of urgency. Then she smiled and rubbed the stubble on his chin with the back of her hand. "In the meantime, dude, you need to clean yourself up and get into wardrobe, hair, and makeup. Do I have to march you back to your cabin and make sure you get showered and shaved?" She gave him a wicked look. Maybe not so sisterly . . . Keegan glanced at Ann, wary about exhibiting their private business in front of her. She grinned knowingly at him. Keegan imagined that the whole crew might be taking bets on when or if he and Jackie would ever get together. He kind of wondered that himself. But not now.

"I can do it." He smiled down at Jackie. "I'll be back for hair and makeup soon. Do me a favor and get Neil and Daya ready. Neil probably needs some caffeine and some B-12."

"Consider it done." She glanced at the digital clock on the

wall behind the cameras. "See you in the control room set in about an hour. I'll send Ann in to you then."

"An hour and seventeen minutes by our best estimates," Neil said. His face was projected up on the wallscreen in the shelter common area, although Barbara and the others still received the same feed through their PDEs. "It'll hit Earth a few seconds after . . ." Barbara could see a makeup sponge or brush in a dark hand cross his face as he talked. Neil sputtered as the tool passed over his mouth. "Oh, come on, Ann! Not yet! . . . Latest data we have is that you are still short on the entrance coverage, Barb. Move it, guys!"

"We're moving it," Dion's voice said, sounding perturbed. "We're shifting half the surface of the Moon onto the other half. It's not that easy."

"You want to come out here and help dig?" Gary added.

Neil's earnest freckled face wrinkled in apology.

"I wish I could," he said. "Look, nothing this serious has ever happened while I've been here. You should see how upset Dr. Bright is. We're all worried."

"Thanks, Neil," Barbara told him. As concerned as she was for the safety of her own team, she felt sorry for their mentor. "We're going as fast as we can. Jan and I've got the power and water hookups tested and ready to operate. The radiation sensor will be online in the next fifteen minutes. The boys are working the bulldozer as hard as it will go. Now that Jan has the sensors and electronics systems under control, I'm headed outside with a shovel to help them finish up. I have Fido on an alarm to get us inside ten minutes before the CME should hit. If you see any changes or anything, let us know. You're the last line of defense."

"I will, Barb." He grinned at her. "Hey, wild first week on the job, huh?"

"Wild doesn't even describe it, Neil." Barbara looked at

the countdown on her PDE and also being projected on the corner of the wallscreen. She glanced down at her health monitor. The air in the shelter had good oxygen levels, and her pulse was only slightly quickened. "I'd better get back to work. Uh, break a leg? Is that right?"

Neil made a face.

"I think that's for stage actors or something. I know Dr. Bright never says that."

"Uh, okay. Then, good luck."

"He never says that either." Neil laughed. "But, thanks. You, too."

"Okay, Barb," she told herself. "There's still time. There's time."

"Time for what, Barb?" Jan asked. Barbara beckoned to her.

"As soon as you're done there, come out and help me with something. I've got an idea."

Jan frowned. "What kind of idea?"

"One that might make things easier for us. I think we have just enough time."

"Okay," Jan said, her dark eyes filled with curiosity.

Barbara turned to the airlock and began her exit process.

"Fido, wasn't there a spoils pile just on the edge of the telescope crater closest to the shelter crater?"

"Yes, Barbara. Would you like me to show you?"

"Yes, please do."

✧ ✧ ✧

Choco327—You see why they need Pam? Everything went wrong when that Barb got there.

NeroliFox—I don't get it. Can't they just live in a cave until the CME goes away?

Keegan#1fan—Where's Dr. Bright?
It's time for the show. Gotta have my fix!

ButchFel9—Barb was awsome.

Chapter 12

"This is not a drill or a simulation," Jackie said into her headset mic, as the control room engineer beside her displayed the opening graphic of the show, the nuclear starburst over a field of electric blue with the title superimposed over it. "The regularly scheduled episode of *Live from the Moon with Dr. Bright*, 'The Moon is a Harsh Mirror, Part II,' will be shown at a later date. Presently, we're experiencing an emergency situation here on the Moon due to a highly energetic solar coronal mass ejection. I am the executive producer of the show, Jacqueline Feeney. We will be broadcasting today live from Dr. Bright's mission control and laboratory headquarters. There have been no rehearsals. None of this is staged. What you are witnessing is the local team led by Dr. Bright doing its best to protect the inhabitants of the lunar colony, Armstrong City, and its new offshoot, Aldrinville, the site of the new radar/radio telescope currently under construction."

The graphic dissolved to display a wide view of the Sparks' laboratory. Camera One panned over a panel of wallscreens and computer terminals. Leona's avatar, this time appearing as a slim East Asian woman in a lab coat, was up on one of the three large screens in the center of the array. Dr. Bright, in a fresh lab coat and jumpsuit, stood over the console facing the display, running over simulations with her. Several other video monitors below the main screens showed images of Aldrinville from above, onsite cams, and PDE cams of the Sparks on the away team. On one of the three big screens, the viewers could see all of the older Sparks huddled around a central monitor and camera system in a dimly lit, sparsely furnished living area, looking at data that Dr. Bright, Neil, and Daya were sending them. As Camera One tilted down to view some of the smaller viewscreens, two of them went black.

"We just lost cameras two and four on the exterior rim of the shelter crater!" Neil announced, without looking up from his computer.

"Roger that, Neil." Dr. Bright tapped at a few more controls and then looked up at Leona. "Leona, run the current space weather false color movie again. Show me particles, fields, and x-rays."

"It is running now Dr. Bright. On screen three."

Screen three filled with bar graphs and data printouts, all moving at different rates.

"Paul," Keegan turned to the tall, thin, hollow-cheeked cameraman running One, and pointed to the image to the right of the main screen, "you might want to zoom in on that or patch the signal direct. People back home will want to see this."

"I've got it," the cameraman said.

"Can you tell us what's going on, Dr. Bright?" Jackie asked, in a light, conversational voice.

Keegan pulled himself away from the console and turned to face Camera Two, run by their new video technician, a plump woman with thick, dishwater blonde hair named Yvonne Walotski. Even though he didn't feel like it, he pasted on a wide smile and assumed his onscreen manner and voice.

"Right. Well, as you all may or may not be aware, we have four of the Bright Sparks on an expedition EVA to the far side region we call Aldrinville. That part of the Moon is currently in lunar day and is in direct line of fire of the coronal mass ejection we're experiencing right now. We have some footage from the solar weather observatory from about thirteen hours ago, which you can see over on monitor number one. This oncoming storm is a monster. I don't think we've seen solar activity like this since 1859. This one may be bigger than that one. Of course, we didn't have anyone on the Moon the last time this happened." Dr. Bright kept his tone positive, but kept glancing back and forth at the monitors over his shoulder. To his dismay, the screen went black, and a cross-hairs logo appeared on it instead.

Daya turned, focusing on him instead of the camera. The one-quarter of his mind that was on the show wished she'd turn toward the lens, but he completely understood. For all her outward calm, she had to be as nervous as he was. Maybe more.

"Dr. Bright, the one satellite that we had permission to keep online, Lunasat 5, just went down. Our remaining eye in the sky and the sat-com over Aldrinville is gone. I hope that it's still operational after the event concludes, but I can't check now. I'll add that we're still getting data through the ground wireless system, but the operating system is showing a *lot* of network resets."

Dr. Bright raised his face to the main scopes.

"Aldrinville shelter, what's the status of your systems out there?" he asked.

On the right-hand screen, Barbara leaned toward the video pickup in the remote console. Like the others, she still wore her EVA suit, but had taken off her helmet and gloves. Good. That meant that they had heat as well as air. The life-support system was working properly. Her light brown hair was all over the place, and her cheeks were flushed. All four of them had sweat running down their faces.

"This is Barbara at the shelter, with Gary, Dion and Jan. We're all okay physically. We've detected very high levels of x-rays on our external sensor. The power systems show a higher direct current voltage bias than is typical for them. Jan tells me that we're still within tolerance levels. I've confirmed that reading." Barbara turned to her left. "Dion is checking the internet connectivity right now. Dion?"

The big African-American youth leaned in and gave the camera a worried smile.

"Right, Barb. I just posted some pics of us to the Internet a few seconds ago and got a confirmation, so we're still up for now. I did get a 'lost server' error twice in the process, so the whole thing's going intermittent."

A klaxon interrupted him, followed by flashing red lights from ceiling fixtures and emplacements above the doors. For a split second, Keegan thought the alarm was at Aldrinville, then realized it was going on around him. Shutters rolled down over the windows, and the doors slid shut and sealed themselves with an ominous BOOM. He looked up.

"WARNING! WARNING! WARNING!" a robotic female voice announced. "This is a loss of pressure alert. All citizens of Armstrong City are warned to immediately don protective environment suits and gear as a possible loss of pressure is highly likely! Repeat! Don environment suits immediately! This is not a drill!"

Keegan waved to the camera crew and headed for the locker that was in every room in the city. The laboratory closet contained one of his environment suits and half a dozen spares of assorted sizes, as well as secondary suits for each of the Sparks. He beckoned to Neil and Daya. "Kids, come on!"

"What the heck?" Neil asked. He seemed frozen at his desk, his hazel eyes wide. Keegan gestured to him with his whole arm.

"Not the time to question, Neil! Get your suits on. All of you! Now! Set the cameras down and get your suits on!" Keegan pulled out one of the adult spares and tossed it to Paul, then a smaller one to Yvonne. He strode back to the desks, grabbed Neil and Daya by the hands and rushed them to the locker. He handed them their emergency gear. "Get these on *now*, you two!"

"Yes, sir!" Daya exclaimed. She turned her back on the others, stripped off her saffron coverall and shoes, and sat down on the floor to stuff her feet into the legs of the suit. Keegan undid his lab coat and threw it over the nearest desk. This was life or death. If Armstrong City was experiencing a real catastrophe, there was no time for modesty or concern with finding a dressing room. Neil followed his example.

Keegan grabbed his environment suit with one hand and kicked off his shoes with the other. He unzipped his flight suit, dropped it to the floor, and stepped out of it. If a breach was imminent, there could be only seconds before there was a decompression that sucked the life-giving air from the room, and, following that, the temperature would drop rapidly. They had to get suited up and sealed as quickly as possible.

Every single individual on the Moon had been trained for rapid pressure loss emergencies. The administration ran weekly drills to make sure even temporary visitors knew what to do when the alarm sounded. Everyone was required to know the protocols for getting dressed in a hurry, much like passengers on a cruise ship who had to participate in mandatory lifeboat drills. At least on Earth, there would be air. Not on the Moon. They were *wearing* their lifeboats.

Keegan applied the compression garment to his legs and then jumped as he pulled the arms upwards and over his shoulders to help yank it into place. The Kevlar-and-carbon-reinforced neoprene material snapped like a rubber band against him with a *schlurp*! Keegan cringed.

That's going to leave a mark, he thought.

He yanked the zipper fastener up from between his legs and then up and over his shoulder. Out of the corner of his eye he could see the rest of the crew working feverishly to get their gear on. Neil and Daya were already putting their boots and gloves on. Keegan was proud of them. They reached for their helmets and fastened them.

He stepped in his boots. As soon as his feet hit the insoles, the shafts sealed around his shins and compressed against his feet. Then he slipped on the gauntlets and grabbed his full dome helmet and popped it over his head. Once he had slapped his PDE against his wrist and started the suit startup sequence, he turned to see if anybody else in the crew needed help.

Yvonne, the Camera Two operator, was having a bit of difficulty reaching the pull cord for her fastener. The heavyset woman was fairly new to both the crew and the Moon, nor was she necessarily the most flexible person on it. Keegan stepped in behind her and poked the cord up between the woman's legs so she could reach it.

"Thanks, Doc," she said. "I always have to have someone help me."

"When you use your own suit, you should tape that thing to the inner leg, Von. It'll make it easier to get to."

"Good idea, Dr. Bright." She had a good attitude, he had to say that for her.

"All right, team," Jackie announced over the intercom. "Once your suits are on, pick the cameras back up and keep speeding. We still want to get this. We're streaming live."

"Dr. Bright, I have kept the interior video cameras operating while you were getting dressed," Leona said, pleasantly. "I can send the video file data stream to Ms. Feeney's console. I have blurred the images of the crew's bodies."

"Do it," Keegan said. "We have to get back to work. Got it, Ms. Feeney?"

"I've got it! Thank you, Leona!" Jackie replied. "All right, we're all suited up here in the control room. Any idea what just happened?"

"No, I'm sorry. I do not know yet," Leona answered. "But I am searching the emergency instructions announcements for information."

"I think I know!" Neil announced from his console. Keegan realized that he had not even seen the boy finish getting dressed, much less going back to work. But he was sitting there hacking away as best he could in his gloves. So was Daya. He shook his head in admiration. Best team *ever*. "Listen to this. It's on the emergency broadcast frequency."

Neil tapped a couple other controls, then swiped at one last switch several times until he finally got it to connect.

"*. . . Roger that, control,*" a woman was saying. "*Auxiliary thrust is down as well, and there's nothing on primary. Orbital descent will intersect as expected but we cannot slow the approach.*"

"Hey, that's Commander Harbor's voice!" Neil said excitedly.

"Shhh! We need to hear this." Keegan waved at the youngster and held his finger in front of his helmet as close to his lips as he could get them.

"*Understood, Commander. At this point, Flight Control recommends that the flight crew and passengers evacuate the shuttle.*"

"Oh, no!" Daya cried.

"*Roger that, Flight! We're already making way to the escape pod,*" Harbor said. She and the flight controller sounded unnervingly calm.

"*Understood. Godspeed! Search and rescue teams are being assembled.*"

"Jesus," Jackie whispered.

"Leona! Get me the radar track on that shuttle right now!" Keegan exclaimed. He turned to Neil. "Neil, I need you to get the trajectory optimization simulation up and pull the two-line element data from the radar tracks Leona is sending to you."

"Right," Neil said, his hands flying. "I know exactly what you need."

"Dr. Bright?" Daya asked.

Keegan waved a hand behind him.

"Hold on, Daya." He bounced into the circle of desks behind Neil and loomed over the boy's shoulder as he tapped at the console cumbersomely with his suit gloves. Keegan pointed. "There, right. Good work, Neil. Now run that trajectory on the big monitor in the middle."

"Oh, my God," Neil moaned, his eyes wide. Keegan's eyes were equally wide open. He had a horrible feeling that he knew where the wayward shuttle was going.

"Leona, overlay that trajectory on a three-dimensional map of the city!"

The projection popped up on screen, taking the place of Leona's avatar. To Keegan's horror, a red line tracked towards a false lunar surface, and a blue line representing where the trajectory was headed continued right into the surface and terminated.

"Right away, Dr. Bright." The screen filled in behind the projections with the topographical map of Armstrong City and its surroundings.

"Dr. Bright?" Daya asked again, more insistent.

Keegan held up a finger for patience. He peered at the image. He knew the lunar grid very well, and he had an instinctive understanding of the calculus of falling objects, but he had to be sure.

"Run it again, Neil."

When the track of the shuttle was overlaid on the city, the descending arc passed straight through one of the hotel towers and landed in the heart of Armstrong City. He sucked in a breath. There was no mistake. If they didn't do

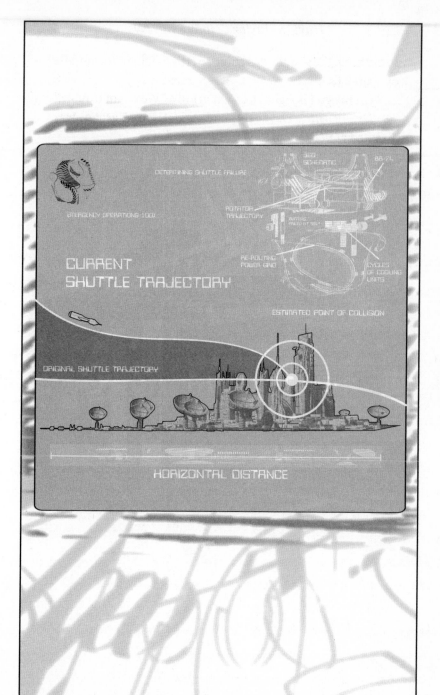

something, the shuttle was going to strike right in the middle of Sparks Central.

"Oh my god is right," he said, grimly. "We've got trouble."

"Dr. Bright!" Daya shouted this time. Keegan was alarmed at her tone.

"What is it, Daya?" he asked, turning to her.

The petite teenager was almost trembling with anxiety and fear. She pointed to the scope, now black.

"We just lost all signals from Aldrinville, sir!"

Keegan reached for her gloved hand and pulled her up out of her chair.

"We'll have to deal with that when we can, Daya. Right now, everybody out! Move down and out from the studio as fast as we can! That shuttle is going to hit right on top of us!"

✧   ✧   ✧

SwitchViewDan—What happened to the feed?

ZetaMoto—Commander Harbor is my hero. Don't let her die!

GaMeRgirl873—The shuttle could kill everybody in Armstrong City! Where can they go?

Chapter 13

Barbara stared at the black screen. Dion had been in the middle of a sentence when the communications link went down. His mouth was still open.

He clapped it shut. The faint noise echoed off the bare, stiffened fabric ceiling. The sharp-smelling glue resins had yet to harden completely, but the thin material layer with several meters of lunar dirt on top of it caused the interior to have the same acoustics as a cave.

Still in shock, Barbara turned to look at the others. Gary sat wide-eyed. Jan had her fists clenched in her lap.

"Well," Barbara began. Her voice seemed to echo in the silent room. She swallowed hard. Fear threatened to overwhelm her. She felt it wrap a cold hand around her heart, but she forced herself to think, to drive back the sensation. That was it. *She* was in control, not her emotions. There was nothing to do but follow the protocols and safety training and to stay alive. Her throat felt tight. She cleared it and took a deep breath. "Well. We knew it was going to happen sooner or later. We're as prepared as we can be. We've got the supplies and equipment for a whole settlement here in this habitat. Let's make the best of it. They're still out there in Armstrong City. They're fine. We're fine. We just can't get back to them right now."

Gary's face went from pale to red.

"You sound so calm. How can you be calm? We're cut off! We just lost all communications with the base!"

"I'm not calm!" Barbara said, forcing the words out. She swallowed again. "I'm shaking like a frightened rabbit."

"What're we going to do?" Gary asked. He pointed to the console. Most of its lights had gone from green to red. "The satellite's off line. Even the relays are fried. Who knows when we can talk to the others? The radiation might kill us before anyone can get out here!"

"Hey!" Jan sprang up in front of Gary, shaking a finger in his face. "Calm down! We're safe here. We're under two meters of rubble. It insulates us from the CME. You know that! You ran the calculations yourself when you proposed this project! This was all based on data you gathered. You know that!"

"What if we missed a spot?" Gary asked, the desperation he felt clear in his voice. "You heard Dr. Bright. He said it was vital to make sure we had complete coverage."

"Dude, chill!" Dion said. He looked calm, although his rich voice was squeezed thin. "Nothing's different now than it was five minutes ago. Neil gave us the thumbs-up that we had the whole place tucked in. We *got* this!"

"Yeah, but we don't know if everything's going to keep running! We could suffocate or freeze to death!"

"Gary, the power truck has enough juice for over two weeks," Jan said. "Once the CME ends, we can get it back out there gathering sunlight. It was designed to make it through a lunar night."

"What if burying it did something to the solar panels?" Gary asked.

"Knock it off!" Jan said, fiercely. "I mean it! You know too much! You're just trying to find something wrong. Do you want us to panic and die? Huh?" They stared at each other. Barbara felt as if she should say something, but her mind was blank. Dion stepped between them.

"We need something to eat," he said. "We missed at least one break and one meal."

"How can you think of food now?" Gary demanded.

That made all three of the others turn to gawk at him.

"Okay, now I know that it's the end of the world," Jan said, throwing up her hands. "You, refusing *food?* Who are you and what have you done with Gary?"

Barbara listened to the argument, looking from one indignant face to another. The absurdity bubbled up inside her until she started giggling, first nervously, then with relief from the terrible tension that had taken hold of her, until she was laughing out loud. The others turned to stare at *her*. She gasped in a breath of air.

"Is it too late to tell Dr. Bright that I wanted to have a little time to acclimate before I went out on assignment?" Barbara asked, giggling until tears leaked out of her eyes. "I mean, after all, I'm new here and I've never been to the Moon before."

Gary and Jan howled almost in unison. Dion's big laugh boomed out. He picked Barbara up in a bear hug.

"Lady, you are a hoot," he said, setting her back on her feet. "We're okay. All right, now. We're overreacting because we're tired. We've been hustling all day to get this shelter set up and buried. Let's blow off some steam, but I need a square meal *stat!*"

The others laughed, too. Barbara wrapped her arms around Dion and squeezed hard. Human contact helped dispel the terrifying feeling of isolation and peril. Her tight nerves relaxed. Dion turned her loose. She gave him a grateful look.

Gary stared at his feet.

"Sorry, guys. I know I blew it. I just feel responsible for the success of this project."

"We get it," Barbara assured him, with a friendly pat on the arm. "Your project is still going forward. Your plans were good! Nothing has failed. Look, we're only human. There's no way to foresee when the sunspots are going to erupt. This could have happened when we were halfway here, instead of with the habitats ready to move into. *That* would have been a disaster. This is just a delay, nothing else. In fact, I'm glad we were here and able to shelter in these things rather than in the water truck. That would have been a tight fit for us all. Can you imagine?"

"Well, we'd have been clean," Jan said, her eyes dancing.

"You're right." Gary sighed and stretched his arms over his head. His spine cracked as it straightened. "I could eat. In fact, I just realized—I'm starving!"

The Sparks laughed again. Barbara felt a rush of relief.

"It'll do us good to slow down and take a rest." Dion glanced at Candy, still in place on the back of his environment suit sleeve. "I'll get something going. Jan, is the kitchen set up?"

"Yep," the dark-haired girl said cheerfully. "All the supply boxes are on the racks."

"You all sit down. I'll get some food for us."

"I'll help," Barbara said, following him out of the control room. As they moved from one chamber to another, motion sensors turned on LED clusters to light their way.

The food preparation center lay adjacent to a bathroom so all the plumbing was fed by one long pipe from the water tanks. Off-white ceramic heat transfer coils surrounded the pipes like radiators in an apartment building. As heated water flowed through the radiator it provided constant living temperature for the shelter. Barbara held her hands out and warmed herself as if she was standing by a fireplace. Dion hauled the heavy food crate up from the lower shelf and browsed through the vacuum-packed containers, frowning at labels. Barbara smiled inwardly, seeing how at home he made himself, even in the strangest kitchen in existence on the far side of nowhere.

"What do we need?" she asked, coming over to join him. He gave her a friendly glance.

"A little of this and a little of that. No reason not to spoil ourselves a little and rustle up one of the big packages of food," Dion said, handing her a couple of packages, and topping the stack in her arms with a handful of utensils from another plastic box. Barbara wrinkled her nose at the puff of dust that blew into her face as he shut the lid. They had been in such a hurry to offload the crates from the truck and get them into the kitchen that they hadn't taken the time to clean them properly. Regolith flew up in small clouds around the room as they moved packages. The pale gray dust settled in slow Brownian motion paths that reflected in the room lighting like little fireflies. Small dunes formed all around them and next to the door and in the corners near the shipping containers. Barbara knew she ought to get a vacuum-broom and sweep the mess up and get it out of the habitat, but she was too tired to think of anything but a meal.

"Aha! Just what I was looking for." Dion pulled a two-liter sized canister of freeze-dried entrées from one of the heavy plastic crates and surveyed the label. "How does beef stew sound?"

"Like heaven," Barbara said. Dion collected the packages from her arms and set them on the food prep table next to the sink.

"It'll be better than the quick meals and snacks we've been eating for days. I've got some hot sauce and spices I'll share that'll make this taste pretty good. You want to activate one of those packages you've got there? It makes hot bread rolls."

Dion pulled the zip-strip from around the top of the canister and filled it with water from the spigot, then activated the heat element in the base. He retrieved his personal pack from the piles of cases just inside the airlock, and added a pinch of this and a dash of that to the bubbling stew. Barbara put down the flat rectangular package, unwrapped it and set it to heat, using the solenoids embedded in the base. Soon, the habitat filled with the savory aroma of hot food and fresh bread. Just inhaling it made her feel better. She peeked out into the main room.

While they were making dinner, Gary and Jan had set up a table and pulled the work chairs around it. They had also changed from their suits into their pajamas. She'd seen Jan's yellow cats, but Gary's were red-and-black plaid. Barbara thought it was such a good idea that she went to change, too. Motion-sensor LEDs lit the way on either side of the corridor floor. In the room she and Jan would share, she saw that the Nerd-Twins had also set up the beds. Her bunk, its coverlet turned down to show the pillow, called enticingly to her. Her muscles ached. She longed to crawl onto the inflated mattress, but her rumbling belly said food was much more important than sleep.

Barbara emerged into the corridor to see Dion, in bright orange PJ's and thick black slippers, coming out of the boys' bedroom. She raised an eyebrow at him.

"In an emergency, they can be used as a distress beacon," he said, with a grin. "I like bright colors, hey? The landscape around here is exciting, but it's dull in terms of color."

On the table, each of them placed the big spoon and flat bowl from their canteen kits on the table alongside one of the company's small all-purpose towels. There was no need for a butter knife, as they had liquid spread in a squeeze bottle. Liquid salt and pepper were in dropper bottles. Since they weren't in zero-gee, they didn't have to worry about particles of liquid floating into the machinery. In fact, any additional moisture in the atmosphere was welcome.

"Food!" Gary said, reaching for the canister and the serving spoon when Dion set them in the middle of the table. Dion stiffarmed him and pushed him back in his chair. Gary wobbled in his seat. "What did you do that for?"

"Uh-uh, brother. Let Barb and Jan get theirs first."

"Ladies first?" Gary scoffed. "We're all equals on this team. That's sexism."

"No, practicality," Dion said, narrowing an eye at his roommate. "If I let your hungry butt at this food first, there won't be enough left for the rest of us. I've watched you eat for months, now."

Gary had relaxed enough to laugh. He plunked himself down on the rolling chair and slid back and forth.

"You're right about that, big bro," he said. "Okay. You all take what you want, and I get everything that's left!"

A drop of gravy jumped from the spoon to the back of Barbara's hand while she was ladling stew into the bowl, and she licked it off. It melted onto her tongue, making her crave more. She was surprised how hungry she was. The food tasted better than anything she had ever remembered eating. Dion was an amazing cook. She handed Jan the spoon and dug in with her own utensil. Soon, the room was silent except for the sounds of the ventilation system and eating.

"Have you always traveled with your own spices, Dion?" Barbara asked, mopping the empty bowl with one of the last of the rolls to keep from missing any of the sauce. "That was fantastic!"

He grinned at the compliment.

"I started when I went away to college, and discovered that dorm food has practically no flavor. My granny writes cookbooks, so we all grew up knowing what good food ought to taste like. When I told her I was going to the Moon, she whipped up some extracts and spice packets for me. She sends me refills once in a while on the supply shuttles. Because the low pressure of the habitat is like high altitude and there's an extreme lack of moisture in the air, your tongue can't taste subtle flavors, so these are pretty intense. You probably wouldn't like them if you tried them on Earth."

"She's a chemist as well as a chef," Jan added, chasing the last drops herself. "You ought to take a look at Mama Purchase's online bio. I'm going to go worship at her feet next time I'm on Earth."

"I owe her a thank you note," Barbara said, sitting back with a sigh and fighting back a yawn. "That's just what I needed."

"Utterly fantastic," Gary said, savoring his last spoonful. As he had foretold, there were no leftovers in the canister. He cleaned the big container out under the tap, capped it, and put it back in the case to be reused and refilled back in Armstrong City. He even rinsed out the rest of the team's bowls and spoons. "Compliments to your granny, Dion."

"Thanks, brother." The big youth slid his chair back from the table and stood up.

"We ought to get some rest," Barbara said.

"I'm too wired to sleep yet," Gary said, finally. "Still thinking about being cut off like this. I wish I could get it out of my mind. I just can't. Not yet."

"It's our first night in the habitat," Jan said. "It's kind of an occasion. Why don't we just hang out for a while? I brought my guitar."

"I saw that," Barbara said, with a smile. "I'd like to hear you play."

"Yeah, why not?" Dion said. He smiled at Barbara. "She's pretty good, you know."

Jan got up and ran to their room. She came back with a heavily padded case that Barbara had noticed in the corner beside Jan's inflatable bunk. The instrument that emerged from the bright gold felted interior was a gorgeous acoustic guitar with a chocolate-brown face, blond wood neck and back, and polished bronze tuning pegs. Jan pulled it into her lap as if it was a beloved pet.

"That's beautiful," Barbara said. "I've never seen one like it."

"It was adapted for the Moon by the manufacturer," Jan explained to Barbara. "I couldn't have afforded this brand on my own, but they *gave* it to me. It's good publicity for them and a dream for me. I call her Trang Chim, after the Vietnamese moon goddess."

Barbara sighed. More detail she'd missed not reading the For-pay Forums. Jan began to tune it. The guitar had a warm, resonant sound. The others pulled their chairs into a circle around her. Jan drew her legs up to sit crosslegged on the padded seat, and fanned her fingers down over the strings.

The first few chords made the weirdness of sitting in a hollow habitat under a thousand tons of regolith rubble on the far side of the Moon seem a lot more normal. Barbara relaxed in her seat as her roommate picked out one familiar song after another. Now and again, Jan lifted her voice to sing along. She was a good singer. Barbara could tell that she had been trained. Jan glanced at the others, inviting them to join in. Gary jumped in right away, with Dion a couple of beats behind him. Barbara felt shy at first, but the others didn't grimace or faint dead away when she sang. In fact, the small group sounded pretty good together.

With a wicked glance at the others, Jan struck up an energetic introduction, which Barbara recognized after a few bars as a classic more than a century old, one that she and her parents loved.

"'Dark Side of the Moon,'" she said, with a laugh. "Talk about appropriate!"

"Neil would want to vlog this, you know." Dion chuckled. "That kid puts *everything* on the net."

"Well, he gets a kick out of it." Jan said. "It's kind of cute. That didn't sound too bad, you know. Maybe we should record the song for posterity." She laughed again.

"Not sure we're ready for primetime yet," Barbara said. "Maybe after a few more rehearsals. This must be the first time that song has actually been played on the dark side, except it's not dark out there." She glanced at the monitors on the wall. All of them were off except one feeding from a camera perched on a mast on the lip of the crater. It was their only source of sunlight in the habitat.

"I know," Dion said, making expansive gestures with his arms, and started talking faster. "'There really isn't a dark side. The song makes no sense! It's the *far side*. It's not dark except at night!'"

"Dr. Bright!" Gary laughed, and started making his own emphatic motions. "'Far from it, Dion, and that's exactly right. The Moon is just like the Earth and has both day and night that moves around it as it spins on its axis.'"

"You two do good impressions of him," Barbara said, laughing. She poked Gary playfully in the arm. "Has he ever caught you doing it?"

"Not yet, or at least I don't think so." Gary looked thoughtful. "I know Leona snoops on us once in a while. The way Dr. Bright asks us questions sometimes makes me think he's getting some kind of updates. Wish he was here with us, though. It bugs me that we can't talk to him if we need him."

Barbara hesitated. She glanced at Jan, who shot her an encouraging look.

"Maybe we can," Barbara said. "I was going to wait until we've had a chance to get some sleep, but I suppose I don't mind discussing it now."

"What? Have you been running underground telecomm lines while we were bulldozing the crater full of dirt?" Dion asked, his eyes crinkling with humor.

"Kind of," Jan said, with a grin. She executed some complex fingering with the tips of her nails that filled the air with notes. "It'll be underground, anyhow."

"What is it?" Gary asked, eagerly.

"You know the spoils pile up against the wall of the main crater near the shelter and the supply truck?" Barbara asked. "Behind where we buried the feedhorn and the rest of the equipment?"

"How could I forget it?" Dion asked, sardonically. "I must have driven near it sixty or seventy times today. What were you two doing out there by it anyway?"

Barbara retrieved Fido from the darkened communications console and showed them the diagram that the PDE had called up for her before they had closed up the shelter. Inside the habitat, the three-dimensional rendering rose up bright and clear.

"Jan and I checked the vector. Do you know that that part of the crater right there is pointing directly at Mars?"

"So?" Gary asked, wrinkling his forehead.

"So, I was thinking about Commander Harbor," Barbara said. "She just came back from setting up a high bandwidth relay ground station on Mars."

"So?" Dion asked.

"*So*," Jan added, with a flourish on the strings for emphasis, "we could dig a tunnel into it. A miniature radio telescope, just like the one Neil and Daya were going to make! We could beam a signal from here, bounce it off Mars, and back into the receiving stations on Earth. From there, they could relay it to Dr. Bright. We can talk to them! It'll just take a little work."

"Using what for equipment?" Dion asked, skeptically. "As you just said, we buried the feedhorn under two meters of regolith. In any case, we don't have the equipment to broadcast a signal."

"We do, as a matter of fact," Jan said, with a toss of her head. She held up Ms. Scruffles. "These."

"Our PDEs?" Gary asked, squinting at her. Then his eyes widened. "Oh, yeah! That could work. But they'd take some adapting."

"We have other comm gear," Barbara pointed out. "The PDEs have complete software-defined radio apps that span across most of the communications spectrum. I've checked: they can generate a signal in the band of the Mars station. We downloaded the waveform the system uses before the communications went out, just in case. Jan is pretty certain she can tinker something together she can use to rig a miniature feedhorn that, when combined with a crater dish, will transmit in a tight beam to that relay on Mars."

"Isn't it too small to transmit that far?" Dion asked.

"It's not the size, it's the power and dish size combination," Barbara said. "Power's my specialty, remember. The SDR app can be ramped up so it runs at max transmit and receive power, but the feedhorn will need to be as high gain as we can manage. That's going to take some real fiddling."

"We can do that, no problem," Gary said, gesturing to himself and Jan. "Fiddling is *our* specialty."

"Also, the app will drain the battery on the PDE in minutes so we'll need to take a big battery outside with it and connect a charger plate to it." Jan said. She wiggled her eyebrows. "I know it's wild. When Barb tried her idea out on me, I was sure it couldn't work, but look at the schematics and the link budget calculations! It all works out in the math."

"Dr. Bright was just about to do the same thing with a miniature dish dug into the Armstrong side of the Moon," Barbara added, seeing the hope dawn on the boys' faces. "We can carve out a five-meter depression under the rim of the crater in no time."

"We can't go anywhere until the CME is over." Gary said, worry warring with optimism on his face. "And then, shouldn't we just go home?"

"I'd rather call home first and get updated orders from Dr. Bright." Barb replied. "This idea will work. I think." She watched the boys' expressions for reassurance. "What do *you* think?"

"We need to look it over," Gary said, after checking calculations on his own screen. "It sounds good. Beam us the schematics."

Barbara sent the file that she and Jan had been working on to both of the guys' handhelds. Each of them studied the diagrams. Within a few minutes, both of them were grinning.

"I get it," Dion said, scrolling up and down with one big finger. "Yeah, if we can boost the signal enough, we should be able to dig a crater that will aim the radio signal in the right direction. We got this!"

"That's great!" Gary exclaimed. "Let's get to work on it!"

"Not now," Barbara said. The heavy meal and the hard day's work had finally hit her system. Her whole body felt like it was encased in lead. "In any case, like you just said, we can't go outside until the CME ends. I need some zees. We'll all have clearer heads after some rest. And maybe by morning it will be safe to go outside."

"If the roof doesn't collapse on our heads," Gary said, darkly. Jan battered him with her free hand.

"Will you stop that?" She pulled back when she saw that he was grinning. "You geek!"

"That's it," Dion said, raising his palms in the air in mock surrender. "I'm going to sleep."

Barbara and Jan followed the LEDs in the floor to their room.

"Nice job, Barb," Jan said, putting her guitar in the corner and settling into her wheezing bunk. "Your idea snapped everyone out of their gloom. We'll get through to Dr. Bright. He'll be pretty impressed."

"It'll be a nice job if it works," Barbara said, climbing into her own bed. "If it doesn't work, well, I'm sure we'll figure something else out."

Jan chuckled.

"*When* it works, girlfriend. When. I won't let you settle for anything less."

✧　✧　✧

Choco327—They're gonna freeze to death!

ZetaMoto—Commander January is in trouble. Can she eject in time?

SwitchViewDan—Relax, I ran the figures. The shuttle can't hit the city.

5X5Power—This is irresponsible! Those children shouldn't be out there alone. Somebody ought to be arrested.

Chapter 14

"We're trending all over the world, on news programs and social media," Neil said, putting the scrolling feeds up on Einstein as he, Daya, and the video crew ran behind Dr. Bright heading toward the lake shelter. Others joined them, rushing through the corridors, impatient to get to the safest place in the colony. Neil dodged around an environmental tech team pulling a cart of equipment down the passage and ducked under the arm of a woman with her laptop clutched to her chest. Sparks Central was at the farthest edge of the colony from the lake. "People are worried about our away team. Some are wondering why you sent them out without more backup. Wow! The comments are pretty vicious. They say you're endangering children. But Jan and the others aren't children. They're all legal adults. They knew the risks, and I think they're better trained than anyone except astronauts. Right, Dr. Bright?" The boy turned a hopeful face to him. Keegan wasn't in the mood to play four million questions, but the boy meant well.

"They *are* astronauts, Neil." Keegan had been berating himself for the same reasons. But what was done was done. He had to be certain that the team he had picked could and would take care of itself. Thank goodness that he, Neil, Daya and the show crew had their in-suit radios tuned to a dedicated channel. He didn't need everybody in the colony listening in and adding their two cents to his concerns. Comments were the least of his problems. He'd deal with the fallout later, once the Sparks were all back safe in the colony.

Keegan couldn't help but let his mind race ahead. Once the CME was over with, lunar engineers, the Sparks among them, would have to rebuild the links to the Aldrinville site. Somehow, he needed to make sure the kids were safe and could return home safely. But for the meantime, they were probably safer where they were on the far side of the Moon than everyone else in Armstrong City was at the moment. If Keegan understood the shuttle's trajectory right, the city was about to take a beating. And to top it off, if it landed where he thought it might, Bright Sparks Central was ground zero. They would be the last ones to make it to the safety zone.

". . . Now they're talking about Armstrong City. What can we do?" Neil asked. Einstein had escaped from his hand and was fluttering along beside him at shoulder level.

"Don't respond just yet, Neil," Keegan said, beckoning to them to hurry up. Jackie brought up the rear, making sure everyone kept up. He exchanged a quick glance with her. "We're going to work this out. But first, let's get everyone safe and in the shelter. Hey, Leona, how are we doing?" Keegan turned to his PDE on his sleeve. He did his best not to pay attention to the camera that was currently zooming in on his face. He just kept reminding himself that it was part of the job.

"I estimate it will take four and a half minutes for you to reach the shelter, Dr. Bright." Leona responded over the PDE's speaker. He glanced up. The corridors were deserted now. The technicians and the retail staff were long gone.

"How long until shuttle impact?"

"Three minutes and thirty seven seconds." Leona's voice

sounded somber. "We' are not going to make it to the shelter in time."

Keegan stopped dead in his tracks. Daya managed to slow down by grabbing the wall, but Neil plowed right into him. Keegan reached out and caught him by the shoulders and almost had to bearhug him to keep him from rolling onto the floor face first. In the low lunar gravity, the boy seemed weightless to Keegan. The camera crew crowded in and zoomed in on his face again, picking up what he knew would be a really dramatic shot. Keegan didn't like having the world's attention at the moment, but he had to accept that it was just something that wasn't going to change. He had to put that potential embarrassment out of his mind and think of the right move. And he had just little more than three minutes to figure that out.

"Everybody, hold quiet for a second." He held up a hand. "I need to think."

"There are no nearby secondary shelters reachable in time, Dr. Bright." Leona added.

"What about the residential emergency shelters?" Paul asked.

"Already sealed," Neil said, after a quick check on Einstein.

"Keegan, you better think of something fast." Jackie sounded more alarmed than he could remember ever having heard her in the many years they'd been filming together.

"I know. I know. It's gonna be like an earthquake in here soon." Keegan spun about, looking wildly at the corridors around them for ideas.

Ahead of them were the restaurant and casino and hotel lobby, and the passage that led on to the lake. Up ahead and to the left was a corridor that led to more quarters and offices. Just behind them and to the right was a corridor that led out to Armstrong Park and Museum. The only other door, a couple of meters from them, was an exit to a maintenance air lock. None of them was an absolute safe choice. If the shuttle crashed through the roof, they were in danger from flying shards of ceramic and metal, not to mention smoke or fire. The safety doors had closed behind them, sealing off the lab and studio. The AI running colony security would have sealed all the other sectors as they were evacuated. In a moment or so, the only passageway left open would be the one to the lake. The lunar gravity was light, but Keegan wished they could fly.

"Aren't you supposed to get under a doorway or something during an earthquake?" Neil asked.

"Move out into the open would probably be safer," Daya whispered.

"Shhh. Let him think," Paul added. But then Keegan let out a hoot of glee. He beamed at the girl.

"Daya, that's it! You are a genius, young lady. Everyone, faceplates locked and airtight. We're going on an EVA!"

"*Now?*" Neil asked, his expression wavering between worry and excitement, as the crew fumbled at their seals with the heavy gloves. All the lights on their wrists shone green.

"Now." Keegan stepped back between the two kids and cycled the maintenance hatch. "You wanted to go outside. Now we're going outside." He pulled them into the small chamber. The show crew crowded in behind, cameras and all. "Everyone in! Go, go, go!"

The airlock hatch cycled, sucking the air out of the small chamber. Keegan slapped the big red button for pressure release and danced impatiently up and down during ten seconds that they didn't have to spare. As the atmosphere was sucked out, Neil's PDE started to fall. He caught it with one hand and popped it against the magnetic holder on his suit sleeve.

Finally, the outer hatch released and popped open. Keegan pushed the door free and bounced through, making way for the others. He bounded to a stop on the lunar regolith a meter from the open hatch and scanned the twilit sky for the shuttle.

"Where is it, Leona?" he asked. Her voice came through clearly on the speakers in the collar of his suit.

The AI didn't have to ask him what "it" was.

"The hotel towers are in the way of the shuttle's trajectory, Dr. Bright," Leona replied.

"Yeah, I was afraid of that," he said. He turned back toward the bulkhead and gestured. The crew had finished cycling through the airlock. "Jackie, dog down that hatch."

The producer palmed the controls, then secured the lock on the door, making sure the green lights came on to prove that it had sealed behind them.

"What now?" she asked.

Keegan did a calculation in his mind, then pointed in a general direction that was orthogonal from the crash trajectory path and free and clear of buildings. "That way! Bounce as fast as you can!"

"Dr. Bright, what about the CME? Are we safe out here?" Yvonne asked, dithering back and forth between the mound of regolith and the safety hatch. "I mean, radiation and all?"

"Don't worry, Yvonne," Daya said, as the camerawoman turned toward her and zoomed in. The girl faced the lens and spoke directly to it. *Bless her*, Dr. Bright thought with pride. "We're on the dark side of the Moon right now. The CME is hitting the Sun-facing side where the other Sparks are. We're fine. It's the others that have to worry about the CME."

"Yeah, we're fine all right, if you don't consider a shuttle about to crash on us," Paul added sarcastically.

"It's not coming this way," Neil said, patiently, pointing back toward the door through which they had just run. "It'll be over there."

"Bounce!" Keegan shouted, turning up the volume to get their attention. "Don't get distracted! This is *life and death*!"

The group started running, kicking up huge clouds of regolith dust with every leaping step. Keegan kept glancing back to make sure the crew followed him.

"Leona, update." he snapped as he bounded across the Moon, doing his best to be patient and not run off and leave the slower members of his EVA team behind. He made sure to keep close to the younger Sparks.

"Yes, Dr. Bright," the calm voice said. "The shuttle is fifty seconds from impact and still on the same trajectory as before. I calculate, based on position knowledge error and radar position error, that there is a fifty-seven percent chance that the shuttle will hit the hotel and a seventy-two percent chance it lands on Sparks Central. There is almost a one hundred percent chance that it will pass through the main antenna farm for Armstrong City between the hotel and Sparks Central."

Keegan turned in briefly to the admin channel, listening to the colony administrator giving orders to the rest of the settlers and visitors. Under the circumstances, she sounded reasonably calm. From what she was saying, everyone else had made it to the lake, and the rest of the complex was locked down.

"Right. Let me know as soon as we're clear enough to stop running." He glanced back at the others and pointed to the complex antenna array on the top of the hotel tower. "Those dishes right there are where the shuttle is going. Draw a line between the hotel, the dishes, and the habitat module. We need to get clear of that, and far enough away that nothing can fall or land on us."

"You heard the man!" Jackie said, waving her arm forward. "Keep moving, people."

With the constant chatter from the colony and the shuttle, plus the sound of his own breathing in his ears, the minute that passed felt like an eternity to Keegan. On an ordinary day, bouncing over the Moon's surface was one of his favorite things to do. With the threat of a spacecraft that might crash on their heads at any moment, it wasn't anywhere as pleasurable. He checked on Yvonne, who had never been on an EVA before. She looked torn between enjoying herself and worried to death. He had to give her credit for never letting her camera lens drop. *A real pro.*

Keegan dashed between the humped shapes of items left out in the vacuum underneath tarps to protect them from the dust, then bounded over the rim of a shallow crater that formed part of the margin of the plain on which Armstrong City had been built. Behind him, the crew and the kids scrambled to follow.

"You are clear now with about a ten percent safety margin, Dr. Bright," Leona said.

"Ten percent ain't good enough for me," he replied, glancing back. "We'll keep moving for another ten or twenty seconds."

Keegan counted Mississippis in his head and finally reached the bottom of his last bounding step at the center of the crater. He held up a hand, motioning everyone to stop. He took a knee and turned to view the crash direction. The city was still intact. He couldn't see the shuttle yet.

"Everyone all right so far?" he asked. They nodded. Through their visors, he saw worry and fear in their faces. "Give me a sound off of name and status."

"Neil. Okay!" The boy waved both arms from the crater's edge. He came springing toward Keegan, raising puffs of dust that settled almost immediately. He bounded to a stop at Keegan's side.

"Daya is okay." The girl followed in smaller leaps.

"Yvonne, okay." The camerawoman's voice sounded strained. The unfamiliar movements were tough on a newcomer's knees.

"Paul, fine."

Keegan waited and tallied the crew names in his mind

until he heard Jackie. He knew she'd wait until last. They huddled together quietly as Leona counted down for them.

"Twenty-seven seconds to impact. Twenty-six. Twenty-five . . ."

"Stick close, everyone," Keegan said, staring at the city's outline.

"We should see it by now," Daya said, shielding her visor with her glove. "Why can't we see it?"

"That's a bad sign." Neil added.

"It must be directly behind the city buildings," Dr. Bright acknowledged.

"Ten, nine, eight . . ."

"Oh, my God!" Neil shouted, stabbing a finger toward the tower. The array of dishes and antennae on the steel framework was framed by lights for a split second, then the view was obliterated by a hurtling body.

"Everyone stay calm!" Keegan clapped his hand on the boy's shoulder and the other on Daya's and held tight. "You two stay close."

The stubby white ship, which looked like a loaf of bread with delta wings and a black nose, had come in over their heads from the left, tore through the top three or four stories of the Armstrong City Hotel, then tumbled down over the mass of the colony complex. Keegan's gut turned upside down as the exterior walls of the tower vented and popped like balloons, throwing glass, concrete and steel in all directions.

The impact with the hotel sent the shuttle on a wild spinning frenzy as it plowed through the communications antenna farm affixed to the roof of the central atrium dome of the colony museum. The main communications antenna in the middle, an array of transmission circuitry poking through the center of a huge white satellite dish, took the full brunt of the collision from the shuttle fuselage. The antenna instantaneously separated into millions of shiny pieces that were strewn about the other two antennas flanking it. Once its tailfin caught the main structural pier of the dish, the spacecraft tumbled upward. The multiton lunar concrete post cracked and started to sway. The tailfin section tore free and tumbled off in a slightly different direction, then crashed through the dome that marked the main chamber of the museum. The debris expanded into a cloud that tracked across the sky behind the falling shuttle, all in terrifying slow motion.

Behind the falling hulk, orange and black fireballs burst out from the twisted structure like fireworks going off, from the mix of combustible materials and what oxygen had been in the rooms. With each bone-chilling burst, Keegan thought he saw tell-tale signs of orange plasma and soot from rocket fuel. Perhaps the reaction-control thrusters of the shuttle were leaking as well, but there was no way to be certain at that distance.

"Why are the fires going out?" Yvonne asked.

"No oxygen," Keegan explained, tersely, staring at the destruction with growing horror. "The pressure doors in the hotel sealed off the damaged sections as soon as there was a breach." He scanned the outline of the tower, searching for bodies, but as far as he could see, there were none being sucked out behind the shuttle. Keegan felt his knees wobble with relief. That was a great sign. That meant the hotel had been warned with enough time to be fully evacuated. Hopefully, there was only material damage.

The nose of the shuttle rolled down amidst debris flickering in the city's external lights like glitter and confetti at a rock concert. It landed nose down on the surface of the Moon, then tumbled tail over fuselage past on the outer periphery of the Sparks' habitat module. A wing snapped off and spun, skipping over the ground like a stone. Out of pure instinct, Keegan jumped backward, dragging the youngsters with him. The bulk of the damaged spaceship bounced and flipped upward, then skittered to a stop in a massive cloud of dust on the other side of the settlement, several tens of meters from any buildings.

"Wow," Neil breathed.

"Holy cow!" Paul squawked.

"Are you getting this?" Jackie asked, always the professional.

"Every bit!" Yvonne said. "Wow!"

Gasses vented and escaped the battered hulk in jets of white steam. Pieces of the hotel walls and the antenna dishes tumbled down on top and all around it. The complex itself was peppered and pockmarked with debris, but as far as Keegan could see it was still intact. He leaped up to the rim of the crater and scanned the city for signs of escaping atmosphere. Neil pointed to the low dome at the north end.

"It missed Sparks Central!" he cheered.

"But it didn't miss the hotel or the antennas," Daya noted. "A terrible mess! What about the shuttle crew?"

"Leona, did the crew escape?" Keegan asked.

"According to the radar tracks there was a second object that separated from the shuttle several minutes ago. It settled to the surface about seventy kilometers from the city. That's most likely the crew emergency module. I have yet to detect any communications from them," Leona said. "The city communications officer is attempting to make contact."

"The survivors might need medical attention," Daya said, fretfully. "We must pick them up."

"That'll be up to the Emergency Response Crew," Keegan said. "When they're ready to muster, I'll be going out with them."

"Any casualties reported, Einstein?" Neil asked his PDE.

"There are no casualties reported so far, Neil," the old man's voice replied.

"What about in Armstrong City?" Keegan asked. "Anyone missing or injured?"

He chafed at the brief pause until Leona spoke again.

"All inhabitants have been located and accounted for except for the shuttle crew and complement, and our EVA team in Aldrinville."

Keegan and the others let out gusty sighs of relief.

"Keep trying to contact the Sparks, Leona," Keegan said. "I know they're still battened down because of the CME, but keep trying anyhow."

"Yes, Dr. Bright."

"Look!" Daya pointed at what was left of the antenna farm. The two main antennas that remained standing started to sway. Their frameworks buckled visibly, bulging at their joints.

"They're going to fall!" Neil shouted.

"If those go down too, we'll lose contact with Earth," Keegan said.

He watched in horror as the first antenna's superstructure folded over to a ninety-degree angle and fell across the second one. That one tumbled down like a second domino and collapsed on the colony roof.

"Earth, if you can still see us, this is Dr. Bright signing off for now . . ." Keegan said into the camera nearest him. Halfway through his statement the green light on the transceiver blinked and turned red.

"We've lost connection with the repeater, Dr. Bright," Yvonne said.

"Yes. The communications link between the Earth and the Moon has been severed." Leona hesitated. "Sir, you have an incoming emergency call from the emergency response chief."

"Put it through."

✦　✦　✦

GaryFan—That's it? What happened?

TeamSparks090—Did Armstrong City get hit?

M0on1969—I lost my internet for a while.
Can anyone see this?

SalchichaPequena—Dios mio! Las auroras son muy
hermosas!

Chapter 15

"Yeah, chief, I can see it from out here where we are and it doesn't look pretty," Dr. Bright said, walking up and back with nervous tension evident in his bounding stride. "The hotel is going to need a *lot* of work. Are we certain the hotel is structurally sound and isn't going to fall? What do the engineers say? Uh huh . . . I see . . . The antennas? Well, as best we can see it's bad. All three comm towers are down. No, they're toast. The collision did serious structural damage. We might never locate some of the components. I'm not certain about low bandwidth stuff but the Yagi farm was under the dishes and is most likely smashed as well. We were lucky that the shuttle bounced over the outer habitat and the museum. Any known casualties? . . . That's wonderful, Chief." Dr. Bright replied. Neil watched him closely, hoping to get an inkling of their next move.

Neil wasn't scared any longer. He wasn't sure that he ever had been. Even when the hotel erupted into pieces on the upper floors, it didn't seem any more real than a movie or a computer game. Maybe he had never felt scared at all. Or, maybe it was his ego saying that after the fact. He shuddered to think about the other Sparks trapped on the far side of the Moon, with no communication links and no way back . . . ! What if the colony had collapsed completely, leaving them out there in the airless void?

His mind was beginning to wander down that dark path just as a light flashed on his PDE, distracting him.

"What is it, Einstein?" he asked.

For answer, the PDE scrolled out a text.

Turn to the Sparks' private channel, it said. He glanced up to see Daya looking at him, her dark eyes intent.

With one gloved finger, he tapped the PDE and slid the bar to the right that tuned the digital transceiver to their marked frequency. Daya's voice filled his helmet.

"Neil, we need to figure out how to reach Barb and the others," she said. "What if they go outside and there turns out to be a second wave and it starts to hit? They're out there all by themselves. They need help."

Neil laughed a little ruefully.

"I was just thinking the same thing," he said. "Well, we estimated this CME to last eighteen hours, but it may be more. They know to stay put, and they have the radiation sensor."

"It could fail," Daya said.

Automatically, Neil opened his mouth to protest, then stopped. "You're right. It could. They might accidentally go outside during the next wave and not realize they were being fried until it was too late. They've got basic first aid supplies, but nothing to deal with radiation exposure. Even a mild dose could make them pretty sick. We'd better figure it out."

"Yes, we had. And quickly," Daya said.

Neil started pacing, just like Dr. Bright. He kicked up dust clouds with every step.

"But how do we get a message to them? Comms are down here in a *big* way and all the routers between the day-night line and Aldrinville are probably shot. Those Yagi routers aren't designed for the kind of bombardment they're taking."

Daya stayed still, watching him.

"We must find a way to communicate. What if something has gone wrong out there? There is no way to know. I don't like it."

Neil made a face at her. "Worrier." She frowned back. "Okay, I'm sorry. That was harsh. I'm sure Dr. Bright doesn't like it either." Neil noticed that Dr. Bright was looking at him expectantly. He tilted his head in that direction.

Daya nodded. "Better open the main channel again."

Neil switched back to the open frequency in time to hear Dr. Bright finishing up his PDE conversation.

". . . All right, I'll be at the hangar in about five minutes. Go ahead and let the first truck leave without me. Who knows what difference five minutes will make to the astronauts out there? Every minute counts. I'll take the second truck and follow along as fast as I can with whatever rescue crew is left."

Dr. Bright tapped his PDE and looked at the rest of the group. They gathered in around him.

"Listen, everyone," Dr. Bright began, meeting each of their gazes in turn. "Communications with Earth are temporarily unavailable right now, maybe for quite a while. All our satellites are fried or offline and, well, you saw our main and backup antennas go down. Pretty dramatic, wasn't it? Gonna make great video." His eyes crinkled, but the usual humor in them was muted. "I have to go help the fire and rescue teams find those astronauts. I can take Jackie and one camera operator." Paul raised a finger. "Great. You're with me. Yvonne, would you go back to Sparks Central with Neil and Daya and stay with them for me until we know what the situation is?"

"Sure," the camerawoman replied, looking relieved to have something useful to do. "I'd be happy to."

"Yvonne, get some footage of them checking out the damage and doing whatever they plan to do next," Jackie added. "Once we're back on line, we'll want to upload that."

"Right," Yvonne said, hoisting her unit up beside her helmet. Neil threw his shoulders back and tried to convey an air of confidence and responsibility. He could hear Daya clicking her tongue in amusement. Dr. Bright turned to them.

"Neil, Daya, you two get back to Central and do *whatever* it takes to get comms back up with Aldrinville. We have to keep them apprised of the CME situation. Don't want them wandering outside if wave two kicks up. And let me know whatever it is you come up with and how they're doing."

"Yes, sir!" Neil and Daya replied eagerly.

Daya crept into Sparks Central, watching the ceiling and walls as though they were about to collapse on her. Neil got impatient with her dawdling and plunged past her. He stood in the middle of the lab and turned three-sixty to take it all in. Yvonne followed him with her lens.

"Well, it looks just like we left it." Neil turned and smiled at the camera. "As it should, I guess."

"Yes, we were very fortunate," Daya added. She bent over her console and tapped at the touchscreen. The system sprang to life and the lights of the control room popped on, causing them to squint a bit from the bright white illumination. Power did not seem to have been affected at all. "Pressure is fine at zero point nine eight atmospheres, twenty-one degrees Celsius, and standard O2 to N2 twenty-two to seventy-eight mix."

"In other words, Daya, we can take the suits off?" Neil asked sarcastically.

"Well, we could, but not until the all-clear has been sounded by the colony administrator," Yvonne told them from behind the camera. "I had that drilled into me when I got here, along with all the other survival regulations."

"Awww, that's just a formality!" Neil protested.

"But, it's the rule, none the less," Daya interrupted. "They stay on."

Neil hesitated. After all, Yvonne was the only adult present. Daya would listen to her, but Neil chafed at having authority imposed on him, even if it had been at Dr. Bright's order.

"Roger that!" he responded in his best astronaut fashion but made a sour face. "But we can open the visors at least, right?"

"Yes, that's protocol." Daya said as she flipped open the front half of the bubble on her head, letting in fresh air. "Ahhh." She sniffed. "I can smell smoke and chemical residue in the air, more than usual. It must be from the firefighting modules. At least there was no life lost! Achi has a message from my mother to tell me there are only a few bruises from anxious people crowding into the safety zone."

"Good! Okay, we have an important job. Let's get down to business." Neil sat at his console and started tapping at the screen and keys with a frenzy. He glanced up toward Yvonne's lens with a conspiratorial look. "You know, a lot of people probably think that the modern spacesuit gloves that are practically skin tight, have a tactile surface on the fingertips, and are able to activate touchscreen technology, were invented by the space program. Well, I actually looked it up. They were invented by a company making winter gloves that could still activate PDE touchscreens, back at least seventy years. Go figure."

Yvonne laughed. "That's an incredibly useless bit of trivia, Neil."

"It wasn't meant to be funny," Neil grunted under his breath. Daya raised an eyebrow at him. He grimaced at her. "Einstein, run a complete system diagnostic on the communications link between Aldrinville and here, okay?"

"Right away, Neil," his PDE replied. "There are connections active out to the edge of the day-night line, but beyond that there is nothing. The surge suppressors have shut off the circuits beyond that."

"What about the satellites, Achi?" Daya asked, scanning her own screen.

"There are no currently functioning orbital platforms."

"Hmm. What about any Earth-Moon links? There has to be something somewhere!" Neil banged his hands on the desk in frustration.

"None," Einstein said. "All links beyond the day-night line have been terminated. The CME is ongoing, so no satellites will be reinitialized until that event has passed."

"None?" Neil repeated in disbelief. "Then how are we going to check on the others?"

Daya sat up straight at her terminal, then turned to him.

"Neil, I've been thinking. Remember how Dr. Bright explained that long long ago people used to bounce old radio messages off the Moon and back to Earth? They had done it more than a hundred years before we were born."

Neil flipped a hand.

"Yes, they did, but those were old-fashioned analog radios. Everything nowadays is based on software-defined radios with digital encryption sequences or spectrum-hopping bands that require a key to detect. It isn't as simple as building an old radio out of copper wire some metal plates and cans. Modern digital radios are more complicated, and difficult to detect. Probably why SETI will never work."

Daya pursed her lips in annoyance. Neil stopped. He was explaining the history of radio to her like she didn't already know that. After all, she had been a Spark before he was— by several months. And the two of them had argued about the Search for Extraterrestrial Intelligence forever.

"Sorry," he said.

Daya understood. "I know you like to dive into a problem, but if it becomes knotty, you fall back on repetitious facts."

"Hey!" Neil protested.

She smiled. "I think that a high dextrose-content treat,

perhaps with a chocolate coating, might help both of us now, but we need to find a direction."

"What do candy bars have to do with radio?" he asked.

"Nothing, Neil, but, I mean, aren't our PDEs software radios?"

Neil shrugged. "Yeah, sure, but they don't have the range to reach all the way around the Moon. Besides, they'd need either line of sight or relay transceivers, which is what the systems along the road to Aldrinville would use if they were online." He scratched his head and then added. "Or the satellites if they were working."

"There has to be a radio in line of sight with Aldrinville. It shouldn't be this difficult! Radio is a simple device." Daya leaned back in her chair and slumped down. Her bubble helmet annoyingly hit the back of her chair. "I'll be so glad when we're allowed to take these things off!"

"Well, maybe there's something in view of Aldrinville, but I don't know what it would be that would be safe from the CME." Neil pursed his lips and made a motorboat sound ended with a slight sigh, as if he was channeling Dr. Bright. "Let's ask. Einstein, are there currently any functioning transceivers in line of sight with Aldrinville and us?"

"I'm sorry, Neil, not that I can find," the PDE replied.

"So, that's that." He tossed up his hands and shrugged his shoulders. "I'm going to go find some chocolate. That's a good idea. Do you want some?"

"Wait. Einstein," Daya interjected, holding her hand up to shush Neil. "Are there any functioning transceivers in line of sight with Aldrinville only?"

"Yes, there is one," Einstein replied, in its pleasant voice.

"Well? Which one is it?!" Neil and Daya said at the same time and then looked at each other and then back to the PDE.

"The Mars High Bandwidth Manned Mission Transceiver is fully operational and in direct view of Aldrinville."

Daya's eyes shone as they met his.

"Neil! If *we* thought of it . . ."

He caught fire from her excitement.

". . . So would they!"

"Einstein, can the Mars transceiver be seen from *Earth* now?" Daya asked.

"That's a leap of logic, Daya," Yvonne began.

"Yes, Daya, it is," Einstein replied.

"Of course it is." Neil slapped the console top. "We've got to contact Earth!"

"How? Our PDEs?" Daya asked.

"No. Not powerful enough." Neil felt the devilish grin forming on his face. Daya didn't look as though she liked it.

"What is, then?"

Despite his EVA suit and space helmet, Neil arranged himself in as casual a pose as he could in his desk chair.

"We *know* where there is a digital video transceiver system and a dish pointed right at Earth. We just have to go out there and set it up."

"You do?" Yvonne asked, looking from one youth to the other. Her forehead wrinkled.

"Yes, we do!" Daya understood immediately where he was going. Her eyes danced. "It's mere meters from the edge of the city. It's all ready to use. We just have to go outside and set it up. Right now!"

Yvonne looked up from behind her camera and shook her head no at the two of them. Neil wasn't sure if the camerawoman was afraid to go back outside, or if she just didn't want *them* to go outside.

"Come on, Yvonne!" Neil was almost bouncing out of his chair. "We were already going to do it. We've trained on it. We know what has to be done. It'll be simple."

"Not on your life, Neil. Dr. Bright told me to keep an eye on you."

"Yes, he did. And you will," Daya said, joining in. "But he

also said, and I quote, 'Neil, Daya, you two get back to Central and do *whatever* it takes to get comms back up with Aldrinville,' unquote. Those are his exact words. He stressed 'whatever.'"

"But . . ." Yvonne protested.

"Play them back if you don't believe her." Neil grinned. "She has a near perfect eidetic memory."

"I do. You know that, Yvonne." Daya smiled triumphantly. "That's what Dr. Bright said for us to do."

"But . . ." She looked helplessly from one to the other.

"Then it's settled," Neil said, rising to his feet and heading out the door of the module. Daya bounced after him. "We have to do it. Dr. Bright said to."

Yvonne had no choice but to follow them.

✧ ✧ ✧

Captain86—The whole Moon is off line, not just Sparks Central!

HalifaxNox—Is everybody dead?

NeroliFox—Someone? Anyone?
I can't reach my sister in Armstrong City! Help, please!

TruBlues—It's a sign we're not meant to be out there.

MoonLoves—It's a sign yr uh idiot.

Chapter 16

"No, Daya, the five mil socket driver." Neil held out his left hand. He propped the feedhorn on his right shoulder, doing his best to hold the metal can and balance it while threading a bolt into the predrilled and tapped hole with his right and standing on a ladder at the edge of the pre-excavated miniature satellite dish. The ruins of the antenna farm and the hotel tower were behind him. Yvonne thought that it made a better backdrop for her video than the bleak lunar landscape. He felt the socket driver land in his outstretched palm and closed his fingers around the shaft. "Great, thanks. Now, hold that boom up another centimeter if you can."

"Okay, I've got it." Daya grunted, not because the length of aluminum was heavy but because it was cumbersome. "This was a lot easier with Dr. Bright's added two hands."

"Yeah," Neil panted and strained a bit to reach the bolthole pattern with the socket driver without falling off the ladder. "This was clearly planned as a six-handed job, not four. And Dr. Bright is a lot taller than either one of us."

"Maybe we should ask Yvonne to put down her camera and help?" Daya pleaded.

"No!" Yvonne said, from two meters away. "I don't want to be in the scene. I still don't think this is a good idea."

"It is!" Daya said firmly. "It's the only answer."

"We don't need her," Neil said, dismissively, ignoring Yvonne's exclamation of annoyance. "We've got this, Daya." He managed to get the bolt started and then placed the driver socket on the head and zipped it in. "Not too tight," Daya said.

"Will that hold the boom?" She asked, peering over his shoulder. He turned his head up. She squinted as the worklight attached to his helmet shone straight into her eyes.

"Not yet. Two bolts at least." He grunted and stretched as far as he could to get the second bolt into the hole. His shoulder held the center connector plate up to the tripod legs. "Almost . . . there . . . *got it!*" He cheered as the metal screw slotted into place. He wriggled under the boom so he was close enough to the head to apply the socket driver, then inserted a third. He ratcheted the wrench a couple of times on each bolt, then drew his arm back, surveying his work with satisfaction.

"Is it in?" Daya asked. "Can I let go now?"

"Yeah. Back out from under the rig and see if it stands up on its own three feet." Neil wiggled his feet a bit to get a better foothold on the ladder rung. When he did the ladder jiggled under him, threatening to jar him loose. He windmilled his arms, sending the tool flying. "Whoah!"

"I got you," Yvonne said. The metal steps stopped vibrating. Neil looked down. Yvonne had moved up to put one foot and one hand on the lower part of the ladder. Her other hand still worked the controller slung at her side that operated the camera on her shoulder mount. Neil grinned at her.

"Thanks! Don't know why I'm nervous. I could jump from here or even twice as high and still land safely in this lunar gravity." Neil shook his head at himself in exasperation. "Okay, I'm going to let off it now and see if it holds."

Neil slowly bent his knees and dropped away from the tripod-mounted feedhorn until he was no longer touching it. It looked good. As far as he could tell, it was holding. With a look of exasperation, Daya held out the tool, which she had retrieved from the regolith in which it had landed. He reached his hand down toward Daya. She slapped the socket driver into it.

"Give me the rest of the bolts now and I'll finish this part."

"Very well," Daya said, transferring the packet to him. "I'll start running the cable to the remote console. That's next on the checklist."

"Got it," Neil said. "We'll be done in no time."

"Neil! Daya!" Dr. Bright's voice blared in their ears, not sounding too pleased. "Where are the two of you? Report, stat!"

"Uh-oh," Neil said, shooting Daya a rueful glance. "Looks like he's back."

If he had been his own mother, Keegan would have been tapping an impatient and disapproving toe on the floor of the lab. Instead, he stood with his arms folded, a glare fixed on the two young people. Neil fidgeted as he described what he and Daya had been up to in his absence. Yvonne stood in a corner with her camera rig, very carefully not saying anything. Jackie loomed in the door of the lab, her arms crossed, too.

When the alarm lifted, they'd compared notes, and realized that the trio had been nowhere within the confines of Armstrong City. She was mighty ticked, but Keegan wanted to give the youngsters the benefit of the doubt.

". . . So, you see, Dr. Bright." Neil concluded sheepishly, his freckled cheeks red with embarrassment, "we're ready to throw the switch and go online as soon as Daya activates the app on the control panel. See?"

"You went outside by yourselves?" Dr. Bright asked through tight lips.

"No, sir! Yvonne was with us. We had an adult present at all times," Daya insisted, talking faster than usual. "You said for us to get communications up with Aldrinville, and this was the only way we could think of to do it."

"We were never in any danger!" Neil said. "Well, not much. We followed all the safety protocols!"

Keegan hoisted one eyebrow high on his forehead. He shot a glance at Jackie. She rolled her eyes. It was a good thing everyone was back safe.

"We will talk about this later, you two," Keegan said, unfastening his helmet and setting it on the desk. There hadn't even been time to change after his rescue mission. He was covered with regolith and sweat.

"Yes, sir," Neil said. "Um, is Commander January okay?"

Leave it to the boy to try and change the subject. Keegan had to stifle a grin. He was a personality and a half. He retrieved a shop cloth from one of the work tables and wiped his face.

"She's fine, son. The whole crew's just a little shaken up." He flicked a hand toward the control panel. "All right, then. Turn it on and let's see if we get a comm signal with the downlink station on Earth. I'm sure the colony administrator will be happy to plug the main communications bus into our antenna if it works." Dr. Bright nodded. "It'll still be days before the antenna farm is back online. I saw it up close. It's torn to shreds. We'll never find all the pieces. This could solve a lot of problems. If it works."

"Uh, yes, sir. Here we go." Neil said, as he slid several control bars on his desktop touch screen to tune the SDR to the right frequency-hopping spectrum and modulation scheme. He glanced up at his colleague. "Okay, Daya."

"Ready." The petite girl tapped the big red circle on the app screen before her, and it turned green. A waterfall chart scrolled across the console screen, then also projected onto the big center screen on the wall. A modulation spike bounced about in a sea of noise, then Neil's slidebars all turned green. He glanced back at his mentor, hoping for approval. "Dr. Bright, I think we're on."

They were indeed. The signal was a strong one, clear as a bell.

Keegan watched them, his chest about to burst with pride. It looked like they had done it. Clever, smart kids. *His kids.* He felt honored to be their guide and guardian into the world of science. Pretty soon, they wouldn't need him any longer.

"Looks like we are. Leona, take control of the hopping key and modulation. And open a voice and video channel with Ground Control in Houston."

The artificial intelligence's warm voice rang out.

"Done, Dr. Bright. Ground Control watch commander is online, sir."

Keegan leaned forward toward the audio pickup beside Daya's desktop.

"This is Dr. Keegan Bright in Armstrong Central Control. Do you copy?"

Almost as soon as Dr. Bright had started talking, a video image popped up on the first and third screens on the wall, the flight control officer of the day back on Earth, a tawny-skinned, black-haired man in his thirties. He looked startled. Neil glanced at Daya with a smug smile on his face and cheered inwardly.

"We've got you, Keegan, loud and clear," the controller replied. "Lieutenant Jack Ferrar here in Houston. Glad to hear from you folks. Kind of an unfamiliar frequency you're broadcasting on. Can you give us a status update? A lot's been happening since y'all went dark."

"My AI is sending you a detailed report now, but the short version is that the CME fried the inbound shuttle's control logic and it crashed into Armstrong Tower One, destroying a good portion of it *and* the communications antenna farm. I'm happy to say that we have recovered all of the astronauts and passengers on the shuttle and they're all safe. The city also sheltered according to plan, and there were no casualties here, either. We're broadcasting from a homemade antenna temporarily until the others are back online."

"That's great news, Keegan. Why are you talking to us and not the colony administrator or someone from Lunar Control Station up there?"

"Two reasons, Jack." Dr. Bright paused, with a shared glance at Daya and Neil. "One, this was an experiment and we weren't sure if it would work this well. We just this second turned it on, and I'm as pleased as I can be that it's nearly perfect for such an improvised setup. My AI is setting up a channel for Lunar Control as we speak. They'll get on to you just as soon as they can. There are a lot of frustrated people up here who are probably busting to make contact. We've got a bunch of completely destroyed equipment, including one permanently retired space shuttle. You can imagine that it was a distraction for a while, but the colony administrator and Lunar Control will be on this line soon."

"Of course it was. And we'll keep an ear out for them. I'll relay them over to EarthComm, no problem." The control officer laughed. Keegan grinned. Jack was an old acquaintance who understood just how much Keegan was understating the situation. "And the second reason?"

The worry overwhelmed Keegan all over again.

"Jack, we have crew of four of my Bright Sparks on EVA on the far side in Aldrinville. Communications went down right as the CME started and we're desperate to get in contact with them. We hoped they might have found a way to contact Earth."

Jack shook his head.

"Nothing as of yet, but the CME is still going strong, and it looks like there might be a second eruption brewing. Hopefully, they're staying put in safe shelter. We've been keeping apprised of the situation up there. If we hear anything we'll let y'all know."

"Okay, thanks, Jack." Keegan's shoulders slumped. It was too soon for the away team to be able to do anything outside the habitat. Not that he wanted them to endanger themselves, but it would have put his mind at ease if they could have made contact.

"Glad everyone is okay up there," Jack Ferrar said. He glanced down at his console. "I'm getting a signal from Lunar Control right now, demanding access to the White House, the news services, and the Internet, not in that order. I'd better start linking them up. Good job getting back on line so soon."

Keegan laid a hand on Daya's shoulder.

"You can thank my Bright Sparks, it was their idea and their prototype we're using." he said.

"Thanks, kids," Jack said, grinning at Neil and Daya. Both of them straightened up with pride. "Keegan, I recommend y'all get some sleep. If we hear anything from your team, we'll let you know."

"Jack, I want a direct line as soon as you hear anything."

"Will do, Keegan. Now, y'all get some rest."

✧　✧　✧

NeroliFox—She's all right! My sister is okay! I just heard from her main office.

M4r1a—What about Dr. Bright? The program stopped in the middle.

YuBaitu—The shuttle stopped transmitting, too. Does anyone know its fate?

RutaAust—What about the Bright Sparks?

ButchFel9—I need to see my Barb!

Chapter 17

"So, let me get this straight." Dion shook his head over his coffee cup. "The radiation sensor shows a normal environment outside, meaning that the storm has passed, but you're concerned, Barb, that the thing was damaged by the CME somehow and that as soon as we go outside we'll start getting fried by high-energy ionized particles?"

"Well, uh, yeah, sort of." Barbara finished off her morning coffee and pushed the cup away from her. "I know it sounds paranoid, but how do we *know*?"

"My roommate there has a point." Jan backed her up. "The sensor could be damaged."

"Maybe, but aren't we getting an ambient signal from the sensor now that's indicative of sunlight on a normal day as it should be?" Gary asked, running a finger around the inside of the container of scrambled eggs with chopped bacon to see if there was any left. "I mean, if it was broken, wouldn't the signal just be garbage, or nothing at all?"

"It might be," Barbara said. "But we can't get confirmation from Armstrong City. We need something to verify the reading independently."

"What?"

Barbara gave him a cheeky smile.

"Fido, play the 'toon we were watching last night," Barb said, pointing her PDE at the shelter wall. "Projector mode, please. And dim the lights."

"Certainly, Barb." She let go of the PDE. It floated into the center of the room. A light lanced out from its end and projected a colorful image onto the far wall. A small cartoon yellow canary with a giant head swinging on a perch in a cage appeared. The canary was singing an old-fashioned song in his high-pitched nasal voice.

"What?" Dion laughed as the cartoon continued to sing. "Tweety Pie?"

"Exactly." Barb tilted her head playfully at them.

"What?" Gary asked. "An ancient cartoon?"

"This is what we need to check the sensor." Jan raised an eyebrow at him. "We need a canary."

Dion gave her a look that said he doubted her sanity. "A bird?"

"Yes, a mine canary. That's exactly what we need," Barbara said.

She admitted that it was a leap of intuition. She and Jan had awakened in the middle of the night. They had chatted for a while about getting up and working on the interior of the shelter, but they knew they were still overtired. Both of them were worried about the CME, being out of touch with Sparks Central, and whether they would know for sure that the radiation danger had passed. The electronic gauge on the main console seemed stuck on 450 mrem, when it ought to have been going down gradually. They had to get a second opinion before exposing themselves to radiation.

They decided to go through their video collections to find something to watch that would relax them back to sleep. Close to the bottom of the list, Barbara uncovered Jan's collection of Warner Brothers cartoons. Some of them were almost a century and a half old, but still funny. Jan put on her favorites: Bugs Bunny, Daffy Duck, and Tweety Pie. They had laughed at Sylvester the cat trying to catch the little bird and failing every time. Then, almost at the same moment, an idea had struck them.

In the light of Ms. Scruffles's glowing screen, they had turned to look at each other. They had talked over the idea, coming up with a plan of operation in case the radiation readings were inconclusive, which was just what they had proved to be.

"How is a bird going to help us even if we had one?" Gary asked. "I'm not a zoologist, or even a biologist."

"I *am* a biologist, and I don't know what they're talking about," Dion said.

"Well, long ago before sensors, miners used to take birdcages with canaries in them down into the mines." Jan started explaining. "The canaries were more susceptible to high carbon dioxide, carbon monoxide, or low oxygen or toxic gases or something. Their systems were far more sensitive, so they would pass out or die before the humans would. So, if the miners saw a lifeless bird in a cage, they knew they had to get out."

"Well, we don't have any canaries here on the Moon that I know of. At least not out here in Aldrinville. I could double check the manifest for you if you'd like, but I'm pretty certain we're fresh out," Gary said. "They probably have plenty of secondary sensors back on Earth." He gestured toward the door. "Should I just run out and get one?"

"I wish we had access to something like Goddard Space Lab's Cosmic Ray Telescope for the Effects of Radiation, but we don't," Barbara said. "We'll use an electronic canary."

"Yeah, but CRaTER was a long time ago," Gary said. "Even if it was still operational, we couldn't communicate with it anyhow. So where are we going to get a canary?"

Jan grinned and held up Ms. Scruffles.

"Here's one. Our PDEs can be the canaries. We just slide

one of them out the door into the sunlight and see if we lose comms with it."

"If the canary stops singing, then we're in trouble," Barb added. "If it keeps going, we're fine. Then I'll admit the CME has passed."

Dion watched Tweety finish his song.

"I haven't got a better idea. Go for it, Dion said."

"Who's going to volunteer their PDE as our mine canary?" Gary asked, cradling Turing with a protective hand.

The Sparks looked at one another. Barbara shook her head.

"I will," she said. "It was my idea, after all. If the radioactive puddy tat gets Fido, at least we'll be safe. But we have to know."

Once the guys were on board, Gary and Jan started tossing ideas out over Turing's screen on how to expose one of the PDEs with the least possible risk to the interior of the habitat.

"The trouble is that there's only one way in or out of this shelter," Gary said. "We've got one big door. No hatches, no ports, nothing but the conduits for electrical connections and plumbing."

"Well, it's supposed to be buried deep," Jan argued. "We didn't anticipate having to send a makeshift probe out."

"We didn't work in double-redundancy for a situation like this," Dion said. "Shame on us."

"You hear that, Turing?" Gary said to his PDE. "Make a note: we've got to back-engineer at least one equipment access hatch for sensors and things. Give me all the optimum locations, too."

"Noted, Gary," his PDE said, in its pleasant tenor voice.

"And we'll have to deactivate most of the airlock functions to get the PDE out there," Gary said. "If we attach Fido to a tether, we can't seal the room airtight."

"I'll put up with a little air seepage in exchange for being able to get out of here safely," Jan said.

"We don't have to deactivate anything, really," Barbara said. "I'll stand in the airlock and put the PDE outside."

"Without exposing yourself to the CME?" Jan asked. "Do you have a handy little robot in your luggage to carry the PDE into the sun?"

Barbara laughed. "I wasn't going to go that high tech. We have rolling chairs. I can attach it to one of them and push it out the lock. I don't have to put myself in any danger."

"The chair's wheels are too small." Gary jumped up. "They'll get swamped in the regolith. I'll get the skid loader from the engine room."

Jan laughed. "Let's do it!"

"I'll monitor the O2 levels," Dion said. "You get our mine canary out there."

Barbara's nerves jangled as they prepared to push Fido into the sun. She and Jan suited up in full gear on the inside edge of the airlock. Behind them, Dion had set up a decontamination chamber in the bathroom in case any of them got a dose of solar radiation. She hoped it wouldn't be necessary. If they were exposed this far away from medical help, it could be catastrophic.

With the big-tired cart taking up most of the room, the airlock was more of a squeeze than usual. They watched the indicator lights nervously cycling from green to yellow as the air was sucked back into the habitat.

Jan took a deep breath, and gave Barbara a thumbs up. The door slid open. Barbara felt a little shock to see brilliant sunlight again after so many hours in the dimness of the shelter. Instead of welcoming it, she worried whether it was still the enemy. If she put her arm out into it, would she be exposing herself to danger?

Her little silver PDE looked like a patient on a too-big

gurney, strapped down with one of the cargo ties. As soon as the gap was wide enough, she shoved the skid loader outside. It went rolling out of the shadow of the habitat's overhang. Fido's screen winked blindingly with reflected sunlight just as Jan hit the control to cycle the airlock door again. Barbara blinked at the afterimage, trying not to worry.

Once there was air in the airlock again, Jan held out her sleeve and her own PDE. Barbara pulled off her helmet.

"Can you hear me, Fido?" Barbara asked, speaking into Ms. Scruffles's audio pickup.

Loud crackling erupted from the speaker. Barbara and the others looked at one another in dismay. Barbara felt as though a piece of her had been ripped away. She had only had the PDE for a little while, but it was an awesome piece of electronics, and Dr. Bright had personally given it to her. She let out a deep sigh. She would have to go back to Old Fido as soon as they could return to Armstrong City. Sympathy in his deep brown eyes, Dion patted her on the shoulder.

On the console behind them, a female voice burst out.

"All clear, Barbara," Fido said. "Radiation levels normal. The sensor needs to be reset, but is otherwise functional."

Barbara turned to stare at the board. She let out the breath she didn't realize she had been holding.

"You're alive!"

"Correction, Barbara. I am operational."

Barbara clapped her helmet visor down again and stepped back into the airlock. She could hardly wait to get outside.

She reeled in the skid loader and seized the PDE in a hug, ignoring the scatter of moondust that came with it.

"I could just kiss you," she said, regarding the slim device with delight.

"Not necessary, Barbara," Fido said. "I am just fulfilling my functions."

"Yay!" Gary cheered. "We can get to work on the dish now! Wait until I tell Dr. Bright about this."

"Got another old movie quote for you," Dion said, beaming with relief as Barbara came back inside, holding her PDE triumphantly aloft. "'ET, phone home.'"

"Got it, Jan?" Dion stuck one long arm down into the hole they'd dug in the side of the crater. Jan's feet were all that stuck out into the sunshine. "Here are the other two bolts."

"Thanks," Jan said. Her voice sounded hollow.

Barbara only looked up for a brief moment from hauling a spare battery out of the rear of the partially unburied power truck. Dion and Jan had the task of mounting the makeshift feedhorn and the PDE connections under control. She concentrated on steering the large black box down the truck's rear ramp, accompanied by the driving beat of her grandmother's old-school hip hop. She was so glad to have Fido back that she was running through her playlists one by one, but for her ears only. The others had their own preferred music to work by. Once in a while, she could hear a few notes or a riff under their voices when they spoke to one another.

Behind her, Gary was dragging a cable through the trench they had dug to the shelter that would be attached to the mechanism. The large solid battery would certainly have been too heavy for her to move back on Earth, but on the Moon it seemed very light to her. The power cable clamp bolts, on the other hand, must have been put on by a bodybuilder.

"Ugggh!" She tugged her wrench handle as hard as she could, but it didn't budge. "That thing is *on* there."

"Who you talking to, Barb?" Dion straightened up and looked over at her. Barbara felt her sweating cheeks burn.

"Oh, sorry, nobody," she said, a little embarrassed to have been overheard. "Just this bolt on the battery cable clamp won't budge."

"Need a hand with it?" Gary looked up from his cable dragging.

"No. I can get this," she said testily. She grunted again and strained against the bolt, but it went nowhere. "Okay, okay, so you're probably heated up and swelled together. So, I need to either cool you off or get more torque."

Barbara set the wrench down and paced a few steps back and then forth, nibbling at her lower lip. The bolts gleamed silver-white in the sunshine. It wasn't as though they had gone rusty over time. She wished she had a can of spray lubricant or solvent that would work in space. From her practical studies, she knew there were very few chemical solutions that worked in vacuum. Instead, she needed to rely on physical strength. Her dad had done the trick back on their farm many times.

"If it worked on Earth, it should work on the Moon," she whispered to herself, pointing a finger at the bolt. "You stay put. I'll be right back." She shouldered the wrench and bounced back to the equipment truck.

That morning, they had taken the Cat and dug away part of the rubble pile behind where the big hauler had been buried, forming a kind of artificial cave where the cargo doors opened up. Over the course of the next day or so, they could start uncovering all of the gear and components, but first things had to come first. They needed communications with home base before they did anything else. She cycled the electronic hasp on the door. It had worked right away when they first unburied it, but Barbara worried that it might seize up again. Instead, it cycled through and went green. The doors opened slightly as the bolt retracted.

"That's a good sign," she muttered.

Barbara climbed up into the container and began rummaging through the hardware and materials until she found what she was looking for.

"Aha! Just what the doctor ordered." Metal vibrated

against metal as she pulled a piece of pipe about a meter long and about two and a half centimeters in diameter out of the pile in the back. She grimaced to see how their previously well organized stores had fallen into a haphazard mess, but there would be time to straighten it all up once the crisis was over. The water truck was still buried and would remain under the regolith until they were ready to drive it back to Armstrong City. Most of its contents had already been piped into the shelter's tanks. The heavy hauler with the pieces of the framework and feedhorn for the big telescope also remained under its bed of dust and rocks.

Barbara could see Jan crawling from the hole in the spoils pile and Dion bounced to a stop beside her almost as soon as she had landed. Jan worked herself to her feet and bounded in her direction as well.

"Finished, roomie." Jan said. "Just curious what the doctor is ordering over here."

"I keep forgetting I have the mic open." Barb looked sheepish as she held up the metal pipe. "I guess I'm used to talking to myself."

"Well, you understand what you mean," Jan said. "Can we help?"

"You shouldn't have to," Barbara said. "I hope."

"What're you going to do with that, Barb?" Dion asked. "Beat the bolt loose?"

"Not really." She smiled as she dropped the handle of the wrench down into the end of the pipe, leaving only the box end sticking out, making it almost a meter long. Barb slotted the head over the bolt head and worked it in place. "This is my dad's version of a torque bar. He always liked to quote Archimedes at this point, whether anyone is around to hear it or not; 'give me a lever and a firm place to stand.'"

With a grunt, she leaned into the end of the pipe and pushed hard. The bolt broke free. Barbara almost staggered over the battery, but she regained her footing. She held the wrench up to the sun in triumph. "'And I can move the whole world.'"

"Or the Moon," Jan said, with a laugh. "But I'll settle for moving our voices from one side of this sphere to the other."

Neil hadn't been able to sleep all night. He had gone to bed exhausted, but at the same time he was so wired up about having done the EVA and getting the communications system working just like they had designed it to, that his mind kept racing with a couple of nightmare scenarios. One of those mental vids that played over and over again was a vivid picture of Dr. Bright kicking him out of the Sparks for going outside without him. The other was him telling Daya and Yvonne it was fine to go out, just as he opened the door and stepping into the teeth of another CME that inexplicably was pounding the Armstrong City side of the Moon with rains of hot silver radiation. Those two nightmares dragged him out of a sound sleep over and over throughout the night.

A gentle, grandfatherly voice interrupted his uneasy dreams.

"Neil, it is time to wake up." Einstein said softly, from the nightstand beside his bed. Neil rolled over and pulled the covers over his head.

"Thirty more minutes, Einy."

"I'm sorry, Neil, but Dr. Bright is being very insistent that you join him in Sparks HQ."

Neil's eyes opened, giving him a close-up view of the fibers of his quilt.

"It's a bad dream."

"No, Neil, I assure you this is not a dream. Dr. Bright has called more than once. You must hurry."

"Okay, okay! I'm getting up." Neil threw the covers back and stared at the ceiling for a moment. He let out a heartfelt yawn. "Did he say what he wants?"

"No. He just said to meet him as soon as you can."

"Uhgh." Neil grunted and pulled himself out of bed. He bounced softly to the floor and then to the bathroom. The floor felt warm under his feet, which meant the circuits had turned over from the cooler nighttime power-saver setting. "What time is it?"

"It is 8:42. You have slept in this morning."

"Oh, no! When did he first call me?"

"Thirty minutes ago. Daya has already responded to the summons."

"Has the CME stopped?"

"Yes, it has."

"Hey, maybe he's heard from Aldrinville."

"Yes, he has."

"Wow," Neil said, fully awake now. "Tell him I'll be there in less than ten minutes."

Neil bounded excitedly over the threshold into Sparks Central and leaped over the circle of desks to land in his chair. Dr. Bright and Daya were gazing up at the middle screen. The picture was of pretty poor quality, but all four of the elder Sparks were in it. They looked well and healthy, if a little sweaty.

". . . as far as we can tell all the equipment survived the CME. We're getting everything dug out from under the rubble piles and hoping to hear instructions on what to do next. For now, I'm hesitant to get back to work until we know more." Barbara's voice sounded as strong and confident as ever.

"Hey, guys!" Neil said, waving at them. "Boy, am I glad to see you! How are you? Are you okay? What was it like being in the middle of an ejection event? Did you hear anything? What were the radiation levels like? We were really worried about you!"

The elder Sparks stared at him blankly.

"Hello, guys?" Neil asked. He glanced at Dr. Bright.

His mentor burst out laughing and slapped Neil on the back.

"You're going to have to wait a little while for an answer, Neil," Dr. Bright said. "It's gonna be twenty minutes before your questions get to them. Mars is about ten light-minutes away right now, and the data packet has to bounce there and back."

Neil felt foolish, but he straightened his back.

"I knew that," he said.

"Of course you did," Daya said, doing her best to spare his feelings. "It's perfectly understandable. We're so used to speaking in real time at much shorter distances."

Soon, though not nearly fast enough for Neil, the Sparks on the screen seemed to come to life. They laughed.

"We're fine, little bro," Dion said, with a broad grin. "We took a leaf out of your book and built a mini-dish to reach out to Armstrong City. Barbara thought of bouncing the signal off the new relay array on Mars, then route it through Earth's system."

"That's just what we did!" Neil exclaimed. Dr. Bright put out a hand to stop him. He remembered about the time delay and subsided.

"This is hard," he said.

"I know," Dr. Bright told him. "I'm feeling just as excited as you are. This isn't too bad. Imagine what it was like for Mission Control to operate the Cassini probe over the distance between Earth and Saturn. Or the Newton orbiter that explored Ceres."

". . . We've got most of the equipment unburied again," Gary was saying. "In another day, we can have everything laid out and ready to start work on the crater."

"We plan to leave this little dish operational until the satellite communications are restored again," Barbara added, leaning forward toward the camera. "We won't clear that part of the crater until then."

"They can't do that," Neil said, alarmed. "Didn't Lieutenant Ferrar say that there might be another wave from the sun? Have we got any more information on that?"

"That's right, and I've sent them the download from the orbital telescopes," Dr. Bright said. "They haven't seen it yet." Even as he said it, on the screen, the elder Sparks' faces changed from joy to dismay. "All right, they've got the data." He raised his voice. "Sorry to ruin all your hard work, kids, but as you see, the early warning systems on Earth detected a second blast a little while ago. I had to confirm it before I sent it to you. Because of the shuttle crash, we're having to share the bandwidth with everyone in Armstrong City. It's been a little chaotic around here. You've got just about thirteen hours. The colony administrator's going to send out a warning in about ten minutes as soon as we have more data gathered on the magnitude of the storm."

"Oh, how could I have slept through all that?" Neil groaned. He felt under his desk for a container of cola. They were all gone. He'd have to go down to the commissary and pick up another bunch.

"You needed the rest," Daya said, reassuringly. "We did good work yesterday. Without us, there would have been no communication between Earth and Armstrong City." She turned a cautious eye toward Dr. Bright. Remembering his nightmares, Neil followed suit. Dr. Bright seemed to have forgiven their tacit disobedience, but they knew he certainly hadn't forgotten it.

"Well, at least now we can get updates from Aldrinville every ten or twenty minutes," Neil said, doing some mental calculations. He glanced up at the other Sparks, who seemed to be talking among themselves while they waited for the next message from Armstrong City to arrive.

If they sent a message to Mars, it would have to travel the ten minutes to Mars and then ten more minutes back to the

Moon. So each message one way had a twenty minute travel time. It would take forty minutes just to say "hi" and then to hear "hello" back. That was going to make detailed conversations difficult. They needed better.

Daya seemed to read his thoughts.

"We will have long waits in between messages. Much too long."

"I know," Dr. Bright said and nodded. He stood up so he could see both of them and the main screen. "That is one of the other reasons why I called you both in here."

"Huh?" Neil asked, puzzled. "We can't fix the speed of light."

"Of course not!" Dr. Bright laughed. "I wish. But we can move our relay station a lot closer."

"How's that? Anything in orbit will pass through the day side and get fried by the CME," Neil asked.

"So, we don't put it in a standard orbit." Dr. Bright raised an eyebrow at the two of them like he always did when he knew the answer but was waiting for one or all of the Sparks to catch on.

"A nonstandard orbit?" Daya asked.

"But, we'd need constant propulsion to manage that unless we were in a Lagrange point or something." Neil scratched his head and pulled out Einstein to check. "We'd have to have a *lot* of propulsion one way or the other. Either to maintain a non-Keplerian orbit or to get to a Lagrange point which would be waaayyy out there."

"That would mean any craft would be vulnerable to the incoming radiation," Daya said.

"You're both right." Dr. Bright said, purposefully giving them no more information than necessary. Neil tried to figure out where he was going. Usually, he loved the challenge, but he wasn't sure if a major crisis like this one was the right time to make them guess.

"So, we're going to use a shuttle or something?" he

hazarded. Dr. Bright's eyes danced but he shook his head. Neil was tantalized and frustrated all at the same time.

"No. Lunar and Mission Control have grounded all shuttle flights until we know the CMEs are over with for more than twenty-four hours."

"No shuttles, but we have to have propulsion." Daya screwed up her face in thought. "So we have to build something? Something that *we* are capable of creating, here and now?"

"Yes . . . ?" Dr. Bright's look encouraged them to go on with their ideas.

"With propulsion!" Neil burst out in excitement. He could hardly believe it. "My drone!"

"You got it, Neil." Dr. Bright smiled, turning over a hand as if giving him a gift. "You finally get to build your drone." The hand closed and the forefinger extended upward as a warning. "But we need to beef up the communications package."

"We can do that!" Neil said, raking at Einstein's screen to bring up the proposal that contained his detailed schematics. Then a thought struck him. He looked up at Dr. Bright. "Wait, how does the drone not get destroyed by the CME too?"

Dr. Bright turned toward the left monitor.

"Leona, bring up the orbital analysis simulation for Neil's drone comm-relay bird."

"Certainly, Dr. Bright," Leona replied. An image of the Moon appeared on the central screen and a dot labeled Aldrinville was clear just inside the day side.

"So you see," Dr. Bright waved his hand. "If we draw a straight line from Aldrinville at this angle all the way out to here, at this point the line is in the shadow of the Moon and protected from the CME. We'll have to continuously update the orbit to have it move with the shadow of the Moon but it's a straightforward calculation."

ROTATIONAL GEARING INITIATION-ON
Point of entry-On
Power 99%
Life support 97%
Heat barrier 87%
Back-up engines on
Boosters ready
360 SCHEMATIC-ON
CALCULATING DISTANCE TO TARGET
POWERING DOWN AND REDUCING SPEED
LUNA LANDING PROTECTORS 100%
Aldrinville
TIME ELAPSED between boosters
2Hrs
THRUSTERS 0.56

"That's great!" Daya said. "I can't wait to speak to them and make sure they're doing well. I want to hear more of how they have been coping."

"This'll make direct communication a piece of cake," Neil agreed. He was still reveling in the delight of having his project approved. What should he name it? ZimmerStar? NeilSat?

"That it will," Dr. Bright said. "How long will it take you to build it?"

"Build the drone?" Neil rubbed his chin, feeling the few soft hairs that grew on it. He had never felt more and less grown up at the same time than at that moment. "Well, I'm guessing an hour or two to print out the chassis and then another couple hours to wire it all up and test out the flight software. With Daya's help maybe we can shave some of that off."

"Not just Daya's help. Mine, too. This is top priority."

"Uh, okay, then maybe three hours. When do we start?" Neil asked.

"Neil, you misunderstand." Dr. Bright looked at his PDE. "Leona, put the countdown 'til the next CME up on the board and keep it running."

On the right-hand screen, a huge digital clock appeared, reading 12:25:00. The numbers immediately began to count down: 12:24:59, 12:24:58 . . . Dr. Bright looked Neil straight in the eyes.

"The clock is running, Sparks. We just started your project, Neil. You're in charge. What do you want us to do first?"

Neil's mouth dropped open.

"Uh, I, uh . . ."

✦   ✦   ✦

GaMeRgirl873—They're alive! Sparks rule!

HeloFanAx—The connection to the Moon is really crude. Is that the best they can do?

NeilZ—We lost the whole comm array, Helo. Check the upload of our bypass system. It's pretty awesome. Hey, EMDrone coming on line soon!

StrTrk4FR—Another CME? The last one burned out our satellite dish!

Chapter 18

"It seems like we just buried this truck," Dion complained to Barbara. She waved for him to pile a little more dirt over the side to her left.

"Yeah, I know! That looks good there, Dion. One more bucketload for that spot." So much for doing science. She was moving dirt around, just like on the farm.

Barbara adjusted her sun visor dial, and the face mask turned clear enough she could read her PDE screen. She read the digital clock ticking down on the screen and grimaced a little. Eight hours and twelve minutes! They had been working steadily since Dr. Bright dropped the bombshell. Another coronal mass ejection! And it was anyone's guess if this one would be worse than the first one. As best they and Dr. Bright could figure, there was only one shift until the CME blasted them, *again*. They had to get the cable underground as deeply as possible. "I guess this is like camping. No matter how pretty it looks before you go, it always rains."

"That's not a very healthy attitude," Dion laughed.

"It's realistic," Jan said, loyally, from inside the shelter.

"Well, it at least keeps you prepared. I always carry

raingear." Barbara bounced upward in a big leap to the side of the pile and then up on top of the truck, scattering clouds of sparkling regolith dust as she went.

"I used to," Gary said, chuckling. He was inside, too, helping Jan adjust the connections on the console. "Although I haven't had a lot of use for it lately."

"Too true," Barbara said. "Slickers won't keep you safe from radiation."

"Depends on the manufacturer," Dion said. "I saw an umbrella for sale on an infomercial that sounded like it flung the rain back up at the clouds. Only $19.99 plus shipping and handling."

"Can you imagine what shipping would cost to get it up here?" Jan asked.

"Come on, what's a million dollars more or less?" Gary asked.

Barbara laughed, enjoying the camaraderie with her fellow Sparks. She was amazed at how confident she felt at that moment. If anyone had said to her even a week ago that she would be standing on the far side of the Moon with a solar storm on the way and it felt more like an inconvenience than an impending catastrophe, she'd have laughed herself silly. They had gotten through the first storm. They'd handled the lack of a reliable comm link. They could manage this.

"Fido, crank up some hard rock, okay? That seems appropriate."

"Playlist eight, Barbara?"

"Yes, that'll be good," she said.

She surveyed the site from her new vantage point, scanning around her to make sure everything was under cover. Dirt and stone were mounded high on the trucks again. The layers looked thick enough to fend off another blast from the Sun, even one worse than the first.

"I think we're good out here. Let's double check the cable and make certain it's buried and grounded. We don't want our only comm link to blow while we ride out the second storm. We want to be able to check in again as soon as it's over."

"Roger that," Dion said. He turned the Cat toward the makeshift dish. Barbara saw him leaning out the side of the cab, checking that the trench had been adequately buried, as dust kicked up into his face mask. She started to climb down, taking more care than she had jumping up. She didn't want to fall again, not when retrieval was delayed yet another day or more. She followed the cable trench the other way, looking for any shallow spots. As song followed song, her bounding steps seemed to fall into rhythm.

Her music stopped abruptly, making way for Gary's voice.

"Barb, Dion, you need to come inside," he called. Barbara looked up toward the habitat doorway, surprised at the sudden urgent tone.

"Okay, we'll be done out here in about ten minutes. Can it wait?"

"I'm not certain." Gary replied. "We've got a potential situation. . . . Uh, hold on a minute. Jan says you should finish out there first. It can wait until then."

"Okay. See you soon." Barb said, wondering what else could be happening to them. Gary sounded uncharacteristically tentative. Her cheery mood soured just a little. She turned the other way and clambered up over the lip of the big crater. "Come on, Dion. Let's get this job done and see what that's all about."

"Right." Dion rolled the mini-dozer up to a gap in the cable trench and packed the dirt over it. As the high level silicic regolith scattered in the low gravity, it glistened like tiny fireflies in the sunlight before settling to the ground again. Barbara enjoyed the amazing Brownian motion and beautiful sparkles, but only briefly. Her mind had to stay focused on the job at hand, making certain the cable run from the spoils pile antenna to the shelter was covered. She beckoned Dion up to the ridge. He scooped up a load of regolith and rumbled up to her.

After a few extra buckets on the high spot, Barbara was satisfied that the communications cable was protected from the CME ions.

"Looks good," she said. "I'm getting hungry, anyway."

"Me, too." Dion pulled the dozer into the hole he'd previously dug out for it. He climbed out and bounded up to meet her. "We really need to just build a garage out here. *And* some cold-storage areas."

"Yeah," Barbara said. "All of it underground."

"Or, just into the side of a crater. There are plenty closer by. Good inspiration that you and Jan had, digging this emergency dish where it is." He squinted up at the sun. "It's pointing the opposite direction from the CME."

"We just got lucky that Mars was in place for us," Barbara said.

"My granny always tells me that the harder you work, the luckier you get." Dion gave her a grin as they made their way downhill toward the habitat.

The two of them cycled through the airlock. Barbara waited impatiently as the carbon dioxide level light teetered at the edge of green and yellow, then finally and, Barb thought, reluctantly flashed to green. When the inner door cycled, they stepped through to the main chamber and took their helmet bubbles off. Gary and Jan were waiting in the main room for them.

"Hi, roomie." Jan sounded less enthusiastic than usual. Both of the Nerd Twins looked glum.

"Okay, guys, what's up?" Dion asked, peeling off his gloves. "You could have told us while we were still outside."

"I wanted you to see it for yourselves." Gary stated, aiming a thumb toward the airlock. "Did you notice how the carbon dioxide level was very close to the yellow line?"

"Yes, I did," Barbara said. She unfastened her suit sleeves so she could look at the band on her wrist. The CO2 levels were higher than they should have been. "Is there something wrong with the filtration system? Something caused by the last CME?"

"I don't know, and I feel that I ought to." Gary pointed at her PDE. "I just sent you both a graph of the carbon dioxide levels over the past twelve hours and the projection over the next twelve. The level has been growing on a linear progression instead of staying around a mean value. The projection shows the growth way into and past unacceptable levels. It will be dangerous to breathe in here in six hours."

"Wow," Barbara said, feeling the weight of the last several days weighing around her neck. The good mood she had felt while working outside fled. She was suddenly tired. In fact, she was very tired. They had all been working a lot of hours since breakfast. She took a deep breath. It didn't seem to refresh her as it should have. "Sometimes it seems like everything on the Moon is trying to kill us! What could be causing it, Gary?"

"Two of the three carbon dioxide scrubbers have failed. Numbers one and three. Good ol' number two is still humming away, but it wasn't designed for the capacity being asked of it." Gary explained.

"What? Why did one and three fail? The CME?" Barb asked.

"Same question I asked, Barb!" Jan emitted a sour laugh. "Chalk it up to a system built by the lowest bidder, I guess."

"Weren't the vendors vetted by the space program?" Barbara asked. "I thought all the components were supposed to be rated at triple redundancy."

Gary grimaced.

"They're supposed to be. But it's too late to worry about who or what is to blame, at least until we get back to Armstrong. As far as our external diagnostic sensors can tell, the zeolite inside the faulty scrubbers isn't doing the job. The air flow rate is choked there as if the matrix of material that absorbs the CO2 is stopped up. That drove the fans downline so hard that they overheated and burned out." Gary gestured to his counterpart. "Jan has a different theory."

Jan frowned. "I don't think the stopped-up zeolite matrix caused the fan to burn out. I think it was the other way around. I followed the electrical lines and the airflow lines and *I* think we got a charge built up from the CME that caused an electrical arc inside one and three. That's what burned out the fans. The resulting fumes, carbon, and whatever else burned off reacted in the zeolite filters and stopped them up."

Barbara felt a chill in the pit of her stomach.

"But I thought we grounded everything and covered it in dirt. Meters of dirt."

"We did! Maybe too efficiently. Ms. Scruffles, bring up the scrubber diagram and put it on the wall."

"Yes, Jan."

"You see this plumbing line here?" Jan pointed at the chart projection. The others nodded. Barbara studied it closely and thought she saw the problem before Jan finished. She figured that a buildup of static electricity was the most likely culprit. "Remember when I told you we had to leave it free? This is the regen process line. Every so often the filters have to be exposed to the vacuum to regenerate the zeolite material. This process basically releases whatever carbon dioxide has been trapped in there. It also boils off the water absorbed from the atmosphere, too."

"But we did leave it free," Barbara insisted, checking her notes. "It was in the original plans that Gary drew up. Unless some regolith tumbled onto it. I thought we packed everything down around the plumbing lines."

"Yeah, we did, because I recall that from studying the

shelter design, too," Dion added. "It was clear. And only one scrubber is supposed to go into regen mode at a time. That's why there are three. How could two of them fail?"

"Wait, this plumbing is nonmetal, right?" Barbara asked, reading the stats.

"Yes, it is," Dion said. "Standard nonmetallic plastic plumbing line that's space-rated."

"It couldn't be," Barbara said, baffled. The problem wasn't what she thought, then.

"Well, it might be nonmetallic, but I put an ohm meter on it a few minutes ago." Jan shook her head. "It *is* conductive. A length of the line about a half meter long looked like a forty kilo-ohm resistor."

"Really?" Barbara's suspicion was correct after all. "So, the line vents to space and we didn't cover it up for that reason. But the CME still managed to charge it up. Probably like a weird cylindrical capacitor or something."

"That's not what I ordered for the project at all," Gary said, peevishly.

"Right," Jan agreed. "I had Ms. Scruffles simulate it in SuperSPICE and that's exactly what happened. Probably. The tubes charged up, then arced over to the fans, burning them out. The fans burned out, and the smoke fouled up the filters."

"Man, that's bad. We don't have replacements on the manifest," Dion said, dismay dragging down the lines of his face. "I'm not even sure there are any kitchen chemistry tricks we could pull."

"Activated charcoal or quicklime or something would work, but where do you find that on the far side of the Moon?" Barbara shrugged. "I have no idea."

"Me, either." Gary added. "Jan and I sent a request back to Neil and Daya to figure it out but it will be forty minutes before we hear any response."

"Thirty-four now," Jan corrected him.

Gary glanced up at the countdown clock in the corner of the main screen.

"Uh, right, thirty-four."

"We absolutely have to have those scrubbers working." Dion sighed. "No scrubbers, no breathing. No breathing . . ."

"No us," Jan concluded glumly. Barbara gulped.

"Fido, how long until the CME hits Aldrinville?" she asked. "Do we have time to drive out of here?"

"Barb, if Dr. Bright's estimate from the previous message was correct then we have approximately eight hours and one minute until it arrives."

"Even with me driving, that's not enough time to make it to the night side," Gary said. "The day-night line is getting closer, but it isn't that close."

Barbara was nervous now, more nervous than she'd ever been. Hiding in a cave from the sun was one thing that she'd already coped with, but not having air to breathe scared her at a far more fundamental level. This wasn't scuba diving. They were going to suffocate! Her heart pounded so loudly that it overpowered her thoughts. The others stared at her. They must be thinking she was going to go to pieces again.

No. She tightened her fists, forcing herself to stay calm, breathe, and solve the problem. She made herself smile at the others. They were probably as upset as she was. She mustn't add to their worries by freaking out the way she had on the first night. Barbara knew she was past all that. She and the Sparks would figure it out. They had to stay calm and *think*. We got this.

"So, we have six hours until the levels are bad. How long until it starts affecting our performance? Headaches? Lethargy? Blackouts?"

Gary put another chart on the wall.

"It's already slowing down my reactions a little," he said. "You might not notice it, but I do. My pulse has sped up a few points. We're not likely to feel the problem in any significant scale for a bit. First there will be headaches in about four hours. We're already at the level where sailors on submarines complain about sleeplessness. I'm not sure what there is we can do."

"So, that's it then." Dion sat down on the bench by the entranceway and started to pull off his suit. "There's nothing we can do. There's no way out. We'll be safe from the radiation, but our own CO_2 is going to kill us."

"Don't say that!" Jan shouted, her face a fierce mask. "Dion! You don't say things like that! You can't say that! We can't give up. We can't!"

Tears rolled from the corners of Jan's eyes and down her cheeks. For a second, Dion didn't move. He just sat there, his bare chest heaving, looking up at Jan in shock. Barbara felt shocked, too. Jan had always been the most optimistic of them all, keeping her spirits high when she felt ready to give up. The wear of all that had happened to her must finally have pushed Jan past her threshold of endurance. Barbara glanced at Gary, but he had nothing to add. It was up to her to do something. There was no one else.

Pushing aside her own fears, Barbara stepped in and wrapped her roommate up in a big bear hug. She held on to the other girl and rocked her as if she was a baby.

"Jan! Jan! Listen, roomie, we're okay. We're not going to . . ." Barbara just said, ". . . die in here. You understand me? It's okay. We just have a problem to solve. That's what we do. And we're all good at it. Great, even! We've got this, you hear me, girl? We're the Bright Sparks! We got this. We have *got* this! Right, Dion? *Right?*"

Barbara gave him a stern stare, determined that he would look her in the eye. Slowly, he raised his eyes. After a moment, he nodded. She met Gary's glassy gaze until he seemed to snap out of it a little. Jan's tight shoulders relaxed.

"There. Now, listen, all of you. We're fine as long as we use our heads. This is just a problem. We're astronauts on the Moon. If we weren't right for this job, Dr. Bright wouldn't have picked us as Bright Sparks. Even though it's beginning to seem like around every turn we have to rethink, reengineer, retool, rebuild, or redesign something on the fly just to keep from being fried, suffocated, or vacuum packed, we can do it. He believes in us." She paused for a brief moment to gather her thoughts. It was getting harder to think. Was the air getting thicker? No, it was her imagination. Just a little slowdown, as Gary said. She took a deep breath. "We have plenty of oxygen, right?"

"We do but, Barb, that doesn't matter," Dion started to explain. "All the oxygen in the world wouldn't matter if there's too much carbon dioxide in it."

"I understand that, Dion. Answer my question, before I can't think properly. Do we have plenty of oxygen?" Barbara asked, staying as calm as she could manage. For a second there she felt like slugging the young man. She couldn't let herself fall into the same trap and lose her temper.

"Uh, well, I'm not sure what plenty is, but we have a lot," Gary put in.

"Good." She continued to force the scenario through her mind. There was a solution there somewhere. She needed to fight her way through the exhaustion to get to it. "So, we will just have to find a way to breathe the oxygen and not the carbon dioxide."

"How do you expect us to do that, Barb?" Dion shrugged in defeat. "Sounds impossible."

"All right, stop it. No more pessimism. That's not what the Bright Sparks do, is it? You've kept me glued to my seat in front of my television and my computer screen at home because you found solutions to impossible problems. I admired you so much, because you never gave up, no matter how bad things seemed to be going. We can *think* our way out of this. Let's do the math first, then we panic." Barbara rubbed her fingers through her hair, glad to have the helmet bubble off after so many hours in the open. "The shelter is fifteen meters across by three meters high, right? So, that's, uh, seven point five meters radius squared times pi times three, so about five hundred thirty cubic meters volume. We can seal off the chambers we aren't using down to the bedrooms, the kitchen, the bathroom and this room, bringing it to oh, a hundred and eighty cubic meters volume. Assuming there's no scrubber at all and that we become nonfunctional at two and a half percent carbon dioxide and death is at five, then we can figure out how long we could stay in here. The average person exhales about . . ." She rolled her eyes up toward the ceiling, trying to remember her biology classes.

". . . Zero point zero five meters cubed per hour of CO2 when calm," Dion said automatically. Barbara nodded, glad to have engaged him in the process.

"Right!" she said, giving him an encouraging smile. "Assuming we're working slowly but steadily getting things ready for the trip back we should increase that rate to about zero point zero seven five meters cubed per hour. Using the equation we all learned in training that it's the volume of the room times point zero two five, or two and a half percent, divided by the number of people times the expected exhale volume rate . . . uh . . ." The figures in her mind suddenly flew off in all directions. "I lost track of the numbers somewhere. Hold on."

She blinked. She felt as though the lack of accessible oxygen was becoming more evident with every breath. The debilitation Gary had mentioned was beginning to hit. Her ability to do math in her head was suffering.

"Fifteen hours," Jan snapped, holding up Ms. Scruffles. "I thought you were good with numbers."

"Thanks," Barbara said, without rancor. It was the CO2 talking, not her friend. "So, look at that. We have fifteen hours even without the scrubber that's still ticking." Barbara thought for a second about everything she had learned about breathing in scuba-diving, then had a spark of an idea. A *bright* spark, even. "How many times could we open the hatch and blow all the air out of here and then fill it back up with fresh air before we run out of it?"

"That's crazy!" Jan said. "We're doing everything we can to keep atmosphere in, not out."

"Wait a minute," Gary said, his bright blue eyes going wide. She could tell he was catching on, too, fighting his way out of the carbon-dioxide-induced lethargy. She felt that spark warm to optimism. All of them were on board the project again. He fumbled for his PDE. "Hold on, and I'll run some numbers."

"It's like scuba-diving," Barbara said, encouraging them all. "Sometimes you have to blow your mask clear. It seems like you're wasting air, but you're not. You're getting rid of the bad stuff."

"That might just work, Barb, for a while." Dion stood up and grabbed his PDE and started tapping at the screen. Jan did the same with hers.

"But, we can't just blow the door," Jan added without looking up. "That could cause some rapid decompression stuff that might damage the shelter or airlock. We'll have to let it leak out slowly at first, say over five or ten minutes or more."

"Jan's right on that," Dion agreed. "It would be like a rocket engine if we just opened the door. The airlock can be set to cycle on a continuous loop until we're at low enough pressures to open both doors. I can fix that code."

"Three times with just this shelter's supply," Gary said at last. "That will give us about forty-five hours. One point eight seven five days, to be exact," he added with a grin.

Barbara took a deep breath.

"See? Let's say one and a half days for margin, and that isn't counting what's in the vehicles or in our suits. Plus, we have six hours now before we absolutely have to flush the system. We won't be at our best, but we'll be all right. And with the added help of scrubber number two, that will probably stretch to at least two and a half or maybe more days. We need to work a simulation on that."

"Easy," Gary said, already sliding equations back and forth on his screen.

"And maybe see if there's a way to salvage numbers one and three?"

"I'm on that," Jan said, perking up, "although I already went through all the possibilities I know. I'd better reread the manuals."

Barbara watched each of them concentrating on their tasks. They were focused and doing what they did best now: solving hard problems. "We need to send our plan to Dr. Bright and see if they have some other ideas how to stretch out our air supply. At any rate, we're riding out this next wave in here, and in our suits while we flush the shelter. And then, we're getting the heck out of here as fast as we can back to Armstrong City."

"Amen, sister." Dion nodded in agreement.

"Well, we need to get a plan going for the drive back." With a plan, Barbara could fight against the fear that threatened to overwhelm her. She made herself smile, though she knew she must look as exhausted as the others did. "Let's get to work. We have a lot of science to do."

✧　✧　✧

CombatBallerina—So let me get this straight: they're talking from Mars?

JHarbor0562—I think it's immensely innovative. I can't wait to meet these Sparks.

SwitchViewDan—What about the CME? It looks horrible on the website!

OSay5477—Dr. Bright can't leave them out there like that! He has to go get them. This is criminal.

Keegan#1fan—No, it's not! He cares. The shuttle took out half of Armstrong City, too!

OSay5477—This wouldn't have happened if Pam wuz there.

Chapter 19

"How are they?" Jackie Feeney asked, coming around backstage with a steaming coffee pot in her hand.

Keegan plunked his elbows on his dressing room table and ran his fingers through his thick hair. If tearing some of it out would have helped, he'd have done it in a nanosecond. After a couple of hard days, he was frustrated and tired. The city was safe, if a little battered. Commander Harbor and the shuttle crew were pretty much the same. They were in sickbay isolation for a couple of days for mandatory observation. He and the younger Sparks and the whole video crew were safe, so he had nothing but time to worry about the ones he couldn't reach. He looked up at her.

"Jackie, they have a little more than two days before they suffocate. As best I can tell from right this moment they have thirty-one hours of time left in the shelter." Keegan groaned, clutching his hair again. "I can't just go get them. There are no shuttles free and we couldn't drive there in time to get them. The CME will hit in about six hours. Say it lasts as long as the first wave did, which was about eighteen hours. They'll have about thirteen hours left to get a truck loaded for the trip and go. I'd really prefer them to take two in case one goes down. Not sure they'll have time."

"So, *buy* them some time, Keegan. Do some magic of yours and find them the time they need." His producer and friend sat down beside him and handed him a fresh cup of coffee. "How much will be enough?"

Keegan rolled his head back and looked up at the ceiling.

"I'm not sure. They'll need to sleep before driving. Maybe if they did just take one vehicle they could go in shifts of two up and two sleeping." He reached for the coffee and sipped the hot, fragrant liquid. He took a deep breath and closed his eyes for a second as he hovered over the mug. "And who knows if the CME's second wave will be longer or shorter than the first wave. We can only estimate. Dammit!" He slammed the mug down and it bounced. He had to hold onto it and chase the blob of coffee upwards to keep it from splashing out.

"I've never seen you like this before." Jackie raised an eyebrow and frowned at him. Keegan didn't like the disapproving look.

"What is it?" he asked. "What's wrong?"

"Are you giving up on them?" she demanded. She threw a hand in the general direction of Aldrinville. "I'll bet you those kids out there aren't giving up on *you*."

"Maybe they should. I dunno." Keegan was feeling as guilty as he possibly could at the moment. The project had all seemed so straightforward when they had been making plans. Why hadn't he checked the solar charts and calculated that a CME was possible, let alone two? "Maybe all those hater posts were right. Maybe I shouldn't have put the kids into danger out there."

"Keegan, you didn't put them in danger. They're on the Moon, for heaven's sake. This is the definition of a hostile environment. *Anywhere* here is in danger. People back home want to think that Armstrong City is all honey and roses, but it's far from it. Look at the training that even temporary visitors have to go through? You can't forget where you are.

One step out the door without proper protection, and you're dead. It's not television. It's reality. They knew the risks. They were eager to take them."

"Yeah, but . . ."

"Yeah, but nothing." Jackie stood up slapping the table top as she did so. "Snap out of it, Keegan. Those kids are the smartest I have ever seen. They're resilient. They aren't quitting! Now you get off your butt, and don't quit on them. What would they think if they could see you right now?" She peered down at him, her eyes suddenly sympathetic. "They never see the vulnerable side of you, Dr. Mother Hen. Don't collapse now. This isn't the worst thing that could happen. What if the CME hit this side of the Moon, on top of the shuttle malfunction, and you still had those kids out on the other side? What ever happened to 'we can do this'?"

"All right, peace! I surrender." Keegan held up his palms of his hand. His shoulders felt tight as a drum. He worked them back and forth to release the tension.

She was right. There had to be some kind of inherent fudge factor he hadn't thought of. Keegan called all of the parameters of the remote shelter to mind and concentrated on finding variables. The numbers started to fall together in his mind.

"Well, let me see . . . I can stretch the oxygen for them if they reduce the pressure inside to about three quarters of an atmosphere. I'm hesitant to go to half. That would be like on Mt. Everest base camp. Too many people have trouble at that pressure. The habitat walls have stiffened now, so they don't need the air to keep them inflated."

Jackie grinned and patted him on the shoulder.

"See, you already have ideas."

"Yeah, yeah. Get out of here and let me think." Keegan gave her a half smile. "Leave the coffee. And Jackie . . . thanks."

"Bah. Makes good television." She slipped out of the room.

"Hurry up and open it, Jan!" Gary said impatiently, as they crowded around the central computer console. "Who's it from?"

"Now, how would I know that until I open it?" Jan turned from the small screen connected to the Moon-Mars-Earth-Earth-Mars-Moon Relay system they had developed. In a playful moment, Gary had decided they should call it the MMEEMMR, pronounced "meemer" for short. "This isn't like normal messaging." The Nerd Twins made faces at each other.

"All right, you two. Just open the message already," Dion interjected gruffly.

"Okay. Jeez. Don't bunch up your princess panties." Jan tapped the console and ducked to stare into the monitor. Barbara angled her head around, but it was no use.

"Put it on the big screen, Jan. I can't see though all of you."

Jan glanced up and realized her roommate was behind both of the guys.

"Oh, okay. Sorry."

The video started with standard text message giving the date, time, length of the message, and where it originated: Armstrong City, that day, about twenty minutes before they received it. Then, to Barbara's infinite relief, Dr. Bright's smile filled the screen. He looked tired and scruffy, as though he hadn't shaved in at least two days. As if in sympathy, Dion rubbed his own thickening stubble. Neither he nor Gary had bothered with a razor since the emergency began.

"Greetings, Aldrinville!" Dr. Bright began. "I have to say, this mission keeps getting diverted in every different direction. First, I want to commend all of you on your brilliant work thus far. The Mars relay was nothing short of genius. I can't wait to hear the whole chain of ideas of how you guys came up with it when we're all safely back together. Sorry I haven't talked to you in a few hours. I had to wait my turn for bandwidth. There's a lot going on over here.

"Now, about the CME: I just got the latest data in from the space weather group at NASA and NOAA. I don't have good news. It looks like a doozy. We're in for a full up super solar storm. It's possible that this wave could last as long as twenty-four hours."

"Oh, no." Barb gulped as she did the calculations again in her mind. There was not enough air.

"Oh, my God!" Dion shouted, smacking himself in the side of the head. "You've got to be kidding me!"

"We won't have enough time," Gary added, his eyes wide with horror.

"Everybody shut up and listen." Jan shushed them.

". . . First thing you have to remember is to stay calm and don't panic. Guys—no wait, Sparks—no, that ain't it either." Dr. Bright fixed them with a sincere blue gaze. "Dion, Gary, Jan, Barb, I could apologize for getting you into this mess, and I do hate that this has happened. But, I'm *not* going to apologize because that would be an insult to each of you. The four of you worked for your entire lives to be able to have this opportunity. I'm not going to belittle the fact that you are amazing people, young as you are, to be on the far side of the Moon doing jobs that no astronauts in the history of mankind have done. You're intelligent, you're resourceful, and you're brave. So, know this: I have complete confidence that if you follow these instructions I'm about to give you and use your heads to improvise when you need to—the way you have already—then everything will be fine, and we'll see you all back here at Armstrong City in a few days." He paused for second and moistened his lips and rubbed his eyes. To Barbara's surprise, it looked like he was tearing up. As worried as she was about their situation, her heart went out to him. He swallowed hard, and smiled at them again.

"So, the good news. Immediately, I want you to reduce the atmospheric pressure in the cabin to seventy-five percent. This stretches your air by another ten or eleven hours. With your venting rotation plan in place to clear accumulated CO_2, that means you'll have at least a three-hour excess to outlast the projected CME. Let's pray it matches the models. If it doesn't, we'll work contingencies, but we need to do first things first."

"Gary, adjust the air now." Barbara whispered. "We should have thought of that."

"Already did it." Gary held up Turing. The pie chart gauge on the small screen showed three-quarters of a circle in blue.

"Good."

"Also, I want you to take the two down scrubbers apart. You have the manuals in your PDEs. Take the zeolite materials out of them and set them out into vacuum for two hours. Then, put each into a permeable bag of some kind—I'm thinking a t-shirt or a pillowcase, or something similar."

"Pajamas," Jan said at once. "I'll volunteer one of my sets."

"Smash the zeolite up in a hammer once it's in the bag. That will increase the surface area of it so it can capture more CO_2. Then tape the bags over one of the air filter intakes in the shelter's main cabin. This might work as a very inefficient scrubber but should buy some time. Next, I want you to put the dust filter in the airlock on a continuous loop but with the inner door slightly cracked. There might be enough alkaline materials as well as iron and titanium oxides in the dust that some of the CO_2 will also get trapped. My calculations suggest a half of a percent improvement to the removal rate from this, and every half of a percent might prove important."

"Dion?" Barb glanced at him.

"Done." The inner airlock door hissed slightly and slid about a centimeter open. They heard the dust filter vacuum begin to whine. "That's inspired. I'll work it into my program."

"And, finally," Dr. Bright said, his gaze intent, "I want you taking shifts sleeping. No more than two people awake at one time. The ones awake are prepping for the ride back. There are plenty of air and scrubber materials in the suits and vehicles for that duration. As soon as the CME is over with, take one vehicle and drive straight through. Two sleep and two drive. Just get here as soon as it's safe."

He was thinking farther ahead than they were, Barbara noted. The Sparks concentrated on absorbing all the details for their survival as Dr. Bright reeled off his suggestions and the calculations behind them.

". . . So, hang in there. We're doing some things here that might help, but chances are we're going to be cut off again during the storm, so I'll see you all when you get back here. I know you can do it, Sparks! Dr. Bright out."

The screen went blank. For a moment, all of them stood silently. Barbara glanced from one to another, wondering how they were going to react. She knew her reaction. No matter how scared she was, she would just keep trying until they returned safely to Armstrong City. Dr. Bright had their backs, and he was working out ways to keep them safe. She had faith in him. They just had to implement the plan as he had laid it out.

They were just like the astronauts of old. They'd reported to "Houston," and Houston had laid out their best course of action. As long as they were all still breathing, they were going to be all right. She hoped. It might have been her imagination, but adding the filters in the airlock seemed to have improved things already.

Jan was first to break the silence.

"Well, that's it. We're on our own again." She tapped her personal PDE. "I had Ms. Scruffles create a checklist of what we need to do from Dr. Bright's video as he spoke. I'm texting it to all of you now."

"Great work, Jan." Barbara looked at the file on her PDE's

screen, but it was too long to see on Fido. She projected it to the big wall monitor. "Let's divide and conquer this. First things first. Two of us need to go to sleep right now."

"Go to sleep? We should knock out this list first," Gary argued.

"No." Barbara shook her head and held up her right hand waving it back and forth. "We all heard him, and we can always go over the items again later. Dr. Bright was right. We need to prepare for what happens next. So, who's first? I have to be honest, I'm bone tired. *I* could sleep. I need some food, but I'm ready to sack out. Anyone object?"

"No. I'm okay right now." Jan said. "I could get started pulling the scrubbers apart. I put them together. I know how to break them down. Let me grab a pair of my PJs first."

"Gary? Want to flip for it?" Dion asked.

"I don't care, man, but you were out there fighting that bulldozer all morning. Aren't you tired?" Gary asked him.

"I guess I could sleep, then." Dion replied, letting out a long sigh. "Join you for a quick snack, lady?"

"That'd be great," Barbara said. She looked at her team. They were steeling themselves for the effort. The air still made her a little drowsy, but that was all right for now. If Dr. Bright's projections were correct, and she was certain they were, by the time she woke up, the air would be better. She hoped. Were they all on board? Jan glanced at Gary. The two of them gave her a thumbs up. She nodded, relieved.

"Good. It's settled. Dion and I will sleep for the next four hours and then we'll swap out."

✧　✧　✧

MOon1969—Neil's satellite worked! I knew it would.

ZetaMoto—Meemer rocks. Can they leave that up?

5X5Power—They don't have enuf air. They cud sufficat.

TeamSparks090—Isn't it over? Can't they drive back?

Chapter 20

✦

Dr. Bright came bounding into Sparks Central, clutching his ever-present coffee mug. Neil and Daya were glad to see that he'd had a chance to shave and put on a fresh khaki jumpsuit. Neil straightened the collar of his clean blue coveralls and gestured at the left-hand screen over the console. On it, a small spacecraft sat on the floor of the open hangar not far from the shuttle landing and maintenance pad, dwarfed by all the machinery around it.

"This is it, sir. She's ready to fly." Neil felt the thrill of just saying the words.

"We managed to cut some corners on the printing and got it done in about seventy percent the estimated time," Daya said, offering her own calculations for their mentor's approval. "It's been sitting in the vacuum now for about ten minutes with no system hiccups detected." She was pleased, too. Not only had the manufacture been smoother than expected, but Neil had actually let her participate in the fun parts of programming it.

Dr. Bright glanced up at the big screen. The little device had come out looking almost exactly like the rendering in Neil's detailed plans. It measured about one meter cubed, with nozzle exits on each face. He studied it critically. The skin was printed solar panels, with small metallic protrusions sticking out at each corner of the cube—antennas. Various sensor pods were mounted externally on the cube, with a small camera on each face. Imprinted in a different color of plastic on one of the vanes were the words BRIGHTSAT 1. Neil wriggled impatiently and a little nervously while the blond scientist scanned both the video and the stats.

"Looking good, Sparks," Dr. Bright said, straightening up. "How about the comms?"

"Communications link is up, and patched through to the main console, sir," Daya said proudly. "Our PDEs should work as long as we're in line of sight with it. Dr. Bright, I think we're good to go."

"Neil? This is your show. Is it ready to fly?" Dr. Bright asked. Neil swallowed hard. He had only been campaigning for this moment for months. Doing his best to look more confident than he felt, he nodded.

"Yes, sir! Just like Daya said. BrightSat One is good to go."

"Well, then what're we waiting for?" Dr. Bright said, waving a hand at the screen with some of his usual eagerness restored. "Fire up the EMdrive."

"EMdrive startup sequence initiation in five, four, three, two, one, *lift-off.*" Neil touched the glowing green circle on his screen. As the little cube-shaped hover vehicle lifted off the floor of the hangar, he grinned from ear to ear. It worked exactly as it had in testing. On the big center screen on the wall, views of two aspects of the hangar appeared side by side. "Video link from the nose and aft sections," he said. "If you want a different face view, just let me know."

"Star tracker and Earth-Moon sensors are working perfectly, Neil," Einstein's voice announced over the room speakers. Figures scrolled up Neil's desktop monitor and along one of the smaller screens below the main ones. "Would you like me to take control now?"

"Yes, Einstein," Neil ordered, feeling like the real voice of

Mission Control at last. "Initiate automated control and flight path to predetermined non-Keplerian orbit."

The views from the cameras lifted higher.

"Roger that, Neil. I now have control of the vehicle and accelerating to predetermined orbit. Destination orbit ETA is seven minutes and forty two seconds following a nontraditional insertion trajectory."

Daya smiled and looked at the PDE screen. Even though Achi wasn't flying the probe, it was following the flight path she had calculated. Neil shared his delight with her.

"Great, Einstein. Keep a close watch on all systems and keep me posted if any issues occur. And make certain the trajectory stays in the shadow of the Moon and out of the sunlight."

"Of course, Neil," Einstein said.

"This is great work, you two!" Dr. Bright aimed a smile at them. He watched the screen as the small craft's cameras tracked out of the hangar and into the twilit sky. The visuals quickly left the colony buildings behind, flitting out over shadowy craters and pockmarked plains. "Neil, Daya, I should have let you do this a long time ago."

"Thanks!" they chorused. Neil felt as though he could burst with pride. Nothing could bring him down.

"So," Dr. Bright asked, his voice dropping to a monotone that sobered Neil's buoyant mood, "now tell me how long the *battery* is going to last."

"Uh." Neil hesitated. The battery story wasn't great and he knew it. That was the one weak spot in his plan. "My current estimation is six hours with a one-hour charge cycle. Or, similar amount of time to swap batteries out." Neil shot Dr. Bright a hopeful glance. "If we could stay in the sun it would fly for twice that." Even as he said it, he knew that wouldn't be enough. The other Sparks would be stuck in Aldrinville for maybe four times that long, then they had the drive home on top of that.

"Hmm." Dr. Bright rubbed at his chin as Neil watched him closely, hanging on the edge of his seat for further praise from his mentor. His eyes twinkled over his hand. "Then, I guess, you have about five hours to get a second BrightSat built and charged and in orbit before you bring that one back. I want continuous communications with the team from here on in. If you can get a third one going in parallel you are authorized to use whatever resources to do so. I'll make sure you have unrestricted access to the 3D printer. Got it?"

"Uh, yes, sir." Neil sat in his chair, feeling stunned. He'd just pulled off a miracle of engineering, and he was being told to go right back to the design concept environment! "I guess."

"Hey, look at it this way, Neil." Dr. Bright smiled at the look on the youth's face. "You did such a good job you get to do it again."

"Barbara, Dr. Bright wishes to speak with you," Fido said softly. Barbara wasn't sure if she was dreaming or if the low-pressure air and high carbon dioxide content was giving her vivid dreams. No, she was asleep. She had to be dreaming. The CME was in full throttle outside. Earth's satellite relays would have been taken off line for safety. There was no way Dr. Bright could be calling her.

"Barbara, please wake up. You have an incoming PDE call from Dr. Bright."

Barbara's eyes opened. She hadn't been dreaming. It was Fido's voice, therefore there *was* an incoming call from their mentor. All at once, she was fully awake.

She rolled out of her bunk and looked around for her PDE. It took her several seconds to locate it: still on the arm of her flight suit from before her extended nap. She fumbled getting it out of its pouch and sat down cross-legged on the bed with it. According to the digital clock, she had slept for exactly four hours and two minutes. She realized that she was in her pajamas and her hair was a mess, and she didn't remember the last shower she had taken. For a moment, she felt shy at letting herself be seen in that condition, but defiantly pushed that feeling aside. It was just all part of being an astronaut, wasn't it? Pride in her personal appearance had gone out the airlock days ago.

"Video display, Fido." Sure enough, Dr. Bright's face lit up her screen. "Hi, sir."

"Hello, Barbara!" Dr. Bright sounded happy. "I hope I didn't wake you."

"Uh, yeah, but it's okay! It was time to get up and change shifts anyway." She smiled back at him. Then she frowned. She glanced down at her pajamas, then her eyes flew up to him in dismay. "Wait a minute—this is in real time! We're talking!"

Dr. Bright looked pleased.

"Yes, it is. But not being recorded for the show. Good on you for catching on to that so quickly."

"How are you making this call?"

"Aha." Dr. Bright gave her a conspiratorial glance. "You can thank Neil for that. Remember his design for a little EMdrive battery-powered hoversat, the one he told you about on your first day? He built it! It's flown out to a high non-Keplerian orbit just inside the night side of the day-night line. I believe we will now have our Sparks PDEs up for the rest of your trip."

"That's amazing!" Barbara bounced up and down on her bunk, ecstatic. "He *said* it would work and it did. I don't believe it! I owe the little brat a hug!"

"Ha, ha. I'll tell him you said that. But, later. His head is big enough right now as it is." Dr. Bright smiled, but then turned serious. "Barbara, I have to tell you how proud I am of the way you have handled your first mission. This is the most, uh, *extreme* any Bright Sparks mission has ever been. And, I have to say that thanks to you they're coming out on top again. The team is better having you as a part of it, and

I mean that. I'm glad you accepted my offer to join. It's been a privilege having you on board."

Barbara felt her heart swell with pride. His praise was worth all the terror and dread she had been through over the last several days.

"Thank you, sir. I really appreciate that, but it's not just me. If this wasn't such a good team, nothing I did would have made any difference."

He chuckled.

"So speaks a natural-born leader. You're not gonna tell me now that you're not the leader of the group, are you?"

Barbara sat back on her spine. She'd resisted the title when it had first been wished on her back in Armstrong City, but like it or not, she had stepped forward into that role.

"No, sir. If the others want me, I'm proud to do it."

"Glad to hear it, Barb. Are there any problems, other than the obvious? I mean personnel problems? If I need to talk to anyone, I will. You don't have to handle everything on your own, you know."

"Uh, thanks, but we're all good, I think. We know what has to be done and we're all doing it."

"All right. I didn't have a doubt in my mind." Dr. Bright hesitated for a second while he adjusted something off screen and then continued. "The three of us, Neil, Daya and I, will be here around the clock for now on until you four are home safely. If you have a problem or just want to talk, we're here. As long as Neil's bird stays in orbit, we're as close as your PDE. Call if there's anything you need to know. Check in every two hours. Got it?"

"Yes, sir, that's great!" Barbara thought for a second. To her relief, the air felt just a little fresher than it had before her nap. Her natural optimism was returning. "Are there any updates on the CME?"

Dr. Bright looked rueful.

"More updates than you can possibly do anything useful with. They're coming in continuously now from space weather teams around the Earth. The event is about two hours away from the Moon. It probably wouldn't hurt for you all to make one more runthrough of all the circuits and grounding protocols before it hits."

The checklist immediately started cycling through Barbara's mind. She could probably have recited it off the top of her head to him, but he didn't need to hear it.

"I will, sir. Good idea."

"And how are the scrubber modifications working?"

"Uh, I honestly don't know. Jan was going to work on them during my sleep cycle. But I'm about to go check."

He gave her an approving nod.

"Great. Keep us posted."

"Roger that!" Barbara turned her hand thumbs up. He returned the gesture.

"Bright, out."

"How about that? We have communications now," she said out loud as she practically leaped from her bunk. Even considering Moon gravity, her steps were lighter than before.

"I'm sorry, Barbara, I didn't understand your question." Fido announced. She chuckled.

"It's okay, Fido. I don't need anything right now."

Barbara pulled a moist wipe from a tube near her bed and wiped her face and eyes with it. She wished she could take the time for even a dry shower. Then she wriggled into her mission suit and her sneakers. She bounced into the main room, gathering her hair up behind her in a ponytail while holding an elastic band between her teeth. She steadied herself and then applied the band. Her hair felt greasy under her fingertips. Maybe later, she promised herself, she could take a real shower, with cascades of hot water pouring down over her dusty, smelly body, and a long, thorough shampoo.

Jan gave her a sleepy grin from the table where she was working on ventilator components.

"You'll never guess who just woke me up!" Barbara said.

"We know." Her roommate pointed at the wall screen behind her. Neil and Daya gazed out of it at her. "Look who's here."

"Hi, Barb!" they chorused, waving. The two younger Sparks were all smiles.

"I'm glad to see that your physical reactions are in normal parameters," Daya said. "It's been several days since we were able to check."

"What she means is, it's great to see you," Neil added, wrinkling his nose.

"Good to see you two." Barb said. "Neil, I owe you a hug for this."

Neil wiggled his eyebrows at her. "I'm going to collect it."

"Neil!" Daya exclaimed. "Don't be like that."

"Like what?" Neil tried to look innocent, and failed miserably. Jan laughed.

"Where's Gary?" Barbara asked, glancing around.

"Where else?" Jan countered. "In the kitchen, of course."

"I heard that." Gary came in with a mug of soup and a handful of steaming hot rolls. "Because I'm good-hearted, I even left some for the rest of you. I'm going to kick Dion out of bed. Then I'm going to get some sleep."

"Good idea," Barbara said. "And, Jan, time for you to sack out, too."

Jan let out a huge yawn and stretched her arms wide. She pushed back from the table and rose.

"Don't have to tell me twice. I got the zeolite from scrubber one and started on three but had to take a break. My eyes were starting to cross, so I'm replacing pins and clips on the housing. Gary got most of the software overrides and the manifest for the trip started. You can take over where we left off. Neil and Daya can catch you up on where we are in the rest of the checklist."

"Great. Sleep well."

Jan patted her on the shoulder as she passed.

"Goodnight, roomie."

"Boy," Neil said, breathlessly, as Barbara sat down at the console, "have we got a lot to tell you!"

Barbara shook her fingers and put them in her mouth for a second. "Holy cow! That bites hard."

She was two hours into the task of pulling the zeolite package from scrubber number three in the equipment room when the CME started. Jan had been right. It hadn't taken fifteen minutes of exposure to the solar wind, cosmic rays, and whatever else was going on out there for the vacuum pipe on number three to acquire a fierce electrical charge. Barbara had been running a socket driver over the outer manifold that led to the ventilation fan, when a shock so fierce it knocked her back on her bottom crackled out of the pipe.

She sat there on the floor of the equipment room for a few moments, blinking her eyes. That had to have been thousands of volts, maybe more. At least the amperage was low, or she would have been hurting a lot more. Her fingers weren't burned, just a little red. She retrieved the tool from the floor and pointed it sternly at the scrubber mechanism.

"I'd better ground you before I keep going."

As predicted, the relays serving Meemer had gone down when the solar radiation began to bombard the Earth and Moon for the second time. Thanks to Neil's clever little bird—she loved the name BrightSat One—Aldrinville still maintained contact with the lab in Armstrong City. Every so often, Dr. Bright checked in and asked for progress reports. She hoped to have this task finished before he called in again.

With half the team asleep, the habitat was quiet except for the burbling of machinery and the occasional soft footfall of Dion coming and going on his own tasks. She found she was talking to herself more than usual, just to hear the sound of a human voice.

She pulled herself to her feet and rummaged in the components chest for some wire with no shielding. There was a spool of heavy copper wire, about ten or maybe eight gauge, approximately three and a quarter millimeters in diameter. She unreeled a meter or so of it and found a ground screw on the electric breaker box to attach it to. Then she dragged the spool over to the pipe, unwinding it as she pulled it across the room. Cautiously, she draped the reel of wire over the pipe where it fed through the manifold in the shelter wall.

Pop! A white flash arced as the copper touched the pipe. Careful not to touch the wire itself, she wrapped the length of copper around the pipe several times and then just dropped the spool to the floor without cutting it.

"That should do it." Gingerly, she touched the back of her hand to the pipe. This time there was no shock. "Whew."

Once the CME had ended, they could fasten the grounding wire to the wall, so it would permanently bleed off stray charges. When they went back to Armstrong City, they could obtain a scrubber conduit that was guaranteed nonconductive.

She finished removing the rest of the bolts holding the zeolite cylinder package in place. The final bolt dropped to the floor with a CLANK! along with her socket driver. She grabbed the cylinder with both hands and twisted it counterclockwise until the seal broke. Once it was loose she worked it around pipes, structure, and wiring until the package was free.

"Okay, now, according to the instructions I just need to twist here . . ." She clasped the cap and tried to turn it. Her hands trembled as she strained to undo the cap. It wouldn't budge. Her muscles were a little weaker than normal from the buildup of CO_2 in the air, but this was fastened a lot more than hand-tight. She hopped back to the tool chest for a pipe wrench and the crescent-shaped adjustable wrench. Together, the tools broke the seal loose, and the cap turned easily. She turned the cylinder upside down and the zeolite slid out of the tube.

"Aren't you a mess?" Barbara looked at the material. The matrix ought to be pink and white, but it was covered with a gummy tarlike substance. No matter if Jan or Gary was right about the source of the contamination, it *was* a mess. No wonder the scrubber had failed. "Oh, yeah, I need to throw you outside."

Barbara set the sticky mess on a tray from the kitchen and carried it toward the main room. Dion was already in his suit, dragging boxes to the door of the airlock. The plan was to stage the boxes just outside, but still under, the edge of the rubble pile awning they had fashioned. The moment they were cleared to leave, they wanted to be ready to move out at once. He already had most of their empty food containers, the tool and component cases, and his personal duffel bag stacked in place. He gave her a smile as he reached for his helmet on the peg by the door.

"Are you planning on going outside now, Dion?" she asked.

"Yes. You need something?"

"Yes, please." She held the tray out to him. "Could you set this outside and bring in the other zeolite pack from scrubber one? It's sitting on the loader just outside the awning. If you'll just roll it in, swap packs and roll it back, I'd appreciate it. It should be clean by now. That way, I don't have to suit up just yet."

"No problem," Dion said. "But, look at the CO_2 gauge. We'll have to do our first purge in about thirty minutes anyway."

"Oh, yeah, I figured." Barbara looked at the projected CO2 level versus the measured. The measured line was slightly below the projected good. "Sleeping, using the airlock as a scrubber, and lowering the pressure in here has bought us about a half hour more of oxygen. Maybe it will be even better once I get another scrubber pack involved."

"It ought to be, Barb. Be right back." Dion stepped through the airlock with an armload of boxes. The door closed behind him and the lights cycled from green to red. About a minute later, the lights cycled again and the door opened. Barbara shivered. A wave of cold from outside dropped the temperature in the big room by about fifteen percent. Dion dropped the zeolite onto the table to let it warm up. He took off the helmet and set it aside. "That was easier in the suit. Pressure is better than in here."

"Oh, I didn't think of that." Barbara examined the material, not daring to touch it until Fido confirmed that it was warm enough not to give her instant frostbite. It was pink and white again. None of the gummy stuff remained. As Dr. Bright had suggested, setting it in the vacuum had cleaned it. "Too bad we can't just plug it back in, huh?"

"There's time enough," Dion said, and paused. He stood there beside her a bit longer than she'd expect him to. The closeness made her a little uncomfortable. Also, his suit radiated the cold of the lunar vacuum, but he didn't move. She looked up at him. He was studying her with sadness in his big, beautiful eyes.

"Is there something else, Dion?" she asked, feeling a little shy. Her mouth felt dry.

His must have, too. He swallowed.

"Barbara. For earlier . . . I . . . uh, I mean . . . I'm sorry for . . . you know, overreacting. That's not who I am. You were great about calming us all down."

"It was nothing, Dion." Why was it so hard to stop looking into those eyes? She all but shook herself to break the spell and looked down at the zeolite casting a halo of frost on the work table. "I mean, did Jan tell you I panicked in the tents on the way out here? I'm beginning to realize that being an astronaut is harder than I ever dreamed it was! It takes all of us to keep each other from going nuts, getting stupid, and getting killed. Like now." She picked up the cold cylinder of zeolite and brandished it at him.

"Very, uh, pragmatic of you." Dion looked disappointed, as if it wasn't what he expected her to say. She stumbled on.

"No, well, maybe a little. But, we're in this together. We have to take care of each other, until we can get home safe again."

He smiled, and her heart melted a little.

"I can get behind that. I'm on your team, lady."

Reluctantly, Barbara broke their gaze and looked toward her work area. "We'd better get back to it. We're going to have to wake the others up soon so we can, um, clear the air."

"Right." Dion backed away. He put his helmet back on, then went over to pick up another load of crates. Barbara glanced after him, and returned to her own tasks, humming to herself.

✦ ✦ ✦

HeloFanAx—The second storm hit! Will Aldrinville keep working, or do they have to abandon it?

CombatBallerina—They can't get away. Oh, God, I hope they're okay.

TeamSparks090—Neil's EMDrive drone is up at last! He's only been talking about it for a YEAR.

GaMeRgirl873—The away team needs air. Everybody think clean thoughts.

StrTrk4FR—What's zeolite? Is it something I could catch?

Chapter 21

"Look, if the air goes too bad before this thing ends, we'll just put on our suits and stay in them all the way back to Armstrong City. We spend most of the day in them already," Dion said, turning a hand up as if moving his whole arm was too much trouble.

"That's why I don't want to have to put them on again until the last minute," Gary argued. He sat with his chair leaned well back and his feet on the console. All of them had reached a state of lethargy. "I'm not saying it like it's a bad thing, but that suit smells too much like me. Both of us need a real cleaning, not just a dry shower."

Jan hooted and let her head fall back. She lounged cross-legged in her chair with Trang Chim on her lap.

"I'm glad I didn't have to say it," she said, rolling her head toward Gary. "You saved me the trouble. We stink. In a purely olfactory sense, I mean. Otherwise, we totally rock. We're cryogenic, lasting this long with faulty tech and two—TWO—solar storms."

They had just completed the third purge of the CO_2-laden air. Barbara had just finished stripping out of her EVA suit and back into her work coverall. They had finished loading out everything they could for the trip back. Now they were growing impatient for the CME to end. The four of them had slept so much in the last two and a half days that they just couldn't sleep any longer. They just hung out in the main room, relaxing and doing their best not to do anything that would consume more oxygen.

Gary gave her an impatient glare.

"Seriously, okay? The CME is going strong at twenty-four hours now. If it weren't for the makeshift scrubbers, we'd have been out of good air five hours ago."

"You're not helping the oxygen concentration when you both gas on like that," Dion said, with a sly smile.

"Would you two just stop it?" Daya's face frowned back at them from the wall. "According to the data feed we're getting you are well in the green and can make it at least another ten hours or so. All of you are healthy and show good oxygen saturation. The decline in CO2 levels has improved the atmosphere in the habitat."

"They're just bored, Daya." Barbara recrossed her feet on the table beside her coffee cup.

"Right, they aren't happy unless something is wrong," Jan added. "Right, princesses?"

"Right!" Barbara said.

"Hmph!" Gary grunted. Dion just rolled his eyes at her.

"I heard that!" Neil said from the background somewhere in the room behind Daya.

"I'm sure you did, Neil." Jan laughed. Barbara smiled, thinking it sounded like her first day back at Sparks Central, only now she really felt as though she belonged as part of the group. Even though she was thousands of kilometers away on the far side of the Moon in a solar storm, she was right where she was supposed to be.

"Can't I at least be a prince?" Neil asked, his voice almost a whine.

"Self-rescuing princes?" Jan said. She and Barbara exchanged a quizzical glance. "Uh, nope."

"Royalty—how about that?" Neil pleaded. "Gender neutral?"

"Forget it. Its princesses or nothing. We've had to put up with being called guys for decades!"

"But *I* don't call you guys!"

"Okay, fact check. Einstein, count up all the times he called us guys over the last four months," Jan said, a challenge lighting her eyes.

"Barbara, the exterior sensor data has shown a rapid diminishing in cosmic ray detection in the last two minutes," Fido's voice interrupted the chatter.

"What?" Barbara shot straight up from her reclined chair and pulled her feet from the rolling table. "Transmit the data to Sparks Central and display it here on the wall."

"Certainly, Barbara."

The four of them roused themselves to study it. A graph showing the particle incidence on the radiation sensor drew itself on the far blank wall. The left side of the chart showed extremely high in particle count in red, but then it dropped off on a sloped hill shaped curve, approaching the green, nominal levels. Barbara held her breath as the line dipped even lower.

"That's the tell-tale cosine squared drop-off!" Neil shouted gleefully. "The storm's over! I'm calling Dr. Bright."

"Gary, run a quick sensor diagnostic," Barbara said. She read the data, and beamed at the others. "No failure. It's real. No more CME."

"Yeah!" Gary tapped at the console and turned to them with a smile. "It's time for the canary to sing."

"Yes!" Dion slapped his chair arms with both hands. "Play the Tweety cartoon."

"First things first, everyone." Dr. Bright's voice filled the speakers. His face bounced onto the screen as he sat down in front of his console. "You've got the all-clear, Sparks! NASA confirms from half a dozen sources that the

CME has passed. But I like your canary plan. Suit up and give me secondary confirmation."

"Sparks, you heard him!" Barbara said. "Let's get to work!"

Gary turned the oxygen saturation back to its full level. Their lethargy dissipated in moments. With renewed energy, the four ran for their sleeping rooms.

"We are *so* out of here!" Jan cheered.

Barbara and Jan burst in and grabbed their suits off the wall pegs. They were so excited that they had to force themselves to slow down and check one another's seals for leaks. Once Barbara had her compression suit sealed up, she picked up her bubble and dropped it over her head. At last, the difference between the suit's air pressure and the habitat's were the same. They were going home!

She and Jan bounded out into the main room, where Dion and Gary were waiting.

"Fido, run the Tweety video in a loop and broadcast it to the team until I tell you to stop." Barbara smiled, carrying the PDE toward the airlock with the other three in her wake. "Ready? Sing for me, Fido."

". . . Bird in a gilded cage . . ." the little PDE warbled.

Barbara slid the PDE out the door and used the skid loader to slide it all the way out from under the awning and into the sunlight. She held her breath. The blazing light hit the screen, reflecting a blinding square of whiteness. The music didn't stop for a moment.

"It's working fine!" Neil shouted again.

Instead of rolling the cart back, Barbara stepped outside into the brilliant sunshine and turned in a circle, glad to see the sky friendly again.

"Team, I think we can start loading up," she said, unable to stop grinning. "And watch out for shocks. Make sure everything is grounded. Otherwise, I'd say we're all safe out here from dat ol' puddy tat!"

✧　✧　✧

Barbara watched as the others loaded the last armload of things they had planned to take back to Armstrong City with them. The power truck and the water truck were so buried that they didn't bother pulling them out. They only uncovered the top solar panels so the batteries could continue to recharge and keep the water truck from freezing until they came back again. The heavy hauler stood at the edge of the crater nearest the roadway. With only the minimum coverage of lunar dirt protecting it from the CMEs, it hadn't taken Dion long to dig it out with the Bobcat. They had pulled the tarpaulins off, checking for any damage. Under Barbara's careful eye, they had brushed away all the regolith they could see. It was ready to go.

Dion sat in the driver's seat going through the checklists. Gary had vanished into the back seat with his armload of goods. Barbara expected that most of it was food. She grinned indulgently. He would probably be eating to fill his hollow leg all the way back to the city. Jan stood on the step rail of the passenger side front door, waving to her, Trang Chim in its case hanging over her shoulder.

"You coming, Barb?" Jan asked.

"Roger that. Just turning off the lights. You know, we'll want to come back here and finish the job before long." Barbara cycled the airlock for the last time. She bounded over to the power truck, and cycled the control panel to automatic. That had been the last job on the checklist. Everything was done. She glanced down at Fido, now back in place on the back of her wrist.

"Sparks Central, you there?" She knew she was broadcasting to the entire world.

"Roger that, Barbara." Dr. Bright, Neil, and Daya were all sitting at their consoles. They were broadcasting back a wide angle view so she could see them all. The feed was going realtime to the website. Text comments began to pile up underneath at a rate she had never seen before.

"This is Aldrinville Basecamp. We're battened down and about to depart," Barbara reported in her best astronaut style.

"Roger that, Barbara," Dr. Bright said, with a big smile. "You'll be back in plenty of time for next week's show. I can't wait to feature all six of you, with plenty of video of your two improvised dishes."

"I think I speak for all of us, Dr. Bright," Barbara said, calmly, "when I say that before we sit down in front the cameras, we all want to take really comprehensive showers."

Their mentor threw back his head and laughed. "Roger that! Oh, just so you have something really special to look forward to, Commander Harbor wants to take all of you to lunch when you get here. She wants to hear all about *your* adventures."

Barbara caught her breath.

"That will be fantastic!"

The others cheered. Dr. Bright nodded.

"Sparks Central is transferring to the transport comm channel, now," he said. "Adjust your PDE to the Bluetooth link."

"Roger that," Barbara confirmed.

"Hey, you better get on the road," Neil said, looking her square in the eye. "You have . . . oh, maybe six hours before the next CME strikes!"

"Until *what?*" Dion bellowed, almost deafening them over the helmet speakers.

Daya reached over and swatted Neil on the shoulder with the back of her hand.

"Ow!" he yelped.

"Don't listen to him! He's joking. The solar flares are over! You have a clear beam to come back. We look forward to welcoming you home."

"Ha-ha! I got that picture of Barb for the website," Neil crowed. "Posting it! I bet it gets a million hits before you get back."

"Hey!" Barbara protested.

"There's your initiation, Barb," Jan said, chuckling. "If you didn't feel it before, you're really one of us now."

"You all get back here safely," Dr. Bright said. "You don't need any more initiation than you've already been through. Come on home."

"See you soon, guys!" Barbara bounded to the truck, feeling as though she could fly. She climbed up into the rear seat behind Jan and strapped in. As the hauler pulled out onto the narrow road, she watched Aldrinville disappear behind them in a cloud of regolith dust. She was almost sad to leave, but happy to be heading back to Armstrong City. She knew now what Dion meant about a blood family and a brain family. Aldrinville was an adventure, but Sparks Central had become her home.

✧　✧　✧

KeeganMarryMe—That picture of Barb is hilarious! I'm making into my screensaver.

ButchFel9—Already did it.

SwitchViewDan—OMG, I'm just so glad they're safe.

HeloFanAx—They didn't finish the dish!

CombatBallerina—Are you crazy? They're lucky to be alive.

ZetaMoto—Sparks rule! Sparks rule! Sparks rule! Iowa Sparks most of all!

Atlanta-Fulton Public Library